THE TRUST

ALSO BY NORB VONNEGUT

Top Producer
The Gods of Greenwich

THE TRUST

NORB VONNEGUT

MINOTAUR BOOKS

A THOMAS DUNNE BOOK
NEW YORK

THOMAS DUNNE BOOKS.
An imprint of St. Martin's Press.

THE TRUST. Copyright © 2012 by Norb Vonnegut. All rights reserved. Printed in the United States of America. For information, address St. Martin's Press, 175 Fifth Avenue, New York, N.Y. 10010.

www.thomasdunnebooks.com
www.minotaurbooks.com

ISBN 978-1-250-00389-8 (hardcover)
ISBN 978-1-250-01477-1 (e-book)

First Edition: August 2012

10 9 8 7 6 5 4 3 2 1

For Wynn and Coco

ACKNOWLEDGMENTS

I'd like to acknowledge three groups that made *The Trust* possible, starting with those who contributed to the story. Tim Scrantom, a friend for thirty years, told me about a chicken-processing plant in Georgia. Somehow the poultry morphed into an adult superstore inside these pages. I borrowed two separate anecdotes, one from Peter Malkin and one from Caroline Fitzgibbons, which added heft to a character you'll meet. The chapters that start in Miami and work their way to the Turks and Caicos—I could not have written them without the help of my longtime friend Dorothy Flannery and her brother Paul.

While writing, I received lots of technical support. Cort Delaney and Dave McCabe are my go-to lawyers in the field of trusts and estates. Burke Files, author of *Due Diligence*, was an invaluable resource on international money scams. Plus, he opened an important door inside the Turks and Caicos. Tom McNally answered questions above the FBI. Several people from Wall Street firms prefer to remain anonymous.

Next, I owe thanks to my core literary team. Scott Hoffman is my agent and champion at Folio Literary Management. He helped me find David Ratner and Tess Woods, my publicists from Newman Communications. Pete Wolverton, my editor from Thomas Dunne/Minotaur/St. Martin's Press, made this book better while staying flexible and encouraging me to follow my creative instincts. So did Anne Bensson. Special thanks to Andy Martin and Matthew Shear, my staunch allies. And here's where I break ranks and offer a little insight into the author's journey.

There is an unspoken policy, I think, about my publisher's holiday parties. What happens at SMP stays at SMP. Until now. A conversation with Anne at one of those parties—that and one of my innumerable home-improvement projects gone bad—inspired Chapter 8. When you read what happens in church, I hope you will agree the creative juices were flowing.

Finally, I'd like to acknowledge several allies (there are many) who help spread the word about my books. Dewey Shay has been a great friend and source of motivation. Thanks also to Jon Ledecky, Scott Malkin, Mark Director, Tony McAuliffe, Brooks Newmark, Chris Eklund, and Eugene Matthews, who, like Dewey, have been there every step of the way. I am grateful to Tad Smith and Caroline Fitzgibbons, John and Susie Edelman, Cam Burns, Jack Bourger and Selena Vanderwerf, Marlon Young, James Morgan, Mark Sheehan, and Matt Arpano. This list is not exclusive. There are many others I owe a debt of thanks, and I hope to do so in person.

Family is everything to me. Thank you: Tom and Steve Graves, Joe and Wendy Vonnegut, Chris Nottingham and Helene Vonnegut, Micki Costello and Jack (whom I miss so much), Wynn and Coco, and Marion. I could not have written this book without Mary. She helped fill in the gaps in the left side of my brain.

Two disclaimers: In *The Trust*, I created a community foundation based in Charleston, South Carolina, called the Palmetto Foundation. If a real one exists, there is no link between the two. Mine is pure fiction and nothing more. Same thing with the Catholic Fund. The one in this book is my invention.

The Philippines also plays a role in this novel and, I suspect, in my future writing. I reference one of the country's tougher elements, but I hope to avoid leaving readers with the wrong impression. I love the Philippines and look forward to returning one day. It's a country every American should visit and embrace.

I hope you enjoy *The Trust*.

THE TRUST

CHAPTER ONE

In my business, nothing good happens on Friday afternoon.

I've been at the game ten years. I know better than to hang around before the weekend starts. But there it was, nine minutes to the closing bell. Friday afternoon. Tangled in the stretch cord of my headset, I wasn't going anywhere. Not anytime soon.

Elbows on knees and hands cupped over headphones, I perched on the lip of my swivel chair and gazed down at a stain on the carpeting. At this level, I could smell the trace odors from chemicals. Cleaning solvents had washed out the steel-blue fibers but not the soy sauce. Go figure.

Every so often, I glanced sideways. To my right, Cleopatra legs were going toe to toe with a pair of pin-striped pants. And I wondered who would kick the other one's shins first.

If your head is under the desktop, as mine was, chances are somebody will ask if there's a problem. He might even call the paramedics. That's assuming you work in a reasonable profession like food services or publishing. Or you live in a reasonable place like Wichita, San Diego, maybe even Des Moines.

But if you're a stockbroker in midtown Manhattan, nobody notices when you crouch under your desk. That's our cone of silence, our ad hoc refuge when we're on the phone and it's impossible to hear because the bonehead three desks over is screaming, "I just bagged an elephant!"

Some people hear "The Call of the Wild," and their thoughts turn to the Jack London novel.

I associate that title with stockbrokers. We fight and yap all day. We mark our territories. And you can take it from me. We've forgotten more about pack behavior than London's sled dogs will ever know.

My name is Grove O'Rourke. I work at Sachs, Kidder, and Carnegie, or SKC for short. We're a white-shoe investment bank, a place where the elite go for smart ideas and kid-glove service. From the outside, all you see are bright people and lots of panache.

Inside, it's a different story. We could be Goldman Sachs, Morgan Stanley, or any of the wirehouses. Backstabbing. Rival coalitions. There's nothing pretty about slimeballs. Internecine warfare is the same in every firm.

So are the office layouts. Stockbrokers get crammed into tight spaces. No surprise given the staggering cost of office space across Manhattan. At SKC, there are 150 of us arranged in neat rows of high-tech workstations.

We make a ferocious racket: buying, selling, and nagging clients to shit or get off the pot. Throw in a dozen televisions tuned to CNBC or Fox Business, and the noise is more jarring than silverware in a garbage disposal. Our place is a nuthouse.

But stockbrokers, I mean the ones who succeed in our produce-or-perish business, get used to commotion. That includes military brats like me. Long ago I stopped asking, *How'd I get here?* I discarded my old notions about order, because survivors are the ones who adjust to chaos.

Take the phones. There are time-honored techniques for working them. Outgoing calls are easy. We grab mobiles and disappear into empty conference rooms for sensitive or personal topics. No noise. No prying ears. No big deal.

Incoming calls require finesse. Our quarters are so tight that everybody eavesdrops, whether intentional or otherwise. That's why we talk to our wives and girlfriends, anybody phoning with a prickly issue, from down below. There's no telling when loose lips will bite our sorry asses. Most days, crouching under a desk is business as usual on Wall Street.

That Friday afternoon the noise was deafening, over the top. I was on the phone with a client, not just any client, but Palmer Kincaid. I couldn't hear myself think.

Scully, the world's loudest stockbroker, was screaming all hoarse and bulgy-eyed at Patty Gershon, who holds her own in these ax fights. To be fair, Patty isn't a screamer. Not usually. Guile is her thing, the closest you'll ever come to meeting a tarantula in high heels.

The decibels had taken over, though. Every broker and sales assistant in the room gawked as the argument mushroomed louder and more fierce.

Scully: "Stay away from my client."

F-bomb.

Gershon: "Lowell asked me to mop up your mess."

F-bomb.

Back and forth, the two cursed. And I couldn't hear Palmer, my client and mentor, the guy who got me into Harvard. He'd opened all the doors. He was the bigger-than-life presence, the shrewd coach riding a winning streak that would never end. At least, that's what I'd always thought.

Until now.

"I need your help." He sounded shaky. There was none of Palmer's trademark swagger. He had gone off his game, tentative and distracted.

The Palmer I knew was silky and genteel one minute, an invincible, maybe even ruthless, negotiator the next. He was the classic Charleston businessman, all charm and orthodontist smile, kicking the dirt, playing the small-town card, and taking the center cut from every deal.

Don't get me wrong. Palmer was fair. He was honest. He had allies out the yingyang, and I was one of them. But let's put it out there. Real estate developers don't make $200 million playing Good Samaritan.

Palmer was unflappable. For twenty years, I had admired his grace under fire. All hell could be breaking loose, and he'd invite you into his office and chat about the family. He was never in a hurry.

Not today. Those four words, "I need your help," sounded like Greek coming from his lips.

"Name it." I was worried about my friend. I wished Scully and Gershon would shut the fuck up.

Palmer did not reply. Not at first. The seconds ticked by. The silence became awkward. When he finally spoke, I expected some kind of explanation for his change in behavior.

Didn't happen.

"Damn, Grove! What's going on there?" Apparently, the noise was getting him too.

"Hang on thirty seconds, okay?"

"Sure, whatever."

"Thirty."

I put Palmer on hold and stormed toward Scully. His face burned redder than a watermelon. His neck veins bugged out, fat and puffy like thick blue garden hoses.

He stopped shouting at Gershon, who took a time-out herself. The two stared at me, openmouthed at my intensity. So did the 147 other brokers and eighty-some-odd sales assistants scattered across the floor. Suddenly there was absolute silence, the calm before the storm.

Look, I'm not especially big. About six feet tall, and my girlfriend says, "Grove, you could use ten pounds." You see me and think Lance Armstrong with ginger hair. It's not my size that works in these situations, maybe not even what I say.

It's attitude. When I hit my limit, I morph into a human wrecking ball. I become ruthless, brash, capable of flattening anyone who gets in the way. My Southern manners go AWOL. I have a temper.

"What do you want?" Scully boomed, more bravado than brains, surprised anybody would intrude on his two-person hissy fit. He glanced away, a fleeting nervous flicker, and it was game over. I had him.

Patty said nothing, which is typical. She's more cunning.

Slowly, deliberately, I leaned over and squeezed Scully's shoulder hard enough to make a point. I whispered into his ear, soft enough so nobody else could hear. Not even Gershon. I spoke without venom because conviction is ten times more effective.

Scully's eyes dilated, saucer wide and jittery. The world's loudest stockbroker lost his voice. But his face quivered, and his brow furrowed like a scared rabbit's. "What'd you say?"

No need to answer. I stared a hole into Scully until he dropped his eyes again. The trick in these situations is to threaten once. Act like a hair trigger, methodical, outcome certain, ready to snap any second. Repeating myself, even a simple glance at Patty, would have broken the spell.

Thirty seconds are an eternity when you're shredding somebody's self-confidence. It took less than twenty for Scully to cave. "Let's grab a conference room," he told Gershon.

She looked puzzled, waving her hands and trailing after him. "What did he say?" The two left the room, Scully in the lead, trying to regain his dignity.

"Sorry, Palmer." I was back on the phone, sitting upright at my desk. "What's going on?"

But the moment had passed. His head was somewhere else. "I'll call you Monday, Grove."

"Don't you need my help?"

"Give me the weekend to think things over."

"Think what over?"

"Nothing the harbor won't fix," he said, not all that confident but somehow easing into his steady charisma. Palmer had forgotten more about Southern charm than half of Charleston will ever know. "You still seeing Annie?"

"Whenever I can."

"Take her out to dinner. Get to know her."

What's that mean?

"I'll call you Monday," Palmer repeated.

Then he was gone, and the biggest mistake I ever made was not hopping the next flight to Charleston.

CHAPTER TWO
CHARLESTON, SOUTH CAROLINA

Palmer hung up the phone and gazed across his office. Wide-plank floors were the perfect canvas for a scatter of Persian rugs. The pine wainscoting, ravaged by generations of wood-boring worms, was imported from England. And his antique furniture predated the 1900s. It seemed that everything in the room, Palmer included, was clinging to memories from better times.

Dozens of photos lined the walls. There was Palmer—doughy face and twinkly eyes. His hair was either blond or white, depending on his age in the picture. He was shaking hands with Bill Clinton at the presidential library in Little Rock, hobnobbing with the mayor of Charleston, and dining with Pope Benedict XVI deep inside the Vatican. The shots all trumpeted his storied past. But the politics, big-money career, and more recent years of philanthropic service were the furthest things from his mind.

Palmer was worried sick about his family. His daughter, Claire, was bright and beautiful at age thirty-three. But she was unmarried, for now, and sauntering through life like a divining rod for losers. Her marriage had been an epic disaster. The only good news was that no kids had been caught in the crossfire.

Ashley Kincaid, Palmer's first wife, died when their daughter was a young girl. He had never envisioned life without his sweetheart from Bishop England High School. And now, every so often, his thoughts returned to her. He wanted to talk things over, ask her advice. But he was relieved she could not see his distress.

Palmer's second wife was twenty-seven years younger, a different kind of woman, and a real piece of work in the best possible way. JoJo was loving and affectionate, one of those women who touch everyone, fingertips vital to her communication. She was mercurial, the product of fiery Latin DNA. She spent money like a drunken sailor, not that Palmer cared. JoJo had skills, talents like no woman he had ever known.

He faced a Faustian choice, which is to say, no choice at all. The realization was torturous, eating his thoughts like fire ants. If Palmer did the right thing and fessed up, JoJo and Claire would go to jail. Him, too, but that was beside the point. If he kept his mouth shut, there was no telling what would happen. The consequences might be infinitely worse than a few years in jail.

Really. He had no idea what "his partners" would do. They'd once held themselves out as allies. But they played by a different set of rules, and Palmer was an obstacle. He knew it. They knew it. And in their world, he was expendable.

Palmer could hear his heart beat. He could feel the perspiration running down his brow. He could smell his own fear.

Who are these people?

The Palmetto Foundation once offered so much promise. It was Palmer's baby, his gift to Charleston. He could forget his shortcuts through the years, the ones that all real-estate developers take. Cutting corners made tight budgets work. But cutting corners left ugly problems for somebody else down the road.

Those days were over.

Palmer had made his money—enough to support generations of Kincaids. Now he was looking for absolution. And the Palmetto Foundation offered a gilt-edged legacy, one he could burnish over time, one that would eclipse his shortcomings forever. The organization was much more than a trust formed by a strangle of legal documents. It was a living, breathing entity. It was Palmer Kincaid's immortality.

As a charitable conduit, the Palmetto Foundation served everybody in the community. It accepted donations and made grants according to donor wishes. It provided accounting, investment, and administrative services. It enabled families to build philanthropic programs that survived from one generation to the next without the hassle of paperwork. Palmer donated the first $10 million and promised there was more on the way.

Now his dream, giving back to the community and helping others do the same, was a joke. The irony was nobody had a clue. Even as Palmer's world was unraveling, all of Charleston feted the Kincaids because everything looked oh so good from the outside.

In local circles, Palmer's name equaled largesse. His reputation had grown beyond the boundaries of his own resources, which were already vast. As the chairman of the Palmetto Foundation's board of trustees, he signed every single check—whether he was making the gift or honoring the wishes of other philanthropists.

That $100,000 donation to the College of Charleston: Darlene Simpkins chose to remain anonymous, so she channeled her gift through the Palmetto Foundation. Palmer signed the check, which prompted a handwritten thank-you from the college's Director of Development. Same thing with the Spoleto Festival, the Holocaust Memorial at Marion Square, and several dozen other nonprofit organizations around town. They were all good causes. And Palmer was happy to accept thank-yous, even if he was not the force behind the gifts.

Still, his family gave generously. It was Kincaid money that created critical mass at the Palmetto Foundation. JoJo had recently completed renovations at the Cathedral of St. John the Baptist. Palmer was funding a new wing at the South Carolina Aquarium. And Claire had developed into a philanthropic force all her own at the Charleston Library Society. The locals regarded Palmer's organization as their beachhead against exogenous threats to Southern manners, stucco houses, and a way of life distilled over three hundred—plus years.

The acclaim, Palmer knew, would end soon enough. If word leaked out, all of Charleston would scorn the Kincaids and whisper behind their backs. He struggled to his feet and lumbered across the hall to his daughter's office. He felt every bit of the wear and tear from his sixty-six years.

How could I be so stupid?

Claire was the Palmetto Foundation's Vice President of Development. Her job was to identify families with at least five thousand dollars to give away and help them structure their gifts for medical research, children at risk, whatever.

She was a natural, glowing around donors, opening wallets with the best. She made families believe in the power of giving. She taught them the importance of a philanthropic culture in the home. Everybody trusted Claire Kincaid.

Palmer's friends often said she would make an "awesome mom," a high accolade that gave him hope.

"See you Monday, sweetheart." He was mustering his resources, putting on a good show.

Claire glanced at her watch and feigned disapproval. "And where are you going, mister?"

Palmer marveled that his daughter could stay fresh, both clothes and attitude, through a humid September afternoon. She had a sweep of satiny brown hair, tidy and medium length. Her eyes were clear, free of judgment. Her skin was smooth, flawless, unsullied by the worries that come from society games. She was growing more gracious with age, just like her mother, who'd always had a kind word for everybody.

"Night sailing on *Bounder*." He mopped his brow with a handkerchief.

"Oh, fun. May I come?"

"Not tonight, sweetheart."

"I won't ask Mikey," she persisted, slightly hurt.

Claire's latest boyfriend was a turkey. Palmer would rather slit his wrists than spend five minutes at sea with that guy. But he avoided the urge to make a disparaging remark.

Smiling, eyes twinkling, and stomach somersaulting, Palmer shook his head. "He's not invited either."

"Something wrong?"

"Nope."

Claire paused. Her dad's reply felt too breezy for her comfort. "You're not yourself."

"I need some space tonight."

One floor down Palmer stopped by JoJo's office, high ceilings and bold chocolate-brown walls. Her dachshund, Holly, big-dog attitude compressed into a small body, jumped up and sniffed his wingtips. Tail wagging like crazy.

JoJo was sitting on an overstuffed red chintz settee. Her knees were bent, Jimmy Choos tucked underneath. She gunned Spanish into the mouthpiece of her headset, so fast that Palmer couldn't tell where one sentence began and another ended.

He had taken the language all through high school. *A total waste*, he'd realized on more than one occasion. Sometimes JoJo would tease him and deadpan in the slow, elongated Spanish she reserved for foreigners, "Usted habla español como un gringo."

Seeing him, JoJo sprang from the sofa and stuck the landing on four-inch heels. Never stopped talking on the phone. Never missed a beat. Not so much as a pause. Palmer mouthed the words "I'm going sailing," whereupon she fussed his hair into place, shifted her mouthpiece, and kissed him square and sloppy.

JoJo dabbed traces of Crimson Blush, her favorite shade of lipstick, from his mouth. Her deft touch bordered on foreplay, though it was nothing more than simple affection. "Qué pasa? Qué pasa?" she echoed into the phone, happy and excited, unable to rein back her enthusiasm.

The two made an odd couple. Not so much the difference in their ages: JoJo was thirty-nine; he had a false hip. It was the way they paced through life. Palmer was the classic Southern gentleman, never in a hurry, always slow and methodical, as though the earth would delay its rotation until he caught up. She was kinetic, touching, talking, and tempting.

For an instant JoJo fixed on Palmer. He saw the concern flash across her golden mocha features, her brown eyes dark and almond-shaped, dilated with worry. Palmer smiled double wide, as though closing a deal, and cupped JoJo's cheek until she twinkled back and all the angst disappeared.

With that he headed down onto Broad Street and into the Charleston evening, still muggy at 5:30 P.M. Just once he glanced over his shoulder at his building, yellow stucco, big soaring windows, the place he dubbed "our world headquarters," only half in jest.

These days the Palmetto Foundation made him sick. Walking inside was pure torture, the air rank with stupidity and regret. Leaving was hardly any better. Because from the outside, Palmer's house of good intentions looked more like a tombstone than his shot at redemption. As far as he was concerned, the epitaph should read:

HERE'S WHERE KINCAID FUCKED UP.

It was 9:30 P.M.

The sun had gone down. Sea breezes chased the heat, and rising tides drowned the marshy stink of pluff mud. There were no mosquitoes, none of the flying insects that enjoy air supremacy over Charleston. There was just the hypnotizing chop of water, *Bounder* rocking in the ocean's cradle. It was a night that made the day easy to forget.

Palmer stared at the Cooper River Bridge. His eyes traced the pillars to the flickering of traffic overhead, to the soft light of the crescent moon. His lungs savored the salty air, his ears the symphony of buoys and navigational bells playing the harbor at night.

After a while, Palmer's eyes dropped to the ocean's surface. He lost himself in the occasional flash of dolphins breaking the water, the silvery glint of baitfish stirring the surface in desperate attempts to elude their predators. No way he was pulling up anchor and going home, not anytime soon.

Now, halfway through the bottle, Palmer poured another shot of Wild Turkey. He knocked it back and wiped his mouth with the back of his hand. He felt the fire rake his throat, the hot-chill liquid sliding down his pipes.

Alcohol is Advil for stupidity.

Palmer had boiled a pound of king-sized shrimp for dinner and was down to the last few. He peeled one, tossed the head and shell over the gunwale, and thrust the shrimp into a bowl of his special cocktail sauce.

It had taken him exactly three tries to perfect the formula, which was nothing more than the generic brand plumped up with horseradish and Peter Luger's steak sauce. He laughed when he considered all the people who had offered to pay for the recipe.

The stars, the open night, made everything okay. Behind prison bars, he would lose this peace, the swells and salty smell of sea, the shadowy views of Charleston brushed by moonlight.

He might go a year without seeing JoJo or Claire, maybe several depending on how things played out. He had no idea what the courts would decide. But the more he drank, the less he cared about what happened to him. It was time to protect his wife and daughter. No matter what.

In Wild Turkey, wisdom.

On Monday he'd call his lawyer. He'd fall on a sword and take one for the team. Avoiding the law was an unacceptable risk, one Palmer refused to take with his family's safety at stake.

Afterward, he'd call Grove. That kid had navigated more than his fair share of problems. He was a guy Palmer could trust, smart and rock-solid reliable even if a little slow to take action.

"Sometimes you do the best you can and just say fuck it," Palmer observed to no one in particular.

"Is that any way for a good Catholic to speak?"

Palmer almost leaped out of his skin. He whirled toward the cabin. What he saw made him sick.

CHAPTER THREE

Annie and I had driven up to my beach house in Rhode Island for the weekend. Years ago, she was my sales assistant at SKC. Now she's getting her master's in creative writing at Columbia.

I'm glad she decided against law school. Quick and whip smart, my girlfriend would make a great attorney. But the world doesn't need another litigator who bills at nine hundred dollars an hour. And I doubt she'd be happy anyway.

It was 10:15 A.M. Annie was at the house surgically attached to her laptop. She had a short story due Monday. I was laboring through a kickboxing class, my instructor beating the crap out of me.

"Where's your head, Grove?"

"Sorry."

I couldn't focus. I was thinking about Palmer. The coach's three-step exercise was simple enough. Left jab. Right cross. But when I reached the roundhouse kick, he leg-swept my feet from underneath me.

"Pay attention." My instructor is a big guy, solid, six foot two, built like a tank. I had never seen him so frustrated. "You asked to join my academy. Remember?"

"Sorry."

My apology, number two in as many minutes, was lip service. You don't grow up with a self-assured demigod, listen to him shake and hesitate over the phone, and park your concerns at the door to a martial arts studio. Not when the guy's been a pillar all your life.

Last night, I dialed Palmer's cell from the road. Same thing this morning before class. I tried his office. And when that didn't work, I phoned his home on South Battery. I wanted to ask, "Is everything okay?"

A machine answered each time. "It's Palmer. Leave a message." His recorded voice, the trademark whisper of a Southern drawl, resonated just as soft and sweet as the real thing.

"Left jab," my coach barked.

Bam. I smacked his hand pads, the crack from my glove reverberating like a snare drum.

"Right cross."

Bam.

"Roundhouse kick."

No bam this time. My coach took my legs out from underneath me, again.

"What about your bike races?" he growled.

He was right. I had signed up for kickboxing lessons to improve my reflexes for those tight finishes when the slightest hesitation separates first place from fourth. The classes were a good workout. But cycling is my sport, cross training my way to win more races.

"Sorry."

"You say that again, and I'm taking you down."

Try as I might to pay attention, it was all Palmer that morning. His four words were haunting: "I need your help."

I told myself once, maybe a hundred times during the kickboxing session, *Palmer's fine. Stop being so alarmist.*

The admonitions didn't work.

"Left jab."

Bam.

"Right cross."

Bam.

"Roundhouse kick."

This time my coach clubbed the right side of my head with his pads, which, cushion or no cushion, stung like a bastard. "You got no street in you. Somebody's gonna pop you outside of class, and you won't know what to do."

My eyes narrowed.

He saw the anger. "Take a shot."

I took my fighting stance, left leg forward.

He waited, expecting one of those endless combo drills that dominate our exercise routines. My ear smarted. And me being the sensitive guy I am—always sucking it up until my temper takes over—I wanted to kick his ass. I jumped and twisted in midair, my right shin wheeling around and leveled at his head. Make no mistake: I was going for blood.

The coach ducked, low enough to avoid serious contact. I still managed to swipe his clean-shaven pate. After about ten lessons, it was the closest I had ever come to landing a real blow. And cuffing him felt glorious.

He was surprised. His mouth curled up to the right—smile, smirk, a hint of respect. He continued to circle. "Nice, man, real nice. But in a street fight, nobody's gonna wait for you to wake up."

I waited, fuming, not thinking about what he said. I watched for an opening, ready to jump and take down my coach with a spinning hook-heel kick, anything to get even.

"Enough for one day, Grove. Your legwork's good. Must be all that cycling, because it sure as hell isn't your concentration."

"You want to come riding with me?" I was throwing down the gauntlet. I could take him in a bike race, no sweat.

"Thanks, man. Can't."

Palmer never called Saturday, which was odd. We don't worry about bothering each other on the weekends. We're long past that. I knew something wasn't right. And my instincts were eating me from the inside out.

CHAPTER FOUR
FAYETTEVILLE, NORTH CAROLINA

"What's your wife say?"

"About what?" The crew boss rubbed his temples. He was trying to forget last night's special, the dazzling kick line of two-for-one tequila. He wished the kid would shut up and leave him alone.

"Us working Saturday."

"Says she needs the time off."

"From what?"

"Me."

"Hah!" the kid chortled. "Go figure."

"Shut up."

There were five men working a job near exit 55 on I-95. They had taken two pickup trucks, one equipped with a cherry picker. The telescoping boom reached forty feet no problem, important for the big jobs.

Everyone on the crew wore a blue construction helmet and a body harness, company policy at Smithfield Outdoor Media for employees going up. A sticker on the kid's helmet read, I STILL MISS MY EX, BUT MY AIM IS IMPROVING. The decal was not standard at the billboard company.

They had driven south from corporate headquarters, forty-five minutes through the dense stands of pine and cypress. Saturday morning or not, it was like any other day on the North Carolina freeway. Flying insects detonated against windshields, splattering in yellow cones. Heat wafted off the tarmac in double helixes of Southern ennui. And aging northerners gunned their Cadillacs south. The winter pilgrimage to Florida was under way.

An endless procession of billboards broke the monotony of open road. They promoted fast food, hotels, and chains of every kind. By far, the displays from South of the Border were the most annoying, its one-liners legendary. One after another, they exhorted drivers to pull over and flex their credit cards at the decaying theme park on the Carolina border:

FILL UP YOUR TRUNK WITH PEDRO'S JUNK.

HONEYMOON SUITES: HEIR CONDITIONED.

KEEP YELLING, KIDS! (THEY'LL STOP.)

Soon, one lone billboard would steal all the attention from Pedro, South of the Border, and the blight of signs along I-95. The five men were about to ignite a firestorm. They knew it. So did the owner of Smithfield Outdoor Media. He'd agreed to post the advertisement only after negotiating top dollar and a hold-harmless agreement.

Greater Fayetteville, pronounced "Fed-vull" by the locals, is 200,000 people strong. It's an eclectic place, where patriotic residents take pride in the military presence. Were it not for the armed forces, Fayetteville might be another one of those countless two-blink towns that sprout like mushrooms along muggy Southern highways.

Thousands of soldiers, hailing from every state in the nation, are stationed at nearby Fort Bragg and Pope Army Airfield. They train and run military maneuvers, which make armed caravans a common sight. Many troops deploy to the Middle East, leaving their loved ones behind.

When the soldiers return, local television stations broadcast joyous reunions at Pope. Couples kiss. Little kids hug their mommies or daddies. Everybody has a good cry. And during those moments, parents forget their worries about tight budgets and mortgage payments.

Some families—they're more the exception than the rule—have lived in Fayetteville for generations. They're fiercely proud of their heritage and bristle at the occasional mention of "Fayettenam," military-speak ever since the Vietnam War. The historic district, long-timers note, may be small. But it's bursting with Southern charm, with the craftsmanship and detail orientation that predated the military's arrival en masse.

For the most part the communities are full of hardworking families. Parents take jobs with local businesses that provide services to those living steady lives in tidy neighborhoods. There are big wheels in front of the houses, dogs and cats everywhere.

Neighbors are always getting together for backyard barbecues. They talk football and local politics. They plan day trips to places like Mount Olive, birthplace to the pickles that line supermarket shelves across the country. Or they compare notes about more distant locations, historic resorts like New Bern on the coast.

But Fayetteville, however all-American, suffers a unique misfortune. Located halfway between New York City and Miami, it serves as a convenient hub for the East Coast drug trade. The area's combustible mix of soldiers on furlough, lonely spouses, and a steady supply of recreational drugs makes the city prone to spectacular, sometimes sordid events.

In Fayetteville 28312, where the five men from Smithfield Outdoor Media were working, there were fifty-six churches in total. Twenty-four of them were Baptist. The residents, young or old, military or otherwise, were God-fearing folk for the most part. Sunday services buttressed their lives like the pillars inside the various houses of worship.

Neighbors were accustomed to freeway billboards. Many signs were visible from their backyards because of size and shape. But the new advertisement was a real monster. It soared forty feet in the air, high atop a thick metal pylon. The ad space measured fourteen feet by forty-eight feet. And powerful spotlights illuminated the message dusk till dawn.

None of the neighbors would be happy with what they saw. Size was hardly the issue. It was the promise of comfort food, the pledge of clean showers and spotless bathrooms, and the prurient offer of Sodom and Gomorrah to every trucker on the East Coast.

Three members of the team stood on a metal gangway, behind the billboard's face and high over the ground. They clasped sturdy ropes and began to pull, hand over hand.

Smithfield Outdoor Media no longer employed sign painters. They were a vanishing breed. These days, the company hung preprinted tarps on their billboards. Two men at the bottom fed the sign to their colleagues up top. They took great care to prevent the vinyl tarp from flapping in the breeze.

The giant advertisement began to climb, the message strangely fetching. It read: HIP—TWENTY THOUSAND SQUARE FEET OF FANTASIES OPENING NEXT WEEK.

As the men unfurled the vinyl sheet, the middle section hinted at the coming horror. To the left, the tarp listed what customers would find inside those twenty thousand square feet: costumes, novelties, restaurant and bar, shower facilities, CDs, and toys, toys, toys. There was an ad burst proclaiming, TRUCKERS WELCOME.

To the right was a woman's face, not quite in profile but close. Her unnaturally blue eyes were sultry and stylized, one closed in a salacious come-hither wink. Her red lips were pouty and lush. They evoked images of Park Avenue clinics and other epicenters for plastic surgery where collagen sightings are a dime a dozen. She was sucking on the biggest chocolate-covered strawberry ever seen in those parts. And her radiant face suggested steamy sex at its best.

The bottom three feet eliminated all doubt. The ad copy was big, black, and beckoning. It read, HIGHLY INTIMATE PLEASURES. THE SOURCE FOR ALL YOUR ADULT NEEDS.

Next week an adult superstore, twenty thousand square feet of lechery and fetishes, was opening off exit 55. The billboard ended speculation, all the guessing over the last six months about who was putting up what just a few clicks from the Temple Baptist Church.

The uproar, however, had just begun.

CHAPTER FIVE

"Hey, Biscuit." Mrs. Jason Locklear wedged her way to the front of the room. She was a plump woman, her ample bosom jutting forward like the nose cone of a 747. "What do we tell our children?"

The crowd hushed and waited. They were homeowners. They were military families, stretching for their piece of the American dream. Above all, they were kindred souls united by a common problem.

Mrs. Jason Locklear was the reliable neighborhood activist. She had proven herself time and again, whether organizing block parties or staving off tax hikes on their homes. Now she was assembling resources for the fight of the young subdivision's life.

Parents had packed into her 3,100-square-foot colonial with wrap-around porch. It was by far the largest home in the neighborhood, the only residence that came with a bonus room from the builder. Liberty Point Plantations was a community on edge.

Most days the development resembled other suburbs near exit 55. The houses were uniform, two stories, two-car garages, and too much red brick. Their timber trim—whites, blues, and greens bordering on black—kept things interesting.

Bikes were sprawled across front yards. The lawns were a tangle of crabgrass and regret, a dappling of bare spots underneath towering pines that dropped needles everywhere.

The communal swimming pool was a notch too small. Kids were always landing cannonballs on each other, every summer marked by three or four 911 trips to the emergency room for broken bones. Liberty Point Plantations was the kind of place where young families would grow old—were it not for the cycle of active military that moved in and out every few years.

Today the neighbors had forgotten the routine complaints of suburbia in the South. Whose kid was a bully. Whose dog was a menace—lock it up or put it down. Who made too much noise, either partying all night or sitting on a horn in the driveway, trying to hurry the kids off to school, church, or whatever. To a man, to a woman, they had declared war on their common enemy:

Highly Intimate Pleasures.

Biscuit Hughes scanned the crowd of fiery eyes, furrowed brows, and tense fists. He was a towering man, though his size was not especially intimidating. He fell more into the category of lovable bear, his pudding body shaped by Denny's every morning.

Bacon, sausage, scrambled eggs, syrup, whipped butter, and a stack of pancakes—Biscuit believed a Grand Slam breakfast was the only way to start the day. The calorie intake was monstrous, 1,100 of those bad boys, but he insisted his side order of yogurt kept things healthy.

The next few minutes, Biscuit knew, would be critical. It was time to be careful, time to choose his words with the ambassadorial talent of a United Nations diplomat. Because he was about to drop a second bomb on Liberty Point Plantations, and this one packed more explosive punch than the nightmare billboard hovering over I-95.

Biscuit wondered how many in the room had slept. Whether they had stayed up all night, staring across their backyards at the monstrous red lips, illuminated and salacious. Whether residents had vented at their ministers all morning, fuming, praying, pondering what had become of their neighborhood, the place where everybody once felt safe.

Next week exit 55 would become a destination, the place where truckers from New Jersey could buy steamy movies and take cold showers. There was no doubt about it: the neighbors might be in control of their emotions now, but his revelation would whip them into a frenzy never before seen in Cumberland County.

After Desert Storm and four years in the army, Allan "Biscuit" Hughes scraped through the Norman Adrian School of Law, when it was located in Buies Creek. In many ways, grad school was a bust. The town was dry, and the courses made his teeth hurt. He objected to the precise, ponderous language from professors who blurred the distinctions between right and wrong.

Biscuit was not the smartest attorney in Fayetteville. Nor the mean-est. Nor the most ruthless. Biscuit was, however, the most persistent. He practiced law through conviction and war of attrition rather than logic or examination of fact. He was the attorney every underdog admired, once a fixture on the front page of *The Fayetteville Observer*, the hope of ordinary Joes who had been wronged by the powerful reach of big business.

Four years earlier Biscuit sued Cavener Land Development, a NASDAQ-listed company based in Calabasas, California. He brought a class-action suit on behalf of fourteen homeowners in Riverwood South near Fort Bragg. Families from the subdivision complained that the builder's work was shoddy, that their homes leaked like sieves every time it rained. Mold and fungus grew everywhere.

The partners at his former law firm told him to forget the case. "We'll never get paid."

"It's not about the money," argued Biscuit. "My old man was enlisted. And I won't sit here and watch a bunch of assholes from California rip off our sergeants major. I'm suing with or without you."

Without.

The senior partner fired Biscuit on the spot. "We hired you to close property transactions. Not to pick fights that you, of all people, can't win."

Biscuit swallowed the overwhelming urge to say, "Fuck you, sunshine."

He proceeded against the odds and ran the suit from Phil's Polynesian, the tiki bar outside Bragg he co-owned with his brother-in-law. Cavener boasted more money and more investigators. It had more hired guns, all of whom hailed from Harvard and Yale. Just more, more, more. They were competent adversaries, attorneys who kicked ass in court.

Few people had any confidence in Biscuit, other than the aggrieved families. They were living in moldy homes with moist foundations and no roof paper under their shingles. They needed to believe in somebody, any-body, and he was the one attorney willing to take their case on a contin-gency basis.

The other believer was Faith Ann Hughes. She was always telling her husband, "You can win this."

Biscuit compensated for his so-so legal skills with research. He interviewed everybody, all the families in the subdivision, building inspectors, and clerks in the town office. He Googled the senior executives at Cavener and scrutinized their backgrounds ad nauseam. He was looking for a nugget, a morsel, any tidbit that would give his clients the advantage.

He tripped over a mountain. Fayetteville's building inspector agreed to meet at Phil's Polynesian. And their conversation, fueled by three mai tais each, turned an otherwise mediocre legal practice into the stuff of legends.

Inspector: "What do you reckon your clients paid for their houses?"

Biscuit: "Two hundred thousand on average."

Inspector: "I doubt those homes are worth a couple of three thousand."

Biscuit: "What are you saying?"

Inspector: "It's cheaper to knock them down and build from scratch than fix what's there."

Biscuit: "But your department issued the certificates of occupancy."

Inspector: "All crap. My predecessor was on the pad, and I can prove it."

The story dominated Fayetteville's news—partly because of Biscuit's instinctive knack for working with the press. He promised drinks, Navy Grog on the house at Phil's Polynesian, for every story written or television clip aired about Cavener. The developer settled out of court shortly after *The Wall Street Journal* printed a scathing article.

The dollar amount of the settlement was never disclosed. But Biscuit pocketed $2.1 million. And his reputation grew in size and stature.

He explained his acclaim like he was giving the recipe for a drink: "One part sleuthing, one part hyperbole, and three parts media."

There was a new fight now. The residents of Liberty Point Plantations agreed Biscuit Hughes was the right man to protect their patch of the American dream. But they had no idea what Biscuit had already unearthed.

Inside the Locklear family room, its temperature growing warm from all the bodies, Biscuit could almost taste the expectation. He could feel the hope that his words would make everything better. That Highly Intimate Pleasures would go away, and life would return to normal.

"You know what my daughter said?" asked Mrs. Jason Locklear. She had contacted Biscuit first, chased him down yesterday morning. All eyes in the room shifted from him to her. Locklear was large, and for the moment, she was in charge.

Biscuit waited, patient and respectful. He remembered the rancor at Riverwood South. He recalled what it was like as a kid, when the Hughes family of eight crowded round the table. Best to let people vent. Get it out of their system.

Once Locklear spoke, and anyone else for that matter, he'd deliver his thoughts Joe Friday style. "Just the facts, ma'am." At least he'd try it that way.

"My daughter read the word 'costume,'" Locklear said. "She wants to know if HIP is a Halloween store."

"Jason would love to see you in a few outfits," cracked Evans. He was one of the husbands in the crowd, the guy who kept things light, the guy who brokered peace during neighbor-versus-neighbor arguments.

A few people snickered, which prompted Evans's wife to elbow him in the ribs. The chuckles were anemic, though. And Locklear stared daggers at the offenders, her fiery demeanor warning them to keep their mouths shut.

"I can't stop Highly Intimate Pleasures from opening next week." Biscuit shook his head in regret. There were audible sighs across the room, the sound of air hissing from a balloon.

"Hold them up in zoning," somebody suggested.

"How'd an adult superstore get this far along in the first place?" another demanded.

"Yeah?" barked a third. "It's a damn disgrace if you ask me."

The room broke into a low, unintelligible roar. Neighbors talked over each other and gunned questions faster than Biscuit could answer. No one waited for a response. And it was clear that Locklear had lost her reins, the riotous crowd growing noisier by the moment.

Biscuit pursed his lips, stuck his forefinger and thumb in his mouth, and whistled like a steam pipe. The shrill note packed a power more abrasive than fingernails against a chalkboard. The high pitch silenced the angry mob and sent Dodger, the Locklear dog, yowling around the corner.

"I checked out the building," Biscuit said. "Our county law says HIP can't locate within three thousand feet of a subdivision, church, or school.

And they haven't. You need to drive at least a half mile off exit 55 to get to them, which means they don't need zoning approval."

The room grumbled in unison.

"But why let facts get in the way?" he asked, quoting a professor from his law school days. "I'll talk to the county inspectors tomorrow. Get them riled up."

"Attaboy," one of the men encouraged.

"Not so fast," Biscuit cautioned. "HIP most likely complies with our zoning. And I doubt they meet the county's definition of 'sexually oriented businesses.' "

"SOBs," clarified Evans.

Murmurs filled the room again, until Locklear turned around and glared the crowd into submission. "Why wouldn't it be a sexually oriented business?"

"Sales mix. Inventory selection. Those costumes you mentioned, all the lingerie, the novelties, the nutraceuticals—they don't count as adult products. There are superstores like Highly Intimate Pleasures all over the country. Most of them dedicate less space to blue movies and toys in order to avoid the zoning requirements for adult-oriented businesses."

"What about the bar?" she pressed.

"What about it? I didn't see any references to topless dancers."

"We need some of that Cavener magic," said Locklear, reminding the lawyer about the importance of his job. His mission was to stop an adult superstore, at any cost, from defiling their way of life inside Liberty Point Plantations.

Some of the neighbors, just off duty, were dressed in Army Combat Uniforms, or ACUs as they are known among the troops. Military uniforms always filled Biscuit with a sense of mission, with the fight, the will, the energy to redouble his efforts. But he reminded himself not to overpromise. It was the surest way to underdeliver, and his newest clients needed to know exactly what they faced.

"I'll throw everything at them," he promised, "including the kitchen sink. But it's fifty-fifty whether we win."

"Trying to goose your legal fees?" snapped Evans. No elbow to the ribs this time.

"The fees are the fees." Biscuit refused to bite, no matter how provocative Evans's questions. "In these cases, I usually check out the owners first thing. Dig up some bad stuff. Play it up in the press, big-time. And then I bring the hell and fury of political pressure down on the zoning board."

"So do it," urged Locklear.

Every person in the room nodded assent. Their jaws set and their expressions stern, they were ready to take on Goliath.

"Won't work," answered Biscuit.

"Why not?"

"Any Catholics here today?" Biscuit scanned the crowd.

A half dozen or so raised their hands, including Locklear. "What's that got to do with anything?" she objected.

"HIP is owned by a foundation."

"What kind of foundation?" somebody asked.

"The kind that comes with money and a huge congregation."

The expressions changed from resolve to confusion. The room buzzed out of control again, nobody waiting for the lawyer's reply but everybody demanding an explanation.

Biscuit whistled, that shrill piercing call for attention, and the crowd went silent. "The name of the foundation," he said, "is the Catholic Fund."

Stunned silence.

"What's that mean?" demanded Locklear.

"HIP doesn't sell condoms," cracked Evans.

"I'm all over it," observed Biscuit. "You can take that to the bank."

CHAPTER SIX
NEW YORK CITY
MONDAY

"My office, Grove."

It was early, before the opening bell, and that's how my current boss summoned me. No pleasantries from her. Nothing like "How was your weekend?" I wasn't sure what to expect, an attaboy or a beat-down.

Current boss.

You heard me. I've had fourteen managers over the last ten years. I'd call them an endangered species, except the supply is endless. The last one, Kurtz, traded SKC for Morgan Stanley. We called him the "Monthly Nut," as much for his brain-dead decisions as for our belief that he was an extraneous expense, an overhead line item.

Kurtz sent around an e-mail on the way out, something about seeking "new challenges" and treasuring his years "with good friends at the firm." What a crock. The boy got himself canned. Over at the new shop, he'd stop at nothing to eat our lunch.

Ten years. Fourteen bosses.

Katy Anders is number fourteen. She had been on the job all of ten days, hardly enough time for me to break her in. But long enough for my colleagues in Private Client Services to dub her "Pamela Anderson." The nickname was a not-so-veiled reference to her open buttons and pour-over blouses.

"What'd you say to Scully on Friday?"

Straight and to the point. Anders had heard about the F-bombs. She was all business, none of that mealymouthed baloney Kurtz had perfected. I like a boss who speaks her mind, or his, whatever the case may be. It makes life so much easier.

"I implied he might have a career problem."

"How?"

"I said Percy Phillips was on my line."

"Oh." She leaned back and frowned.

"And he wanted to know who was screaming 'Fuck you' every five seconds."

Anders developed a sudden case of thyroid eyes. Percy does that to people. Our CEO is a legend, not only for building SKC from scratch but also for his mercurial decision making. He once fired a stockbroker over the intercom during a companywide research meeting. Some hapless newbie had made the mistake of mouthing off to the press.

"Do I have a problem?" Anders's face was clouding over. She brushed her upper lip with a hooked forefinger, and I made a mental note to remember the nervous tic.

"What makes you think that?"

I was too intrigued to confess that Palmer had been on the line. That I would have done anything to muzzle Scully and Gershon, even if it meant snatching his $125 Hermès pocket square and stuffing it down one of their throats.

Scully believed my Percy story on Friday for the same reason Anders believed it now. I cover our CEO. He became my client a few years earlier, when the Monthly Nut brokered an arrangement to keep me at the firm. That was the last time I got pissed off and threatened to leave. Anders knew Percy was my client. So did every broker on the floor. Politics has a way of getting around at SKC.

"Percy's unpredictable. Two brokers lose control on my watch. And you want to know why I have a problem?"

"Don't worry about him," I said, taking the low road of corporate real-politik and pretending to hold more sway over our CEO than was actually the case. "I got your back."

"Thanks." She kept brushing her lip with that curled forefinger. "He has a short fuse these days, right?"

"No kidding," I agreed, sensing she was about to change topics.

Anders gestured with her eyes toward the door. I stood up, closed it, and returned to my seat. She leaned forward, conspiratorial and buddy-buddy. Her pose was, forgive me here, a boss-with-benefits moment for the ages.

"Did Percy and you talk about anything else?"

"The usual," I said coyly. Our exchange was showing promise.

"Then you know what's going on?"

One thing was clear. Anders suspected a big event, something that would make page 1 of *The Wall Street Journal*. But she had no clue what—otherwise she would never have asked the question. I stayed on plan, pretending to know more than I did, squeezing her for whatever she knew.

"Percy tells me lots of things in confidence."

"Stuff about SKC?"

I studied Anders, her curiosity, her intensity. She was fishing for info, wondering if our CEO had revealed a big strategic decision to me.

Not a chance.

It's not like we shot the breeze about SKC's corporate direction. But my relationship with Percy didn't stop me from pretending. "Nothing I can repeat."

"Hah! I knew it," she triumphed. "All the whispering. The conversations behind closed doors. People who stop talking when they see you in the halls. You know, Grove, what happens in this room stays in this room. Right?"

Tell that to the thirteen managers who preceded you.

A short knock at the door saved me from answering. I whirled around to find Zola Mancini, dark exotic features, unruly shock of curly black hair, and my partner going on two years. We managed over $5 billion together.

"Sorry to interrupt." Zola turned to me. "Claire Kincaid is on the line. She insisted I find you."

A client's daughter trumps a boss with nose trouble all day long. I stood up and asked Anders, "Can we talk later?"

The interruption was odd. Claire calling me at the office. Asking Zola to hunt me down. I remembered the last time we saw each other. It was bad news three years ago. And I had a feeling it was bad news now.

Claire Kincaid was my Daisy Buchanan. Not that she was pampered and superficial like Fitzgerald's siren from West Egg. She was far too kind. Nobody could ever accuse her of being some shallow snot with more money than heart.

If anything, Claire had been friendly to a fault during high school. She'd hang with the cool crowd and then goof off with the dweebs. Afterward, she'd say nice things about everybody. Palmer's daughter was controlled and elegant with her opinions, a regular Madam Ambassador.

Perfection makes me nervous. I like a few warts on my friends. Sometimes Claire's diplomatic polish bugged me—which might be my problem rather than hers. When we were at Bishop England, our high school in Charleston, I often wished she'd break down and gossip like the rest of us.

Claire played it safe, though. She'd never turn on anyone. And it was generosity of spirit that made her vulnerable. She was spread way too thin to develop deep relationships, the kind where somebody's in your foxhole. She was everybody's ally, but nobody's best friend. Still, I wouldn't call her superficial. The word that comes to my mind is "unobtainable."

Let me explain.

The historic part of Charleston is located at the junction of two rivers. The Ashley and the Cooper collide, spill into a harbor bordering the Atlantic, and forever leave behind the stiff-legged egrets with S-shaped necks that fish the marshes day in, day out. These waters are more than a home for shrimp and crabs, schools of dolphin, mullet, and red snapper, the occasional alligator or two. They're walls, natural barriers protecting a way of life that has endured over three hundred years. You're either from the Charleston peninsula or from somewhere else.

South of Broad is the rich end of the historic district. The houses are sacred relics, many built in the 1700s and crafted from mahogany and brick, from materials chosen to withstand hurricanes, termites, and other scourges of nature. The residents pride themselves on handing down a way of life from one generation to the next. If your family hasn't lived there for the last hundred years, you're not part of the club.

Then there's South Battery, the street south of Broad you see in all the tourist photos, the one with the massive mansions overlooking Charleston's harbor. I've heard people call it "High Battery," because in a neighborhood of the elite, this street is hallowed ground. Home to the capo dei capi. The people living here are the lords of Charleston.

Growing up, Claire was next in line to the throne. More money. More looks. More body. Enough sex pheromones to make teenage boys forget all the lingerie in Hollywood. Every guy in high school had a secret crush on her. I know I did. Claire was taller and more athletic than the other women on varsity track, too well built to ever devolve into one of those size 0 anorexia queens prowling around Manhattan. She had it all.

I grew up on an Air Force base. And when my dad retired, we moved into a three-bedroom ranch in the area known as West of the Ashley. South Battery—give me a break. We didn't live anywhere near south of Broad. We didn't even live on the peninsula.

Translation: O'Rourkes were outsiders.

No matter how nice Claire Kincaid was to me, I never dared to indulge my high school crush and ask her out. There was too much distance between us: a caste system of Southern manners, that and about eight miles of fiddler crabs along the Ashley River.

I saw her all the time, in AP classes and outside Cathedral after Mass every Sunday. I drove her home after a party once—me, the designated driver for Daisy Buchanan—when her busted trade of a boyfriend passed out in the back of Palmer's BMW. But we never had one of those moments, two people sharing something intimate, until long after high school.

You know the kind I mean.

It was three years ago at the funeral of my wife and daughter. Claire held me for a long, long while, and when we parted she brushed tears from my cheek. Standing there, dressed in several shades of charcoal, she bored into my eyes. Hers looked like black headlights.

"You okay, Grove?"

Claire refused to let me look away. She wanted to hear everything. How Evelyn and I met in college. What our daughter, Finn, was like. And yes, how they crashed on I-95 heading toward New Haven.

Fucking eighteen-wheelers.

I wanted to put on a game face with Claire, thank everybody who came to the funeral, and then crawl into a spider hole where, alone with memories of my wife and daughter, I could gnaw off my arm in peace.

After the funeral, Claire phoned a few times. She worried about me. She'd ask how I was. And she got nothing in return, because I had perfected the fine art of plastic replies:

"Awesome."

"Fine, and you?"

"Living the dream."

That's the thing about my profession. You talk money. Explain risk. Throw in a few snide cracks about I-bankers, all the toxic crap they cook up, and you have the perfect place to hide when you're brain-dead from grief.

Long before Annie and I became an item, Claire reached out to me. I never gave her a chance, for reasons that elude me to this day. Maybe her deadbeat of an ex-husband was still in the picture. I don't remember.

Anticipation sends time to the penalty box. You watch from the sidelines. You see everything in slow motion. The seconds don't tick by. They get under your skin. It's the wondering, worrying, and waiting for resolution that are so maddening.

After Zola said Claire was holding, I sprinted to my workstation. Ten years had lapsed, or so it seemed, by the time I picked up the phone and stabbed the blinking light to take her call. Inside, I was screaming, *What's wrong?*

But I exercised control and hid my alarm. "How are you?"

"Not great." Claire's voice quivered, the timbre shaky and unfamiliar, a shadow of that rich mix between CNN anchor and Charleston drawl.

"It's your dad, right?"

The question surprised Claire, the way I'd guessed the reason for her call. At some base level, I hoped Palmer was okay.

Then she confirmed my fears with a question of her own. "How'd you hear?"

The room started to spin.

"What happened?"

"Dad's body washed ashore early this morning."

Zola watched my eyes, rolled her chair next to me, and rubbed my arm. I could feel my partner's breath. It was fresh and warm, moist like a heated towel rubbing my face. She knew there was a problem. And without speaking, she was telling me, *We're in this together.*

But inside my head, I left Zola and the buzz of Private Client Services. I returned to that black, barren, bleak place where I had spent eighteen months flogging myself for missing a flight back to New York. I should have been the one driving Evelyn and Finn to our place in Narragansett. Now something had happened to Palmer, a guy who had sounded an alarm only three days ago.

It's on me.

"I spoke to Palmer on Friday."

"He went night sailing and never came back." Claire started to sob.

Her words made no sense to me. "Palmer's an elite sailor."

"The police said he was drinking. They think *Bounder*'s boom hit him in the head."

He's too young. I could feel my eyes welling up.

"Dad said to call you first, if anything ever happened to him."

"I'll be on the next flight to Charleston."

"I don't know what to do."

I wanted to hug Claire through the phone. My wife and daughter—I knew the vulnerability that comes from loss all too well. "We'll get through this. I promise."

"He said you're his 'thousandth man.' Do you know what that means?"

I knew all right. That's when I lost it. Zola's face dimpled with empathy. So did Chloe's. She's our sales assistant. They both saw the tears streaming from my eyes. It's hard to appear stoic when you wear your feelings on your sleeves.

CHAPTER SEVEN
BROKERAGE FLOOR AT SKC

After hanging up with Claire, I called Annie first thing. It's what I do. Those eighteen months of despair I mentioned—she's the one who rescued me. We've been together for two years now, and I've been okay, even happy.

Annie is blazing through life on the verge of volcanic explosion. Not because of a temper. It's her energy. That's what I love about her, most of the time. She doesn't hold back. Opinions, emotions whether happy or sad, and those uncanny observations about details the rest of us miss—she's always erupting about something.

In stockbroker lingo, my girlfriend is "long" conviction. Right or wrong, she thinks she's right every time. And mostly, she is. But I have to be honest. Every once in a while, her certitude bugs the shit out of me. That's when Annie teases me and says, "Come on, Grove. You know I'm adorable."

And I say, " 'Adorable' is such a girl word."

And she says, "It's like our version of 'hot,' except we mean cute women with spunky personalities."

Only now, we weren't bantering with each another. Annie was counseling me, the way she always does. "You belong in Charleston."

"Palmer told Claire I'm his 'thousandth man.' "

"Like the Kipling poem?"

"He made me memorize it one summer."

"That's weird." Classic Annie. She's quick with an opinion.

"Not weird, I worked for him."

"But, Grove, a poem?"

"Just our relationship. I'd drive Palmer out to his developments. And we'd talk business, deals, people, the whole shebang. He said military brats get the big-picture stuff right, but we suck at the instinctive stuff. Like horse-trading with people."

"What's this have to do with Rudyard Kipling?"

"Palmer said he got more out of Kipling than he got from business school."

"I can't remember how the poem goes."

"And I'll never forget:

'Nine hundred and ninety-nine depend
On what the world sees in you,
But the Thousandth Man will stand your friend
With the whole round world agin you.'"

"Wow," she said, almost whistling. "He loved you."

"And I blew it."

"What do you mean?"

"He was odd last Friday. Said he might need some help."

"That's why you were phoning him all weekend?"

"Yeah."

"You're not beating yourself up, are you?"

"No," I lied.

"Good, that's my job," Annie replied, breezy, never pausing to catch her breath. "How's his daughter?"

"About what you would expect. She's a wreck."

"I'm sorry to hear that."

"You want to come?"

"Can't. Two papers due this week." She paused for a moment. "Hey, Grove."

"Yeah."

"You're Palmer's thousandth man based on what you do now. You had no control over what happened Friday."

"Sure."

That afternoon I forgot the markets. I didn't care about the Dow Jones. As far as I was concerned, the index could blow up with or without my help.

Same thing with SKC. I didn't care about the drama du jour. I had no idea why Anders was squeezing me for information. And for the moment, I had no reason to believe anything was out of the ordinary. My shop is a fucking soap opera 24-7.

Palmer Kincaid pounded through my brain the rest of the day. Dead at sixty-six. I couldn't believe he was gone. Frankly, there were a number of things I couldn't believe.

Palmer was a skilled drinker. We had eaten at all the top restaurants, Le Cirque, Le Bernardin, whatever suited his fancy whenever JoJo and he boarded their private jet for New York City. I had seen him guzzle wine, vodka, every form of alcohol you can imagine. Even grappa, which tastes like turpentine if you ask me. He never got sloppy, not once. He was always in command, always in control.

Palmer was also a skilled sailor. He had won countless regattas through the years. He was more comfortable on *Bounder* than he was on land. So he said. I didn't buy the flying-boom-to-the-head explanation. Not on *Bounder*. Not with his experience.

Nor did I buy the news from Chloe. "All the flights to Charleston are sold out," she said. "JFK, LaGuardia, even White Plains."

"There's got to be something."

"I'll keep trying."

Chloe was right.

On Tuesday, I boarded an early flight and arrived in downtown Charleston around noon. Palmer's vigil was that night. And me being an O'Rourke, I refused to miss it.

"Real friends," my dad used to say, "show up at your wake."

If you ask me, the night before your own funeral seems a little late to find out. But I never challenged the big guy, then or now. I make the wakes.

The Charleston Place Hotel was what you expect from luxury accommodations down South: crisp, clean, the temperature cold enough to hang meat. I dumped my bags upstairs and headed outside to Meeting Street, where Charleston remained exactly how I'd left it. Heat that saps your energy. Palmettos everywhere and, because they offer no shade, not much help with the sun. The air smelled sweet, muggy with camellias and horse piss from the carriage rides. There was no hint of the fall, just a few days away.

I began walking toward Palmer's place on South Battery, through the time capsule of buildings two and three hundred years old. And the old feeling returned, the sense that I had joined an ongoing epic with Southern heroes and Yankee barbarians, that I had entered a consecrated land where the families had been hallowing their homes, their way of life, and sometimes each other for generations. Given the circumstances, it was a coin toss whether I wanted to be back.

About ten minutes later, I pushed through a black wrought-iron gate into the Kincaids' front garden. There was a crepe myrtle off to my right, its flowered branches blasting with lavender. Two columns of gerberas, potted in Charleston-green containers, lined the painted wooden stairs. And hanging baskets of pansies, laced with violas, sprayed the porch with violets, whites, and purples so dark they were black.

Nobody does gardens like Charleston.

I'm in good shape, and the hike from the hotel had been short. But I don't care if you're Charles Atlas himself. Sweat was already drenching my white oxford shirt. On the way over, I had draped my tan jacket across my shoulder. I pulled it back on, both to hide the dampness and to afford Palmer the proper respect.

Ferrell opened an arched mahogany door, nearly eight feet high. He was seventy-something, stiff and gray in an ageless kind of way, his manner genteel and distinguished. He had been working for Palmer as long as I could remember. Driver. Butler. Whatever. I didn't know his exact title, only that he was Palmer's go-to guy for everything.

Dark, puffy circles rimmed his eyes. But the lines were not from age. His bags came from tormented nights, from staring at the ceiling fan and remembering a friend. From thinking, *What a waste.*

"Mr. Grove," he said, "the family's been waiting for you."

Some things never change. Ferrell's formal address made me uncomfortable. Under any other circumstances, I would have reminded him to call me Grove. Now wasn't the time. I shook his hand, looked him in the eyes, and walked inside the double-wide foyer with fourteen-foot ceilings. "You were together a long time."

"Mr. Palmer was a good man."

Yesterday morning, Claire had asked me to drop by "Daddy's house" the minute I arrived. "JoJo and I will be there."

I expected to find the two of them, alone with their grief and members of the staff. But a modest crowd had already arrived. The who's who of Charleston were gathering to extend their condolences long before the seven-thirty wake that evening.

Jim and Lita Devereaux were there. So was Gabby Calhoun, who hated her nickname but everybody called her Gabby anyway. I saw Bull Pinckney, Missy Heyward and her husband, whose name I couldn't remember. It was probably Rutledge, but I always confused the guy with Bat Ravenel. The Pritchard sisters were there, identical twins. So were Prawler Condon, Sunny Harken, and Monsignor Manigault. All the faces and unique Charleston names—I knew these people from Cathedral or around town, but we no longer stayed in touch. It felt like I had stepped back ten years.

"Grove O'Rourke, is that you?" called a woman from across the room.

It was JoJo, svelte in trim black pants and a matching top. I would have said Armani, but Annie tells me I think everything is Armani and that most of our older friends wear St. John. JoJo was taller than I remembered. Maybe it was the heels. And her hair was lighter than the last time I saw her. Maybe it was the highlights, but again I'm getting into Annie's territory. She looked fresh off a movie screen: flawless tan, perfect white teeth, and a figure that had grown more provocative on the cusp of forty. Only her moist brown eyes betrayed the reason we had all gathered.

JoJo squeezed Bull's shoulder and walked toward me, stopping to instruct Ferrell where to put two dozen roses that had just arrived. "Give me five minutes," she said, resting her hand on his, "and get Rose on the phone. I want to go over tomorrow's menu with her one last time."

I half hugged JoJo hello, formal and awkward the way O'Rourke men have been greeting women for generations. The fact was, I didn't know JoJo all that well. I felt more comfortable hanging back and letting her take the lead. She had moved to Charleston from San Diego, and she became Palmer's star broker about the time I graduated from Harvard Business School. As their relationship evolved, she phased out of his real estate interests and into the Palmetto Foundation. JoJo and Palmer had married five years ago, and the hug was me erring on the side of caution. We had spent only a handful of evenings together in New York City.

JoJo didn't hold back. She threw her whole body into the embrace. Squeezed me hard. Her storied dachshund, Holly, appeared from nowhere and started to bark. I think from jealousy.

When we finally broke, she cupped my face with her hands and said, "I'm so glad you're here. It means everything to me."

The words surprised me. With her touch, tone, and teary eyes, Palmer's wife conveyed intimacy way beyond the depth of our friendship. "You know I owe Palmer everything."

"He often talked about getting you back to Charleston."

JoJo straightened my jacket, stepped back, and looked me once over. "Don't they feed you in New York City?"

I came up empty on the small talk and shrugged.

"You need to spend some quality time with a fork, Grove. After the funeral tomorrow, I'm feeding half the peninsula back here. And I won't be happy until you pack on ten pounds."

I know the happy-face act, how to pretend everything's wonderful when you're bowled over and ready to throw up your grits and a lion's share of grief. Been there. Done that.

JoJo had gone into funeral entertainment mode. She was rallying with friends and staving off her pain. After the tears were shed, after everybody said, "I'm so sorry," or asked, "How may I help?" after they finished their drinks and paid their respects—she would sit alone in Palmer's big house with nobody but her dog and her despair. The heartache would eat her marrow like myeloma. Nobody ever cheats grief from getting its way.

"Miss JoJo," interrupted Ferrell. "The caterers are on the phone for you."

"Oh, right. Tell Rose," she replied, winking at me, "we need three dozen more of those shrimp kebabs. And more of that red snapper she serves with cilantro sauce."

"Yes, ma'am."

"Let's find Claire," JoJo said, tugging my hand, squeezing and touching her way through the gathering that was growing bigger by the minute.

Roses were arriving left and right. Everybody, it seemed, wanted to talk with Palmer's widow. Or they wanted to catch up with me. A woman whom I hadn't seen since high school said, "Let's grab a drink after the wake." JoJo was on a mission, though, and insisted we find her stepdaughter.

More of a "stepsister," given their age difference.

"I need to talk to both of you," she said, speaking to me, but somehow connecting with everyone in the room.

"Lead the way."

We found Claire staring at the portrait of Palmer over the fireplace, a Warhol no less. She wore a black top and pleated charcoal skirt, the close shades her signature style. She turned, and it was like we had never left my wife and daughter's funeral. No hint of aging. No advance of time. Her skin soft in the afternoon light. Claire still possessed that vulnerable look—buffed, elegant, the expression that asked, "Will you take care of me?"

"Hey, you." I hugged her with my awkward O'Rourke hello.

"I'm glad you're here."

JoJo rubbed both our backs and said, "I spoke to Huitt this morning. He asked if we could all meet at his office on Thursday."

"Why me?" The request for my presence seemed odd. Huitt Young was one of Palmer's lawyers. I suspected he was the executor, because the two men had been friends since they attended Bishop England together.

"Huitt insisted," JoJo confirmed.

"Do you know why?" I asked.

"Just be there," she said. "Oh, there's Gordie. Gotta go."

"Gordie?" I asked, once JoJo was gone.

"One of dad's roommates from college." With that we stood there, alone with our memories of Palmer and each other.

CHAPTER EIGHT

DISTRICT OF COLUMBIA

Back home, everybody called him "Bong." Not that he was a druggie. And not that he abstained. Through the years, Bong had tried everything at least once. There was nothing better than "black hash," opium mixed with hashish, especially when made from the really good shit that's impossible to find outside Myanmar.

Those days were behind him. He was a businessman. He had no time to get Marley'd. And the truth was, his nickname predated all the sucking, snorting, and shooting up. His parents called him Bong as a toddler because he loved doorbells and was always mimicking their sound.

"Bing bong."

From inside his Chevy, a white nondescript rental, Bong stared at an art deco building across the street. ANACOSTIA was posted on the facade in bold, cursive, billboard-sized letters. And underneath, a signpost marked the streets. He was standing at the intersection of Martin Luther King Avenue and Good Hope Road.

"Good Hope" my ass, he thought.

Bong knew a thing or two about poverty. He had endured the worst, seen it, touched it, smelled it, heard it, and yes, tasted it. As a teenager, he lived in a barrio perched on stilts over a river clogged with excrement. There was nothing worse than watching a dead neighbor float facedown and ride the intestine-brown water to wherever. Anacostia was better than the slums back home. But the place was a pit no matter what *The Washington Post* wrote:

"Historic district."

"Home to a growing enclave of artists."

"Safer because Marion Barry is no longer the mayor."

Bullshit.

To Bong's way of thinking, no self-respecting sewer rat would be caught dead in this shit hole of flaking paint and run-down buildings. Southeastern D.C. reminded him of home, of growing up in squalor and making do on what the blowflies ignored. The district also reminded him of prison. Only here, the iron bars kept people out instead of locking them in.

He drove east a block and turned south, the area more residential now. All the air conditioners were hanging out the second-floor windows, maybe for sleeping in the bedrooms, or maybe because thieves could rip window units from ground-floor sashes. Two more turns, three minutes to park, a short walk around the block, and he was staring at Sacred Heart.

The church made him proud. The grainy stucco exterior, a ruddy tan washed out by design, was in mint condition. No cracks anywhere. The light blue trim was pristine. There were no hints of the flaking paint that plagued the rest of Anacostia.

Nothing but the best for Father Mike.

For a moment Bong savored his handiwork. The sign out front, his sign, read SACRED HEART, ROMAN CATHOLIC PARISH. The seconds drifted by, a few cars too, until he remembered there was a job to do. No time for nostalgia. He was a businessman after all.

Sleeves rolled up, Bong was carrying a lunch bag in his right hand. He was hungry and craved potato chips, something salty to tide him over. There was no food inside the brown bag, though, and it sure as hell wasn't time to eat. He'd stop at an Outback Steakhouse later, probably the one outside Richmond off I-95 heading south.

Bong bent over and placed his bag on the sidewalk. The aerosol can inside clinked on the redbrick sidewalk, the only hint of a more prosperous time in Anacostia. He pushed down his sleeves, covering up the tattoo of a frowning sun with eight spider legs. This mark wasn't the kind of thing he wanted Father Mike to see.

With the spider-sun hidden behind pink oxford cotton, Bong bounded up the steps leading to Sacred Heart. Once inside the dark and cavernous room, he filled his lungs with the familiar air. What was it that made all Catholic churches smell the same? No matter the continent, it seemed like every church piped in the scent of old books and burning candles from the Vatican. Bong reminded himself to focus.

Nothing but the best for Father Mike.

Almost on cue, the hoary old priest appeared. Father Michael Rossi was wearing a long black cassock and walked down the center aisle toward Bong.

The pews to the right and left were all empty, no Mass for several more hours.

"You're kind of casual," he said, noting Bong's khaki pants and oxford shirt, the brown paper bag.

"Lots of running around today," explained Bong, shifting the sack and shaking the priest's hand.

"What couldn't wait?"

"You need to hear my confession."

"Okay." The old priest, his eyes somewhat confused, gestured toward the confessional.

"I prefer face-to-face." Bong nodded at the pews.

"Me too. There's something about getting on your knees that makes people go into grocery-list mode, don't you think?"

Father Mike slipped past Bong and sat on one of the long wooden pews. The younger man followed and pulled a twenty-ounce can of Great Stuff Big Gap Filler from his bag. It was the spray insulation used for tough jobs, the sealant that would expand and plug cracks greater than one inch wide. He undid the yellow top and fixed the long straw to the can.

"What's that for?" asked Father Mike.

"A little work before I leave."

"Can't it wait?"

"You know what they say. 'Idle hands are the devil's workshop.'"

"Yes," the priest said, looking at the can, his face dimpled with uncertainty. "Let's get started."

"Bless me, Father, for I have sinned. It's been—"

"We're long past the formalities," Father Mike interrupted.

"I suppose you're right." Bong's eyes glowed with discomfort.

"Go ahead. It's okay."

"I've killed a man, Father."

"Who?" Father Mike's jaw hung slack for the first time in fifty years of hearing confessions. "Who'd you kill?"

"You."

Bong lunged at the priest. With his left hand, he grabbed the old man's forehead and slammed skull and brains hard against the high back of their pew. One lightning motion. A sickening crack. And the sound of pain echoed through the church.

"Ugh."

That grunt was the opening Bong needed. He pinned Father Mike's head down and shoved the Great Stuff straw into the old man's gaping mouth. He pulled the trigger on the aerosol assembly, which hissed from the discharge. "I fucking warned you to keep your mouth shut, old man."

Twenty ounces of Great Stuff emptied from inside the can, twenty ounces that expand into 420 lineal feet. The priest could not gag. There was no room inside his esophagus for anything to escape as the foam swelled on contact. It grew bigger and bigger.

Father Mike writhed. His eyes bulged. His feet kicked. His throat burst at the seams. And suddenly the spasms stopped, save one final flinch of his left leg. The smell of urine wafted through the air.

Bong checked around the cavernous hall one last time. Nobody was there. Nobody saw. He pulled the straw from the dead man's mouth, packed the can into his bag. He rose, headed for the door, and before stepping into the daylight, touched his forehead with holy water from the marble urn with ornate marble carvings.

Nothing but the best for Father Mike.

CHAPTER NINE
MPDC FIRST DISTRICT SUBSTATION
THURSDAY

"Jimmy Hoffa might be buried here." Murphy hoisted a cardboard box from his cluttered desk with both hands. "Let's grab a conference room."

"Lead the way." Agent Izzy Torres swept her arm with a flourish. "After you."

She liked Murphy. He was old-school, had a lovely voice for a guy. Better yet, the detective was respectful. He never called her "Dickless Tracy." Or "Agent Arriba," which was a nickname she hated. Through the years, she had heard just about everything from the D.C. police force.

Torres was one of nine children, five boys and four girls. She was the first of her siblings to drive, the first to get married and have babies. She was the first to attend both college and graduate school. She was also the first to abandon her profession, because like most attorneys she hated the practice of law.

Sitting around an office had been bad enough. But the constant pressure to goose billable hours was a nonstarter. She refused to pad the numbers, which had been a problem with the partners at her firm. Torres once told her younger brother about the FBI, "I found my people."

Through eleven years with the Bureau, she had seen plenty. Meth heads. Her share of gore. Some things would never be comfortable. But the savage murder of an elderly priest, Father Michael Rossi, rivaled the worst of her past investigations.

"Any witnesses, Murph?"

"You know Anacostia. Everybody clams up."

"But a priest, for crying out loud. You'd think somebody would grow a pair."

"Why the interest, Izzy?"

"Father Rossi was part of an ongoing investigation."

Less is more, she thought.

"You gotta give me something." Murphy dumped the cardboard box on the conference room table. "The chief rides my ass every time you Feds get involved."

"Tell him we've been watching Rossi for some time. That we won't intrude on your homicide. That I'll share anything I can." Torres pointed to the contents in the box and asked, "May I?"

"Knock yourself out," he grumbled, not happy with her reply.

"Any theories about the weapon?"

"Yeah. Some fuck knows ballistics don't work on spray foam."

Torres pulled a cell phone from the box. Father Rossi's mobile was sealed in an evidence bag. She scrutinized it through the plastic, holding the contents up to the light. "You have the call log?"

"Next to Jimmy Hoffa," Murphy confirmed. "I'm worried about this one."

"Why's that?"

"The Catholic Church gets enough bad press as it is." The detective shook his head in dismay.

"You're thinking sex revenge?"

"What else can it be?" Murphy was fishing. "Nothing's missing best we can tell."

Torres knew the detective's game, two arms of law enforcement asking questions until somebody gave in. She paused a moment, taking time to craft her words, allowing silence to create an awkward divide. Her boss had demanded absolute secrecy.

"This case is a huge PR problem for the Church." Torres placed the mobile phone, bag and all, on the table. "But our interest has nothing to do with sexual predators. That's all I can say for now."

Murphy gestured for the FBI agent to sit on one of the conference room chairs. The two stared at each other, uncomfortable and uncooperative. They could have lingered in silence another ten seconds.

"Sex crimes aren't your thing anyway," the detective noted in resignation.

As he spoke Father Rossi's cell phone rang, and an out-of-state number popped up on the LCD display. Torres reached into her jacket pocket, searching for the pad and pen she always carried.

"Answer the phone," Murphy demanded.

Second ring.

"No." Torres looked like a statue. Immobile. She made no effort to reach for the evidence bag with the ringing phone. "We get the number and do the research first."

Third ring.

"They're probably calling from a disposable phone. Answer it."

Fourth ring.

"That's a coin toss, Murph. I'd rather go in prepared."

Fifth ring.

"Give me that." The detective snatched the evidence bag from the table and exhumed the cell phone in one fluid motion. He was desperate to answer before the caller went into voice mail.

"Hello." Murphy spoke in a whisper, calm and under control. He reined back the clipped hints of an Irish brogue that Torres found so lovely. JFK or Charles Manson—his phone voice could have belonged to anybody.

The caller spoke.

Murphy winked at Torres. "Who's calling?"

He frowned, as though surprised by a pushback response.

"Father Rossi isn't available."

Torres mouthed the word "speakerphone."

Murphy wrinkled his brow and shook his head no at her.

His attention returned to the caller. "Then you'll be holding a long time, pal. This is Detective Murphy. We have your number. We have your location. Maybe you should answer my questions."

Torres rolled her eyes. She assumed the caller would hang up.

"Is this some kind of joke?" Murphy screwed up his face, making Torres wonder what the caller had said.

CHAPTER TEN

FAYETTEVILLE, NORTH CAROLINA, AND MPDC FIRST DISTRICT SUBSTATION

"No joke. Everybody calls me Biscuit. Why are you answering this phone?"

"I'm investigating a crime. Why are you calling Father Rossi?"

Murphy's words rocked the lawyer. Except for the occasional problem with a tenant, Biscuit seldom spoke with Fayetteville police. And contact with D.C. authorities was out of the question. "Is he okay?"

"Are you a friend?"

"I'm a lawyer," replied Biscuit. "What's this about?"

"I'll call you from a landline."

Biscuit hung up and considered his chaotic desk. The phone was vying for space with legal debris and junk-food wrappings. "What the hell." He slapped his meaty palm on the tabletop.

Ten seconds later, Murphy and Torres connected with Fayetteville. "This is Detective Murphy. Can you hear me okay?"

"Fine. Is anybody else on this call?" Biscuit recognized the tinny sound of a speakerphone. In his profession, there were innumerable horror stories about unidentified listeners.

"Agent Torres from the FBI."

"Good morning, Mr. Hughes." She tried to sound cordial. She might need his help later.

The surprises kept coming. Biscuit had never expected to connect with the police, let alone the FBI. "I take it there's a problem."

"Father Rossi is the victim of a homicide," answered Torres. "Why are you calling?"

"To discuss the Catholic Fund." The lawyer sipped a supersized Coke.

"How was Father Rossi involved with them?" For the moment, Murphy was concealing his lack of knowledge. He knew nothing about the Catholic Fund.

Torres scribbled on her notepad.

"Sacred Heart Parish and the Catholic Fund," drawled Biscuit, "share the same address."

The Southerner's slow speech irritated Murphy. He rolled his index finger in circles, trying to speed Biscuit's answers. "Why do you care?"

Torres remained silent. Murphy's questions were fine. And she'd rather eat nails than disclose anything to some attorney from Fayetteville, North Carolina. Lawyers were all the same. They'd turn her investigation into the three-ring circus known as ABC, NBC, and CBS. She had seen the media spoil too many cases before—both in private practice and with the FBI.

"I represent a subdivision outside Fayetteville—"

"North Carolina," Murphy interrupted, finishing the sentence, still rolling his finger.

Biscuit decided the cop was boorish. "For the most part, my clients are military folk. And right now they're pissed."

"Why's that?" pressed Murphy.

"Because an adult superstore named Highly Intimate Pleasures is opening in their backyard. Because real estate prices will tank when truckers stop for burgers and blue movies. Because my clients are NCOs. It's all they can do to scrape together a down payment for their homes. Soldiers put their lives on the line every day, and they sure as hell don't need twenty thousand square feet of peep shows dragging down property values."

"Noncommissioned officers?" asked Torres. She knew what "NCO" meant. She asked only to curry Biscuit's favor. She already smelled problems around the corner.

"Right."

Biscuit's outburst surprised Murphy. The force, the passion, made him think there was more to the story. "Just real estate—that's the only connection between Sacred Heart and your adult superstore."

"It's not mine."

"You know what I mean."

"The Catholic Fund owns Highly Intimate Pleasures. I want to know if Sacred Heart's passing a collection plate so they can sell vibrators in my neck of the woods."

Annoyed, Torres stopped writing. "Not helpful, Mr. Hughes."

"Neither are perverts."

"Do any of your clients know the victim?"

The big lawyer stopped to consider Murphy's question. "They're not suspects, are they?"

"I've got a badge, a dead body, and a motive. What do you think, Counselor?"

"My clients live in North Carolina. They learned about the Catholic Fund last Sunday."

"I need their names."

"Why?"

"Father Rossi died two days later."

"You should focus on the Catholic Fund." The unexpected turn in the conversation annoyed Biscuit. His lather was growing, his drawl dissipating, his words coming faster and faster.

"Leave the investigation to us." Murphy was just as angry. This lawyer bugged him.

"Maybe I should bring in the press. Reporters make great sleuths. And they'll have a field day with this one."

Biscuit had shut down Cavener with help from the media. He knew journalists would leverage his time and make the cops play defense. He'd dial them in a heartbeat.

"What do you mean 'field day'?" asked Torres.

"Want me to spell out the headlines?"

"Go ahead." Her eyes narrowed.

" 'Forget Bingo. Vatican Sanctions Porn to Raise Money.' That's catchy, right?"

Torres had heard enough. Her investigation could not afford the publicity. Nor did she welcome another pubic relations disaster for the Church.

Her Catholic brethren always got a bum rap, even when they weren't to blame.

In the old days, Attorney Torres would have jumped down Biscuit's throat. That's how it was growing up in a big family. Sometimes, she uncorked just to be heard.

At that moment, her FBI training took over. And it was Agent Torres who stayed calm, no matter how intense. "I doubt the press is in your clients' best interests."

"A bunch of sergeants are depending on me. I don't care who we annoy."

"Suit yourself," Torres replied, her tone mocking and indifferent. "But you're interfering with a federal investigation. My dad was one of those sergeants you keep describing. And I know NCOs don't have time to answer questions when the Federal Bureau of Investigation comes knocking. We burn through hours and mess with day jobs. It could take forever to interview any one of those soldiers. I really don't want the press involved. We clear?"

Murphy raised his eyebrows.

"The subdivision knows about the Catholic Fund," said Biscuit. "The story will find its way to the press. It's only a matter of time."

"Then I hold you responsible." Torres knew her boss would go ballistic if their investigation attracted news coverage. "Maybe it's time you reestablish your chain of command."

"I don't get the hard-ass threats." Biscuit was crushing the receiver with his grip, forgetting himself. "Who are you to hold soldiers hostage?"

"I'm doing my job. And if you want to protect your clients, I suggest you stick to zoning rather than eyewitness news."

"That may be impossible."

"I can refer you to a decent lawyer who knows how to get the job done."

"You have my number." Biscuit clicked off.

Time for hardball. Torres decided to call Biscuit later and apply the pressure. A phone call here. A phone call there. She'd make him think twice about hanging up on the FBI.

CHAPTER ELEVEN

THE LAW OFFICES OF YOUNG AND SCRANTOM

Huitt Young was Palmer's lawyer and best friend. He was slender, 140 pounds in his British wingtips. He was short, no more than five foot seven. His shock of silver hair, swept back high and tight, added a good inch. Maybe two. He was kinetic. Huitt evoked roughly the same reaction from a room as a Jack Russell terrier. He possessed the breed's preternatural ability to stir things up. People were wary. And sometimes, true to his profession and canine equivalent, he left messes behind.

Right now, I felt like one of them.

JoJo, Claire, and I had arrived right on time at 10:00 A.M. Huitt met us in the lobby.

"Thanks for coming," he said. "Grove, you mind waiting here while I discuss family specifics?"

"No prob."

That was ninety minutes ago.

The first time I phoned my office, Zola reported, "The market's melting up."

"Melting up" is the latest jargon from finance. Zola meant that buyers had returned. They were sending stocks sharply higher, 3 and 4 percent in most cases.

A half-dozen calls later, Zola grew tired of my interruptions. So our assistant, Chloe, a single mom who calls it like it is, took over and put me in the adult equivalent of time-out. "We'll let you know if anything happens."

The thing about law offices is they don't keep much reading material in their lobbies. Dentists stock everything from *People* to *Sports Illustrated* for their patients. And my barbershop offers the latest on cars, diets, and cycling, not to mention PG-13 porn like *Maxim*. But there was only one copy of *The Wall Street Journal* in the venerable offices of Young and Scrantom. I had read it front to back fifteen minutes after arrival.

My BlackBerry was running low on juice. I was restless and irritated. I wondered what was taking so long and why I had been summoned in the first place.

What the hell am I doing here?

The last forty-eight hours were a blur. I wore black sunglasses during Palmer's funeral and well into the night, even though the camouflage wasn't necessary. Seeing old friends dulled my pain. Classmates from Bishop England came out in droves to pay their respects to Palmer Kincaid. These were people I had not seen for years. And the funeral was, forgive me here, a reunion of sorts.

Those same friends exacerbated Claire's grief. Don't get me wrong. She had a good cry with many of them. But she never left my side yesterday. And it was my arm Claire clutched for support, even though we had not seen each other for years.

Weird if you ask me.

Maybe the more familiar faces reminded Claire that Palmer was gone. There would be a void in the life that had once been so consistent. Or maybe Palmer's advice prompted her to stay close.

"You're his thousandth man."

At 11:45 A.M. Huitt interrupted my reverie. "Sorry to keep you waiting. I didn't expect us to take so long."

"Is everything okay?"

"Nothing the family can't work out."

Danger, Will Robinson.

Inside the conference room, I studied JoJo and Claire for clues. The two women looked about how you'd expect—wrung out from the ordeal.

Huitt launched right into business. "For the sake of clarity, Grove, all numbers are after tax. Best as we can figure, that is."

"Understood." Huitt was being modest. He was a fine lawyer.

"Palmer left one hundred and fifty million to the Palmetto Foundation."

"You're kidding."

I couldn't help the outburst. Palmer's financial assets totaled about $200 million. Three-quarters was going to charity, a staggering gift by any measure. Instinctively, I checked JoJo and Claire. Both were smiling. Both were crying, tears of joy running down their cheeks.

"Not kidding," Huitt replied. "And that's why you're here."

Growing up in the South makes you diplomatic. You learn how to ask delicate questions at an early age. Me—I apologize all over myself. I'm formal, a bit awkward. And then I rip right into the rough stuff. "It's none of my business. And forgive me for asking. But that leaves fifty million give or take?"

Huitt looked at the two women. He was the consummate professional, a lawyer asking his clients for permission to disclose sensitive information.

"Go ahead," urged JoJo.

Her engagement ring—a three-carat emerald-cut diamond surrounded by baguettes around the band—glinted in the light. I guessed seven figures from Harry Winston. Annie teases me about fashion naïveté. But I know my stores of value, gems included. It comes with the job.

Claire nodded okay and pushed the bangs from her face.

"Fifty million in financial assets," Huitt said. "Plus the houses."

No way!

My lips parted for a moment. "That's after tax?"

He noted my reaction. "That's what I said. Why the surprise?"

Time for diplomacy.

Fifty million dollars before tax made sense. Fifty million dollars after tax did not, unless Claire was cut out of the will. Estate transfers between spouses, Palmer to JoJo, are tax-free. That's just the law.

But estate transfers from a parent to a child are fully taxable. If Palmer left any money or real estate to Claire, the remaining cash and financial assets would have been less than $50 million after all the taxes were paid.

Sitting before the two Kincaids, I chose my words carefully. "The balance seems large given what I know about the family."

"Do you know about Palmer's life insurance?"

"No. But I get it now."

Wealthy individuals often buy life insurance policies to pay their estate taxes. It was possible, I now realized, that Palmer had left assets to Claire. I was not about to apologize, though, and ask what she had inherited. Diplomacy is one thing. Bad taste is another. Better to let the details bubble up naturally.

"Why am I here, Huitt?"

"Palmer requested something from you."

"Anything."

"He asked you to serve on the Palmetto Foundation's board."

Shivers of pride danced up my spine. Pins and needles, the same feeling as a leg falling asleep, crisscrossed my forehead. It's a big deal in my biz, an honor really, to join a philanthropic board. Especially one with $150 million in assets. "I don't know what to say."

"How about yes?" JoJo's face glowed. Her skin tones were as golden as the light beaming through the windows.

Claire suddenly looked fresh. For a moment, all four of us forgot last week.

Caution being what it is, I reverted to time-tested sales lingo for fishing out details. "Tell me more."

"The board membership is a volunteer position," explained Huitt.

"Of course."

"The foundation will reimburse your expenses. And as a member of the board, you will vote whether to approve or reject the charitable projects."

"Including those proposed and funded by donors outside the Kincaid family?"

"Absolutely." Huitt spoke in confident tones, his voice raspy from years of dispensing advice. "JoJo and Claire are your co-trustees. All three of you have one vote each, which makes you the swing vote outside the family."

"I assume it's okay to attend meetings over the phone?"

"Absolutely."

"How soon do you need to know?"

"Monday," Huitt said. "Otherwise, I find alternates."

"We need you," urged JoJo.

"Will you do it?" asked Claire.

"I need to ask SKC."

"Why's that?" Claire pushed the bangs from her face again.

"Company policy. I need approval for board affiliations. Especially one that involves money."

"You're not being paid," objected JoJo.

"Doesn't matter. I'm required to disclose outside activities."

"Sounds like Big Brother." Claire pronounced "brother" with three syllables.

"That's Wall Street."

"Let me know Monday." Huitt stood to leave. "And call me if you have questions."

"I'm flattered."

Talk about diplomacy. My statement was true enough. Palmer's invitation to join the board was an honor. But after my initial groundswell of enthusiasm, the old Wall Street cynicism took over.

I had seen this movie before.

The stronger the patriarch and the more sudden the death, the greater the chaos that ensues. I still had no idea what Palmer had left to JoJo, versus what he had left to Claire. If the two ever disagreed, if there was any hidden jealousy, I could be caught in their crossfire.

Maybe that was the price of being Palmer's thousandth man.

CHAPTER TWELVE
HIGHLY INTIMATE PLEASURES

Biscuit punched off his cell phone. He turned into the parking lot, where the tarmac was crisp, black, and freshly paved. Even though it was late September, waves of heat shimmered off the pavement. Biscuit did not get out. Not at first. Instead, he stewed inside his black Hummer—engine running, air conditioner blasting, Southern sun bearing down two degrees hotter than hell.

He found the river birch surprising. So many of these shade trees had been planted around the lot. They were surrounded by flowering shrubs and at least three different ground covers—variegated lilyturf, cotoneaster, and bishop's weed. The attention to landscaping was not what he expected outside an adult superstore. The grounds resembled a city park.

For a long while, Biscuit considered Father Michael Rossi. He wondered why the FBI was involved and whether the priest's death was more than a coincidence. To some extent, he felt guilty. Biscuit had expected to harangue the good father about Highly Intimate Pleasures, to grill him six ways to Sunday. Only now, a Fayetteville inquisition was impossible.

There was also that hard-ass FBI agent. Torres had done a grade-A job busting his chops. Biscuit could feel his face redden, his attitude sour. He shook his head and muttered to himself, "That woman could start an argument in an empty house."

The moment passed. Biscuit hopped from his truck with unreasonable agility for a big, pudgy man. He surveyed HIP's parking lot. There was not an eighteen-wheeler to be seen, although sedans and SUVs were scattered everywhere. He wondered whether he'd recognize anybody inside the store.

Biscuit had inspected HIP every day since it opened. A couple of nights, too. Much to his disappointment, the bouncers checked the IDs of all entering the bar at the rear of the store. There would be no easy victories. The twenty-thousand-square-foot complex was already operating with the precision of a well-oiled machine.

These guys don't make mistakes.

No matter how many times he visited HIP, Biscuit found the experience entertaining. He'd never confide his fascination to clients, though. If Mrs. Jason Locklear ever heard, she'd crucify him on behalf of the neighborhood association. He had expected a seedy interior—no matter how new the store. He once assumed that soundtracks from sex videos, an orgy of hot pillows and clutching thighs, would pulsate over storewide speakers rigged for wall-to-wall moaning.

Not even close. HIP played provocative songs with upbeat lyrics, like the Lady Gaga number about riding a disco stick. There were no fake orgasms pounding through the store. And the interior almost looked Tuscan. The floors were fashioned from faux marble tiles with a soft, rubbery texture. Easy on the feet. There were two rows of Corinthian columns, fourteen fiberglass pillars in all. They split the store in half and created a corridor leading to the bar. Overhead, its neon sign read THE CATHOUSE CLUB. Biscuit felt like he was walking through a Roman bath.

Except for the merchandise.

To the left, he saw lingerie of every shape and color. Babydolls, garters, and bras—there was a little something for everyone. There was even a section called the "Naughty Brides Collection." The selection was massive, lace and fantasy everywhere.

To the right were a series of smaller departments. A big sign read GOOD

VIBES and promoted the latest and greatest toys underneath. Then there were the videos. The selection seemed small for a twenty-thousand-square-foot superstore. But there was one section dedicated exclusively to Ron Jeremy, the aging porn star of epic disproportions. Beyond the videos, shelves of nutraceuticals promised men they could "grow bigger" or "last longer." And finally there were novelties and gag products. Cooking paraphernalia promoted breast-shaped cakes or penis meat loaves for those occasions that required something extra.

To Biscuit's way of thinking, the people in the store were the biggest surprise of all. The customers were women. They outnumbered men at least nine to one. Biscuit had expected skeevy middle-aged guys with bad skin and bourbon fumes wafting out their nose pores. Members of staff were also women, every single one. They wore black pants and black shirts, with HIP on the front and STAFF on the back. In age, they ranged from their early twenties to their mid-thirties.

One of them, a tall woman with silky shoulder-length hair, stared at Biscuit. She eyed him head to toe, her expression half perplexed and half smile. She was standing behind a table display of vibrators, designed for all occasions and the places where only doctors belong.

"Come over here," she commanded in a throaty, sexy-woman voice. "I've seen you before."

Biscuit looked over his shoulder, wondering if she was speaking to someone else.

"I mean you," she said to him, her shoulders thrown back, her carriage erect and proud. "We need to talk."

Biscuit could hear his bravado disappear. It sounded like air hissing from a flat tire. He had been to Kuwait and back, witnessed horrors no man should see. But for all the hard-bitten experience, or the way he lorded his 260 pounds over legal adversaries, women got the best of him. It had been that way ever since he was a kid.

Usually, trouble erupted over the bathroom. Position of the toilet seat. Length of stay. That's how it was with five sisters. No matter who started the ruckus, sibling squabbles always ended with his mother hollering, "Leave your sisters alone."

Day in, day out, "Leave your sisters alone" became his mother's mantra. No surprise, given he was the only boy.

Once, Biscuit made the mistake of smarting her back. "You want to run that pony by me one more time?" He'd first heard the expression at a barbershop. All the men chuckled when some guy used it as the punch line to his story. To a young, impressionable boy, the remark sounded like a joke about horses.

Biscuit's mother was not amused. She heard the words from her son and whacked his elbow with the closest thing available. Her wooden spoon broke on contact, evoking a right smart "Yeow." The mashed potatoes went lumpy that night, the half-mushed consistency of porridge. And Biscuit got the message to back off. He had been backing off from women ever since.

His wife Faith Ann was the one exception. They were equals raising their three sons.

"I don't bite."

The HIP clerk placed her hand on her hip. She studied Biscuit, her eyes dancing a cha-cha smirk, her smile perfect except for the faintest twist in one of her two front teeth.

The big man spotted her name badge and leaned down for a better look: AMY. STORE MANAGER. WE AIM TO PLEASE.

Remembering his own mission, Biscuit said, "You're the person I need to see."

Amy glanced at the wedding ring on Biscuit's index finger. She was a true salesperson, all warmth and allure. She asked, "Something for the Mrs.?"

"Er."

"Come here." Amy enjoyed home-court advantage. She was in command, confident and seductive. She drew him in, tugging his tie playfully. "I know just what she needs."

Biscuit turned crimson. He checked around the store to see if anyone was watching.

Amy grabbed a translucent green vibrator from the stack on her table. It looked like a happy cactus. With a deft flick of the thumb, she hit the On button. A low droning sound erupted, and a few shoppers turned their heads in Biscuit's direction. The sound reminded him of the spaceship engines from the 1950s Flash Gordon reruns he had watched as a kid.

"Lean down." She issued the order with the command persona of a drill sergeant.

In that instant, Biscuit discovered how a deer feels in the headlights. He lowered his head as instructed.

Amy touched the happy cactus to Biscuit's nose. "That's how it feels on a woman's clitoris. Trust me, your wife will love it." She spoke in a loud, husky voice, two clicks too loud.

Several nearby women tittered. College age. One wore shorts, made from sweatpants cotton, with UNC plastered across her bottom.

Biscuit wanted to hide. He wanted to get away from this woman, so confident, so much in control. He wanted to leave HIP, to vacate the vibes and videos. But he had work to do.

"I'll take it," Biscuit yammered. For the love of humanity, he wished she would lower her voice.

"Your wife will be thrilled." Amy handed him an unopened package. "There's no shame in making a woman happy."

"We need to speak about something else." Biscuit could feel the heat rising from his red face.

"Some lingerie?" she offered, still sounding like her mouth was connected to a megaphone. "We have the most adorable teddies in stock."

"Nothing like that." Biscuit folded his arms, trying to regain control, trying to hide the vibrator.

The manager cocked one eyebrow.

"Sorry to hear about Father Rossi." Biscuit did his best to look haunted, as though the two had lost a good friend.

"Who?"

She doesn't know him.

Biscuit recalibrated. "I'd like to meet the owners of HIP."

"Do you have a business card?"

"Er, yeah. What for?"

"They'll call you."

"I'd rather call them," he told Amy. "It's time-sensitive."

"I can't give out numbers." She folded her arms across her chest.

"Whatever happened to customer service?"

"Do you have a complaint?" Amy flicked on the happy cactus, drawing attention from other shoppers.

"Now I do." He wished she'd turn that damn thing off. "Why can't you connect me with your head office?"

"Company policy."

It was time to scram. Biscuit headed to the cash register, where the clerk insisted that she test his vibrator for out-of-box failure. "It'll take two seconds."

"Don't worry about it," Biscuit protested, aware of the line of women behind him.

"We don't accept returns."

"It's okay."

"Suit yourself. Cash or credit?"

"Cash."

Faith Ann will raise hell if she sees HIP on our Visa.

"You just saved yourself some money," the clerk said. "We discount all cash payments ten percent."

"Are you making any progress?" Mrs. Jason Locklear was calling for an update, the third time that week. She was barking and snarling into the phone, demanding answers and teething the receiver. "We need to know."

"Working it."

Biscuit had just returned. His office was located on the second story of a nothing-special brick building in a strip mall. Ten minutes north was the tiki bar he owned with his brother-in-law. Ten minutes south was his favorite Denny's, where another brother-in-law was the general manager. His other three brothers-in-law lived farther away. Biscuit sometimes told friends his childhood was like living on the set of *The View*. Five sisters—and every one of them outspoken.

" 'Working it,' " echoed Locklear, not at all pleased. "That's what you have to say?"

"The county inspectors are no help," reported Biscuit. "HIP complies with zoning."

Locklear said nothing for a while, her silence reverberating with frustration. "I called you to get results. I made representations to the residents of Liberty Point. My neighbors trust me, Biscuit. And I have a responsibility to them. We're paying you good money, and now I'm wondering whether we need to rethink our decision."

"Mrs. Locklear," he said. "You called Saturday afternoon, and I told you this case would be tough. I've spent all week looking for the low-hanging fruit. Well, guess what?"

"What?"

"There isn't any."

"You're the lawyer. Figure something out."

"I need time to do my job."

"While our homes lose value," she growled. "While every trucker heathen makes pit stops just around the bend from here. Time is one thing we don't have."

"I didn't see any trucks this morning."

"You weren't shopping at HIP, were you?"

Biscuit looked at the orange shopping bag on his desk. It read HIGHLY INTIMATE PLEASURES in big, bold black letters. He buried the bag in a desk drawer and replied, "Just research. Like I said on Sunday, I'm all over it."

"Call me Monday," she ordered. "We need weekly updates."

"You got it." Now was no time to remind Mrs. Jason Locklear that phone calls increased legal fees. The two hung up.

In that moment Biscuit wanted to be the client. To be the guy saying what he wanted, when he needed it, and why the world should drop everything and deliver. Tensions were running high at Liberty Point Plantations. Locklear had grown so unreasonable. And the press would be no help this time. For one, Torres had warned him not to use them. For another, it would be difficult to harness public opinion when a priest had been killed.

Stop making excuses, he reminded himself.

CHAPTER THIRTEEN

Catching up grows old when the venues are a wake and a funeral. Palmer's final request, that I join his board, was both humbling and flattering. His last wishes filled me with a deep sense of responsibility. They saddened me too, the unmistakable signal that one of my most important friendships had come to an abrupt, unforeseen end. I was talked out after two days in Charleston, drained from the confusing mix of old friends and conflicting emotions. That said, my plate was still full of unresolved issues—things not done and words not spoken.

What am I doing in Claire Kincaid's garden?

Let me bring you up to speed.

After meeting with Huitt Young, I phoned my boss first thing. Her assistant said, "Katy's in back-to-back meetings. Mind if she calls you at seven tonight?"

"It's a date."

I assumed SKC would rubber-stamp my election to the Palmetto Foundation's board. But Anders never called, thereby delaying the answer till the next day. Odd. Managers are good about responding to their top salespeople. I made a mental note to send my boss back to obedience school for remedial training.

In some ways, I was glad Anders never called. She would have interrupted my dinner with Claire. We went light on the food at Carolina's, split a Bibb salad and an order of steamed mussels. But we didn't hold back on lubricants. After a couple of martinis, we downed at least one bottle of Pouilly-Fuissé. Maybe it was two.

During dinner, I steered clear of the topic foremost on my mind. Call it professional interest. Or prurient curiosity. I really wanted to know how Palmer had divided the remainder of the estate between JoJo and Claire. I don't care how long somebody's been in my biz. Inheritances are always fascinating, especially when the family situation is complicated. We had a doozy here in downtown Charleston, and Huitt never breathed a word to me.

He's a good lawyer.

I walked Claire home to Legare Street after dinner. Didn't expect to stay. But we were huddling on a Charleston bench—green-black, aged, pitted from countless asses—in the secluded garden behind her house. The night air had finally turned cool. And we changed from white to red, working our way through a heavy Australian cabernet to stay warm.

Claire's features were soft and fragile under shadows from the quarter moon. During high school, I would have given anything to share an intimate moment with my Daisy Buchanan. By "intimate," I mean private, not sexual. Although, who am I kidding? Sexual would have been just fine in those days. More than fine. Claire was the stuff of boyhood lust.

You get the point.

The thing is, Annie and I are a team. She's the one who reached me after the death of my wife and daughter. She's the one who defended me when I ran into a problem with SKC several years ago and became embroiled in the fallout from a Ponzi scheme. She stuck her neck out.

When the dust settled, Annie reminded me that spontaneity and flirtatiousness can be fun. It's okay to lighten up. I think that deep down, it's the stupid stuff I like about her. The way she dresses in an explosion of colors, layers of stripes and prints and renegade textures that somehow work together. I don't think anyone, except for Evelyn, has ever intrigued me the way she does.

Like last week.

Before I heard from Palmer, Annie called me after one of her classes at Columbia. "I have good news and bad news."

"Go with the bad." I knew this game.

"You're taking me to a chick flick in the Village tonight."

"Yikes. That is bad."

"But you get to hold my hand all through the movie. And I'm an absolute marshmallow after a good cry."

How could I resist?

Claire and I were sitting there, drinking too much wine, savoring the sweet Southern scents of tea olive and camellia. With regard to the wine— cabernet sauvignon is a totally agreeable way for a man and a woman to spend an evening, the cool side of mild, under the stars.

There was something different about Claire. She had pushed the bangs out of her face. And it struck me that she had opened a window into her thoughts. I was in her garden for a reason. Maybe to discuss something unsaid over the past two days.

Every so often, a passing car interrupted the rhythmic sounds from her fountain. A marble bull's head, mounted to the garden's stucco wall, spit water into an ornamental pool brimming with mottled orange-white carp breaking the surface. I waited for Claire to take the lead on issues of substance.

"I'm so proud of my dad."

"Because of his gift to the Palmetto Foundation?"

"Nobody needs the wealth we have." Claire was skirting round an age-old question. It's the one that nobody asks on Wall Street: how much is enough? But I wasn't much interested in the debate.

"Did your dad ever mention the gift?"

"Not a word."

"Really?"

"You sound surprised."

"It's so much to give away." I sipped some cabernet.

"Daddy said there'd always be plenty to screw up my life."

"What about JoJo—you think she knew?"

"Are you kidding?" Claire scoffed.

"What do you mean?"

"She's a gold digger."

"Your dad loved her."

"You really don't know," said Claire, pausing for a moment, her words fading into the fountain's refrain, "what happened today."

"Know what?"

"Daddy lit the fuse on JoJo's tampon."

Yuck. Claire had spoken the words with molasses in her syrupy Southern accent. But so much for ambassadorial grace. I was floored. I had no
idea what to say. So I said nothing, which seems like a pretty good strategy
when you hear something that throws the value of speech into question.

"Serves her right." Claire's voice rose like a sudden summer squall. "I
don't like her. I've never liked her. And it's a good thing Daddy made you
the deciding vote. Because we'd never agree on anything."

Danger, Will Robinson.

"Claire, I like JoJo."

"She makes me sick."

"Why?"

"She blew in here from San Diego. The next thing I know, she's doing
splits in my mother's bed and treating me like a kid."

"JoJo's only six years older than you."

"My point exactly." Claire tapped her empty glass.

I filled it to the point where the curve in the crystal indicates headache
in the morning. "There won't be a problem at the board meetings, right?"

"Hope not," replied Claire breezily.

For a while we sat and said nothing. She wanted to gossip, which wasn't
my place. We drank our wine and sat apart on the bench, the earlier magic
gone from our evening. Claire finally broke the silence, her tone somewhat
repentant.

"You think I'm awful?"

"Palmer wouldn't want all the acrimony."

"I doubt there's anything we can do."

"Why not?"

"JoJo got voted off the peninsula." Claire's eyes flashed with victory.
Or maybe it was defiance.

"What do you mean?"

"Dad left me the house on South Battery, plus ten million in a trust to
maintain it forever."

"What about JoJo?"

"She gets our place on Sullivan's Island."

"The beach house is magnificent."

"I bet she's pissed."

"Are you kidding?"

"She got evicted from South Battery," Claire explained. "And I'm moving in."

"That's hardly an eviction."

"It amounts to the same thing."

"The antiques?" I asked, wondering about all the trips to Sotheby's.

"Mine."

"Even the ones JoJo picked out?"

"Mine."

"Did she get anything else?"

"Ten million."

"How can anybody be pissed about ten million and a beach house?" Sometimes, the values get out of whack in my world.

"You've seen the way JoJo flushes money," replied Claire. "She can kiss the private jets adios."

"You got the rest?" I couldn't help myself. The words escaped before my brain engaged.

"Not exactly. Dad left me ten million."

Hmm. That left $20 million in financial securities. I asked about the real estate, though, which seemed more diplomatic. "The South Battery house is the problem?"

"Pride," Claire explained. "JoJo's moving out and throttling back her big lifestyle. Meanwhile, I get the house, ten million to maintain it, ten million in my name, and something else."

"What's that?"

"It's kind of embarrassing," she said, looking sheepish.

"We can handle it."

"There's another twenty million in trust for my kids."

"You don't have any."

"Not yet." Claire's smile was dazzling, a little too flirtatious. "But I'm working on it. Which is a good thing, because there are sixty-one places left in the family plot."

"Your family has that many?"

"Remember the big grassy hill under the oak at the cemetery?"

"Yeah?"

"Ours. Daddy bought sixty-four plots when Mom died. She has a space. He has one. And now I get busy."

"That's two spots. You said sixty-one are left."

"There's a space for JoJo."

It was my time to be the ambassador. "She's suffering like the rest of us."

"You're too nice."

"Like I said before. I like JoJo."

"She just got outed."

"Outed?"

"She's a hobby." Claire crossed her arms. "No kids, and now she's leaving the family house. She's not one of us."

"Not fair."

"A dog would have been so much easier if Daddy needed a bitch."

I was failing at my effort to make peace. It was time to try pragmatism. "JoJo's your equal at the Palmetto Foundation."

"Which is why I need you on the board."

I had no idea what to say. Instead, I took another sip of my wine, and the two of us sat in silence. Me—dissecting the job ahead, wondering what had happened to the woman who was everybody's friend during my childhood. Claire—troubling over thoughts of her father and his wife.

For the first time in my life, I felt like an insider. But I was unsure whether the circles of old Charleston, the brass ring from my childhood, were the right place for me. After a long while, Claire scooted over on the bench and nestled in the crook of my shoulder. I could feel her body shake and realized she was crying.

"I feel like a shit." She sniffled, as though adding an exclamation point to her tears.

What's a friend do?

You give a little when you get a little. You help, and you ask for help. You trade. You open up. That's what Annie says. So does my therapist. They both think there's plenty of vulnerability to go around. They tell me to stop being "so fucking O'Rourke."

Actually, those are Annie's words. My shrink would never say anything like that. They tell me it's okay to open up with friends to reveal some of those foibles. But I wasn't sure what to say.

In the garden, this grieving friend in my arms, I might have asked, "Are you okay?"

Claire might have replied. But if she did, I don't remember what she said.

So instead, we sat there, the night growing colder by the hour. And I stopped judging Claire Kincaid or trying to understand what she had become.

We finished the bottle of wine. The last thing I said before returning to my hotel room was, "We'll get through this."

CHAPTER FOURTEEN

SOUTH BATTERY

FRIDAY

Three Advil into the morning, I was sitting with JoJo on the second-floor piazza outside the family home of Palmer Kincaid. The overhead fans were whipping around and around, stirring the mix of ragweed and mosquitoes. We sipped cappuccino and gazed across Charleston's expansive harbor. Her dachshund, Holly, was sleeping on its back, legs splayed, and dreaming of a belly rub.

I had gone ADHD, my head a mess of random thoughts from the late night, early morning, and lingering tannins. I was trying to focus. But the waterside views—choppy surface and the occasional sailboat—were distractions. Charlestonians, I decided, are charged with a unique responsibility. The old families don't own this city so much as they drag it kicking and screaming into the present.

We could see Fort Sumter in the distance, the place where Confederate troops first attacked the Union in 1861. The island struck me as a harbinger of things to come. As a trustee at the Palmetto Foundation, I might be stepping into a second civil war. That's why I was here to see JoJo.

"You doing okay?"

"About what you'd expect." Big black sunglasses covered JoJo's eyes like a blindfold. "I can't believe Palmer's gone."

"Me either."

"He loved night sails," she remarked in a wistful, longing kind of way, her head turned to the sea. "He'd come home late stinking of shrimp and salt and too much wine. And that stupid cocktail sauce. He made me mad."

JoJo paused and sipped from her cup. I said nothing and just listened. I imagined her brown eyes sweeping the harbor, searching for a memory of Palmer at the helm of *Bounder*. Or perhaps she was thinking about the child they never had. Claire's words from last night were still buzzing through my head:

"No kids, and now she's leaving the family house. She's not one of us."

"Palmer would wake me up," JoJo continued, "and I'd go into a snit, all cranky and groggy. And right now, I'd give anything to take it all back. I adored him."

"Don't beat yourself up."

The sunglasses hid half her face, the high cheekbones, the flawless skin so soft and smooth with hints of gold. I wanted her to take those damn shades off. I wanted to see what she was thinking.

"I've been in your shoes, JoJo. I've played all the mind games myself. And they're no fun, because you can't win. You never win."

A tear rolled down her cheek. The drop emerged from underneath those stupid sunglasses and beat its way toward her long, sculpted neckline, the delicate features of ageless beauty.

"Let me know how I can help." I leaned forward, assuming my words had connected.

"Palmer already did." JoJo squeezed my hand, all touchy-feely the way she is. And I squeezed back because, however non-O'Rourke the bodily contact, reciprocating seemed the right thing to do.

"You're talking about the Palmetto Foundation?"

"We need you." She removed her sunglasses, revealing brown eyes red with grief. The pain was starting to settle in, now that the funeral was over and her crowd of friends had returned to their lives.

"Claire and you have a big job," I ventured, exploring how JoJo would react to Claire's name.

"Did SKC give you approval to join our board?"

"Not yet."

"Claire is a smart girl." I could tell JoJo was starting a sales pitch. "Scary smart. She has a knack for our business, which she gets from Palmer. We'll make a great team, because we've been a great team."

"The best."

"But neither one of us has a head for investments, and Palmer said to forget all our other financial advisers. You're the only one we can trust."

Her words were not what I had expected. Nor was the absence of rancor. I thought Claire's vitriol would spill over. That JoJo would throw her stepdaughter under the bus. But if Palmer's wife felt any bitterness, she kept the venom to herself.

"I'll try my boss again."

"We need you." JoJo was holding both my hands now. "We have an important decision to make next week, and I'm scared."

"Scared about what?"

"Making a mistake. Palmer always says, 'People are dumb as stumps when they lose someone.'"

"I'm here to help."

"Maybe we can take a ride out to the beach tomorrow and talk about money. Not foundation money, but my money." JoJo rested her right hand on my shoulder, casual and intimate at the same time.

"Happy to do it."

"You know me. Palmer made money. And I spent it. I probably need somebody to put me on a budget."

Thar she blows.

But the anger I anticipated never came. Instead, JoJo added, "He made my life better."

"Mine too."

Later that morning, walking back to my hotel, I found myself thinking there was a new Madam Ambassador in town. Her name was JoJo. And I wouldn't give two cents for Claire Kincaid's feminine intuition.

"No. No. No." We had not been on the phone thirty seconds. And Katy Anders had already worked herself into a lather.

"I don't see the problem."

"You've got bigger fish to fry."

"What are you talking about?"

I was walking under the shade oaks of Meeting Street, past the Josiah Smith House and the Calhoun mansion, ready to chuck my cell phone into the next zip code. The horse-drawn-carriage rides weren't the only explanation for the smell of horseshit wafting through the air. My boss might be to blame, too.

"Do the math," Anders said, annoyed, harried. I bet she was looking at her watch. "The Kincaids keep twenty million with you. That's nothing."

What planet do you live on?

"The family needs my help."

"And you know our policy."

"You just got notified. I'm getting approval from compliance, with or without your support." I had been working for Anders less than a month. And already, I was keeping my fingers crossed for boss number fifteen.

"There's no upside."

"I don't care."

"You're a fiduciary," she argued. "If anything goes wrong, you get hung."

"The Kincaids are my friends."

"Get me a box of tissues," she snapped, her tone sarcastic. "Do I really need to spell out the firm's liability for you?"

Somewhere, there was a carrion bird spitting out the rancid flesh from this woman's heart. She didn't get the importance I assigned to a board position at the Palmetto Foundation. No way was I backing down. "The foundation has liability insurance for directors. I already talked to the lawyers."

"Ours?"

"Theirs."

"Ours don't have time anyway."

My boss's snide comment pissed me off. I came back hard, the Wall Street way, and threatened to jump ship. Sometimes it's the only way to get attention in my business. "That's not what Frank Kurtz would say. We have a pretty good relationship now that he's at Morgan Stanley."

"Make my day."

Her indifference shut me up.

"Look, I've said too much," Anders said, her tone softening. "This is not a great time to ask compliance for anything."

"Said too much about what?"

"Just get back here." My boss never answered the question.

"Not happening."

"I like you, Grove."

Uh-oh.

"That's why I'm telling you," she continued, "to forget the Palmetto Foundation and focus on your job."

"Zola and Chloe have things under control. And I have things to do down here, until you explain what's going on."

"Suit yourself."

That was it. We hung up, two colleagues divided by one rat race.

"You're staying in Charleston?"

Anders had just finished flogging me over the phone. Under these circumstances, I call Annie to bitch about the boss. And a good purge—me venting about stupid decisions—usually helps. Only today, our conversation got off track early and never returned to SKC.

"Palmer asked me to be a trustee at the Palmetto Foundation," I replied.

"Congrats. That's big, right?"

"JoJo said there's an important meeting Tuesday."

"So come home for the weekend."

"I promised to look at her portfolio."

"What about dinner with my friends?"

"Oh shit, I spaced it."

Sort of. Annie and I had planned a Saturday night out with her graduate school buddies, which meant I'd pay for everyone. They'd eat. They'd drink. And they'd disappear into the bathroom when the check arrived, leaving me to do the gracious thing and pay the bill because I'm the only one with a fucking job. Bar flight is a form of behavioral entitlement that makes my skin crawl. If you ask me, there's a special place in hell for NYC's dinner deadbeats.

Annie said nothing.

"I'll cancel."

I could almost see her over the phone, the raised eyebrows, the full lips turned up at the corners, the no-dummy expression that says, "Don't bullshit me." Or maybe she was doing that thing where she squints, the look that says she can rip the thoughts out of a skull. My skull. She has a sixth sense about everything.

"You can't. JoJo's a client."

Annie knew these things. She learned the ropes during her first two years working for me. That was before my big fiasco with Charlie Kelemen and his Ponzi scheme: the one that almost got me fired; the one that put me on the cover of the *New York Post*; the one where Annie risked everything to watch my back. A year after we sorted out the mess, she left SKC for Columbia.

"You're right." Any other response would have been disingenuous on my part.

"I've got class. I'll call you tonight."

"On my cell, okay?"

"Why not the hotel?"

"Claire offered me her carriage house."

"You're staying in her home?" Annie asked after a considerable pause. *Uh-oh.*

"In the building out back. But I'm dying to see her place. Claire says the house is pre–Civil War." I was trying to sound chatty. I mean, it was no big deal, me staying with a high school buddy. No big deal if you know how to dance on eggs.

"But you love four-star hotels. Room service and clean bathrooms, right?"

"Claire comes from a family with two hundred million dollars. The bathrooms are okay."

"Yeah, I suppose so," Annie said. "Class is about to start."

"Why don't you come to Charleston for the weekend?"

"I have schoolwork," she replied. "Call me."

Our conversation ended with a dull thud, and I could tell Annie was pissed. Here I was, walking back to my hotel so I could pack up my things and move to Claire Kincaid's carriage house. So I could take her out to dinner and go toe to toe with a few vodka martinis and talk about old times and deal with my own insecurities about Charleston and all my personal crap about not fitting in.

There's a special kind of self-loathing when you double-book the weekend—accidentally on purpose—and disappoint the single most important person in your life.

CHAPTER FIFTEEN

Bong exited I-95 twenty minutes south of Fayetteville and turned onto U.S. 301. Moments later, he parked his Ford rental and considered the spider-sun tattoo on his forearm.

There was no telling what people remembered. He rolled down his long white sleeves and pulled a black baseball cap low over his forehead. No markings on the hat.

The parking lot outside the Lumberton Walmart felt postapocalyptic. Bleak. Buggy. Barren. Bong wondered why the Arkansas company, as rich and powerful as it was, spent so much money on tarmac and so little on plants.

Monstrous lampposts sprouted from the concrete like New Age weeds. The light fixtures at the top looked more alive than the scraggly trees scattered around the lot.

"No attention to detail." He muttered and shook his head in disapproval.

"Hello," croaked the Walmart greeter. The old man's ruddy face was a road map of lines, his voice tobacco-cured from two packs a day. He hunched forward on a stool, his arms slung over a shopping cart, the south side of his pants revealing too much information.

Bong thought the guy an odd choice to welcome customers. Walmart needed some tits out front. Preferably on somebody who could still chew solid foods. This fellow looked several breaths shy of a 911 call.

"Keep up the good work, captain."

Inside the store Bong inspected the layout, the racking, the way different sections were labeled. He found a disposable cell phone in electronics. It cost $19.95 with $10 preloaded in minutes. He selected a $25 calling card with more minutes, paid cash, and headed over to hardware, where he purchased a can of Great Stuff. Again, he paid cash and tugged his cap low.

"Thanks for dropping by," called the greeter bunny.

Bong waved and headed outside. He decided to grab lunch. There was a Dairy Queen on the other side of the lot, and he could use a hit of sugar before calling the franchise.

Clients. Bosses. Assholes come in all sizes, shapes, and labels.

The meeting had occurred twenty years ago.

Bong remembered it like yesterday. He was working in Makati, the business district of central Manila. Earnest and practical, though somewhat brusque, he had earned a reputation for cutting through the nonsense and getting things done. He was a rising young star.

Until he wasn't.

At first, the news had all been good. One boss encouraged him to apply for a work-study fellowship. The firm would pick up his law school tuition as long as he stayed for three years. After graduation another boss encouraged him to spend six months in Hong Kong. There, he could learn the company's infrastructure, really get to know it.

The promotions came fast and furious.

Four years after law school, Bong was poised to take over the division. The prevailing rumor was that his boss would be kicked upstairs to either Singapore or Hong Kong. Both were juicy assignments. And Bong was the natural successor.

"Will you close the door behind you?" The embroidered stitching on his boss's barong Tagalog, the lightweight business shirt favored by the business community, was a little too bold for Bong's taste.

"Sure."

"I guess you heard I'm going to New York for a three-year assignment."

"Wow. Congratulations." Bong could almost smell his own opportunity growing. A shift this big could only mean good things for him personally.

"That's why this discussion is so difficult for me."

Shit.

His boss was wringing his hands, not making eye contact. "Er, I'm not sure where to start."

"I take it you're passing me over?"

"They're giving my job to Bebe."

"Bebe! You've got to be kidding."

"You're reporting to her."

"She's not qualified."

"We want you to run Cebu," the boss said, ignoring Bong's outburst. He was referring to the island near the center of the Philippines.

"I have to move back?"

He nodded his head yes. "Your family will be thrilled."

"Did I do something wrong?" Bong's eyes blazed. He could feel his anger welling over, the overwhelming urge to kick this fop's ass.

"No."

Did you fuck Bebe?

Bong folded his arms across his chest. "I'm not leaving till you tell me why. You owe me that. Because we both know you're shipping me off to the boonies."

"You ask too many questions. The type that doesn't win friends around here. I'll leave it at that."

Bong thought about ordering another shake. But that would only delay the inevitable. He pulled the mobile phone out of its packaging, fussed for a few seconds with the $25 card, and called his franchise client.

"It's me."

"What's taking so long?" Moreno did not speak. His mouth slithered, his *s*'s serpentine.

"I had to tidy some things up."

"Tidy!" scoffed Moreno. "You made a mess in D.C."

Bong held the phone away from his ear until the yelling stopped. "It was business as usual."

"It's not like you to be late."

"I fixed the problem."

"That's what Sammy said."

There was nothing veiled about the threat. Sammy's unfortunate journey through the food chain was legend. Moreno fed him limb by limb into the throat of a commercial-grade wood chipper, fifteen horses that didn't leave much. Then he chummed the hammerhead-infested waters off the coast of Malpelo Island with the remaining chunks. And now Sammy was nothing more than fish turds on the ocean floor. Or perhaps the shit dissolved on the way down, only to be ingested by zooplankton. Moreno was thorough to a fault.

Bong felt queasy. "We've been working together a long time."

"Let's keep it that way. This isn't baseball."

"What's that mean?"

"One strike, and you're out."

"I don't get the threats," Bong protested. "You pay me to watch the details."

"I don't want a perfectionist." Moreno lingered on the *s* in "perfectionist." "I want my money. That's what I want."

Twenty minutes later, Bong stopped at South of the Border. For all the billboards along I-95, the theme park looked empty and decrepit. The place had seen better days. He pulled a hammer from his suit bag, checked to make sure no one was watching, and smashed the cell phone into tiny fragments. He dumped half the pile in the trash can outside the fireworks store.

Forty-five minutes later, Bong dumped the remaining circuits at a Hardee's off I-95 outside Florence. There was nothing like the threat of fish chum to prevent mistakes. He grabbed some fries for the road, something greasy to calm his stomach.

Fucking Moreno.

CHAPTER SIXTEEN
WASHINGTON, D.C.

"Don't do it."

"It's for your own good." Walker stared at her with BB eyes. His features were expressionless, the kind of face you see on passport photos, save one thing. He chewed the inside of his cheek. The right side was more concave than the left.

"Forgive me if I don't see the value." Torres regretted the sarcastic out-burst. But her boss was moving FBI field operations from D.C. to Quantico. The extra forty-minute commute would kick-start high-level peace negotiations with her husband and younger sister, the nanny of first and last resort.

"My job is to keep agents safe. Their families, too."

Torres rolled her eyes. "Aren't you being a little melodramatic?"

Walker's back went rigid. "There's a dead priest in our backyard. And three years ago, Moreno placed a bounty on FBI investigators. Excuse me if I don't see the melodrama."

"That bounty's a joke. You know it. I know it."

"It's a million bucks," Walker said.

"And I doubt some creep will ID me outside our D.C. office."

"That lawyer found you."

"That was different. He dialed an evidence bag and got the surprise of his life." So far, Torres wasn't buying Walker's caution.

"Maybe Hughes is a shill for Moreno."

"No way."

"I don't get your pushback."

Walker stopped speaking for a moment, long enough to work furiously on his right cheek. Torres wondered if he would ever bite all the way through. At least he didn't crack his knuckles.

"Moreno's people just killed a priest," he continued. "You think agents get immunity?"

Walker was right.

Torres didn't like the extra commute. But she'd handle it, like always. That was the thing about her line of work. You lived with the inconveniences. The ankle holster rubs you raw—get over it. The snitch phones during your daughter's play—get your ass down to see him before Prince Charming kisses Snow White in the second act. Arrests made all the sacrifice worthwhile. There was nothing better than the adrenaline rush from mushing some perp's sad-sack puss into the wall.

"Okay. I get it." Torres stood to leave. It was futile to argue anymore.

"Close the door and sit down."

Walker's request was not a good sign. "Is there a problem?"

"Yeah, I'm worried about you."

"Why's that?"

"We've known each other a long time."

"Cut to the chase." Torres landed back in the guest chair with a great whooshing sound. She wished Walker would get on with it.

"You're starting to fray."

"'Fray'!" Her voice rose. Her hands strangled the arms of the chair.

He chewed his cheek. "I wonder if you need some time off."

"No."

"You've got a short fuse around the office."

"I want this case."

"You're too good an agent for me to sit around and watch you burn out."

"I put three years into this investigation," she told Walker. "Pull me out now, and you rip out my heart."

"Nobody's pulling you out. But I wish you'd consider flexible hours."

There it was, "flexible hours," the kiss of death for FBI careers. "That's the fast track to mediocrity. You know it. I know it."

"It's not that bad."

"The thing about women in the work force." Torres paused.

"Yeah?"

"We don't pull stud duty when we're put out to pasture."

"Just think about it. That's all I'm asking."

"I did," Torres said. "The answer is no. We've got bigger issues to address."

"Like what?"

"Biscuit Hughes for one. That lawyer is picking a fight with the wrong guy."

Walker's face reddened with exasperation. "I told you. He may be part of the Moreno family."

"You've got to trust me on this one."

"I hope you're not discussing Moreno with him."

"Maybe," ventured Torres, which sounded too much like "yes" to Walker's ear.

"You'll compromise our investigation."

"Hughes is a bulldog. He'll sniff around Highly Intimate Pleasures and end up losing body parts if Moreno finds out."

"Not our problem."

"Dammit, Walker, he's a civilian."

"Not our problem."

CHAPTER SEVENTEEN
BISCUIT'S OFFICE

Staring down an LCD screen is a loser's game. Computers don't blink.

For the last two hours, Biscuit had studied the Catholic Fund's websites and come up empty. His eyes were red and his mind was fuzzy. The attorney rolled his head in a big circular motion as though to shake free the cobwebs. He racked his brain for ideas, puzzling what next. He owed Mrs. Jason Locklear a phone call and remembered his words to the subdivision two Sundays ago: "My first instinct is to check out the owners."

Yeah, right.

Biscuit riffled his tangled mop of hair. He drummed his porky fingers on the desk and pushed an invoice from his accountant off to the side. He had filed his taxes only two weeks ago—extensions were a way of life given his stake in Phil's Polynesian. And the damn accountant had already sent the bill. The ink on his 1040 wasn't even dry.

"That's it!" roared Biscuit, pumping his fist, radiating the power of a eureka moment.

"You okay?" his assistant, Margaret, croaked from her workstation outside his office. She did not bother with the intercom.

"Happy as a dog with two tails."

Tax returns, Biscuit knew from experience, provided a wealth of information. Ordinarily, they took forever to obtain. But philanthropies were an exception because the IRS required charities to make their filings public. The title of Form 990 may have been the ultimate oxymoron: "Return of Organization Exempt from Income Tax." It was also Biscuit's best idea since last Sunday.

He typed "guidestar.org" into his browser. The site contained 990s for most foundations. And with a few keystrokes, he pulled up the most recent filing from the Catholic Fund. On the first page under the section labeled "Summary," the 990 read:

The Catholic Fund's primary exempt purpose is grant-making. We partner with donors to promote economic justice. We focus primarily on the rights of children and on their ability to live in a healthy sustainable environment where human rights are preserved and protected.

"Where's the economic justice in porn?"

"What's that?" hollered Margaret. His assistant had the ears of an elephant.

"Nothing, darling."

Further down the page under the "Signature Block," Biscuit found the name "Father Frederick Ricardo, President." Even better, he found the San Francisco phone number of the paid preparer, Donald Lim of the CPA firm Bustamante and Lim.

He looked at his watch—a little after nine A.M. on the West Coast—and punched in the 415 number. To his surprise, a man answered on the first ring.

"Lim speaking."

Biscuit introduced himself, stated his profession, and explained, "I found your name on the 990 you prepared for the Catholic Fund."

"Okay?"

"I'd like to contact Father Ricardo."

"To make a donation?" asked Lim. "I can tell you where to mail your check."

"No. I want to discuss the Catholic Fund's stake in Highly Intimate Pleasures."

"Are you looking to buy it?"

Lim's response caught Biscuit off guard. "Is HIP for sale?"

"Everything is on the table—when children's lives are at stake."

Biscuit scratched his head.

The seconds dragged on.

Lim grew tired of hearing the dust settle. "If there's nothing else, Mr. Hughes."

"Actually, there is," Biscuit replied. "I'm surprised."

"About what?"

"That you would sell a business open a little over a week. That a Catholic charity owns an adult superstore."

"Is this why you want to speak with Father Ricardo?" The explanation irked Lim.

"Better him than the NBC news affiliate in Fayetteville." Biscuit had no desire to establish an adversarial position so soon. Nor to call the press, given the warning from Agent Torres. But Lim was about to hang up.

"Whatever."

"Wait till the press profiles HIP." Biscuit was desperate to flush information from the accountant. "I can see it now. Catholics package sex toys with indulgences from the pope."

"Have you ever been to the third world, Mr. Hughes?"

"Iraq. That third enough for you, pardner?"

"Then you've seen the squalor and filth slide downhill." Lim's speech was growing faster, more animated. "Kids get the worst of it. And the good my client does outweighs any wrong you assign to taking such a gift."

"Lemme get this straight. Somebody donated HIP to the Catholic Fund?"

"I've said too much," backtracked Lim. "I'm not at liberty to discuss donors."

"Fair enough. But I still want to speak with Father Ricardo."

"He's a busy man."

"And my clients are furious about Highly Intimate Pleasures."

"Tell them to focus on the kids."

"Easy for you to say," countered Biscuit. "Your backyard isn't a magnet for perverts."

"Like I said before," replied Lim. "If your clients don't like HIP, make us an offer."

Click.

"Why don't you pour yourself a cup of kiss my ass?" Biscuit replied to dial tone. He had Lim's phone number and office address, a respectable location at 44 Montgomery Street. The accountant would talk, if not over the phone at least in court.

Maybe.

It was always fifty-fifty whether Biscuit's assistant would mash down the Talk button or holler from around the corner. This time Margaret used the intercom. She spoke in a hacksaw voice, raspy from Lucky Strikes and the nightly marinade that included two drinks of gin.

"Biscuit honey. Mrs. Locklear is here to see you."

"Shit."

"I heard that," growled Mrs. Jason Locklear. Much to his growing consternation, Biscuit realized his thumb was still on the intercom's Talk button.

Short, stout, seething, she stormed through the door even before he could say, "Send her in." The woman's face was red, the bridge of her nose a whopping wrinkle. For just a moment, Biscuit wondered if he should fire his client before she fired him. But he thought better of it.

"Nice to see you."

"Why didn't you call this morning?"

Biscuit rounded his desk and held out the guest chair. "May I get you some coffee?" He knew the only way to disarm an angry crowd, or five sisters, was to listen with compassion. Mrs. Jason Locklear was a mob of one.

"I don't believe in caffeine."

"Water?"

"Cut the crap. We have a big problem."

"Oh?"

"One of my girlfriends just took a job with HIP."

"These are tough times." Biscuit thought the Swiss solution best. He intended to stay neutral.

"That's my point. The heathens are paying us to work."

"Okay?"

"You don't bite the hand that feeds you," she snapped. "We're losing our will to fight."

Biscuit's expression remained blank.

"They throw thirty pieces of silver at a few employees," Mrs. Jason Lock-lear ranted. "Meanwhile, home prices are dropping like hot horseshoes."

She had a point. Nobody wanted a truck stop in his backyard. Biscuit tried to soothe her anyway. "Maybe HIP has its own problems."

"How so?"

"HIP's been open a little over a week," he explained. "And they're al-ready recruiting new employees. I wonder if somebody quit—if they have personnel issues." Lim had suggested that HIP could be bought. Biscuit knew that organizations sometimes put themselves up for sale when prob-lems cannot be cured.

"Issues? Yeah, they can't handle the foot traffic."

"How do you know?"

"The manager told my girlfriend. The store's putting up thirty new bill-boards this week."

"HIP doesn't sound like a company that's up for sale."

"What are you talking about?"

Biscuit described his conversation with Lim and repeated the accoun-tant's exact words: "Everything is on the table."

When he finished, Mrs. Jason Locklear asked, "Can't we take a petition to our congressman?"

"If you like. But there's not much he can do."

"It's not right, Biscuit."

"I'm working it."

"It's not right," she echoed, throwing up her hands and shaking her head.

Ten minutes later Mrs. Jason Locklear exited like a tempest, draining the law office of all oxygen in her angry wake. Biscuit hated arguing with clients. The process made him uncomfortable—the hashing and thrashing out of details. To his way of thinking, there were more productive ways to waste time.

Biscuit glanced at his watch. Too early to head home for dinner. Right about now, he'd kill for a Navy Grog down at Phil's Polynesian. That and a plate of sweet-and-sour wings. But he eyed the Catholic Fund's 990, still open on his computer screen. It was time to pay attention, time to unclutter his mind and focus on the details.

Easier said than done.

The 990 was the print equivalent of sleeping pills. Boring, boring, boring. His mind drifted, which Biscuit suspected was the body's natural defense to the fucking insufferable parade of forms from the IRS. But when he came to Schedule I—"Grants and Other Assistance to Organizations, Governments, and Individuals in the United States"—the answers piqued his interest.

The Catholic Fund's accountant won't talk, reasoned Biscuit. *But its grant recipients might.*

Last year, the Catholic Fund had supported dozens of nonprofits located in cities around the country: Los Angeles, New York, and Spokane among others. There was the Catholic Victims Fund, the Catholic Endowment for Children, and the Catholic Center for Mercy. Most received large eight-figure grants, although Biscuit noted that Sacred Heart Parish in Anacostia received only $100,000.

"Father Mike got hosed."

Biscuit searched for Sacred Heart's 990 without success. He assumed the diocese, or a more senior entity in the Catholic hierarchy, handled the parish's paperwork. He found the 990 for the Catholic Victims Fund, though. He was curious what the charity did to earn a $50 million gift.

Its summary of activities read: "The Catholic Victims Fund aids families in crisis. We fight domestic violence and work with donors to shield children at risk. We defend those who can't defend themselves."

The language sounded similar to the Catholic Fund's summary. Biscuit scrolled down, thinking it would be odd if he found the same accounting firm—Bustamante and Lim at 44 Montgomery in San Francisco.

He didn't.

The accounting firm was Foz and Associates, based in Spokane. Michael Foz had signed the 990. Biscuit dialed his phone number, which was listed on the form.

"May I tell him what this is in reference to?" asked the receptionist.

Fifteen seconds later, he was speaking with Michael Foz.

"How can I help, Mr. Hughes?"

"I was looking at the 990 for the Catholic Victims Fund."

"Right. They're a fine organization."

"Can you describe its relationship to the Catholic Fund?"

"Are you with the IRS?"

"I practice law in Fayetteville, North Carolina." Biscuit rolled his head.

"Right. What makes you think the organizations have a relationship?"

"The Catholic Fund made a fifty-million-dollar gift to your client."

"Right. Can I get your phone number?"

Biscuit sensed Foz was about to hang up. "What for?"

"I'd rather my client answer all your questions," the accountant explained. "That way I don't make any mistakes."

"Fair enough. When should I expect to hear back?"

"Give me a call if you haven't heard anything in a week."

"You're kidding. That long?"

"They run a lean ship." Foz spoke with an accent, which Biscuit could not identify.

The big lawyer hung up a few moments later. There was something about Foz. Nice, but in a pasty kind of way. Too breezy. Too Left Coast. Biscuit's prodigious gut told him the Catholic Victims Fund would never call back.

For a while, he considered the $50 million gift from the Catholic Fund to the Catholic Victims Fund. It was so disproportionately large relative to the $100,000 Sacred Heart had received. The more Biscuit pondered the difference, the more it nagged him. He scrolled down to Schedule I for the Catholic Victims Fund, wondering whether its grants would offer any insight. Catholic Fund. Catholic Victims Fund. The names were so similar, so close, so hard to remember what was what. He wondered whether there was any real difference between their philanthropic missions.

Again, Biscuit found dozens of grant recipients. But one caught his attention, one that received a $20 million gift last year. He had seen that name before, somewhere, somewhere recent. The big attorney clicked back to the Schedule I for the Catholic Fund, back to a $30 million gift made last December. Just as he recalled.

Both organizations had made eight-figure donations to the Palmetto Foundation.

"What's with that?" Biscuit asked aloud. He still couldn't tell the difference between the Catholic Fund and the Catholic Victims Fund. But the good news was that he could see the principals at the Palmetto Foundation in person. Charleston was only a four-hour drive from Fayetteville.

"Hey, Biscuit," Margaret called. "Everything okay?"

"Fine, darling. You mind sending out for some food?"

"So that's why you keep talking to yourself."

"I'm working late."

CHAPTER EIGHTEEN
THE PALMETTO FOUNDATION
TUESDAY

Claire, JoJo, and I were sitting in the conference room with Father Frederick Ricardo of the Catholic Fund. Both women had stressed the importance of this meeting several times since my arrival in Charleston.

His organization had made a $65 million gift to the Palmetto Foundation. Today he was updating us on the progress of the charitable project for which the money was intended—what had been done and what was left to do.

I wasn't sure why the Catholic Fund needed an intermediary. The Palmetto Foundation offered anonymity and the expertise to manage a long-term gift. But as the newest trustee, I intended to find out more about our role.

My job was to evaluate the charitable projects of donors, while protecting the Palmetto Foundation's interests. Trustees can't wire out money willy-nilly. We have a fiduciary obligation to investigate the recipients of our donor gifts. Otherwise, the IRS would question whether we're entitled to tax-free status.

Technically, the $65 million belonged to us. But Father Ricardo gifted the money with a specific purpose in mind. So in all honesty, I expected to rubber-stamp his proposal. The Palmetto Foundation would never stay in business if we gummed up the wishes of our donors.

I confess. I was feeling good about myself. It was an honor to sit on the board of a charitable organization that already had $140 million in assets. With Palmer's gift, the Palmetto Foundation would soon oversee an additional $150 million. It was a lot of money, $290 million in total. It was a lot of power, all those contributions targeted for a greater good. My position as a trustee afforded me world-class bragging rights back at SKC.

And therein was the crux of my problem. On Monday I had faxed disclosures to SKC's compliance people—me joining the board of the Palmetto Foundation. They had not replied. And given my boss's lack of support, I probably should have waited to accept the position.

But Palmer was my friend and mentor. Deceased or not, he had invited me into his inner circle. He was always saying, "Sometimes you do the best you can and just say fuck it." My exact thoughts now. I couldn't turn my back on his request

Or wait for SKC's Business Prevention Unit to get back to me.

Father Ricardo was well put together, five foot nine and built like a mailbox. His eyes were brown, his hair the color of coal. He wore a black suit, a black shirt, and a white clerical collar. There was an aura about him, the freshness I sometimes notice in people with a spiritual calling.

I rolled up my sleeves and invited him to take off his jacket. "Make yourself comfortable, Father."

He stayed formal but welcomed me to the board. "I look forward to working with you, Grove."

Claire and JoJo flanked the reverend, who was sitting at the head of the table. The two women insisted he take the seat reserved for guests of honor.

Father Ricardo turned to JoJo and held her eyes for a good five seconds. Same thing with Claire. He appeared to absorb their pain and replace it with his inner strength, a potent trade coming from a priest. "I'm making a nine-day novena for Palmer."

We all paused for a moment of silence, letting the good father decide when it was appropriate to continue. And sure as I'm the life-support system for a mouth, Wall Street had nothing on that priest. He was one helluva salesman.

"Some of this may be repetitive." Father Ricardo glanced at the Kincaids for their permission. "I want to bring Grove up to speed."

"Good idea," agreed Claire.

"But just so you know," he said, still addressing the women, "we stumbled across a new opportunity. It's big. It means everything to us. And I need to discuss our funds."

We trustees exchanged glances.

With an overhead projector, Father Ricardo flashed PowerPoint slides against the wall. My first thought was, *Not the Church.* PowerPoint is the great enabler of Wall Street's toxic waste. Derivatives, CDOs, the securities nobody understands till somebody gets hurt—it takes slick presentations to hawk that crap.

No matter my misgivings, the good father hooked me within thirty seconds. It was his focus on the kids, their faces, those smiles that still haunt my dreams.

"Mahatma Gandhi once said, 'There are people in the world so hungry that God cannot appear to them except in the form of bread.'" He paused to gain my complete attention.

I could taste his bitterness.

"There's an evil more sinister than hunger. It's more vile than malaria, AIDS, and other problems you associate with third-world countries. And the Catholic Fund needs your help to fight it."

Every so often Claire and JoJo checked my reactions. Unlike me, they had embraced his mission long ago. I was completely mesmerized, waiting to hear what was next.

Father Ricardo zipped through head shots of orphans, one after another. They were all smiling, scrubbed and squeaky clean the way kids are. "Here's Grace. And Jacinto." And so on.

Once, he stopped to describe a five-year-old boy with a Magic Marker mustache. "Eduardo asked me to draw it so he would look fierce." I smiled at the child's innocence and half chuckled until Claire shot me a look.

What's that about?

The answer came when Father Ricardo clicked on a photo of Grace. Her whole body, not just her face. She had no foot.

Then he showed Jacinto, no arm. One after another the priest scrolled through photos, all the bright faces. Every one of the kids suffered a dismemberment of some kind. Eduardo was the one who got me. His right hand was gone. He couldn't draw his own mustache.

There were tears streaming down JoJo's face. I almost lost it on the spot. "Were the kids born like this?" I had to ask.

"Afraid not." Father Ricardo shook his head from left to right. He bristled with anger.

"What happened?"

Claire's face clouded. Her bangs fell low, her face full of distress. I had never seen her in such distress. "There was this kid in Manila. Mabini Street. One foot. He saw me and came racing over on crutches."

"I don't understand."

"He was a beggar," explained Father Ricardo. "Just like my kids in the photos. At one time, they all worked for men who maimed them."

"What!"

"Crippled kids get more money." Claire's blue eyes moistened.

"Sick." JoJo bent down to pick up Holly. Her yappy dachshund had just run into the room. She snuggled the dog in her arms.

"And I refuse to sit back and watch." The priest's face grew cold and steely, his jaw set. His knuckles grew white from clenching the side of the table. "Which is why our opportunity is so important."

"Sorry, Father. I still don't know what you do."

"You're right. I'm getting ahead of myself."

"Grove needs to hear the whole story," observed JoJo.

Claire nodded her head in agreement.

"We get the kids. We make them safe and give them the tools to live their lives with dignity. That's one reason our relationship with the Palmetto Foundation is so important." He looked at Claire and hesitated.

"Go ahead." She leaned forward.

"I doubt you understand, Grove."

"You're probably right." Eduardo's photo was still showing against the wall, sweet face, black ink mustache, no right hand.

"We're dealing with gangsters. Cruel men who regard the kids as their slaves. They won't let the kids come with us."

"What do you do?"

"Take them." Father Ricardo spoke in a low voice, guarded, almost a whisper but one vibrating with rage.

"Excuse me?"

"We pay men to rescue the children."

"You mean mercenaries?"

"That's not how we think of them."

"How do you think of them, Father?" Priest or not, the reverend was mincing his words.

"Rescue teams, bodyguards, ex–Special Forces—they're angels if you ask me. We hire guys with training you can't get in the seminary. And our team, as you might guess, is a highly sensitive issue for the Catholic Church."

The revelations floored me. I think Father Ricardo stopped speaking because of what he saw in my face. I finally said, "You're a priest."

"Yeah, a Maryknoll priest. Our mission is to 'foster self-worth and dignity.' Look at Eduardo." Father Ricardo pointed to the PowerPoint slide. "You think he had much dignity before we saved him?"

When I was a kid at the Air Force base, the Maryknoll priests visited our church on a regular basis. They described poverty in third-world countries and talked about water-purification plants, classrooms, and facilities to treat tuberculosis. There was always a second collection plate on the days they visited. But there was never a hint of missions like the one Father Ricardo had described.

"You grabbed Eduardo! Isn't that a job for the authorities?"

"Yeah, if they weren't so corrupt. And prayers don't stop them from taking bribes."

Father Ricardo was intense. He was pragmatic. I liked him and was beginning to understand the reason behind our involvement. "The Palmetto Foundation enables you to remain anonymous?"

"We do things the public would never understand. Things that would bury the Catholic Church if the press ever found out. And the last thing we need is another PR fiasco." He glanced at Claire and hesitated again. Even here, inside our private conference room, he worried his secrets might slip out.

"It's okay, Father. Grove's one of us." She swept the bangs from her face.

"We maintain safe houses across Manila. First we get the kids away from their captors. Whatever it takes. Then we relocate them off the island of Luzon."

"Why?" I asked.

"If we kept the kids in Manila, the gangsters would find them and put them back to work. That's why I'm so guarded."

"You relocate kids out of the country?"

"Too complicated. The culture shock would overwhelm them. But we have seven thousand islands in the Philippines. We hide our kids with families on Cebu and the surrounding islands, fit them with prosthetics, and teach them skills. They never leave the country."

I started to think about the operation. The logistics were massive: maintaining safe houses, evacuating the children, and finding homes with families in other regions. It was a noble cause. But it was time- and labor-intensive. "How many kids can you rescue?"

"Every child we save," Claire interrupted, "is a victory."

"But we have an opportunity to do more," added Father Ricardo. "Which is why I'm so excited."

"Tell us," Palmer's daughter urged.

"How much do you know about the Visayas?"

"The region in the middle of the Philippines?" JoJo sipped coffee, her words half question and half answer.

"Right, the Visayas are the islands I mentioned before. Cebu and maybe one hundred and sixty others surrounding it. We have the opportunity to buy a hotel on one of them. It's perfect for an orphanage and school. We can buy it, refit it, and not worry about finding foster families in Cebu before we get the kids out of Manila."

I didn't ask how much it cost. I had a different concern. "Where do we wire the money, Father?"

"Same as before. The Manila Society for Children at Risk."

"We fund your programs in our name, and nobody can tie the Catholic Fund to your activities in the Philippines."

"Right," he confirmed.

"Did Palmer sign off on this?" I asked the other trustees.

"One hundred percent," replied JoJo.

Claire nodded yes. "Why do you ask?"

"We're linking the Palmetto Foundation to mercenaries."

"You're saving kids," protested Father Ricardo, his voice testy.

"What if the gangsters visit Charleston?"

"Why would they do that?" He threw his palms in the air, exasperated with me.

"We threaten their income."

"That's alarmist. They're small-time hoods operating out of Manila." Father Ricardo shook his head in a wistful way. "They don't even follow us into Cebu."

I suddenly regretted my words. "How much money do you need?"

"We've budgeted for all of it," he said.

"Sixty-five million?"

"Minus your fees," he confirmed. "We have acquisition and renovation costs, not to mention our operating expenses. It's expensive to hire angels, lease safe houses, and find families on the islands. We have too much momentum to stop our good work."

"When do you need the money?"

"Now."

"Why the urgency?"

"The seller's about to declare bankruptcy. If you think American courts are slow, you should see them in the Philippines. If the seller files, we lose our chance. I'm not talking about saving hundreds of kids. I'm talking thousands."

"How'd you raise the money in the first place?" I asked, switching gears.

Claire glanced at her watch and then at me. I didn't understand the signal. There was no time constraint, to my knowledge.

The reverend smiled. "Palmer asked the same thing. We target Catholics in the United States through different websites focusing on specific cities. New York, Los Angeles, San Diego—to name a few."

"No mention of your activities in the Philippines, right?"

"Too risky."

"I'd love to see your websites."

"Can we break for a few minutes?" Claire spoke in her Southern-syrup CNN voice. Something was eating at her. But I had no idea what.

Father Ricardo checked his watch, twisting his wrist to expose it from underneath his white cuff. "I had hoped to wrap this up."

"Just fifteen minutes," soothed Claire. "JoJo, Grove, and I need to talk among ourselves."

We do?

"Well, I'd love coffee and a doughnut," he said.

"I'll order something from the café across the street," offered JoJo. "You can use my office while you're waiting."

"Don't bother. I need the walk. So does your dog."

"Charge it to the Palmetto Foundation," JoJo said, passing Holly to the priest. "We have an account there."

"Do you have a leash?"

Holly looked happy. I had never seen the dachshund snuggle up to anyone but JoJo.

"On the hook next to the door."

When I turned around and saw Claire, she was staring daggers at me.

CHAPTER NINETEEN
THE PALMETTO FOUNDATION

"What are you doing?" Claire was pissed.

I had no idea why. "What do you mean?"

"Father Ricardo. I don't get the inquisition."

"We're fiduciaries. It's our job to investigate grant recipients."

"I've been to Manila." Claire leaned forward. "I've seen the kids for myself."

"What about the safe houses?"

"And blow their cover—are you kidding? We've been working with the Catholic Fund for two years. What more do you want?"

"Your dad's money isn't here yet. Sixty-five million is almost half of our total assets."

Claire folded her arms, the right hook of nonverbal communication. "It's the Catholic Fund's money."

"It was."

"They're paying us six hundred and fifty thousand dollars to stay invisible. The last time I checked, we have competitors and they have options. Why are you being such a hard-ass?"

Claire had a point. But I was still right to exercise caution and watch the details. "I'm sure your dad described our due diligence to Father Ricardo."

"The Palmetto Foundation agreed to fund his cause a long time ago."

"Did you sign something?"

Our exchange resembled a tennis match. JoJo watched in silence, her head turning back and forth with each volley.

"Dad did it on a handshake," replied Claire.

"I don't see the problem with my questions."

"You're wasting Father Ricardo's time."

"Palmer's word was his bond," added JoJo.

"I wasn't here."

"We still need to honor his verbal commitments," Claire pressed. "It's good business."

"How did you meet Father Ricardo anyway?"

"Referral from one of my husband's friends." JoJo touched Claire's forearm and leaned toward me, the two united in their opposition. "But the Catholic Fund is Claire's baby. She built the relationship from scratch."

Claire flashed a wan smile at her stepmother.

I looked at Claire. I looked at JoJo. The voting math was clear. "Can't I have one week to study the organization?"

"No," insisted Claire.

"You heard Father Ricardo. He needs the money." JoJo squeezed my hand. The gesture filled my head with images of Eduardo and the other orphans.

"So if we vote right now, the Palmetto Foundation will wire the funds?"

The two women checked each other. Then they looked at me, nodding their heads in unison.

"Fine, I quit. I won't be bullied into a decision I don't understand." I regretted my words at once. The petulant-little-boy crap worked at SKC, but it could destroy my lifelong relationship with the Kincaids.

Fortunately, Claire softened. "Come on, Grove. We need you."

"It's the kids." JoJo reached across the table for my hand again, trying to defuse our tension. "Their faces. Their wounds. They're tearing us up inside. And Palmer's gone."

She was right. I had joined the board as a swing vote, and right now there was no deadlock. Far from it. Frick and Frack were on the same page. "I'd feel more comfortable doing my homework on the Catholic Fund."

Claire unfolded her arms and reverted back to Madam Ambassador. "We've got our fees and the future of this relationship to consider, Grove."

JoJo smiled her assent.

"I'm okay if we wire twenty-five million now and the balance in a week."

"Father Ricardo will hate the delay," JoJo objected.

"Twenty-five million goes a long way toward keeping a project on track," argued Claire.

"We're going back on my husband's word. How do we explain that?"

"Blame it on me. This is my first meeting as a trustee. And this is our first important decision since Palmer's death. A priest, of all people, will understand our need to regroup."

"Father Ricardo won't like it." This time it was JoJo who folded her arms across her chest.

"We need to decide." Claire spoke with the conviction of a veteran horse trader. And it dawned on me that the Daisy Buchanan of my youth was taking charge of her father's empire.

I insisted on playing bad cop. It was my fault, after all, we weren't wiring the full $65 million. Father Ricardo would be ticked off. I had no doubt.

"How was the doughnut?" Claire smiled brightly, relaxed, confident, ambassadorial. She was sitting next to the priest.

"We both enjoyed it." Father Ricardo passed Holly back to JoJo. Then he looked at me and confirmed my childhood conviction that all men of the cloth come with a sixth sense. "What's the problem?"

"I need time to review your proposal."

He said nothing at first. He just stared at me with the glacier face that priests reserve for confession. When you grow up Catholic, it's really uncomfortable to be sitting across the table from a guy who's hot under the clerical collar. He finally asked, "How much time?"

"One week."

"We need our money now. The seller will declare bankruptcy, and then all bets are off."

"We'll send twenty-five million today. That will buy your seller time with his creditors."

Father Ricardo turned to Claire. "You agreed to this?"

"Yes." She nodded, but her eyes blinked.

"We had a deal, Claire."

"We still do," I intervened, trying to regain control of the conversation.

"Palmer said the money would be available whenever we need it."

"One week, Father."

"It's our money, Grove. You're going back on my handshake with Palmer."

"I don't see why seven days are a problem."

"And I'm not sure what you hope to accomplish."

"If it were my decision, we wouldn't wire any money until I finished my due diligence." There it was, me throwing myself under the bus. I glanced at Claire and JoJo, acknowledging Father Ricardo's allies on the board, and added, "But given our relationship with the Catholic Fund, I'm okay with twenty-five now."

"Anything can happen in a week. We've been waiting too long for me to lose this property now. And frankly, it troubles me your organization doesn't have the integrity to stand behind its word. This would never happen with Palmer at the helm."

"No, I suppose not," admitted JoJo, sitting apart from all of us. The reverend's rebuke was a bitter pill for her to swallow.

"We needed a partner." Father Ricardo addressed Claire, laying the guilt trip on her. "We chose your organization for its stability. Now I realize we were mistaken. And ordinarily, I can work through mistakes. Everybody blows it at one time or another, even priests. But it's the kids who are suffering. How can you be so indifferent?"

I almost caved, Eduardo's photo still on the wall. "How much does the property cost anyway?"

"Immaterial. It's the principle. Where I come from, a man's word counts for something." Tension growing, Father Ricardo rubbed his collar to emphasize the point.

It was Claire who emerged from the shell of her father, Claire who offered a solution à la Madam Ambassador. "Maybe there's a way to make the week more comfortable."

"Wire us sixty-five million," Father Ricardo snapped. "That'll make us comfortable."

"Why not seventy?" Claire countered.

Three heads snapped around, Father Ricardo's, JoJo's, mine.

"What do you mean?" asked the priest.

"We'll stick to the schedule," she said. "Twenty-five today, forty in a week, and five thereafter. Call it our apology for making you wait."

For a moment, Father Ricardo considered her words. He looked at all three of us before addressing Claire: "We could use ten."

"We're not that sorry," Claire said, laughing, leaning forward, grasping both his hands. "No harm, no foul?"

"It's a fine solution," urged JoJo. "We can fund the last five when Palmer's bequest comes into the foundation. He'd be thrilled."

"How about waiving your fee?" Father Ricardo smiled. Less money for us meant more money to his mission. He was a shrewd, no-nonsense negotiator.

So was Claire. "No."

Most of the tension had left the room. But no one was feeling victorious, least of all me. We sat in an awkward silence, not sure what to say. After a while, I tried to bring closure to our conversation. "Well, I know what Palmer would say."

The others looked at me, waiting for a punch line.

I wasn't trying to be funny—which is my usual crutch in these situations. Humor, I've learned through the years, never solves the problem. It just masks the hard feelings for a while. It was more effective to say something wise for all parties to consider:

"'A good deal is where everybody leaves—'"

"'The table unhappy,'" Claire interrupted, finishing Palmer's words, friendly with me, again.

"Well, I'm unhappy." Father Ricardo held his mouth between his thumb and forefinger.

That's how the meeting ended. That's how our new board made its first decision. And in my view, we ensured that nothing would ever be the same among the three trustees again.

CHAPTER TWENTY

Torres grabbed a coffee and a buttered roll. She also snagged *The New York Times*, *Wall Street Journal*, and *Washington Post*. She preferred the *Times* to the other publications. Didn't matter. Over the next two hours and forty-six minutes, she would read all three cover to cover.

The agent glanced at her watch. She had five minutes to catch the six A.M. Acela Express from D.C. to New York City. She picked up her pace, annoyed by a helter-skelter lifestyle that was growing old in a hurry. This morning, there had hardly been enough time to kiss her babies good-bye.

All this for what?

Murph and the D.C. police had turned up nothing new on Father Michael Rossi. The medical examiner confirmed that asphyxiation was the cause of death. His finding was hardly a revelation.

Fingerprints produced only one hit in the federal databanks. One of Sacred Heart's churchgoers started a bar fight twenty years ago in college. There was nothing, however, to link the parishioner to Moreno.

Nor was there anything to suggest a motive for Father Mike's brutal death. Sacred Heart's clergy reported no suspicious activity, and members of the staff were distraught.

"Father Mike was a saint."

"We all miss him."

"Sacred Heart will never be the same."

Torres assumed the priest had discovered something that jeopardized the Colombian drug lord's U.S. operations. But she didn't know what. And there was no record the good reverend had ever approached D.C. authorities.

The agent put her thoughts on hold for the time being. She found a seat, unwrapped breakfast, and opened *The New York Times*. She thumbed to the business section first, curious how the day would look to employees at Sachs, Kidder, and Carnegie.

The headlines jumped off the page at her. And she had no chance of stifling the "Oh my God" that escaped from her lips. Katy Anders was about to have the day from hell—a pink slip in the making and a visit from the FBI.

DENNY'S

It was 6:30 A.M. Biscuit parked his black Hummer and lumbered into the restaurant. Once seated, he unfolded his copy of the *Fayetteville Observer.*

"You want the usual, Biscuit honey?" His waitress poured him a monstrous cup of coffee, the rich scents of bacon and java beans filling every nostril in the room. She was a sassy young thing—rhino nose, straw flyaway hair, and razor-blade wit that made the world forget how she looked.

Biscuit nodded his head as he sipped the morning joe. "Darling, they don't come any better than you."

"One heart attack on a rack coming up."

He scoured the sports section first—every score, story, and statistic. Then he skimmed the front page, not bothering to complete articles that continued inside. When Biscuit hit the business section, however, he stopped cold. He even forgot the rest of his breakfast. And food was one thing he never forgot.

Yesterday, Biscuit had chatted up the receptionist at the Palmetto Foundation. He'd learned all about Grove O'Rourke, both on the phone and later courtesy of Google. And today in bold print, Sachs, Kidder, and Carnegie was the lead story. O'Rourke had not returned his calls yesterday. He doubted the guy would call him back today.

He wiped his mouth, signaled for the check, and called Faith Ann:

"Sweetie, I'm driving down to Charleston."

PALMER'S OFFICE

I should have flown back to New York. There are plenty of flights that leave the Holy City before eight A.M. I should have engineered a day that landed me in front of my LCD screens by noon.

That way I could have returned to Wall Street's all-important mission, the frenzied commerce that keeps the wheels on our economic bus. Like arguing with bond traders and telling them to go bang walruses off Alaska's coast. Apologies to the wildlife. Or explaining to clients why it's important to invest for the long term, even though their stock portfolios haven't made a dime over the last ten years.

But after a week in Charleston, I had succumbed to the stealthy charm of old stucco and genteel manners, to the soft Charleston dialect where locals conjugate their verbs with saccharine tenses: "We might could grab a bite to eat."

Maybe it was the low-country pace I found so alluring. By the time I reached the Palmetto Foundation that Wednesday morning, I had already run three miles and eaten a breakfast of shrimp and buttered grits. I had even chatted with a lady, her skin the color of chocolate milk, who was selling sweetgrass baskets near the corner of Meeting and Broad.

"Women in my family been weaving five generations," she told me. "Bet my baby will too."

Back in New York I would never have stopped to talk. Of course, I don't see artisans first thing in the morning. Usually, it's homeless guys sleeping off benders on their cardboard mattresses.

At dinner last night, Claire and I made nice. We drank too much Gavi di Gavi Black Label, which is a kick-ass bottle of white if you ask me, and put the testy meeting with Father Ricardo behind us. She told me, "Your Southern accent's coming back."

"You think?"

"It suits you."

Claire insisted I use Palmer's office. So did JoJo. At first the room felt uncomfortable, me surrounded by photos of my mentor amid all the luminaries. But Wednesday morning, I felt like Palmer was sending me alpha waves to relax. Maybe even to stay. For a moment, I sipped coffee and fantasized about opening up a branch office down here.

The morning news snapped the spell. I booted my laptop and navigated to Bloomberg's website. The headline popped up, big and bold: MORGAN STANLEY AGREES TO BUY SKC'S BROKERAGE UNIT. Not the whole company. Just my division.

"Shit."

Anders's suspicions were right. Our CEO was shedding Private Client Services. I should have seen it coming—fourteen bosses in ten years who never got the mix of profits and services right.

Soon I would be working for a new company. Sort of. My industry plays an ongoing game of musical chairs. And ironically, my next boss— number fifteen—was also number thirteen: Frank Kurtz.

Zola answered on the first ring, her voice crisp and husky. "You read the news?"

"Every word."

"What's it mean to us?"

"Opportunity."

"How so?" she asked.

"Change creates winners and losers. Time to keep our eyes open."

"You think Morgan Stanley will pay us a retention bonus?"

"Who knows?"

When one brokerage firm buys another, the acquiring firm sometimes pays stockbrokers to stay. Otherwise, competitors swoop in and pay ridiculous signing bonuses to steal away top producers. Retention bonuses can be big—50 percent or more of last year's revenues. If I was right, Zola, Chloe our sales assistant, and I would split about $10 million just to stay with SKC as it folded into Morgan Stanley.

Of course, there are trade-offs. Stockbrokers sign noncompete agreements and agree not to jump ship. It's like enlisting in the Marines, except we make more money and nobody shoots at us.

"Don't bank on a bonus," I told my partner. "When Dean Witter and Morgan Stanley merged, stockbrokers never saw a dime."

"Percy's addressing the firm this morning."

"Is there a dial-in number?"

"No way," Zola said. "The last time, a reporter called in and taped everything he said."

"Take good notes."

"When are you coming back?"

"Friday. I need to wrap up some business."

"I'm not sure how I feel about working for Morgan Stanley." There was hesitation in Zola's voice.

"Be happy it's not Goldman."

One thing was certain: nobody was getting any work done back at my shop. Sales assistants would gather, three or four strong around the coffee machine, and whisper what so-and-so said. Like their source had all the answers. SKC brokers would talk to UBS, Bank of America, and other firms to test the market for signing bonuses. And managers would schedule meetings, more meetings, meetings about meetings, until they were blue in the face from talking and we were begging them to stop.

"This transaction is good for biz," senior management would tell us, over and over, waterboarding us with talking points for our clients.

The only way for me to investigate the Catholic Fund was to stay right here in Charleston. Otherwise, there'd be too many distractions. I expected to make a few phone calls, Google a few names, and learn the charity was just fine. Don't worry. Be happy.

But here's the thing. My career was taking a nosedive back in NYC. And I didn't see it coming.

CHAPTER TWENTY-ONE
PRIVATE CLIENT SERVICES

Torres was sitting in a posh conference room at SKC, her spiral-bound notebook open on the table. The place smelled like old money—tiger maple walls, Italian-leather chairs, and brushed silk curtains framing the floor-to-ceiling windows that overlooked Rockefeller Center.

For a moment, she considered her days in private practice. It had always troubled her that lawyers built financial stability on the backs of clients. This place was more of the same. The modern paintings and aging Chinese pottery looked like a long stretch of rapacious fees.

The agent glanced at her Timex. She had been waiting fifteen minutes, plenty of time to grow annoyed. She wondered whether her strategy of arriving without an appointment had been such a good idea after all.

"Sorry to keep you waiting." Katy Anders opened the door, shook the agent's hand with a fish grip, and led her five colleagues into the conference room. "You caught us on a busy day."

"So I heard."

"We didn't expect the FBI to come knocking."

"And I didn't expect your head count," Torres said, surveying the group. She spoke in a monotone, distant and aloof. She was scarier that way.

Anders wore a black Chanel suit. Not one of those classic tweedy numbers. This one cleaved to her body like plastic wrap, smooth, tight, and provocative. Her heels, designed by some guy with ten vowels in his last name, soared four inches—making the agent wonder when Wall Street's piranhas had taken to stilts.

The other five introduced themselves. There were three men and two women, all lawyers from SKC's internal staff. The one named Stevenson winced when Anders asked, "Will this take long?" She was a saleswoman. She had no business copping an attitude with the FBI.

"Depends on your answers." Agent Torres sat bolt erect, the posture of a gymnast.

"Our CEO is addressing the sales force." Katy Anders spoke with funereal gravitas, as though Wall Street's future hung in the balance. She checked her watch once, twice, and made no effort to hide the unfriendly smoke signals.

"We may need to depose him." Torres knew her words would alarm the lawyers in the room. SKC would do everything to prevent Percy Phillips from speaking to the FBI—especially today of all days.

"How can we help?" Stevenson tried to defuse the threat.

Torres ignored the lawyer, eyed Anders, and pushed back. It felt good to tweak a woman whose outfit cost half the agent's monthly salary. "Your colleagues can leave if that's helpful, Ms. Anders."

"No, no," Stevenson replied. "Tell us why you're here."

"To discuss Grove O'Rourke."

"Has he done something wrong?" Anders shook her head in exasperation. She suddenly experienced an insatiable urge to take that pompous broker down a notch. What the hell had he done?

"Why don't you question Grove directly?" interrupted Stevenson.

"He's not to know about our meeting today."

"We have an obligation to disclose your interest to Morgan Stanley," blurted Stevenson.

"And interfere with a federal investigation?" Torres stared at the lawyer until he turned submissive. Then she held up her right palm, calling for attention. "Here's how it works."

The room went dead silent.

"I ask questions. And you answer best you can. We clear?"

Six bobble heads nodded yes. Nobody peeped.

"Good. Because our interview will go faster. And nobody wants Ms. Anders to get a stiff neck from checking her watch every five seconds."

Fuck you, thought Anders.

"Yes," acknowledged Stevenson. He eyed the other lawyers to ensure they kept their mouths shut.

"Good."

Over the next forty minutes Torres learned that O'Rourke had been with SKC for ten years. That he was a top producer in the Private Client Services division. That he had been forced into a leave of absence two years ago following a sordid murder. That O'Rourke had cleared himself of all wrongdoing. That the Boston and New York police departments had honored him for solving the murder and exposing the financial scam behind it.

Torres distrusted the police. They overlooked clues all the time. "The missing jewels," she said to the branch manager, "were they ever found?"

"No," replied Anders. She wished that this agent, who dressed off the rack from T.J. Maxx, would go the hell away.

"What do you mean, 'top producer'?" Torres changed topics with no rhyme or reason. The tactic put interviewees on their heels—made it more difficult to lie. Interrogation 101 at the FBI.

"They're stockbrokers who make the most money for our division."

"Is O'Rourke important to the deal with Morgan Stanley?"

"His team generates twenty million a year in revenues." Anders tried hard not to look at her watch. "But it's O'Rourke who built the team's business. Morgan Stanley will ask about him."

"Yes or no?"

"He's one of one hundred and fifty brokers. But a scandal can tank any deal," replied Anders. "That's why we wish you'd tell us more about your interest."

Torres ignored the request and shook her head, feigning disappointment at the response. "Why isn't O'Rourke here today?"

"He's visiting a client."

The agent leaned forward and drilled into Anders's brown eyes. "What do you know about Palmer Kincaid and the Palmetto Foundation?"

The question took her by surprise. "How'd you know where he is?"

"I'm asking the questions." Torres hesitated, feeling the vibration of her cell phone. She checked the LCD and said, "Let's take a five-minute break."

"Percy's gonna shit," one of the lawyers ventured inside the conference room. Torres was outside in the hall, taking her phone call away from the SKC employees.

"Is that your professional opinion?" Anders was in a snit. The FBI irked her. So did the five lawyers vying for airtime. Even worse, she was miffed that her brokers were getting a 50 percent retention bonus while she might rate an attaboy at best. As a manager she had no personal clients. Nobody would care if she jumped ship during the deal with Morgan Stanley.

Translation: no payola.

Anders turned to Stevenson and asked, "We need to tell Morgan Stanley, right?"

"I think we need outside counsel."

"Five people in this room have law degrees. And you need more lawyers?"

"We don't want to piss off the FBI," explained Stevenson. "Or Morgan Stanley. They'll sue us if there's a scandal and we don't give them a heads-up."

"Can't we fire O'Rourke and eliminate the problem?"

Stevenson couldn't believe her question. "Grove's our number one salesperson."

"He's expendable."

"Since when are twenty million in fees expendable?"

"You forget Zola," scoffed Anders. "We keep her, and we keep his clients."

"They're loyal to Grove."

"His clients will stay at SKC if nobody hires him. Don't forget, Grove is tainted goods once we fire his ass."

"Why are you horsing around with the guy's career?" the lawyer demanded.

"Because he's fucking mine. If our deal blows up from bad press, it's me who gets fired."

"How so?"

"You know Percy," she said. "Grove reports to me."

"We don't even know if Grove's done anything wrong."

"Call it a preemptive strike."

"Call it a lawsuit for wrongful termination."

"You won't support me?"

"Based on what I know," replied Stevenson, "no."

"I guess we'll have to take this upstairs." Anders buttoned her white blouse another notch and snugged her Chanel jacket into place. She was digging in for the fight.

"Suit yourself."

Torres rapped on the door and walked into a conference room full of hangdog faces. She offered no explanation for her absence, not so much as an "I'm sorry."

There was no reason to tell Morgan Stanley about Murph's call. The D.C. police were getting nowhere on Father Mike's death. The detective had called to ask if the FBI had learned anything new.

"I need a history of all wire transfers to and from the Palmetto Foundation," announced Torres, picking up where she'd left off.

"We never opened an account in their name." Anders smirked ever so slightly. It felt good to say no to this woman.

"How do you know?"

"O'Rourke and I discussed the charity on Friday."

"Really?"

"They asked him to join the board."

"And did he?"

"I hope not." Anders shot a glance at Stevenson, who shrugged. "I advised against it."

"Why's that? Do you know something about the Palmetto Foundation?"

"I know Grove's board activities would be a distraction. He manages four billion in assets. He doesn't have time for anything else."

Torres narrowed her eyes. "Would you get me a history of all the Kincaid family's accounts?"

Stevenson shook his head no. "Do you have a court order?"

"You really want to play it that way?"

And the lawyer, yet again, understood the threat. "When do you need the info?"

"Now would be good."

Stevenson nodded at a subordinate to get moving.

Whereupon Torres began listing her other needs. "I need O'Rourke's employee files and a copy of everything on his computer. Can you get it without making a fuss?"

"We'll pretend it's a software update."

"Good. Do you tape phone calls? If so, I need a record of every discussion with Palmer Kincaid."

I need. I need. I need. Torres was relentless. The four lawyers still in the room scribbled furiously until she asked for a list of O'Rourke's clients.

"That's confidential." Anders crossed her arms.

"Don't be ridiculous."

"We have an obligation to protect our clients," the branch manager argued.

"Our job is to protect the firm," countered Stevenson, staring at Anders. He clearly disagreed with his colleague.

"Where'd you say Phillips is?" asked Torres, her threat clear to everyone in the room.

"We'll get the list of clients." Stevenson had no desire to see the FBI interrupt his CEO.

But Anders pressed the agent for more information anyway. "Why can't you tell us more about O'Rourke's trouble?"

"Palmer Kincaid may have been part of a conspiracy."

"What kind?"

"Providing material support to a criminal enterprise."

The color drained from Anders's face.

Three hours later, Torres left with a treasure trove of papers and electronic files. She also knew exactly how to turn Grove O'Rourke into an asset, whether he liked it or not.

Anders glanced at Stevenson and asked, "You still want to protect O'Rourke?"

"I don't know," he said. "I don't know."

CHAPTER TWENTY-TWO
BROAD STREET

Every so often, thick billowing clouds rolled through the Charleston sky like tumbleweeds from the West. They hid the sun and protected the city from its fierce rays—if only for a moment. Bong decided the cottony clouds looked just slightly out of reach on the blue mantle overhead.

He pulled his black baseball cap down, as much to escape the clammy autumn air as to stay hidden. He hunched behind the steering wheel, the car windows rolled down, and pretended to read a book.

Through black wraparound sunglasses, Bong gazed at the front door of the Palmetto Foundation. The answer, it seemed, was beckoning him from inside. The plan was the plan, the recent turn of events nothing more than a temporary complication.

"Palmer was a dick," he reminded himself, "a loose end like that damn priest."

The bad news was $33.5 million. Bong owed it to Moreno, a ridiculous debt to a guy who was certifiably loony tunes. This morning he had gone berserk, yet again, screaming over the phone, "You're a fucking maggot, Bong. You're small, blind, and worthless."

The good news was $33.5 million. Moreno could rant and rave, threaten all he wanted. Psychopath or not, he was a businessman. He was practical. He was hard-nosed and analytical. He would not touch Bong until he got his money back.

Who am I kidding?

Bong shuddered as he recalled their conversation that morning. After the last month, he had finally blown a gasket and made the big mistake of mouthing off. "I can't think with you threatening me every time we speak."

"Maybe you'd concentrate better without a thumb," Moreno shot back. "Increases blood flow to the brain."

Claire Kincaid was just the distraction Bong needed to forget his client. She walked toward him, west on Broad, and he slumped a little lower. Claire had once offered so much promise. Now she was just another sour-assed chick.

"The bitch needs a good beefing," he cursed to himself.

Claire walked inside the building, which was probably just as well. Bong had a business to run. And she was the wrong Kincaid.

By and by, his thoughts turned to JoJo. She was just another whore with a dazzling ass, higher priced than most, but a streetwalker all the same. He'd be doing the world a favor by cleansing the streets of her kind.

Almost like a gift from the fates, JoJo walked past the right side of his car. Holly trailed after her on the leash, long body, wirehair, short dachshund steps. Bong watched the two go by, and in a stunning instant of inspiration, understood what was necessary.

He started to open the door. He'd have to be quick. *Careful, careful,* he thought, pulling his cap lower still.

The opportunity disappeared with the same speed it had surfaced. Down at the corner of Broad and East Bay, a tall man ambled in their direction. Bong had seen that guy somewhere before. Where? He was immense, too big to forget. He walked with grace for a fat man, long elegant strides that would make ballerinas take notice.

JoJo stopped in front of the Palmetto Foundation and gestured for the big man to enter. He stepped back and waited for her to go first. Bong kicked himself for being so impulsive.

What was I thinking?

One way or another, he'd get the $33.5 million. He'd get Moreno off his back and make enough to retire many times over. Better yet, he'd have some fun with the Kincaids. Perhaps Moreno was onto something, specifically his comment about "blood flow."

There were all kinds of possibilities.

CHAPTER TWENTY-THREE

"What's he want?"

"Didn't say," replied Jill, our ageless receptionist at the Palmetto Foundation—sixty going on forty, or the other way around. "But he's filling the lobby like he's wearing it."

"What do you mean?"

"You'll see."

"Send him up."

Biscuit Hughes stood about six foot four. Short-sleeved shirt. Tie loosened around his neck. Jacket draped over his shoulder. I guessed he was closer to 300 pounds than 250, given how his stomach lopped over his belt. But he wasn't obese. He was just big, still rippling with muscles from his youth. The lawyer was a walking lunar eclipse.

"How can I help?"

"You can call me back." He handed me his business card, which looked like a coupon special from Staples. "I drove four hours to see you."

Dozens of phone messages were piled on my desk. The stack broke ground yesterday, while I was researching the Catholic Fund and tending to brokerage business. Today the unanswered notes gained height and momentum, especially after the news broke about SKC's deal with Morgan Stanley.

Clients phoned New York, found my coordinates in Charleston, and asked, "Is my money safe?" I couldn't keep up with all the calls.

There were three messages from the big man. "Sorry," I said, riffling through the stack. "Have a seat."

The antique chair, built for lighter bodies from leaner times, groaned under his wide load of a physique. He spoke at a snail's pace, his words slow and Southern, poetic in their cadence. "I'd like to understand your relationship with the Catholic Fund."

I don't discuss clients with anybody. The Catholic Fund was not a client. But it had donated $65 million to the Palmetto Foundation and sure sounded like one. If it looks like a duck and quacks like a duck—you know what I mean? I was intrigued and locked down in security mode at the same time.

"What makes you think, Mr. Hughes—"

"Biscuit," he interrupted.

"That we have a relationship with the Catholic Fund?"

"Last year's 990."

He had me.

It was time to clam up and shuffle my feet. Time to play good ol' boy and pretend I knew nothin' about nothin' and maybe even less. Southern-style business is an art form, one which Palmer Kincaid had mastered in this very room. I leaned back in the chair, like my mentor before me, and waited.

Biscuit launched into a rant I can only describe as stream-of-consciousness. "We just met, and I appreciate your reluctance to speak. I also understand why you have so little time today, the Morgan Stanley deal and everything. But trust me when I say, 'We need to talk.' Because I think you're dancing on turds, which may be nothing new given that fiasco two years ago. Frankly, I'm surprised your record is clean."

"You checked me out with FINRA?"

The government agency offers a Web-based service called Broker-Check. Anybody can use it to check out the compliance records of stock-brokers.

"I've done my homework," he confirmed. "But something ain't right, the Palmetto Foundation and the Catholic Fund. I think you're holding a pair of threes against a full house, captain."

"Whoa, slow down there."

"What do you know about the Catholic Fund?"

"You want to catch me up, Mr. Hughes?"

"Call me Biscuit."

"Maybe you should explain your interest, and we see what happens."

"Your donor," he said, lingering on the words, "owns an adult super-store off I-95 in Fayetteville, North Carolina. It's located in my clients' backyard, and they don't like it."

"Excuse me?"

All of a sudden the big man's comment, "Something ain't right," sounded like an understatement. I tried to play it cool, labored to stay calm.

Father Ricardo had been so confident yesterday. On the way out the door, he assured me, "We'll check out just fine." But let me tell you, my face was about to shatter from the way his charity was checking out.

The stockbroker's mantra is "Know your client." The Patriot Act, Uncle Sam's response to terrorism post-9/11, imposes severe penalties if you don't. There are stiff fines when you get in bed with the wrong people. The sanctions can be levied against companies or individuals, who risk jail time for violations. And there are two words that accompany any discussion of the Patriot Act, two words that were tying my stomach into knots.

Zero tolerance.

I was clueless about the Catholic Fund. Ten years of finance under my belt, and I had no idea who it was or whether Claire and JoJo knew about its investment in the adult superstore. For all I knew, we had just wired $25 million to some al-Qaeda splinter group in the Philippines.

Oh-shit moments trigger a hierarchy of reactions. I'd compare them to Dante's descent into hell. But he laid out nine circles. And I lose count after the first three steps.

First comes denial. There was a logical explanation for the Catholic Fund's investment in an adult superstore. Palmer had done business with the Catholic Fund for two years. Claire knew Father Ricardo well. So did JoJo. Even her yappy little dachshund liked the padre. And dogs are uncanny when it comes to sniffing out problems and squatting on trouble.

Next comes remorse. Katy Anders warned me not to join this board. Why hadn't I paid attention to my gut and resigned from the Palmetto Foundation yesterday? But no, I made nice. I joined the board, all sunshine and Gucci loafers, because Palmer was a friend and I was his thousandth man.

Then comes the gripping realization that you're fucked. I didn't need the hassle—explaining to authorities why we wired $25 million to the Philippines at the request of a priest who was long video porn. I knew what the Feds would say:

"Zero tolerance."

Even worse, investigations have a way of finding their way into the press. I'd soon be explaining this fiasco to my clients, who were already stewing about SKC's merger with Morgan Stanley.

"Just tell us our money is safe, Grove."

Problem.

I had been flogging myself, mentally that is, for about five seconds. It felt like five years—me lost in the private reverie that Annie calls "Grove's world." Sometimes, it's a tortuous climb out of there.

Biscuit rested his thick fingers on the edge of Palmer's desk and leaned forward. He was wearing a class ring from the Citadel, Charleston's proud military college that some describe as the "West Point of the South."

It's a place steeped in core values, where cadets take a lifelong pledge not to "lie, cheat, or steal, nor tolerate those who do." It's a place I respect.

"Something wrong, captain?"

Biscuit, I realized, was talking to me. "Sorry. Tell me what you know."

Over the next fifteen minutes, the attorney outlined his findings about the Catholic Fund, the 990s, the accountants with whom he had spoken, Sacred Heart Parish, and his inability to contact Father Frederick Ricardo. "It's like asking for an audience with the pope. I can't get near the guy."

"Father Ricardo and I met yesterday."

"Wish I'd been there."

At first, I wasn't sure what to tell Biscuit. He already knew the Catholic Fund had donated money to the Palmetto Foundation. And when we filed this year's taxes, he'd see all our grants on the 990, hundreds of them. There was no direct link between the Catholic Fund and its secret rescue activities. But after pausing a few seconds to think, I decided to make the connection.

"Have you ever heard about the Manila Society for Children at Risk?"

Biscuit screwed up his face and tilted his head to the side. "You're full of surprises."

"What do you mean?"

"They're another shareholder."

"Of HIP! You're joking, right?"

"Not at all. Do you have a cell number for the reverend?"

Now I was freaking out. Father Ricardo was pressuring us hard, insisting we wire out the $40 million balance of his charitable grant. The investment in Highly Intimate Pleasures, from his operations in the Philippines, made no sense.

For a moment I wondered whether there were any commercial ties beyond the equity investments. Whether the orphans manufactured adult toys and sewed lingerie. Something to supplement their dividends from the superstore. I hoped the kids weren't performing in the movies. The more I thought about Father Ricardo and Highly Intimate Pleasures, the darker my thoughts cycled.

"Oh, I'll do better than the phone number."

Maybe it was Biscuit's lumbering good nature. Or maybe it was the Citadel background. It was certainly one of those moments when your instincts take over. I found myself trusting the big attorney more and more, which isn't at all like me.

"What do you mean?" he asked.

"Can you attend our next board meeting?"

"I'll clear my calendar," he said.

"And there's one other thing."

"Which is?"

"You've heard that old expression 'Follow the money'?"

"Of course."

"Biscuit, we're following the priests."

CHAPTER TWENTY-FOUR
CHARLESTON INTERNATIONAL AIRPORT
THURSDAY

Erica Jong once said, "Jealousy is all the fun you think they had."

It had been ten days since I arrived in Charleston. Sitting in the airport lounge, plugged into my cell phone, I was about to grasp the wisdom of her observation.

"We invite zone one to board," a woman announced over the loudspeaker.

"I'm coming home tonight. You want to go out?"

Annie ignored the invitation. "I thought you had moved in."

"You mean Charleston?"

"I mean Claire Kincaid's carriage house."

"I keep telling you. It's no big deal."

"Okay," Annie said, with breezy indifference. Her voice was light, the freshness that says, "I don't have a care in the world." But I knew the tone, the battery acid underneath. She was pulling back, still pissed about my decision to stay with Claire.

"Let's do something fun. See a movie or head down to Chinatown."

"Fine."

Oh, brother.

"Come on, Annie. Don't turn this into something it isn't."

Deep down, I acknowledged what she suspected. Most of the time, it had been fun to hang out with Claire. When we were sitting and drinking on the long, narrow Charleston porches with friends from high school. When we were away from the Palmetto Foundation offices, at venues where she had nothing to prove. Claire gave good dinner conversation and seemed to enjoy mine. She hung on to my words like I was the second coming of George Clooney. But we weren't sleeping together. Not even a little.

"We invite passengers to board with seats in zone two."

"Just come home," Annie told me.

"I can't wait to get out of Charleston."

She hesitated for a moment. I pictured her sitting on our bed, legs crossed Indian-style. In my head, she was wearing a loose-fitting sweater, a T-shirt, or maybe a clingy camisole, and baggy pants that made me wonder how all the soft layers could hang together so well. "Did something happen?"

"I'm not sure."

"What do you mean?"

"I'll explain later. You wouldn't happen to know an easy way to measure website traffic?"

"Yeah, Alexa.com."

"What's that?"

"Just give me a Web address, and I'll tell you how popular the site is."

I opened my notebook to the list of URLs Father Ricardo had given me. According to him, his websites raised money from Catholics living in Los Angeles, New York, and other hubs. I gave Annie the one in Chicago.

She navigated to Alexa.com and plugged in the Web address. "Why do you care?"

"Due diligence. I'm curious whether the sites are viable for raising money."

"How much money?"

"Hundreds of millions."

"I bet Chicago is lucky to raise one hundred dollars."

"What do you mean?" Suddenly my stomach twisted into a knot. Annie has many talents. One of them is her instinct for numbers, which I first noticed when she worked for me. "The website looks pretty slick."

"Nobody goes to it."

I just listened.

"I'd be surprised," she added, "if Chicago gets ten thousand hits a year."

"You don't know exactly?"

"I know that Alexa ranks your site seven million something on the Internet."

"Meaning seven million other sites are more popular?"

"We ask zone three to board," the airline representative announced.

"Right," Annie confirmed. "Ten thousand hits is probably generous. And what, maybe ten percent of all visitors donate through online forms?"

"Try one percent. If that." I knew where she was going.

"One percent of one thousand is ten. That means ten donors must make average gifts of one hundred thousand dollars just to reach one million. That's fantasy on the Internet. And you're talking about a charity that receives hundreds of millions."

"Shit."

"What about the other sites?" she asked.

"Zone four."

"I have to board. Can you check out New York?"

Same story. On the jet, I asked about Los Angeles and Spokane. It really didn't make much difference. The traffic was about the same for each of them, next to nothing. And one thing was clear: the Catholic Fund's donations weren't coming from its websites.

"Anything else?" asked Annie before we clicked off.

"Google Biscuit Hughes."

"Who?"

"He's a lawyer from North Carolina I met yesterday. I think he checks out fine, but I'm curious what you think."

Annie's last words were "Get home safe."

CHAPTER TWENTY-FIVE

ANACOSTIA

"Sacred Heart's a money pit."

Father Andy, the acting pastor, pointed toward the church's steeple. He was a young priest, late twenties, reedy and tall at six foot one, his features talcum fresh and worry free. He was showing Biscuit the parish grounds. And every so often, the two men stopped to discuss repointed bricks or freshly painted windows.

"The roof, Father?"

"Brand spanking new. I remember when it leaked like a sieve."

"And the Catholic Fund paid for all the renovations?" Biscuit already knew the answer. The charity had reported a $100,000 donation on its tax return. But his goal was to sound sympathetic. To wring every ounce of information from the young priest.

"Without Father Ricardo, we wouldn't be here."

"What do you mean?"

"Our bishop told Father Mike, rest his soul, to raise money for repairs. Or else the diocese would shut us down."

"Gives new meaning to produce or perish."

"So to speak," the reverend said with a chuckle. "Father Ricardo solved our problem. Pews, roof, steeple, and stairs leading to the sacristy—we refurbished everything with gifts from the Catholic Fund."

"I'm confused." Biscuit scratched his forehead, as though struggling with a complex algorithm.

"About what?"

"I thought Maryknoll priests raised money from local congregations. Not the other way around."

"Father Ricardo can shake donations out of a parking meter." The young priest gazed into the distance, nodding his head with visible reverence.

"That's a real skill."

"We should all be so blessed, right? The Catholic Church is under real pressure these days."

"Do you know why Father Ricardo is so successful?"

"Charisma. He makes people feel good about themselves."

Biscuit scrunched his face again. "How's that possible?"

"What do you mean?"

"I thought the Catholic Fund raises money over the Internet."

"Websites legitimize the Catholic Fund. But the real money comes from face-to-face meetings. Father Ricardo has a knack for getting in front of big donors."

"You've seen him in action?"

"I only know what Father Mike told me. And he said Father Ricardo is one of the best."

Biscuit paused for a moment, as though summoning his resources to ask a difficult question. "I don't want to offend you, Father."

"I can turn the other cheek." Father Andy thought his reference to the Sermon on the Mount was wise beyond his years. "Just speak your mind."

"I'm not sure why the Catholic Fund donates to Sacred Heart. Its mission statement focuses on the rights of children. Not the renovation of churches in Anacostia."

"We provide administrative services for the Catholic Fund."

"Like what?"

"Answer phones. Forward its mail. Whatever it needs."

"Not bad for a hundred thousand dollars." Biscuit regretted his words at once. He had revealed too much information from his investigation.

"What do you mean?"

Hands in his pockets, the big man backpedaled. "I mean that's good business. Sacred Heart serving as the back office and all."

"That's one way to put it."

"Who negotiated the arrangement?"

Father Andy stopped walking and faced Biscuit. "You ask lots of questions. You said you're a real estate lawyer?"

"Yes. And I don't mean to be intrusive but—"

"Are you suing the Catholic Fund by any chance?"

Uh-oh, thought Biscuit.

"Litigation is no good for anyone," he replied.

"You didn't answer the question."

"No, I suppose you're right, Father. The truth is that my clients don't much like your benefactor."

"And why's that?"

"The Catholic Fund owns an adult superstore outside their subdivision."

"I know nothing about it." Father Andy started walking, his pace hurried and curt.

Biscuit could feel the conversation coming to an abrupt end. "The fact is, I want to work things out. And I haven't been able to contact Father Ricardo directly."

"He's out of the country a lot."

"How often does he stop by?"

"There you go again." Father Andy stopped at the curb. "More questions."

"One of his accountants said the adult superstore was a gift from a major donor."

"Wouldn't surprise me." The young priest spoke in a matter-of-fact tone. There was no outrage in his words, which confused Biscuit.

"And you're okay with his source of funds?"

"I'm sure the Catholic Fund's good work outweighs its association with a retail store."

"That's a big hurdle, Father. The store is twenty thousand square feet."

"Thanks for stopping by." Father Andy offered to shake Biscuit's hand, his message clear. The interview was over.

CHAPTER TWENTY-SIX

Stockbrokers are nomads. We travel to see our clients, not the other way around. We pack cell phones, Bluetooth earpieces, and laptops for remote access to Bloomberg. Even with these mobile devices, we carry others: iPads, Kindles, Nooks, not to mention Android anything.

We believe in redundant systems, in part because we're technology junkies. We like our toys, the more expensive, the better. But there's a more compelling reason than the dweeb factor to carry two of everything. We can't afford for communications to break down. If they do, we're dead in the water.

Gadgets have yet to replace human interaction. They miss the innuendo. And that's a communication failure all its own. Same thing with being away for ten days. I had missed the whispers around the coffee machine. I never saw the boss rolling her eyes. Or checked to see who was visiting whose office.

Closed doors are always the first hint of trouble around the bend.

At 7:30 A.M. I marched past Katy Anders. She was leading three visitors across SKC's lobby. The suits carried briefcases and wore grim expressions. I recognized several SKC employees trailing behind them—the staff lawyers and human-resource types that come equipped with nose tethers.

The group was trudging toward a conference room. Their bearing was heavy, their morgue faces drained of energy. And I wondered whether the Morgan Stanley deal had cratered. But Anders was the wrong person to participate in those discussions.

She busied herself with the outsiders and ignored me. A woman from human resources caught my eye and flashed a wan, humorless smile. "Welcome back," she said, which struck me as weird, uncomfortable. I knew her face but couldn't remember her name.

"Thanks." I pressed on.

It took me twenty-five minutes to reach Zola, Chloe, and my workstation. On the way over, stockbrokers buzzed with excitement. They wanted to talk. Not that I had any inside knowledge about our deal with Morgan Stanley. I offered a fresh take, however, on the same old questions that had been posed a million times since the deal was announced on Wednesday.

Scully looked left, and he looked right. He whispered, his voice uncharacteristically low, "Morgan Stanley's a boiler room. My clients won't go."

"Yes they will." Casper pushed aside his fingernail clippers.

Scully, who's a big hitter on the floor, was not accustomed to the pushback. "Who pissed in your Cheerios, bright boy?"

"I'll make this easy for you," snorted Casper. "You answer the phone 'Morgan Fucking Stanley.' Nobody gets hurt, and you take home a fifty percent retention bonus."

"Nothing wrong with that deal," I observed.

"It's about time we got paid around here," Casper said.

In a room full of stockbrokers, everybody has an angle. Especially when it comes to money. Financial advisers claim to be resolute in their convictions, adamant until a better idea comes along. In practice, the vast majority of us change our minds the way pigeons change directions— straying and cooing from one leader to the next as we move inexorably toward the dough.

Patty Gershon, my nemesis on the floor, stopped me before I reached my team. Her revenues were second only to mine. But frankly, she did a better job keeping her finger on the pulse of SKC. "Thanks for coming in, Grove."

New day. Same joke as yesterday and the day before and . . . You get the point.

"Any idea who Anders is meeting?"

"Lawyers from Morrison Foerster," Gershon reported.

"Well, that's emphatic." Her recon surprised me.

"Jane told me."

The explanation sounded reasonable. Gershon was a magnet for every woman in the office with something on her mind, including Anders's administrative assistant, Jane.

"MoFo's bad news," I observed, referring to the law firm.

Morrison Foerster prides itself on the nickname. A line on its website reads big, gray, and in your face: "This is MoFo." It's an image, I think, that hard-boiled litigators embrace during court battles.

It was Gershon's turn to be surprised. "What's the big deal?"

"We only use them when there's a problem."

"Which is what?"

"Who knows? I've been keeping a low profile in Charleston."

"What do you think about the deal?"

"I'm still gathering facts."

"Better hurry up." Gershon picked up her phone. "Anders is leaning on me to sign the paperwork. And my team is scheduled to meet with Morgan Stanley on Monday."

Back at our workstations, Zola high-fived me hello. She was on the phone, already locked into a client conversation. Chloe, our sales assistant, pulled off her oversized headset, vintage World War II, and asked, "Did you bring me a present, Dad?"

We played this game whenever I returned from trips. Usually, I made some wise-ass remark. But this time, I handed her a tin of Charleston benne wafers. They're sweet, sesame with a milklike buttery flavor. I can eat them by the handful.

"I was kidding." Chloe turned crimson.

"I'm hoping you'll share."

"Depends how much I like them."

"Hey, do you have my paperwork?" Our phones were lighting up, but we let the calls go into voice mail. Wall Street could wait another few minutes.

"The Morgan Stanley stuff—Anders has yours."

"What about Zola?"

"She has hers," Chloe confirmed. "She refused to turn it in until you got back."

"It'd be nice to have mine."

"Anders wants you to stop by anyway."

"Did she say why?"

"Oh my God, these are good," Chloe exhaled, grabbing another benne wafer. With that she offered some to me, and we began sucking them down, using sign language to urge Zola to follow our lead.

Old-time Charlestonians believe benne wafers bring good luck. But it's like I said before: in my business, nothing good happens on Friday afternoon. And by the time the day was over, Wall Street's voodoo had more than trumped the positive juju from our cookies.

"It is what it is."

I hate that expression, the inherent fatalism, the callous marching orders to deal with a decision that sucks. Those five words mean somebody got hosed. Today, that somebody had been me.

Outside Anders's office, the beat-down over, I decided she could screw herself. She had outpointed me and eliminated all my options. I couldn't even complain to the client, which is the one thing every broker does in these situations.

Seething, taken aback, I turned philosophical. I decided there's no such thing as halftime in the rat race. The contest grinds on, day in, day out, forever unraveling with no rules and no end in sight. And because there's no clear way to win, I wondered if we all lose.

The meeting with Anders had lasted all of fifteen minutes. It began the usual way. "Chloe said you want to see me."

"Do me a favor and close the door."

Uh-oh.

My thoughts jumped to the Palmetto Foundation. My decision to join had been eating me for any number of reasons. First, there was Biscuit Hughes. From abso-fucking-lutely nowhere, he walked into Palmer's office and linked our charity to an adult superstore.

Ordinarily, I would have thought him nuts. But there was something about the big attorney, something that made me trust him. From the start, he passed my smell test. And later, he withstood further scrutiny when Annie and I Googled him. Biscuit was onto something.

Then there was the modest traffic to the Catholic Fund's websites. Father

Ricardo's story was not hanging together. And when I closed the door to Anders's office, my misgivings gained momentum. Patriot Act. Fines and jail time. I could be going away.

Wall Street runs from trouble. Firms do everything to protect themselves rather than their people. The brass at SKC would throw me, or any stockbroker, under the bus without a second thought.

Which meant I wasn't about to confess my misgivings to Anders. I tried a little misdirection instead. "Is this about Morgan Stanley?"

"Everything's about Morgan Stanley." She paused and confronted me head-on, obliterating my strategy. "Did you join the board at the Palmetto Foundation?"

"I had no choice."

Anders shook her head in dismay. I saw trouble in her eyes. There was something deeper than disagreement between two colleagues. Something more profound and, I would add, something more unsettling.

"That's too bad."

"Do you have paperwork for me?" I asked, retreating to the big deal.

"It's all here." Anders handed me a large manila envelope with a computer-generated label bearing my name.

"I understand several teams are meeting with Morgan Stanley next week."

"You aren't. Not yet anyway."

"What's that mean?"

Anders leaned forward, her usual pose for the big show of cleavage and trust-me body language. Not today. She was attacking. "A bunch of your clients already have accounts at Morgan Stanley."

"Every broker on the floor has the same problem."

"But you cover our chairman."

"So."

"We're moving his account to a team over there."

"Excuse me." Percy Phillips was not my biggest client, not by a long stretch. But no stockbroker wants to lose the CEO's account.

"You heard me."

The scummy reality—firms can reassign clients anytime they want, even though brokers are paid to develop new relationships. I was growing angrier by the minute. I could feel my forehead throbbing.

There are bragging rights when you cover the CEO of your employer. He's the king of the chessboard, the piece every player will protect no matter the cost. I was being sacrificed and had no idea why.

"It's part of the deal." Her words were crisp and cold. But she brushed her upper lip with a hooked forefinger, the nervous tic I had noticed before.

"That's fucked up. Revenues are the same, whether Percy works with me or somebody else."

Anders shrugged. "My hands are tied."

"He agreed to this?"

"Don't go running to him." She leveled her stare like a 12-gauge.

"And if I do?"

"Insubordination. Our lawyers say it's grounds for termination."

"Is that why you met with MoFo this morning?"

"That's none of your business." Anders blinked and averted her eyes. The flicker lasted less than a second. But I knew. I was right. This was one of those times when I would have paid to be wrong.

"What aren't you telling me?"

"Our deal with Morgan Stanley is a big win. You should be thrilled about the payday."

"You're taking my client. I'm not feeling the love."

"This conversation is exactly why I don't want you talking to their management."

"Gershon's team is meeting with Morgan Stanley on Monday."

"Patty is none of your business."

"And you're holding back."

I was bullshit. Ready to blow a gasket. Awareness was the only thing that saved me. Awareness of myself on the brink. Of management's nonsense. Of MoFo's involvement. I began to speak in controlled bursts, my words softer and softer, a steady, seething soliloquy that forced Anders to pay attention. "We all have a few clients who keep money with Morgan Stanley. If they didn't, we probably wouldn't want them as clients."

"Let me say something."

"Don't interrupt."

She backed off.

"Other brokers are meeting Morgan Stanley. I'm not. You're pushing people for their paperwork. But you're not pushing me, which is pretty fucking strange because our team generates more revenues than anybody else on the floor."

Anders started to speak.

"Don't interrupt." I stared her into silence. "And now you're telling me Percy's account is a deal point. It doesn't square with the facts, Katy, and I'm wondering what's happening behind the scenes. Are you taking any other clients?"

"Everything is on the table."

"Does this have something to do with the Palmetto Foundation?"

"Not at all. I love when subordinates ignore my instructions." Anders sounded hard, the sarcasm sharp. But her eyes glowed like a cornered rodent's.

"Why don't you level with me and save the money you're spending on MoFo?"

"I think we're finished."

Anders stood and folded her arms across her chest. The posture, about as subtle as Times Square, said: "Don't let the door hit you in the ass on the way out."

"This thing with Percy," I told her while leaving, "it's not right. I don't understand your game. But we both know it's not right."

"It is what it is."

CHAPTER TWENTY-SEVEN

OSSINING, NEW YORK

Westchester is nothing if not affluent. Big houses. Big taxes. The county is a place where the usual suspects of wealth—doctors, lawyers, financiers—pay for a view. Though, arguably, the best vistas belong to state employees: the guards stationed atop lookout towers at the Sing Sing Correctional Facility in Ossining.

The prison overlooks the Hudson, a wide stretch where riverbanks are steep and trees shoulder each other for slivers of sun. But for all the feral beauty of unruly thickets, the area is best known for jailhouse colloquial-isms like "up the river," "the last mile," and "the big house."

Fifteen minutes east of Sing Sing, around the fjordlike bends, reform is spiritual rather than correctional. The Maryknoll Fathers and Brothers, blessed with a separate zip code, make their world headquarters in a for-tresslike campus. Massive buildings are hewn from great beams and rough-cut stone. And were it not for the Asian motif, at least one pagoda roof, the structures would resemble their razor-wired neighbor on the Hudson.

It was Tuesday when Father Ricardo had visited the Palmetto Founda-tion. Afterward, I Googled the Catholic Fund, the Manila Society for Chil-dren at Risk, and Maryknoll every possible chance. That was between calls to the office, clients, and everyone else. Over the phone, Father Tom Ford agreed to meet me. A Maryknoll priest, he pushed papers for their adminis-tration.

Ossining is cycle heaven. Ordinarily, I would have thrown a bike on top of my Audi and banged out twenty-five miles after wrapping up busi-ness. That Friday afternoon, however, I was in no mood to ride. I was too preoccupied with Katy Anders, the impending merger with Morgan Stan-ley, and the CEO's account that had been snatched from me.

Anders was behaving like an alien. Her job was to make nice and deliver brokers, who could generate fees and commissions to our new owner. She should have been puckering those glossy red lips, all swollen from collagen and other adventures in self-love science. She should have been kissing me square on the patoot. Because that's what overhead line items do on Wall Street.

Anders was hiding something, that flicker of her eyes. Driving up to Ossining, I brooded about my boss. What she knew. What I didn't. I ground through the Palmetto Foundation, my promise to wire $40 million within a week, and the sparse traffic to the Catholic Fund's websites.

Its Internet pages looked legit. In fact, they resembled Maryknoll's three separate websites: one for priests, one for nuns, and one for laypeople. There are three separate Maryknoll operations. But they maintain strong operating bonds and share their focus on the overseas mission activity of the Catholic Church in the United States. The Catholic Fund websites employed the same color palettes and type fonts as their Maryknoll brethren. Even the photos had the same look and feel.

The Donate buttons really piqued my curiosity. They were located in the upper-right-hand corner of most Maryknoll pages. Underneath were the words: "86 ½ cents of every dollar donated goes directly to our work."

The Catholic Fund's websites, even the ones targeting smaller cities like Spokane, included the same gold button. Not similar. The same. The graphics and shading were ditto déjà vu. Only the numbers were different. The Catholic Fund claimed that ninety-three cents out of every dollar donation went to its work.

When I finally reached Ossining, I parked my car and all my preoccupations at Maryknoll's headquarters. I headed inside and shook hands with Father Ford. His modest office was neither spartan nor over the top. He acted like a man in a hurry, short and twitchy. I soon learned he was prone to repeating himself, as though his inner thoughts were echoing out of his mouth. He proceeded right to business.

"How can I help?"

"I'm trying to get some information, Father."

"What kind?"

"Things you might not say over the phone."

"I might not say them in person." The reverend's demeanor was guarded. Priest or not, I could see he was like any other bureaucrat. Careful.

"I may have a problem, Father. A serious problem revolving around sixty-five million dollars. One that will attract the authorities, if my fears are justified. The thing is, I don't know if there's really an issue. And I need information about a member of your order to understand what's going on."

He leaned forward, engrossed. "Who's the priest?"

"Father Frederick Ricardo."

"Nope. Don't know him. Never heard of him. Sorry I can't help."

The speed of his staccato repetitions surprised me. "How can you be so sure?"

"Five fifty. We have about five hundred fifty priests. I know most, but nope I don't know Father Ricardo."

"Do you mind checking your records, just in case?"

Father Ford turned to the computer. His fingers danced over the keyboard. He blinked several times in a frenetic-little-man way, anxious to wrap up and return to his other duties. He removed his rimless glasses, fogged the lenses with his breath, and wiped them clean. "Nope, nope. There's no Father Ricardo."

"Dark skin. Curly hair."

"That could be any of our missionaries."

"Father Ricardo said this would happen."

"What would happen?" Father Ford opened and closed his hands repeatedly.

"Maryknoll would disavow his existence."

"Don't know him. We're not in the lying business. Nope, nope, that wouldn't do."

"Father, I don't mean to suggest you're lying. Father Ricardo said his job is sensitive. That his mission could embarrass Maryknoll, not to mention the Catholic Church."

"This isn't Missionaries Impossible."

"What if I get you a photo?"

"What if whatever." Father Ford spoke like a machine gun, sharp little bursts. "You can get me all the pictures you want. We don't have a Father Ricardo, and we don't employ shady Catholic missionaries. Won't do it. Never have. Never will."

I rose to leave, absolutely dejected. "Thank you for your time."

"Nope. No operatives," Father Ford added gratuitously, a smile returning to his face. "But we could always use some extra money to feed the hungry and heal the sick."

"You know," I said, turning back to him, "the Catholic Fund says ninety-three percent of their donations go toward their mission."

"Hah!" he exhaled. "That's rich. Rich, if you ask me. No charity's that efficient."

Fresh air. I needed fresh air. The walk to the Maryknoll parking lot felt like "the last mile" so infamous just around the bend. The walls were closing in, and Father Frederick Ricardo was turning more suspicious all the time. The Patriot Act says, "Know your client."

Hell, Maryknoll didn't even know him.

CHAPTER TWENTY-EIGHT

Somewhere on Wall Street, there's a how-to guide for screwing employees.

Firms pay big bucks and extoll their workforces in public. "Our assets take the elevator down every night." The expression is a tribute to personnel, spoken with reverence.

Percy Phillips, my ex-client and SKC's CEO, refers to employees as "assets" all the time. I don't get it. In my opinion, the word "assets" dehumanizes people. I don't understand how comparing employees to property is some kind of compliment.

Whatever. Companies lay the legal foundation, day in, day out, to crush their "assets." In theory, litigation is only a matter of time. Sometimes I think our entire industry is bipolar. And the two faces—what senior managers say versus what they do—make me want to gag.

You can see the "bad moon rising." You can smell trouble all you want. But stockbrokers don't know how bad things are until we wade knee-deep into a steaming pile of our firm's advance preparations.

Try getting a lawyer. They all have conflicts.

It was 4:30 P.M. when I called Ira Popowski from the road. He was an estate attorney, one of the best. I had referred him plenty of business through the years. And although his expertise was not what I needed, Ira was a mensch—as close a friend as billable hours allow.

"Maybe it's nothing."

"That bad?" he asked. There was no starting slow with him. He knew me too well.

First I told Ira how SKC had snatched the CEO's account from me. Then I briefed him on the Palmetto Foundation, our $25 million wire, and the fact that Maryknoll had never heard of Father Frederick Ricardo,

Highly Intimate Pleasures, or the Catholic Fund. "I think SKC caught wind of something. But I can't figure what they know or how they found out. Or if my imagination is getting the best of me."

"I bet the Feds knocked on their door."

"The Palmetto Foundation isn't even a client."

"No, but Palmer Kincaid was," Ira explained.

"Why wouldn't my boss tell me?"

"Her job is to protect the firm, not you. If SKC thinks you're toxic, they won't tell you a thing. Especially given the deal with Morgan Stanley."

Toxic?

"But the FBI should visit me, right?" I had a thousand questions. It took every ounce of self-control to hold back and listen to my friend's counsel. "I'll tell them whatever they want to know."

"Not without a lawyer present." Ira stopped talking. He was waiting for my affirmation.

"Got it."

"And it might not be the FBI."

"What do you mean?"

"It could be the Secret Service."

"What's this got to do with the president?"

"I knew you'd say that. The Secret Service protects the president. And they police our financial infrastructure, everything from counterfeit currency—"

"No way that's the issue," I interrupted.

"To money laundering," he finished.

"That's just fucking peachy."

"But it sounds to me like you stepped on a pile of tax fraud. And the FBI is building its case."

"How'd you get there?"

"The Palmetto Foundation received a sixty-five-million-dollar gift. It then wired twenty-five million to an organization related to the original donor. The money's going around in circles, which sounds like a tax scam if you ask me. Maybe Palmer was providing material assistance."

I paused a beat and said, "Right."

"Come on, Grove. You know this stuff."

"I was so focused on the Patriot Act, I didn't think about the tax fraud. And what the hell is 'material assistance'?"

"IRS for 'You're screwed.'"

Suddenly, I regretted my phone call to Ira. "Glad you chose law over medicine."

"Why's that?"

"Your bedside manner sucks."

"Sorry. But the facts are the facts. If the FBI visited your boss, we know they went through the U.S. attorney's office. And the U.S. attorney is the IRS's lawyer."

"This makes no sense, Ira. I've never even seen Palmer's tax returns."

"You're a trustee of the offending organization. And when it comes to tax evasion, the Feds play one way."

"Which is how?"

"They hit hard."

Neither of us said anything. I had turned off the radio. And for a few merciful seconds, the steady hum of my tires rolling against the freeway offered a painless alternative to Ira's cat-o'-nine-tails. But me being a glutton for punishment, I invited him to continue the flogging. "And I thought the Patriot Act was my problem."

"Who said it isn't? But I think tax fraud is more likely, not to mention the best-case scenario."

"How's that?"

"The fines are lower, and there's less jail time."

"Excuse me if I'm not seeing the sunshine."

"I'm no expert on the Patriot Act." Like every other attorney, Ira came fully loaded with disclaimers. "But it empowers the government to freeze your accounts and sentence you to up to twenty years."

"Do you have a partner who can represent me?"

"No."

Talk about a dull thud. My friend's word hit me like an ax. "Your shop has twelve hundred lawyers."

"Right. And SKC pays us a retainer."

"For what?"

"Not to take the other side."

"That's it?"

"It's cheaper than facing us in court." I could almost hear Ira smiling through the phone.

"Can you recommend another law firm?"

"Could be a problem. SKC pays most of the top lawyers in Manhattan, one way or another. They have conflicts too."

"Great. That's just great."

"Look, I'll talk to my partners and get you some names of lawyers who know how to cut a deal."

"A deal. What kind of deal? With whom? I haven't done anything wrong." I was firing objections left and right. Ira's answers were going from bad to worse.

"Dealing with the Feds is tricky. First you need to identify the right agency."

"And tell them what? That my foundation wired twenty-five million to a black-ops Catholic missionary? That Maryknoll doesn't know a priest who claims to be part of their order? For all I know, Father Ricardo kicked the habit."

"Your lawyer will go fishing and pose hypothetical questions."

"I still don't understand why you can't represent me. My problem is with the Feds, not SKC."

"It's only a matter time until your issues bleed over to SKC."

"So what?"

"You want one team. Not two law firms sparring over your case."

"I don't have a case. I have a hunch."

"Don't kid yourself. I need to find you a lawyer."

"This isn't right."

"There's one other thing." Ira paused to make sure he had my complete attention. "How long have you known the other trustees?"

"Claire, since we were kids." A horn honked, and a guy in a convertible passed on my left, flipping me the New York turn signal. "JoJo, not so long and not so well."

"Make sure your lawyer advises you how to interact with them."

"You think they've done something wrong?"

"Maybe. Maybe not." Ira was measuring his words now. "But if you're in trouble with the Feds, so is the Palmetto Foundation. The other trustees will protect the organization because—"

"Because it's everything to them in Charleston."

"Right. Plus, I can't get one thing out of my head."

"Okay?"

"You joined the Palmetto Foundation on Tuesday. And you already ferreted out a problem."

"All I have is a hunch."

"Whatever. How long have Claire and JoJo known this priest?"

"Eighteen months. Maybe longer."

"It strikes me as a little strange."

"Don't go there." I could feel my anger returning.

"I'm just saying."

"The Kincaids are rock-solid reliable. They do great things for Charleston. And Palmer Kincaid left three-quarters of his estate to charity. Don't even think about dragging his family into the muck."

Ira heard the anger in my voice. He backpedaled in tone but not conclusion. "I don't mean to insult your friends. But I'd keep an eye on them. In my experience people take time to go bad. A few white lies, pretty soon they're cutting corners. And they get sucked into a vicious cycle that feeds on itself. I think white-collar crime is evolutionary. Not revolutionary."

"No way. They're worth over ten million each. What's the play?"

"Too bad you're not Jewish. We don't operate on blind faith."

"We don't operate on blind faith."

I considered Ira's words all the way back to New York City. I chewed over his comments while playing the blues. Like I said before: in my business, nothing good happens on Friday afternoon. And Billie Holiday set the perfect mood. Her wailing. Her lyrics. Her somber notes are about as depressing an experience as you can find outside the boss's office of any financial services firm.

CHAPTER TWENTY-NINE

I hate to admit it. But after ten days in Charleston, I could not help but compare Annie to Claire Kincaid. Even with the dozen or so shit buzzards pecking through my thoughts.

Claire dresses in tans and muted blues, subtle shades of gray. Clothes serve as a canvas for porcelain skin and satiny brown hair, her unruly bangs the only hint of imperfection. I look at Palmer's daughter and think she's either leaving a polo match or heading to a cocktail party for some charity in desperate need of cash. Her style is controlled, elegant, and vulnerable.

Annie is a different story. She layers on colors—reds, purples, prints— the way I hang ornaments on a Christmas tree. Her clothes buzz with energy, fresh and sassy.

Tonight she had opted for something simple by her standards: blue jeans and wedge sandals. I think that's what you call the shoes. She wore a lacy camisole that would have been banned in my hometown, her striped blouse carelessly open, double-take style. And the red, yellow, and blue buttons looked happy on her white cardigan.

We had just walked into Shun Lee, not the main dining room, but the small café with the black-and-white floor tiles. Comfort food is usually my first line of defense. That night, in the wake of my conversation with Ira, I was ready for a couple of drinks. Maybe more.

In typical fashion we inspected the room and reached unique conclusions, a man and a woman caroming through life, driven by different hormones and dissimilar observations. I checked out all the faces in the small restaurant to see if I recognized anyone, especially one of my colleagues from SKC. I worried about being overheard.

Clear.

Annie adopted a more holistic approach. She surveyed the couples, who was with whom, what the women were wearing. Had she come to Shun

Lee with one of her girlfriends, they would have worried themselves about the woman's handbag in the corner table. Or wondered why a pretty woman was stuck with such a loser.

We ordered spring rolls and grilled scallops to start. And I ground through my discussion with Ira. Annie listened without speaking. When our Peking duck, crispy beef, and pork fried rice arrived, she asked, "Have you ever heard of Thomas J. Rusk?"

"No."

"Texas governor during the 1800s." She topped up our wineglasses. "He's the one who said, 'We're in a hell of a fix. Let's go to the saloon, have a drink, and shoot our way out.' Or something thereabouts."

"Not funny."

"Not meant to be."

"And your point is?"

"Lawyers don't solve problems." Annie paused a beat. Her eyes locked onto mine. "And SKC doesn't ask questions. They shoot first and ask questions later."

"Keep going."

"You need to fight. Throw some punches."

"At whom?"

"Father Ricardo."

"For chrissakes, Annie. He's a priest."

"I don't care if he's Saint Peter. You wired twenty-five million to his charity. Three days later, you have a problem with SKC and the Feds for all we know. And what was the word Ira used?"

"Toxic?"

"Right. The link seems pretty clear to me. The Palmetto Foundation is the source of all your problems. And I don't care what you say. Claire Kincaid is dirty."

"She's my friend." I knocked back my wine.

Annie poured more. "Don't you see it?"

"See what? She runs a community foundation."

"Who insisted on sending money to this rogue priest?"

"Claire."

"Who handles the Palmetto Foundation's relationship with him?"

"Claire."

"And who makes mistakes with men?" Annie was not asking questions. She was hurling them, one after another, rocks against a window.

"What are you saying?" But I knew where she was headed, that irreverent spot we call "Pagan Place" in our lighter moments.

"Isn't that what Palmer always said about his daughter?"

"Ricardo's a priest."

"He has a penis."

"Enough!" Several other diners looked in our direction. I swigged wine and lowered my voice. "Claire hasn't done anything wrong. She can't."

Annie eyed me, her expression suddenly curious. "What, she's too fragile?"

"Yes, she's too fragile. I've known Claire all my life. She doesn't have the DNA for monkey business." I paused before adding, "And don't play the feminist card with me."

"Whatever." Annie stopped eating. She stopped drinking. She pulled back and stared through her glass of amber-colored wine. Listless. She saw something other than the wine.

Uh-oh.

"Did I say something?"

"No."

"Come on, Annie." Her mood had changed. It went from vine to sour grapes without the rot in between. "What is it?"

"Nothing."

"I know that 'nothing.' What is it?"

"You still have a thing for her, Grove."

"That's ridiculous."

"You ever read romance novels?"

"Of course not. What—"

"They're all the same. The women fake orgasms. And the men fake fidelity."

"Not fair. Why are you picking a fight?"

"Who's fighting? I'm trying to save your career." Annie leaned forward, intense, focused. "And you're defending Calamity Claire because you can't get over high school. That sounds like self-immolation to me."

Annie paused and pulled from her drink, long, slow, and languid. I chugged mine, filled my glass, and signaled for another bottle.

"Which," she added, "is killing me to watch." She reached for my hand and stopped me from raising the drink. We held hands for a long, long time, me savoring her strength, loving her more every second.

"Only you," I finally said. "Only you, okay?"

"Okay."

Annie stared at me hard, an unsettling look that hinted at the fresh wound in our relationship.

"There's a lot I don't understand," she said. "Your Father Ricardo for one. But somehow, some way, I bet Claire got a piece of that wire transfer."

"The Palmetto Foundation received a fee."

"I mean her personally."

"I'm not defending Claire." I had to choose my words carefully. "But she's already rich. What's she gain from another twenty-five million?"

"Twenty-five million."

"By that logic, JoJo should be the one on the receiving end. The money means more to her on a percentage basis."

"Now you're thinking," she said. "You should absolutely check out JoJo Kincaid."

"She's clean."

"What makes you so confident?"

"The timeline."

"How so?" For a moment, Annie's curiosity took me back to the old days when she was my sales assistant.

"Six weeks ago, the Catholic Fund placed sixty-five million with the Palmetto Foundation. And the two organizations have been working together for eighteen months."

"Why is that important?"

"Whatever Father Ricardo is cooking up, he started while Palmer was alive."

"So?"

"So JoJo wasn't involved. She had no incentive to get more. Because she had everything while Palmer was alive."

"I've got good instincts on these things, Grove. And I'm telling you. Claire's a different story. She's dirty."

"Claire is Palmer's daughter. She inherited forty million, plus the mother of all houses."

"I bet," Annie persisted, "that Palmer kept a tight rein on her?"

"On what basis?"

"She got divorced. She never remarried. And didn't Palmer call her boyfriend 'a prenup waiting to happen'? Sounds to me like Daddy controlled the purse strings."

"Palmer bought sixty-four plots in the graveyard. I think he supports her marriage and place in the family."

Annie blinked, and I realized my response was a mistake. "How many plots did you say?"

"It's not important."

"She was in your class, so she's thirty-four?"

"Thirty-three actually."

Annie's eyes grew distant. I expected some crack about Claire's need to get busy. Instead, the silence hung in the air between us. Finally, Annie said, "Daddy-daughter relationships are a weird thing."

"Yours wasn't around." She grew up with her mom, a single mother who made ends meet waiting tables in a Wichita diner. Long hours.

"That's how I know."

There are some things about feminine intuition I will never get. This time, I knew better than to press Annie about her expertise. "You sure I should do the Rusk thing—return to Charleston, knock back a drink, and shake things loose?"

"You don't have any choice. You fought your way out once. And you can do it again."

"What do people from Kansas know about homespun Texan logic anyway?"

"Honey, we taught them everything they know." Annie tried to sound impish, that Wichita accent of hers. But I knew my friendship with Claire troubled her. "When are you meeting Father Ricardo?"

"Tuesday."

"Get down there and fight. And do me a favor."

"What's that?"

"Stay away from Claire Kincaid's carriage house."

CHAPTER THIRTY

"You need to fight."

Annie's advice, coupled with Ira's observations, stayed with me all week-end. There was not one legitimate reason, to my way of thinking, why a Filipino charity would invest in a North Carolina porn shack. All of which spelled big trouble for the Palmetto Foundation's board.

Conversely, my girlfriend's suspicions about Claire were over the top. Or were they? After forty-eight hours of intense soul-searching, fueled by Ira's crack about blind faith, I was still wondering what Claire and JoJo knew and when they knew it. I kept searching for reasonable explanations—or perhaps, looking for excuses.

Did you ever see such a thing in your life,
As three blind mice?

That morning I hopped a flight back to Charleston and avoided the air-line's ham-and-mold breakfast, still thawing after a hard night on dry ice. I checked into the Charleston Place Hotel—you know why—and headed over to the Palmetto Foundation with a plan.

Nobody likes surprises, least of all members of a charitable board, good people who care about their philanthropic mission. I decided to report my findings to Claire and JoJo, the fact that Maryknoll had never heard of Father Ricardo or the Catholic Fund. It was better to share the information first, test reactions and gain trust, rather than surprise them in front of a priest.

Somebody's lying.

Tomorrow's confrontation would be tense, I had no doubt. But today the three of us would join hands and become one. We were all staring down the gun barrel of the same federal investigation. And the only wrinkle, as far as I could see, was tax fraud. If JoJo or Claire knew something, then our alliance would collapse.

"Is Claire upstairs?" I asked Jill, our receptionist.

"Playing hooky."

"Hooky?"

"Packing her things for the move to Palmer's house." Jill leaned forward, her body language conspiratorial. "But you didn't hear it from me."

Charleston's gossip had already kicked into overdrive.

There were at least twenty messages for me on Palmer's desk. Riffling through the stack, I called my office first and reached Zola. "Do me a favor and don't tell anybody where I am."

"I got your back."

Pumped and ready to fight, I bounded downstairs to JoJo's office. Holly was lying on an ancient oriental carpet. The dachshund jumped and started yapping, until Palmer's wife declared, "Friend." Then it was the cute dog thing: Holly lying on her back, making nice, inviting me to scratch her belly.

"I'm buying lunch, under one condition."

"Which is?"

"You pick the spot."

I tried to play it cool. It's best to ease into a tough conversation. The question I really wanted to ask: "Who the hell is Father Ricardo and what have we done?"

"Anywhere is fine." JoJo took my arm. "As long as it's not one of those 'eat all you can' spots."

"All you can eat?" I knew what she meant. Her rework of the colloquialism was cute.

"That's what I mean." JoJo blushed through her golden tan. She grabbed her handbag, hugged me hello, and instructed Holly to stay. "I have good news."

Glad somebody does.

"Tell me."

"Our lawyers say we can get all one hundred and fifty million into the foundation by Friday."

"Huitt's okay with that?" I asked.

"Totally fine."

"I'll call him this afternoon and ask whether he needs anything from SKC."

"Palmer's account with you?"

"Right."

JoJo glowed as we spoke. She brimmed with strength and happiness of purpose, driven by the desire to bring closure to her husband's last wishes. I decided, one more time, that Claire had been wrong in the garden on Legare Street. Dead wrong. Her stepmother would soon become my first ally in the imminent fight. There was no way we were sending another dime to the Manila Society for Children at Risk.

Not on my watch.

"I have a surprise for you," she said, all smiles and sunshine.

Two hundred million dollars is stupid money. With $10 million you fly first-class. With $50 million you fly private, NetJets or one of its competitors. With $200 million you're wondering where to park your Citation X in Monte Carlo. And whether to take the superyacht, three decks and 180 feet long, for a night cruise around the harbor.

Somehow, JoJo had risen above the consumptive spiral of more, more, more. Her $10 million trust account, a fortune by all reasonable standards, amounted to a $190 million lifestyle haircut. She took it in stride, though. She never complained, when it would have been so easy to whine about flying first-class.

I saw no anger in JoJo, no bitterness over her eviction from her residence on South Battery. I never heard a peep about the trust fund that would maintain the house into perpetuity. Taken together, those two bequests signaled one irrefutable truth. The Kincaid bloodline, sixty-one cemetery plots ready for generations of action, mattered more than Palmer's second marriage.

Through the years, I have grown to believe trust funds are oxymorons. There is no trust in trust funds, only acrimony among related parties. It surprised me that my mentor had missed the obvious implications in his will. Maybe Palmer and JoJo had talked things through.

Doesn't matter.

For here, in the Palmetto Foundation's elevator, I saw a woman who appreciated her lot in life. Not that she had a right to complain. Ten million dollars and a beach house on Sullivan's Island—that's big-time in the real world. Everybody's dream.

Outside, JoJo and I steered toward Magnolia's restaurant on East Bay. She pulled close as we walked, her talking and touching so intertwined, her perfume more invigorating than an ocean breeze.

I liked the way she made me feel. There's something about a pretty woman hanging on your arm, no matter how grim the surrounding events. And I suspect that JoJo appreciated my support. Charleston's uneven sidewalks can be treacherous. They ripple like harbor waves and rock even the most graceful women in heels.

"What's the surprise?" In the elevator, I had avoided all discussion. My reticence was, I suppose, force of habit from New York City. You never know who's listening.

"Today calls for a celebration." JoJo sparkled, her teeth dazzling and white, her manner flirtatious.

"Why's that?"

"Claire and I are moving the Palmetto Foundation's accounts to you."

"I'm flattered but—"

"We're making the change this week."

I didn't feel much like celebrating, even though a $150 million account meant at least $300,000 in my back pocket, before taxes of course. The whole world is before taxes. I faced bigger decisions, like the recommendation from an attorney I couldn't hire:

"Cut a deal."

At our table JoJo ordered a 2007 Kistler "Cuvée Cathleen" chardonnay. Before I could blink she raised her glass, took one look at me, and abandoned the toast. "Your eyes look like plates."

"I can't manage our money and serve on the board. It's a conflict of interest."

JoJo placed her wine on the table. Never took a sip. "I'm sure we can do something."

"Five to ten."

"Percent?"

"Years." The regulatory environment was toxic. Financial impropriety, even a whiff of it, would land me in Club Fed.

"You're exaggerating." JoJo squeezed my hand. And for the first time I noticed that hers, while small and delicate, was somewhat coarse to the touch. Blue-collar. Competent. The imperfection appealed to me.

"We can get another team from my shop."

"It won't be the same, Grove."

"I'll find somebody we can trust."

"You seem distracted."

"We have a problem."

JoJo pushed her shellfish and grits around her plate, thinking, not looking up. "Watch your sleeve."

"What?"

"You're about to drag it through your buttered beans."

"Er, thanks." I can never figure out why women mother me.

"So what's the problem?" she asked, now that my sleeve was safe.

"How long have you known Father Ricardo?"

"About two years."

Annie once told me I tilt my head left when speaking. I could feel myself doing it now. "I mean really known him."

"That's a weird thing to ask."

"Maryknoll has no record of Father Frederick Ricardo." I described my visit to Ossining and discussions with Biscuit, every last detail.

"He said they would deny his existence."

"I don't buy it. And I refuse to wire another cent to his project. Not until we get some answers."

"He's good people." The expression "good people" sounded odd coming from her lips.

"Did you ever see the safe houses?"

"Of course not." Same tone as Claire. She rubbed her earring, an emerald-cut ear stud. I guessed Harry Winston, six figures, and life with Palmer.

"Did you ever review any of his organization's paperwork?"

"We're a charity. Not an auditor."

"Did Palmer ever express misgivings about Father Ricardo?"

"No way. Two martinis together, and they behaved like twins separated at birth." JoJo grabbed my hand again and squeezed hard, really hard. "Why are you so worked up?"

"The Catholic Fund owns part of an adult superstore in Fayetteville. So does the Manila Society for Children at Risk."

"Are you sure?"

"I have no idea who Father Ricardo is."

"He's a decent man who'll have a good explanation." JoJo fidgeted with her earring. It made me wish she would take the damn thing out.

"I hope so. Because the alternative sucks."

"Which is what?"

"Prison. Frozen bank accounts." I spent ten minutes describing the Patriot Act: Know your client, and what happens when you wire money to the wrong people. But tax fraud—I steered clear of that discussion. If Palmer had been cheating on his taxes, JoJo would have benefited directly. And I couldn't risk alienating her.

"You think he's a terrorist?"

"It doesn't matter what I think. We can't take the chance."

"Shouldn't we call the police?"

"That's not fair to Father Ricardo. He may have a good explanation."

"What can I do?"

"Ask questions tomorrow. Push him hard. Me too. Make sure I'm being fair. But afterward, once all the talking is done, vote with me. Follow my lead."

JoJo got the math. "You think Claire's a problem?"

"No. But Claire's out of the office. And I'm counting votes today. What's it going to be?"

She drummed her fingers and then reached across the table for both my hands. "This is exactly why Palmer named you a trustee. I'm with you."

We left, and the white wine stayed behind, a good bottle half empty. I had done a perfectly good job of ruining JoJo's meal. And the discomfit showed, her happiness gone. "I'm taking the afternoon off."

"You okay?"

"I want to spend some time at our place on the beach."

"Let me walk you to the garage."

Afterward, I headed back to the Palmetto Foundation. I felt bad about upsetting JoJo. But strangely, I felt the relief that accompanies action. From fighting and setting things straight. I had thrown the first punch, and it felt cathartic. That's the thing about dropping your guard. You never recognize a mistake until you're facedown on the mat.

CHAPTER THIRTY-ONE
THE HOT SEAT

"There's a woman waiting for you upstairs." Our receptionist at the Palmetto Foundation likes to gossip. But here in the lobby, dusty from old money and Confederate ghosts, Jill spoke with the urgency of a 911 call.

"Where, in Palmer's office?"

"She said you'd understand."

Like hell, I thought. Guests wait in lobbies or conference rooms, not people's offices. Suddenly I did an attitudinal 180. "Is it Annie?"

"She's from the FBI."

Two floors up, Agent Torres was inspecting the photo of Palmer and Pope Benedict XVI. Her features were Hispanic, the color of coffee and milk. Her body was hard and angular, chiseled either from granite or long hours in the gym. Torres stood about five foot six, was in her late thirties, and had the demeanor of a scorpion tail.

Stress turns me into a smart-ass. It's a defense mechanism I owe to Wall Street, where each and every day is an outing with the unhinged. After Agent Torres introduced herself, I was stressed. "Don't you guys travel in packs?"

"No."

"I thought cops have partners."

"I'm not a cop."

"You know what I mean."

"We're not here to discuss FBI procedure."

In my business, we learn how to size up people in a nanosecond. Who's decent? And who's a jerk? There was no mystery where Torres fit on the spectrum. "How can I help?"

"Stop interfering with a federal investigation."

"Excuse me?" The blood was pumping to my head and heating my face.

"Where were you Friday afternoon?"

"What's this about?" It was an honest question. I wasn't trying to be combative.

"Let's set some ground rules." Torres walked around the desk and sat in Palmer's chair. "This won't be hard. I ask the questions. You answer them. Are you ready to cooperate, or should I repeat steps one and two?"

Cooperate!

The C-word scares everybody in finance. It's code for being in deep shit with the SEC or those bombastic Senators that investigate everything and agree on nothing. "Can't you tell me why you're here?"

"Another question. You're not too bright, are you?"

"Look, Ms. Torres."

"Agent Torres."

"What's with the attitude? I can always call my lawyer."

"Suit yourself." She stood up and swept her hand toward Palmer's phone. "In my experience, it's lawyer up today and Miranda rights tomorrow. Or better yet, if you don't like due process here, we can get you on a treaty violation. Deport you to South America for a taste of theirs. I wonder if they do house arrest in Colombia."

Scared? You could say that. American justice is one thing. But I had no idea what treaty violation Agent Torres was wielding like a club. I sat down. She sat down. And after considerable silence, me wondering how the United States could deport one of its own, I rolled over. "I was at Maryknoll head-quarters on Friday. Now will you tell me why you're here?"

"You met with Father Ford?"

"Were you following me?"

"All these questions." Torres stood to leave.

"Yes."

"What did you discuss?"

"I was doing my job. Know your customer, right?"

"It's a little late for that, don't you think?"

Oh shit.

"You talked about Father Ricardo. Am I right?" Torres inspected her fingernails, long and sharp. She had the world's most lethal hands for squeezing somebody by the balls.

"Yes."

"What did he tell you?"

"That Maryknoll doesn't know him."

"When are you meeting Father Ricardo again?" The agent drilled me with her eyes.

"Tomorrow."

"Why?"

"For the board to tell him our decision."

"What decision?" she pressed.

"Whether we're funding the Manila Society for Children at Risk."

"And?"

"And what?"

"Don't go stupid on me," snapped Torres. "Are you wiring them money?"

My head was swimming. "I'm not sure what we're doing anymore."

"How much money are we talking about?"

"Sixty-five million total."

I thought my response artful. I never hinted that $25 million had already left the building. The disclosure, it seemed to me, would be an admission of guilt. That's assuming our wire triggered Patriot Act problems or qualified as material support of a tax fraud.

"Ricardo expects the funds tomorrow?"

"Yes."

"After the meeting?" The agent was relentless, all her questions. She was ripping off my face one freckle at a time.

"What are you, some kind of badger? Tell me what you want."

"What I want," she said, and paused, "is for you to speak my language. I say, 'Jump.' You ask, 'How far?' I tell you to get something. You gift-wrap the package. Every time you speak with Father Ricardo, you report back to me. We clear?"

"Got it."

"I'm not finished, Grove. I can call you Grove, right?"

"Yes."

"You're Father Ricardo's new best friend. You ask questions. You learn his habits, his contacts, everything. Even if it means putting the toilet seat down for him. And then you report back to me."

"Okay, okay." I was rubbing my temple, but it didn't help.

"Names are good. Places are better. Travel itinerary is best. We clear?"

"Yes." My goal was to buy time, maybe a little information, until I found a lawyer. "Did you talk to my firm?"

"Another question. And you were doing so well."

I was sick of Agent Fang rubbing my nose in the dirt. "Maybe we need to speak through my lawyer after all."

"That's fine, Grove. But just remember, I'm a freight train. One call to my boss Walker, and we'll send a dozen agents to SKC."

"Make my day."

"Or maybe we'll toss your condo."

"You need a warrant."

Torres smirked. "Your girlfriend's name is Annie, right?"

"Kiss my ass." I knew where this conversation was headed.

"We go into the classroom, twelve agents wearing FBI Windbreakers, and Annie will be the toast of Columbia's campus."

"You wouldn't." All of a sudden, my nerves were shot. The threat to me was one thing. But Agent Torres was dragging my girlfriend through the muck.

"We clear?"

"Yes." That one-word response was about the closest I've ever come to saying, "I'm your bitch."

"Good," she said. "First things first. I want everything you have on the Catholic Fund: account paperwork, history of wire transfers, the files. I want it all."

"I don't know where half the stuff is. I've been a trustee at the Palmetto Foundation for a week."

"Not my problem."

"What's your phone number?"

"Now you're asking the right kind of question." Torres scribbled her number and handed the paper to me.

"Should we wire sixty-five million tomorrow?"

I was fishing, hoping to learn why the FBI was so interested in the Palmetto Foundation. And deep down, I wanted her to say, "Yes." If the FBI instructed me to wire money, it seemed I would be off the hook. Even for the $25 million we sent last Tuesday.

"Kind of stupid, if you ask me."

"What's that mean?"

"If you wire sixty-five million, that takes you up to ninety million total. You really want to wire more money than you received from the Catholic Fund?"

"How'd you know?"

"Class is over, boys and girls."

Agent Torres left Palmer's office. And I decided that the South hadn't seen so much scorched earth since Sherman sacked Atlanta.

Torres was tough. I've seen tougher. Most days, I know how to handle difficult people. Stockbrokers work with powerful men and women. Our clients get what they want, when they want it, and where they want it in all aspects of their lives.

Life in the Armani Lane.

There's this client in London who's a big-time liquor distributor. His date, on a dare, crawled under the table during one of those insufferable dinners on the rubber chicken circuit. Black tie, black gown, and Black Label scotch. With everybody laughing and clinking glasses up top, she gave him a Lewinsky down under.

The two married shortly thereafter. During the ceremony she toasted him in front of all their guests: "Honey, I'd go under the table for you anywhere, anytime." Lots of laughter. But if you ask me, saying yes gets you more control than saying no. That and two or three carats.

I have a dozen more stories with similar themes. It's the nature of our business. Stockbrokers learn how to handle demanding individuals, people who expect to get their way. Only, "frozen bank accounts" or "twenty years" behind bars have never been at stake for me.

Thank you, Ira, for your reassuring counsel.

I wanted to help the FBI. I wanted to do the right thing. But I didn't trust Torres. She hadn't explained the purpose of her investigation, and I feared that one slip, one false move, something I might say, would land me back in Ossining. This time I'd have one of those kick-ass river views from inside Sing Sing.

It was the fight of my career. And I was about to pursue a strategy every stockbroker knows, the one that Muhammad Ali turned into an art form:

Rope-a-dope.

After Torres left, I phoned Biscuit first thing. "You're still coming to our board meeting tomorrow, right?"

The FBI agent and my fellow trustees might object. But I didn't care. The big man would work the HIP angle. And I'd follow with questions driven by Maryknoll, more aggressive this time, about why the Catholic order had no record of Father Ricardo.

"On my way," he replied.

"Great. But there's one other thing."

"Always is."

"You ever hear of an FBI agent named Torres?" I was still smarting from her visit.

"She'd boil water just to scald dogs," said Biscuit, using the Southern vernacular for a nasty person.

"Torres showed up today, unannounced."

"And busted your chops," the big man observed.

"You got the same treatment?"

"She had me sweating like a whore in church."

"Me, too."

"Everybody's got an Achilles' heel." Biscuit sounded rueful.

"You know hers?"

"If I did, I couldn't do anything about it."

"Why's that?"

"She knows mine."

"Let's grab breakfast," I suggested. "Maybe we can figure something out."

"How about Denny's?"

"Oof."

"A couple of Grand Slams." Biscuit heard my hesitation, but extended his words like a doughnut.

"Eat all you can—I'd fall asleep during the board meeting."

I hadn't been on my bike for two weeks and didn't need the massive breakfast. Even worse, Annie had taken to rubbing my stomach over the weekend and calling me "fat boy."

"You ever been to the Philippines?" Biscuit asked.

"As a kid." His question surprised me. "How'd you know?"

"That expression."

"What expression?"

" 'Eat all you can.' "

"They say that in the Philippines?"

"According to my dad."

"You don't miss a thing, big fellow. When was your dad there?"

"Shore leave during Vietnam. How about you?"

"We were stationed at Clark Air Base. But I was too young to remember anything."

"It's a funny expression," Biscuit remarked.

"That's what I told JoJo Kincaid. She said 'Eat all you can' during lunch today." My watch read 3:17. I was growing restless. Long ago, I had succumbed to the ADHD attention span that plagues Wall Street. I didn't have time to dwell on colloquialisms.

"Is she from the Philippines?" Biscuit missed the cues in my voice. Either that, or he chose to ignore them.

"San Diego."

"But her family. Is she a Filipina?"

"Hispanic." I was keeping my answers terse, hoping Biscuit would get the message. It was time to address more pressing matters. Time to move on.

"You sure?"

"I guess so."

"There's a big naval base in San Diego." Biscuit was thinking aloud, trying to explain the coincidence to himself.

From my perspective the conversation was growing old, like waiting for Noah's flood to dry. "I need to hop."

Biscuit got the message. "See you tomorrow."

Next, I dialed Claire. She answered her cell phone on the first ring and came out swinging. "You're getting on my last nerve."

Anger was the last thing I expected. "What are you talking about?"

"Why did you visit Maryknoll's headquarters?"

"Who told you?"

"Father Ricardo," she explained.

"How'd he find out?"

"From one of their priests."

"Father Ford? He lied." The words burst from my lips before I could stop them.

"Who's he?"

"The priest from Maryknoll."

"What were you thinking?" Claire's voice was growing hard.

"We have a problem."

"You," she agreed.

"I'm sorry you feel that way."

"You went behind Father Ricardo's back."

"I can explain."

"All this," Claire continued, "after he said Maryknoll would disavow his existence. Now I doubt the Catholic Fund will ever do business with us again. A big donor relationship gone because you have nose trouble."

She had a point. I assumed Father Ford was the one who told Father Ricardo about my visit to Maryknoll. In which case—he was legit, Maryknoll was operating a clandestine operation, and the FBI was harassing me for reasons other than a $25 million transfer to some rogue charity.

"Donors are one thing. But I'd rather know why the FBI came knocking on my door today."

"What are you talking about?" Claire's fury vanished. She said nothing while I described the visit from Torres. Not one word as I told her about Highly Intimate Pleasures and the Catholic Fund websites that generated so little traffic.

When I finished, Claire said, "I guess we'll find out tomorrow."

"And you still think Father Ricardo is on the up and up?"

"Yes."

"Why are you so confident?"

"Dad trusted him. So do I. And it's time you gave us the benefit of the doubt. Especially Father Ricardo."

There was the Claire Kincaid I remembered from high school. Rushing to the underdog's defense. Operating above the fray. I admired her ambassadorial instincts, always had. Always will. But this time something was wrong, and I doubted diplomacy was the answer.

CHAPTER THIRTY-TWO

STATION 23

Sullivan's Island is a beach community located about twenty minutes northeast of Charleston. It's a place where the air hints of salt and mollusk shells, where the dunes are a rolling tangle of sea oats, horseweed, and saltmeadow cordgrass. The sandy beaches are wide and beckoning, the Gulf Stream waters just the right temperature.

During summer months, Charlestonians gather at the shore to flee the downtown heat. Picking crabs, boiling shrimp, shucking oysters—there's always an excuse to chase tequila shots with longnecks. The best parties take place during the fall, however, when great bonfires leap high into the night. There's something about the chill ocean air that sates the senses and makes people drop their guard.

Bong parked near the corner of Atlantic Avenue and Station 23. He had rolled down all four windows in his car, light drizzle misting the seats. Most days, he savored the ocean's scent. Its briny smell was reassuring, consistent the world over, whether here or back home in the Philippines. But that Monday night, Bong was distracted. He had work to do.

Where is she?

Bong looked at his watch. It was 9:47 P.M., black outside, fog cloaking the stars, surf crashing the shore. He wondered when JoJo Kincaid would get home. He was growing cross, annoyed that she wasn't here.

For the thirtieth time, maybe it was the fortieth, Bong checked his roll of duct tape. It was sitting on the passenger seat. Primed and ready for action. He had already folded back the edge, sticky side facing sticky side. Advance preparation reduced the number of screwups.

That morning, Bong had spent fifteen minutes with the clerk at Home Depot. The two men compared one roll of tape with another. Bong opted for a cheap, nonpremium brand. It unraveled so much easier than the high-end Gorilla product. The last thing he needed was to get stuck while wrapping JoJo. Speed and surprise were the essence of a good show.

Even better, the cheap roll came in royal blue. The institutional gray, standard across all lines of duct tape, did zero for JoJo's skin tones. And while black would make her gold mocha hues pop, really zing, Bong feared the contrast would be far too stark. It was important that she look good on camera.

Bong prided himself on watching the details. He was obsessive, his precision born from martial arts and the stage. As a kid, school plays helped Bong forget the barrio. With the exception of rats, there had never been enough to eat. The theater, however, required him to mimic, pretend, and disappear into another world—thereby offering a short reprieve from the squalor.

For all the prep work now, this job had been one fiasco after another. Moreno was riding his ass every bungle of the way, and one thing was clear: Bong did not have the luxury of making another mistake. Not if he wanted to celebrate his forty-third birthday.

He waited. He watched the clock. Perspiration poured from his brow.

Around 10:13 P.M., Bong heard a car. It was JoJo's Mercedes. There was no mistaking the custom paint job, the cream top and navy blue body. He grabbed the blue tape and slouched low. He popped the trunk and started his car, waiting for her to get out.

JoJo opened her door, and Holly leaped into the night. The dachshund scurried around the front lawn, scratching and sniffing for the right place to pee. When JoJo walked around the back of her car, Bong turned on his brights and hit the gas.

He hurtled toward the Mercedes. Hit the brakes just before crushing JoJo's legs against its fender. She raised her arms in surprise. The oncoming brights blinded her eyes in the cold, drizzly night. The pounding surf drowned her screams.

Bong shot out of his seat, tape in hand. He lunged at JoJo, squeezing between the two cars, and tackled her hard. Drove her face into the oyster-shell driveway. Pinned her fast, his knee pushing against the flat of her back, his hands controlling her arms, dominating her. Endorphins surged through his body with the most glorious tingle of skin.

JoJo tried to scream. Bong was too fast, too powerful, awash in a sea of adrenaline. The veins under his spider-sun tattoo bulged as he wrapped the blue duct tape around and around JoJo's head, gagging her mouth, muffling her cries for help.

Bong coiled her wrists in blue. JoJo kicked and writhed. She lost her flats in the commotion, the Manolo Blahnik snakeskins skidding into the bush. The Atlantic Ocean roared, drowning their noise.

Holly charged to JoJo's defense. Fifteen pounds soaking wet, the tiny dachshund was all grit and gristle—the life-support system of bared teeth. She barked and circled, then darted forward. Bong swung his anvil fist. Holly ducked and fanged his wrist. Blood spurted everywhere.

"Pakshet!" he screamed in Tagalog, his native language from the Philippines. The word almost means "fucking shit," but not quite.

Bong loosed his grip on JoJo. In a flash of blind anger, oblivious to the bite, he snatched the dog's throat and squeezed hard. She yelped. Bong squeezed harder. The yelps turned to dog whimpers, Holly's stubby legs twisting, her hot-dog body wriggling.

With his free arm, Bong grabbed JoJo's waist and picked her off the ground like a rag doll. He threw her over his shoulder, Holly still whimpering in the other hand. He marched, all powerful, to the trunk and dumped JoJo inside with a thud. Holly too. He slammed down the trunk and jumped into his car.

Bong flicked off the brights, backed up, and headed west away from the beach. Total time elapsed: thirty seconds. He caught his breath. And as he drove away, considering the delicious surprises awaiting the very rich Mrs. Palmer Kincaid, Bong realized the most curious thing:

He felt great.

CHAPTER THIRTY-THREE

"Where is she?"

The four of us were sitting in the conference room. Claire wore a light gray sweater, the soft cashmere at odds with her angry words. She drummed her fingers on the ancient table, knotty and gnarled. She checked her watch at 10:04 A.M., 10:05 A.M., and so on.

Father Ricardo wore his black suit and white clerical collar, heavy on the starch. He was commanding in a priestly way, confident that his chain of command trumped all others. But his eyes were hostile. And I could tell he was annoyed.

Biscuit loosened his tie and rolled up his sleeves. His clothes were a mass of wrinkles, not that he avoided the cleaners. His girth tugged and tested the fibers, stretching them this way and that.

We had tried small talk, which didn't work. And I kept the requisite introduction vague on purpose. "Biscuit's here to discuss my findings."

Now our eyes darted back and forth, all of us uncomfortable. Claire tried JoJo on her cell phone but reached voice mail as we waited. Whereupon Father Ricardo placed his own mobile on the table. Biscuit said nothing.

At 10:17 A.M., Claire said, "Let's get started."

"I've never known JoJo to be late." Father Ricardo was sitting at the head of the table again.

"Let's get started anyway," said Claire, taking control, assuming Palmer's role.

"Is there a problem?" Father Ricardo leaned back in his chair, steepling his fingers. He was reserved. No smile, the air toxic—he sensed what was coming. His innate priest senses had kicked into gear.

"Frankly, Grove's findings are a surprise." Claire spoke in her CNN anchor voice, the inflection weighty and ominous.

I glanced in her direction, grateful for the support. Disappointment flashed across Father Ricardo's face. But no more than a hint. He waited and said nothing.

"Grove, tell Father Ricardo what you learned."

All eyes focused on me.

As a kid, Henry Kissinger wanted to be a weatherman. I wanted to be him. I know how to broker peace. But for all my diplomatic prowess—the occasional "Fuck you" notwithstanding—I had never interrogated a priest. And my words proved a struggle.

"Father, I know you had an understanding with Palmer. And it probably feels like we're reinventing the wheel. When we parted last week, I fully expected to wire funds today. But I have questions now. Serious questions about activities that don't fit our mission."

"You need to be comfortable." Father Ricardo registered zero stress. His voice soothing, his smile wan—he spoke with the reassuring manner of a man from the pulpit. "But you're right. Palmer and I reached a deal. We shook hands. The holdup is, well, it's troubling."

"Let's start with Highly Intimate Pleasures."

Father Ricardo looked at Biscuit, who said, "Liberty Point Plantations is my client."

"Who?"

"A subdivision off exit 55. Military people for the most part. All of them churchgoers."

"They're unhappy?" the reverend asked Biscuit.

"It's the view from their backyards. There's a massive billboard promoting vibrators around the corner. How would you feel?"

Father Ricardo turned to Claire. "That store, however offensive to Liberty Point, has nothing to do with my money." His mobile vibrated on the pad of paper. He studied the caller ID before switching off the phone.

"That's true," I said, searching for the right words. "But Maryknoll doesn't know who you are. Which makes the Catholic Fund's investment much more troubling."

"I told you they'd disavow any knowledge."

"I'm sorry, Father. But I need a better explanation."

"You're a stockbroker. You, of all people, should know the importance of discretion. Palmer did."

"Did he know about Highly Intimate Pleasures?"

Claire and Biscuit watched us like tennis fans, their heads turning back and forth every time someone took a swipe.

"Would you accept money from the Kennedy family?" asked Father Ricardo. He was calm, but his voice was growing more and more assertive.

"Huh?"

"A donation."

"I don't see the relevance, Father."

"Just answer the question. Would the Palmetto Foundation take money from the Kennedy family?"

"I suppose so."

"And given the chance, you'd manage the family's money, right?"

"Yes, of course."

"Here's what I don't get." Father Ricardo's voice betrayed his exasperation.

"Okay?"

"Joe Kennedy broke the law. He ran illegal whiskey. And yet you're willing to give the family a pass. Highly Intimate Pleasures was a gift from a wealthy donor—"

"That's what the accountant said," Biscuit interrupted.

"And I'd like to remind you," Father Ricardo continued, "it is a completely legitimate business."

I said nothing.

"Did we violate any building codes, Biscuit?" The father's eyes, intense and determined, locked on mine even as he questioned the lawyer.

"No. But—"

"Has the bar ever been found guilty of serving minors, Biscuit?"

"No."

"Has any female employee ever filed harassment charges, Biscuit?"

"No."

"In fact, women are running the show at HIP. Right, Biscuit?"

"Yes."

"And, Grove, you work on Wall Street, home of the glass ceiling. Can you name one woman CEO of an investment bank?"

"No."

"And you need a better explanation? Even though our charity owns a legitimate business that's never violated the law and, if anything, is a good community citizen, given its progressive hiring practices. What am I missing?"

"How do you raise money, Father?"

"We covered that last week." He sounded less like a priest and more like a guy out $40 million. "My seller is declaring bankruptcy any second now—"

"But we wired twenty-five million."

"Wasn't enough, Grove."

"But—"

"But nothing. I'm about to lose my chance to make a difference because you're dragging your feet with our money."

"There's no way," I replied, forcing myself to remain cool, "you're raising big dollars from your websites. Not with the traffic you get."

"How do you get clients?"

"Referrals, word of mouth."

"Right," he said, again steepling his fingers. "And how do you close them?"

"I visit them."

"Right. So you should be the last person to question me. I visit donors. I make presentations. And when all is said and done, I ask for the order from really wealthy people. You know what that means, right?"

Snide or not, Father Ricardo had a point. Big money requires in-person meetings. But his explanation still troubled me. "Then why did you emphasize the websites?"

"They're placeholders. I see rich people. We talk. We smile. We shake hands, and when I'm gone, they Google me. That's what you did. Websites legitimize the Catholic Fund, and they cost nothing to maintain."

As quickly as I was raising objections, Father Ricardo was knocking them back. "There's one more thing, Father. I hope this question doesn't offend you."

"Why stop now?"

Claire's eyes widened. Biscuit nodded at me. His expression said, "Go for it."

"The Manila Society for Children at Risk invested in HIP. Why's the cash going around in circles?"

The room went silent. Claire, Biscuit, and I stared at the reverend. After a considerable pause, he said, "Sweat equity."

"What are you talking about?"

"My kids sew the clothes that HIP sells. They get paid. And just so there are no conflicts of interest, the orphanage owns a piece of the store."

"Like a sweatshop?"

"Knock it off!" snapped Claire. "You're badgering him, Grove."

"I'll pretend you never said that." Father Ricardo's tone chilled me. "Do you know what it's like for my kids? The lucky ones are missing an arm or a leg. Some lose their eyes. How easy do you think it is for them to get jobs?"

I sat stone-faced.

"Answer me."

"I don't know, Father."

"My kids will never worry about meals. We teach them skills and give them dignity."

I was about to speak, Father Ricardo about to continue. Claire had said enough, and I suspected Biscuit might weigh in somewhere. That's when the intercom buzzed, and Jill said, "I'm sorry to interrupt. There's a delivery guy here, and he's pretty insistent about giving you a package."

"Just sign for it," Claire instructed.

"He won't leave unless I put it in your hands myself."

All four of us shrugged our shoulders.

Claire punched the intercom. "Bring it up."

Jill handed Claire a manila parcel and left the room.

It was a book mailer, bubble wrap inside, approximately nine inches by eleven. The contents bowed at the center. The item inside was neither big nor heavy. It was chunky and irregular. It bulged with what could have been a cell phone for all I knew.

"Are you expecting something?" Father Ricardo glanced at his watch.

"No." Claire pushed the bangs from her forehead.

Biscuit watched.

There was no return address. There were no stamps. There were no labels from one of the major delivery services. The package simply read: "Claire Kincaid. Grove O'Rourke. Open Immediately."

"You think it's from JoJo?" I ventured.

"Not her handwriting." Claire tore the mailer at its edges. She struggled with the tape and glanced around the conference room for scissors.

"Let me help," Biscuit volunteered, his expression cautious. Father Ricardo, Claire, and I were more curious than circumspect.

The big man ripped open the top of the package and glanced inside, his quick peek imperceptible. But I could almost hear his thoughts as he handed it back to Claire:

Easy.

She pulled out a standard envelope, the kind used for business correspondence. It was flat. I assumed there was a letter inside. It contained the same message as before, written in block letters with a black Sharpie: "Claire Kincaid. Grove O'Rourke. Open Immediately."

A second envelope dropped onto the conference table. It was small, but there was something thick and chunky inside. There was no message. Only layers and layers of tape. The second envelope had been mummified.

Claire pulled a letter from the first, white copy paper, same neat black letters as the addressee.

Biscuit mumbled, "This isn't good."

"What's it say?" The suspense was killing me.

She scanned the letter. A look of horror engulfed her features.

"Tell us," demanded Father Ricardo. For the moment, he had forgotten his $40 million. He had forgotten the property in the Philippines. He was consumed by Claire's angst. We all were. The three of us stared, every second an eternity.

Claire's hand flew to her mouth. Her eyes brimmed with tears. When she read, every word proved arduous, every sentence a Herculean task to complete.

" 'We have JoJo Kincaid. You will do exactly as we say. If you don't, the woman dies. If you contact authorities, the woman dies. If you look for us, the woman dies. If you alarm us in any way, the woman dies. And know one thing. Everything makes us nervous.' "

"Good lord." Biscuit swept a meaty hand through his thick mop of hair.

" 'Wire two hundred million dollars to the address below.' " Her face ashen, Claire did not read the wiring instructions.

"Is there more?" Father Ricardo's face was aging before our eyes.

"Yes." She nodded, her expression grave. " 'We know you have the money. Our deadline is tomorrow, five P.M. Don't miss it. Don't ask for more time. We will send body parts, a different limb every day you are late. Unwrap the envelope, and you will see. We are the judge, jury, and executioner. You fuck up, and the woman dies.' "

Claire dropped the letter as though it were toxic. She backed farther and farther away from the table, distancing herself from the second envelope, which was layered in tape and still unopened. Biscuit wrapped his bear of an arm around her, instinctively comforting her. Father Ricardo followed the big man's lead, flanking her from the other side.

I grabbed the misshapen envelope, pulling at the layers of tape. The work was infuriating. The tape would not come off fast enough. I tore. I yanked. Again, I checked the room for scissors. None. When I finally fought my way to the paper part of the package, Claire's eyes widened in horror. She begged me to stop. "No, don't."

Too late. With one final heave, I ripped open the package. Ice, a big wad of plastic wrap, I wasn't sure what. Bits and pieces exploded everywhere.

Something fleshy landed on my tie. Something bloody. Something hidden from the others by the conference room table.

I looked down and almost retched.

CHAPTER THIRTY-FOUR
BOARD MEETING

It was most of JoJo's pinkie.

To this day, I'm embarrassed by what happened next. Disgust, revulsion, nausea—that would be putting it mildly. I lurched backward, almost toppling over. JoJo's finger disappeared between my legs onto the chair. I would have done anything to get away from the severed digit, as though it contained a contagious disease, some kind of necrotic leprosy.

"What is it?" Claire hid behind her bangs. She watched in horror.

Nobody saw but me. The finger was gray and withering in its gore. It was clean cut, severed two knuckles down from the nail, about an inch long. I never answered Claire.

I couldn't.

That big wad of plastic wrap—I bent over and picked it up off the floor. Layers were stretched around and around a folded sheet of paper. Inside, protected from moisture and the melting ice that had scattered through the room, was a photo printed on 8½-by-11-inch copy paper like the ransom note.

There were no block letters this time. It was JoJo. Her mouth was wrapped in blue duct tape, her left hand taped to her cheek, her stump exposed and bleeding. But it was her face that got me, the terror, the dried tears, the loss of dignity.

For a moment I forgot JoJo's finger, the mutilation that made me flinch. I wanted to kill whoever had done this—if only as an act of vengeance on behalf of Palmer. I wanted to find JoJo and save her. Some goon was watching us, reveling in his power. I wanted to reach down the fucker's throat and pull his ass out his mouth. "Is there anything else in that letter?"

"No." Claire craned her neck, trying to see over the table, but not daring to peek.

"A name, anything?"

"No."

"Is that what I think?" Biscuit remained calm, his voice steady, military training in every word.

"Yeah."

Father Ricardo crossed himself.

"Put it on ice," Biscuit instructed.

No need to ask twice. I concealed the finger in my hands, shielding Claire from the sight. Downstairs in the kitchen, I wrapped JoJo's pinkie in tin foil and stuck it in the back of the freezer, behind the ice bucket. Where nobody would discover the foil and investigate the contents. I had no idea when time ran out for reattaching it.

"I'll call the police," announced Biscuit, back in the conference room.

Father Ricardo stood up and shook his head, looking to Claire and me for support. "You heard the letter. 'The woman dies.' "

Tears streamed down Claire's cheeks. "Who would do this?"

"We're in over our heads." Biscuit reached for the conference room phone, one of those gray triangles, a big round speaker built into the middle, and started to dial 911.

"They'll kill JoJo." Father Ricardo was adamant, incensed. He punched down the End Call button before Biscuit pressed the final digit.

"They'll kill her anyway, Reverend. This matter is totally out of our control."

I agreed with Biscuit. "Every second we wait is too long. There's nothing worse."

"How about dead?" Father Ricardo leaned forward on the table, his wide physique imposing. "You call the police—you send JoJo to her grave."

"What makes you so sure?" I had to ask. The priest was in the soul business, not hostage rescue. No matter what he did in the Philippines.

"Don't you get it?" he snapped.

"What?" Claire appeared dumbstruck.

"Maybe you'd better level with us, Father."

CHAPTER THIRTY-FIVE
BOARD MEETING

"I know who these men are."

Father Ricardo gazed out the conference room window at St. Philip's, the Anglican church dating back to 1680. His eyes were glassy, his back bent, his wide physique no longer imposing.

The confidence and spiritual aura—they were gone. He was a man overwhelmed by circumstances. His tortured expression reminded me of JoJo's face in the photo.

Despair?

The three of us waited for him to continue. Father Ricardo didn't say anything at first, because he couldn't. The silence grew ponderous, and I wanted to dial the authorities on the spot. "Who are they, Father?"

He leaned forward, elbows on the conference room table. And using his thumbs, he massaged his temples as though summoning a higher authority for strength. For a moment, I thought he was praying. But when Father Ricardo looked up, I was stunned. We all were. There were tears streaming down his cheeks.

"I've made a terrible mistake."

"What do you mean?" My voice was low, controlled, my heart pounding.

"I held back." His suit was crisp, his face a mask of regret.

"What, Father? What did you hold back?"

"The kids. It's not petty criminals who maim them. It's a crime ring. A huge, sophisticated network of Filipino beasts that could teach the American Mafia a thing or two. I don't know what all they're into."

"But you think they took JoJo?" The words were more accusation than question. I could feel my anger welling inside.

"I'm so sorry." The floodgates opened. Father Ricardo's tears flowed like the Ashley River.

"I told you they'd come looking for us." Last Tuesday, he was the one who threw up his hands in exasperation. This time it was me. "You said Cebu and the surrounding islands were safe. And by default, everyone in Charleston."

"I'm so sorry." He kept wailing, repeating himself. "We're just not worth their time."

"Goddamn it, Father. What have you gotten us into?"

Claire's jaw dropped, dumbstruck by my temper. She was too numb to speak. But words weren't necessary to understand her message. The man was broken. I had no right to badger him, a priest of all people.

Biscuit, his words soft and slow as molasses, tried to ease the tension. "Why did the gang come here?"

"I don't know," the reverend bawled. "These men have never followed us outside Manila. That's why I thought the other islands were safe."

"JoJo Kincaid!" I bellowed. "Two hundred million dollars! What were you thinking?"

"All our plans. I was so wrong," sobbed the priest. "Now everything is at risk."

He was frustrating me. I reached over to the phone, ready to call the police.

"Don't," Father Ricardo pleaded. "You don't know these men."

He wiped the tears from his face, pulled a handkerchief from his pocket, and blew his nose. Claire slid next to him, leaned over, and hugged him with her right arm. The sight—the man in black crumbling and a woman comforting him—stopped me from dialing.

But not from snapping. "Apparently, you don't either."

"Why Charleston?" pressed Biscuit, his voice gentle. "Why'd they grab JoJo Kincaid?"

"I don't know." His tears started to flow again.

The big man was onto something. His questions fueled my own curiosity. "Biscuit's right, Father. The authorities will ask the same thing."

"We've always been insignificant," he started. "Nothing more than nuisance priests."

"I get it. A gnat on an elephant. What changed?"

"They learned about our twenty-five-million-dollar wire?" Father Ricardo was struggling to find an answer, anything to end the barrage of questions.

"So they have a guy on the inside. Big deal. Happens all the time in bank operations."

Claire pushed the bangs from her face and cautioned me with her eyes.

"The Palmetto Foundation," I continued, my voice more respectful, "wired money to the Manila Society for Children at Risk in the past. And you've always been able to hide your activities. There's got to be something different."

"I signed a purchase and sale for the hotel."

Biscuit, ever the real estate lawyer, looked like someone had hit his internal light switch. "Your name is on the contract?"

"My name and the Manila Society for Children at Risk."

"What's the price?" I asked.

"Thirty-eight million."

"We only sent you twenty-five."

"We forfeit our escrow if we don't wire the balance in three days. Now do you understand my urgency?"

"The whole thing?" I asked, incredulous. "You forfeit one hundred percent?"

"Yes."

"How could you be so stupid?"

Father Ricardo glared at me. "I never anticipated a problem, because—"

"Because of what?"

"My deal with Palmer. Which you blew."

Biscuit shook his head. "Here's how I see it, Padre. In the past, you operated under the radar. Rent payments, payroll, and ordinary expenses that people forget. Nothing major. Now you commit to a thirty-eight-million-dollar purchase. Twenty-five down. Thirteen to follow. And the bad guys ask, 'Who is this priest?' They start their homework."

"With the help of an insider," I reminded everybody.

"And before long," Biscuit drawled, "they wonder, 'Who's the sugar daddy funding our boy?'"

"And stealing our workforce from the streets." I couldn't keep myself from interrupting. I liked Biscuit's clarity.

"The bad guys Google the Palmetto Foundation. I know that's what I would do. And they find Palmer and JoJo all over the Internet, where the whole world can see their money." Biscuit sat back. "You think that sums it up, Padre?"

"It's the foundation's money," corrected Claire, returning to her seat.

"Palmer and JoJo Kincaid have always been targets." Father Ricardo sounded defensive, but for the moment his distress was over. "And everybody at this table knows it."

"We're in a helluva fix," I said, parroting Annie's story about the Texas governor. "You risk losing twenty-five million dollars, Father. This gang wants two hundred million from the Palmetto Foundation. And we don't know if they'll return JoJo in one piece."

Father Ricardo was right about Palmer and JoJo. They had always been the prey. I tell clients all the time, "Big lifestyles make big targets."

More than once, Palmer rejected my advice to hire bodyguards.

He dismissed it as too alarmist. "For chrissakes, Grove, we live in Charleston."

Not everybody is so cavalier. That's why I maintain a short list of security services for clients and prospects who express an interest. Same thing with kidnap and ransom insurance, or "K&R," as it's known in the trade. When my guys travel to Mexico or Venezuela, I tell them, "You're crazy if you don't look into a policy."

One of Microsoft's billionaires is the gold standard for personal protection. Journalists love to write about his 414-foot yacht. The helicopter pads and attendant submarines make for good reading. But the ship's crew is what interests me.

It's a team of ex–Navy SEALs.

Father Ricardo surveyed Claire, Biscuit, and me. His tears were gone, his resolve back, both of which were a relief to me. When he spoke, his voice was soft, no more than a velvety whisper. But his message reverberated with the power and gravitas that come only from men of the cloth.

"I've been fighting these beasts a long time. And, right now, I regret my errors in judgment more than anything else in the world. I'd do anything to turn back the clock. To rescue JoJo. To heal her wounds. If I'm guilty of anything, it's trying to save more kids. Because I saw no end to the butchery." He paused a beat. "But know this. If you go to the authorities, if you delay payment, if you second-guess their ransom note, these men will kill her."

Claire was transfixed.

"You know them personally?" I asked, recalling how his confession began.

"Only as adversaries."

"But you can get to them, right?"

"Through my team, yes."

"The mercenaries?"

"I don't like that term. But our men, one in particular, know the world of these gangsters."

"Fine. We go to the authorities, Father, and make sure they talk to your guy."

"U.S. law enforcement can't move fast enough," he objected.

"There's an FBI agent riding my ass. Trust me, she'll drop everything." So much for me keeping secrets.

"FBI?" Father Ricardo asked, hearing about the Bureau's interest for the first time. "What do they know?"

Claire, who had been silent, stood up. She folded her arms across her chest and paced in one direction, then the other, as though organizing a jumble of thoughts. Biscuit, the reverend, and I looked at her.

At first, she addressed me. "Right now, only one thing matters. That's JoJo. And I want her back. No matter what it costs."

I bit my tongue, praying she would stop.

"We don't have two hundred million." Claire swept back her hair. "Not yet anyway."

Please don't go there.

The Palmetto Foundation had $140 million in assets. By Friday, Palmer's gift of $150 million would take our total to $290 million. In my business, we treat everything on a confidential basis. And neither Biscuit nor Father Ricardo needed to know the extent of our resources.

"Dad's gift to the Palmetto Foundation—"

"Is irrelevant," I interrupted. "We need the authorities."

"Totals one hundred and fifty million," Claire finished, overriding me.

"It won't be in the account until Friday."

She wriggled her palm back and forth, the *Whoa* signal. "I'll have the money tomorrow."

I wanted to scream but tamped down my emotions. "A two-hundred-million-dollar payment includes funds from other donors. That's not right, Claire."

"Use our forty," the reverend argued. "That takes you to one ninety."

"But your escrow?" Biscuit leaned into the conversation. Everybody was talking at once.

"I don't care if we lose the property," said Father Ricardo. "I can raise more money. But I can't live with JoJo's death on my hands."

"Your goons will take the money and kill her anyway." It was so obvious to me.

"They're businessmen." Father Ricardo dug his elbows into the table. "If they kill hostages, families will stop paying ransoms."

Around and around we went, until my phone rang and "I Walk the Line" shattered the tense air. I let my boss go into voice mail. Anders dialed a second time, more Johnny Cash, more "I Walk the Line."

On the third ring, Father Ricardo barked, "For the love of Christ, will you answer that thing?"

"Katy, I'm in a meeting. I can't talk."

"Fine, but get back to New York City tonight."

"Why?" Claire, Biscuit, and Father Ricardo stared at me.

"You're meeting Morgan Stanley at eight tomorrow morning."

"No I'm not."

Before she could reply, I said, "Hang on. There's another call coming in."

Ordinarily, I would never put my boss on hold. But my phone said, "Blocked." And it occurred to me—I don't know why—that JoJo's captors might be on the line. "Hello?"

"Hello, sweetheart." It was Torres.

I stood up, excused myself, and walked down the stairs to the kitchenette, away from the ears in the conference room. "What do you want?"

"That's no way to talk to a lady."

The sarcasm was getting to me. Everywhere I turned somebody was copping an attitude, even a damn priest. "You're right. Call me back in five. By then, I'll be primed with F-bombs."

"Hey, we're partners," she soothed. "You getting anywhere with Ricardo?"

"Hang on."

I introduced Torres to my Hold button and returned to Anders. Not much of an uptick. She snapped, "Don't do that again."

"Tomorrow is a nonstarter."

"You're gumming up the works," she growled.

"What are you talking about?"

"Morgan Stanley. They fast-tracked the due dilly. We don't expect any antitrust problems. We only need to check one more box, and that's getting brokers in front of their people."

I looked at the freezer door and thought about what was sitting inside. I remembered how Palmer Kincaid had guided me. Helped me through the years. Been there every step of the way. Wall Street could stuff it. I didn't care about "gumming up" a deal with Morgan Stanley. There was only one thing on my mind: JoJo Kincaid.

"You yanked Percy's account from me."

"Knock it off."

"Remember the last thing you said to me?"

"No."

"It is what it is."

"And your point is?"

"Why didn't you tell me about the FBI?"

"Who told you?" Anders sounded uncomfortable, really uncomfortable.

"Reschedule the meeting."

"This isn't a negotiation."

"Exactly." She knew what I meant. My way. Not hers.

"You're putting me in a difficult situation."

"It is what it is."

I hung up on Anders and clicked back to Torres. "I have no idea why you're riding me. Or what I've done. But right now, I don't care. Got that? I don't care. Last time I checked, you weren't my biggest problem."

"What's wrong?" Agent Torres detected something new in my voice.

And I heard consternation in hers. She wasn't an ally. Nor a friend. I didn't like her. I didn't trust her. I didn't understand why she came at me like a Mack truck the first time we met. Or my firm for that matter. I eyed the freezer door again, long and hard. I may never know what possessed me, how I found the resolve to mouth off to an FBI agent. Especially when I needed the Bureau's help. Maybe all the hostile phone calls in the middle of a board meeting made me crack. Or maybe it was that refrain in the hostage note: "The woman dies." Whatever. I wasn't thinking straight.

"Frankly, Torres, it's time you reimburse the FBI."

"For what?"

"Salary, pension, medical benefits. That's a start. You probably owe them interest and penalty fees too. Don't tell me they provide you with a vehicle."

"You need my help." That's the last thing Torres said before I clicked off.

Dial tone.

Claire, Biscuit, and Father Ricardo stopped squabbling the second I returned. The reverend asked, "Everything okay?"

"Peachy. Now, about the money." I placed my mobile on the table, but it interrupted again, vibrating with the annoying hum of metal against wood. I almost threw it out the window.

"Can't you turn that thing off?" implored Claire.

"Sorry." I looked down at the LCD display. It was my firm's CEO.

CHAPTER THIRTY-SIX
BOARD MEETING

Call me cynical. But hear me out.

I work for a big investment bank, a sprawling empire of combatant egos. The best way to deal with managers is to avoid them. Their annoying memos sprout mushrooms near the bottom of my in-box. Their incoming phone calls go straight to voice mail. Caller ID has increased my productivity tenfold at the office.

Here's the thing. I avoid the brass. If I stay out of the pasture, I can't step in the bullshit, right? Most days the strategy works. Managers leave me the hell alone, because I deliver revenues, year in, year out. And everybody on Wall Street knows, "It's the fees, stupid."

Every strategy has a flaw. The one in mine is the CEO. It's impossible to ignore him.

The LCD on my cell phone read PERCY PHILLIPS. I knew what to expect. SKC's CEO was coming after me. A journalist from *The Village Voice* once described him as a bipolar pit bull stuck on manic. If you ask me, the guy nailed it.

For the third time that morning, I stood up and left. Which was nerve-racking because Claire, Biscuit, and Father Ricardo continued their discussion from my previous absences. And I was missing out.

"Grove here."

"You hung up on Anders." Percy spoke in a controlled Chicago accent, da Bears, da brats, interrupted by the occasional burst of squeaky inflection. "Last I heard, insubordination gets you fired."

"I have issues with a client."

"You have a problem with me."

Strike three. First it was JoJo's severed pinkie. Then it was an FBI agent demanding that I snitch on a priest. And now it was the CEO busting my balls with career threats.

"We're meeting Morgan Stanley tomorrow morning," Percy continued. "You're at that meeting."

"Not happening."

"Excuse me?"

Pawns are blind, and kings don't negotiate. I could tell Percy was pissed. But for the first time in my career, I didn't care what he said. Or thought. Or demanded. As long as JoJo's life was on the line, everyone at SKC could go screw themselves. My gut said Palmer's wife was close, that she needed me, that the next twenty-four hours were critical. There was no way I was leaving Charleston until she was safe.

Percy paused to sort through his thoughts, unaccustomed to pushback either from me or from the other minions on our floor. I could almost hear him frown at his need to shift tone. "Private Client Services does four hundred million in revenues. Your team is twenty million of the total. I need your help, Grove."

His words sounded like another hand job from above. "Anders pulled your account. And now you want my help?"

"Morgan Stanley insists on meeting you."

"My team's only five percent of department revenues."

"I doubt fifty stockbrokers in the world run a twenty-million-dollar business. Especially in this market."

When commands fail, bosses hit the sycophant switch.

I suddenly understood Percy's urgency. "Your deal's on the ropes?"

"I can't answer that."

"You just did."

His jaw probably hit the floor.

I was worked up. Didn't care what happened, either to my job or to Percy's deal. Indifference, it seemed to me in that mother of all eureka moments, was the most luscious feeling in the world. Whoever cares the least enjoys the most power, corporate titles notwithstanding.

"Why can't our lawyers make up their minds?" I demanded.

"They have nothing to do with this."

"The hell. Agent Torres of the FBI stormed through SKC's doors. You recognize her name, right?"

"Grove."

"She scared the crap out of our lawyers. Tax fraud. Patriot Act violations. Wire transfers to the wrong guys. You name it, Torres implied it."

"I'm begging you to give it a rest." Percy's tone had turned sarcastic.

I pressed on, empowered by my detachment from SKC. My diatribe was gaining speed and building momentum. "MoFo comes in and distances you from me. And me from Morgan Stanley, because the hired guns think I'll fuck up your deal."

"I don't have time to sit here while you get it wrong."

That comment shut me up.

"I need your help," Percy echoed from before. The CEO was not one to ask for anything. He usually snapped his fingers and got what he wanted.

"I'm listening."

"You're right about what happened. More or less. But ultimately, it was my decision to tell Morgan Stanley about your FBI problems."

"Sounds like we need new lawyers."

"I've been your client for two years. I know you make good decisions, even if you're on a one-man mission to save all the world's underdogs. I know you play aboveboard. That you didn't do anything wrong. On purpose, that is."

A little late for this, Percy.

"Are you afraid of what happens after I handle the FBI? You think I'll sue SKC for wrongful termination?"

"Just attend tomorrow's meeting, Grove. We'll pay your legal bills."

"Why?"

"SKC needs this deal."

"You sound desperate."

"Banking revenues are way off. Unless we sell your division, our share price tanks."

I almost hung up on the spot. "So this is all about SKC missing its numbers?"

"Yes."

"Sounds like it's time for you to manage expectations. Because I won't be present tomorrow morning."

"Come on, Grove."

"Just do the deal without me."

"We tried."

"Why am I not surprised?"

"I advised Morgan about the FBI's interest in you. And they want to cool things off until your problems play out."

"Even with me out of the picture?"

"Afraid so. It's not like we can indemnify them for bad press."

"Then what does my presence accomplish?"

"It takes bad press off the table. You turn your business over to Zola. Morgan Stanley pays you a whopping big number to ensure your cooperation. Say twenty million. And you sign a nondisclosure agreement so nothing ever hits the press. We all make money and move on."

"Why didn't you tell me this at the start?"

"I tried."

"You said I have a 'problem' with you."

"I'm trying to make you a rich man," Percy insisted. "You'll never work another day in your life. Unless, of course, you want to open your own hedge fund. And if you do, SKC will invest fifty million and raise another fifty million from clients. That's a hundred million, bud."

"One of my clients was kidnapped. She may die, depending on how her family and I respond to the ransom demands over the next twenty-four hours. I don't have the bandwidth for you or your share price or your one-hundred-million guarantee."

"What are you talking about?"

"And for the record: selling PCS to hit numbers is a really stupid idea." With that I introduced the chairman of SKC to my old friend in these situations:

Doctor Dial Tone.

When I returned, Claire was standing near the window. Her jeans were tucked into her boots. She wore a wide leather belt, cinched at the waist. Her gray cashmere sweater looked like the color of stone. In a way, she reminded me of Palmer. She had his pluck. She was pure granite, chiseled cheekbones, her vulnerable bearing gone.

"We've decided to pay, Grove."

Claire swept the unruly bangs from her face. She was my friend, a great friend. But as an equal trustee of the Palmetto Foundation, I had my own ideas about our next steps. Nobody was wiring money without my approval.

"All two hundred million?" The question sounded innocuous. But I was gathering info to make my play.

"No. Fifty."

"Are you telling the police?"

"We decided against it."

"Who's the 'we'?"

"Father Ricardo and I."

To this day, I don't know what possessed me to look at Biscuit. He was not the foundation's lawyer. He was smart, thorough. I wanted him in my foxhole. But he had no vote at the table. The big man, as though reading my thoughts, shrugged his enormous shoulders.

"I'm just a spectator," he ventured. "But in my opinion, y'all are punching outside your weight class."

"What's that mean?" The boxing jargon puzzled Claire. It annoyed her. A lawyer, one from Fayetteville of all places, had no right to interfere in her family's affairs.

"Contact the FBI before it's too late."

"It's been lovely to meet." Her words smacked of pralines and cream. Claire returned from the window and offered her hand to Biscuit, a clear dismissal. Nobody can say, "Get the fuck out of here" with the sugary charm of my brethren down South.

Which, of course, pissed me off. "Biscuit's not going anywhere."

Most times, Southerners are never so definitive. We prefer flanking maneuvers to head-on clashes. We hide behind manners, and sometimes it takes us a while to say what we mean. Charming and disarming—sure. But make no mistake: Southerners recognize disputes for what they are. Cyanide served with syrup is still lethal.

Claire blinked, a fast, almost imperceptible flutter of the eyes. She retreated to the reverend, allied with him, and said, "We don't need another opinion."

"Biscuit's here by invitation, same as Father Ricardo."

"There's a difference," the reverend snapped. "You have forty million dollars of the Catholic Fund's money. If that doesn't buy me a seat at the table, I don't know what does."

I ignored Father Ricardo, signaled Biscuit to stay, and addressed my fellow trustee. "What happens when the goons get fifty million, Claire?"

"They negotiate for the balance."

"Which is a euphemism. It means we lose our money, they keep JoJo, and the Palmetto Foundation gets her body parts in courier bags."

"I told you," Father Ricardo argued, "one of my guys knows how to reach them. We can negotiate."

"You flip-flopped. Before, you said they don't negotiate."

"We've got to try."

"Waste of time, Father. I just hung up on my friend from the FBI. I'm calling her back."

"You do that, and I'll be offering up prayers at JoJo's funeral."

When it comes to investment advice, guys with all the answers scare the crap out of me. They're dangerous. Because nine times out of ten, they're wrong. Right now, Father Ricardo was jamming us, pushing too hard. He was too inflexible about police involvement.

"If we wire fifty million," I said, returning to the money, "they own us."

The priest looked at Claire. "Can he veto you?"

Biscuit cocked his eyebrow. He sensed that Father Ricardo had just lit my fuse. He was right.

"Go ahead," I told Claire. "Get Huitt and his lawyer bees on the phone. You have a vote. I have a vote. And JoJo is recused for reasons beyond her control. Let's see what the mouthpieces say about my veto."

"You're not being rational," the priest said.

"The goons don't get one dime till JoJo's safe. I don't care what you say. Or what the FBI says for that matter. There's one thing I understand, and that's money. How people behave when they have it. When they want it. Or when it's slipping away. If we wire money, we lose our leverage."

"You're playing chicken with the wrong people."

"It's time we change the dialogue, Father. I fly wherever they say. Cook Islands, Cayman Islands, whatever. I open an account. Claire wires me two hundred million. The goons trade JoJo for me. Once she's safe, they get the money."

I stared at him until he averted his eyes. But I was no rock. I was a wreck. I had never been more conflicted in all my life. One wrong move, and JoJo was dead. One wrong move, and I'd live with the guilt that my intransigence had cost her life. More baggage in my growing collection.

"Just give me twenty-four hours." Father Ricardo looked like he might add, "I'm begging you."

I couldn't take any more tears. That didn't stop me from pushing back hard. "What, before I call the FBI? Give me a break."

Claire slapped her palm on the conference room table. The thump sounded like an angry gavel. "Hear him out, Grove. Dad said you're his 'thousandth man.' So act like it."

I eyed Claire, her comment too personal for the setting.

Father Ricardo did not cry. Far from it. "Grove, last Tuesday you asked me for seven days. I'm asking you for twenty-four hours. That's it."

"To do what?"

"To reach my guy. To negotiate with the gangsters. To get JoJo back."

"We're talking about a woman's life, Father. Not money."

"Which is why I'm asking for twenty-four hours. Are you willing to bet JoJo's life that my way is wrong?"

"Why wait, Father? Get your boy on the line now."

"It's not that easy. Time zones and the kind of man he is. Know what I'm saying?"

"Try."

Father Ricardo dialed a long stream of numbers. His eyes flickered for a second. "Voice mail."

"Leave a message, Father."

"Call me." He clicked off his mobile and turned to me. "Then we have a deal—twenty-four hours?"

"You can trade me for JoJo," I repeated. "But no money until she's safe."

Nobody said a word. The silence grated on me. It felt intrusive. And I could tell we were all sharing the same sense of self-doubt and apprehension. The odd thing was, Father Ricardo never suggested a prayer.

He bowed his head once during the board meeting. Big deal. I've been around priests all my life. And there's one thing I know for certain: when the chips are down, priests pull out the beads. There hadn't been a Hail Mary all morning.

CHAPTER THIRTY-SEVEN

THE STREETS OF CHARLESTON

Bong tossed his black gabardine jacket on the passenger seat. He slid into the rental, powered down all four windows, and cranked the AC. He could use a beer. Maybe a couple. Even though the Holy City was cool for early October, he was perspiring like a pig.

He was shaking.

It had always been that way. First came a delicious high from skirting the edge, the rush that accompanies fear. Because deep down, every actor is scared of being revealed as a fake. No problem this time. Bong had just delivered the performance of his life. And he knew it.

Next came the exit to accolades. There was no audience today—just players. But his heart was pumping, his adrenaline surging. And his glands were pouring out their sweaty applause. For a brief moment as he left the garage, he remembered the ovations from his theater days in school.

Near the corner of East Bay and Calhoun, Bong braked hard at the stoplight. As he rolled up his black shirtsleeves, a tan Mercedes pulled up to the right. The driver was blonde. Mid-thirties. Peach lips. She glanced over and smiled with enough wattage to light Yankee Stadium.

The traffic light was slow. The pleasant woman gazed ahead but glanced at Bong every so often. She appreciated his gentle features. Wavy black hair and reassuring, if not classic, good looks. Deep down, the adulation pleased Bong. A lot.

Returning to character, he etched a cross through the air. He assumed the blessing would make her happy. But when the woman spotted his spider-sun tattoo, her stadium-light smile disappeared. The body ink didn't fit, nor did the careful white bandages wrapping Holly's bites.

"I need to be more careful," Bong muttered, noting her reaction, shaking his head, rolling his black sleeves down again. Soon enough he would be lounging on a beach, maybe at the Amanpulo resort south of Manila. There, he could chug Dom Pérignon a million bubbles at a time and drink the ocean air—assuming no more mistakes.

The light turned green. The Mercedes shot forward. The blonde never peeked over, no crinkle of her nose good-bye, no bat of the eyelashes sayonara. Bong continued straight and told himself to focus. He needed time to think. And the drive back to the beach was just what the doctor ordered.

His initial problem had been old man Kincaid. Palmer talked to Father Mike and figured out what was going on. Which jeopardized Moreno's $33.5 million. Which turned the Colombian into a dangerous client. Which put Bong in a pickle. There had been no choice but to eliminate the Charleston developer turned philanthropist.

But now Bong considered the next generation—whether taking his chances with them had been such a good idea. Claire was the poster child for gullibility. She was not a problem. Nor was JoJo, who had always been full of herself. The issue was Grove O'Rourke, an insipid, unexpected, and inconvenient trustee. Bong wished he had never heard of the Palmetto Foundation.

If he let O'Rourke operate unchecked, then Moreno would come looking. And one thing was certain: The Colombian was a vindictive son of a bitch. He would never stop searching. No matter how often Bong moved, no matter where he hid, Moreno would find him.

Halfway over the new Cooper River Bridge, Bong pushed the car to seventy. Maybe closer to eighty. The damp ocean air rushed through the open windows. *The nerve of that O'Rourke.* Bong began muttering to himself: "Are you threatening me?"

Next time he saw the patsy-assed suit from Wall Street, he'd kick the shit out of him. Take out his legs with a sweep kick. Or snap a size 10 shoe to the guy's speed bag. Then he'd stomp O'Rourke's nose until oatmeal was draining through the nostrils. What was that word he kept using in the meeting today?

"Goons."

The more Bong considered O'Rourke, the angrier he became. And Moreno was running out of patience. The Colombian's muscle could arrive in Charleston any minute. And who knew what O'Rourke would say to the FBI? Or when the Feds would come storming through the doors?

He had worked so hard to build his business, the scrimping, the scraping, the long hours. He remembered the first pitch, which had been the mother of all opportunities, no matter how dangerous. "I'm here because you're about to get caught."

The crazy Colombian had shaken his head in disbelief. "And you're about to get dead."

"That would be a mistake."

"You got balls, kid. I'll give you that." Moreno pronounced "balls" with a snaky, lispy sound.

"I can show you how to do the job right. And never worry again."

"Who else knows what you know?"

"Everybody if anything happens to me."

By the time Bong reached the Isle of Palms, just north of Sullivan's Island, his face was beet red, his neck a coil of tense muscles. He attributed his best thinking to fits of violent rage. He was about to have one of those moments.

Near the corner of Rifle Range Road and the Isle of Palms Connector, Bong parked in the hotel lot. From the outside, the place looked okay. More likely to be clean than not. But inside, it was a dump. Breathing was the same as snorting mildew.

A few more days—$200 million in cash, of which $33.5 million went to Moreno—and Bong would never sleep in a shit hole like this again. Nothing but the Four Seasons. The Ritz-Carlton would be roughing it.

He charged down the hallway, choking back the fungus fumes, gaining fury with every step. He charged into his room and saw JoJo lying on the bed. Half asleep. Her right eye was closed from the beating last night.

Quietly, silently, he pulled a video camera from a blue canvas gym bag. Holly started to growl. And Bong started to tape.

The dachshund jumped off the bed, and Bong kicked her against the wall. Airborne at least twelve feet, the dog yelped and hit the floor with a thud. Bong was gaining more power every second.

"Guess who," he announced, his voice halfway between game show host and crazed lunatic. "Bong or Father Ricardo?"

"Don't hurt my dog," JoJo gasped.

"I'll give you a hint. Psalm 137:9. King James version. And I quote, 'Happy shall he be, that taketh and dasheth thy little ones against the stones.'" He liked this priest shit.

"No, Father Ricardo!" she screamed, seeing his wrath.

"Wrong."

With the back of his right hand, he smacked JoJo's face. Hard. He could hear the sweet crunch of hand against cheekbone. Back and forth, he beat her with his open palm. Left. Right. Left. Right. And with every swing, he chanted the same four words:

"Happy shall he be."

When he was finished, JoJo lay on the bed. Out cold. Her left eye was already swelling. Pretty soon it would match the right. She made such a pretty picture, her nose dripping like a leaky faucet, her left hand bandaged in a swath of bloody hotel towels and blue duct tape. Face gray, the color of death.

Violence, he decided, was a beautiful thing. The surge of adrenaline. The rush of oxygen. They delivered a one-two punch of mental clarity, and a video was so much more compelling than photos. "We'll see who plays tough."

With that, Bong pulled off his clerical collar. He had been hot before. Now he was boiling from the exertion, and the damn thing felt like an octopus around his neck. Plus, JoJo's blood had splattered all across the white. He reached into the hotel's refrigerator and grabbed the six-pack inside. He ripped one can from the plastic rings, popped the top, and repeated a mainstay from GI jargon when he was a kid:

"Now comes Miller time."

One beer, two at the most, and he'd find O'Rourke. Push up the time-table. They weren't expecting Father Ricardo to report back until first thing in the morning. Beer in hand, he looked down at JoJo and smiled.

I do God's work.

CHAPTER THIRTY-EIGHT

THE STREETS OF CHARLESTON

It took some doing.

We had all snapped at each other in the Palmetto Foundation's conference room. But Father Ricardo, Claire, Biscuit, and I finally agreed on three actions. We were in a state of shock, each one of us sick with worry. JoJo's life rested in our hands. And the responsibility was killing us.

We tried to rise above our limitations. To be efficient, we circulated phone numbers on contact sheets like the ones I-bankers use during initial public offerings. But our efforts were almost laughable. We were clueless amateurs, floundering over what to do. We lacked the street skills to negotiate with violent men who played by different rules.

Our plan, in my humble opinion, was crap. We were waiting to react, hoping events would turn our way. And the worst thing was, our strategy didn't include the authorities for twenty-four hours.

One: Wait for Father Ricardo.

The minute his mercenary made contact with the goons, the priest would ring us. We'd meet and reassess. Negotiate. Trade me for JoJo. Whatever.

Two: Wait for five o'clock Wednesday afternoon.

That was the deadline in the ransom note. I said, "Screw that noise." If we paid, we lost our leverage. If we held on to the foundation's cash, one of the goons would contact us. I had no doubt. If they didn't, we'd call the authorities no later than 5:30 P.M.

Three: Wait for tomorrow morning.

Which was more of an afterthought than anything else. Father Ricardo, Claire, and I agreed to reassemble at ten A.M. no matter what. Biscuit was not invited. He was not part of the Kincaid family, nor one of their friends. And the Catholic Fund could be at loggerheads with his clients.

I wanted Biscuit's help. In my opinion, he had already proven his value as an ally. But I threw Claire and Father Ricardo a bone because they both wanted to pay the ransom. And I was firm.

No JoJo—no money.

Nobody agreed to a fourth action point.

Office politics being what they are, every stockbroker knows how to say one thing and do another. That includes me. I had my own agenda. As Biscuit and I walked back to our hotel, I realized so did he.

Jacket draped over his shoulder, the big man buried his left hand in his pants pocket. "You think it's okay not to call the police?"

His words, opinion delivered through the interrogative tense of the South, translated, "Are you out of your mind?"

"Keeping silent is just plain stupid," I replied.

"So you're calling the authorities?"

"Yeah, without a doubt."

"Good." Biscuit smirked. His eyes sparkled. And for all our nagging fears, he found humor in the moment.

"What?"

"You're saving me," he confessed, "from calling Torres."

"Why her? I don't trust that woman. I don't like her. And she can go to hell for all I care."

"Why?" the big man asked.

"She's a bull in a china shop. I still don't know why she trampled me at SKC. Or in Palmer's office. But if you ask me, the more heavy-handed, the more likely the breakage. And I'm not taking chances with JoJo's life."

"But she's been working the case a long time."

"So."

"Torres knows the players. She may be a hard-ass. But she's the fastest way to get JoJo Kincaid back. There's no need to bring her up to speed. And besides."

Biscuit was logical. I had to give him that. "Besides what?"

"The FBI has jurisdiction. You don't want to waste time on politics between different law enforcement agencies."

"You got that right, bubba." A couple of weeks in Charleston, and I was already sinking back into the Southernisms.

"So you're calling Torres?"

"Okay."

She answered on the first ring. "Tell me—"

"Are you still in Charleston?" I interrupted.

"Yes."

"Where?"

"Behind you."

"What are you talking about?"

A horn blared, and I whirled round. So did Biscuit. Torres had pulled off to the right side of the road and pushed open the passenger door.

"Hurry up." She signaled us to get inside. "We're backing up traffic."

Torres caught me off guard.

Standing there on Meeting Street, I was a guy on the edge. I could almost feel my veins from inside out, the nanosecond of calm and then the surge of blood through vessels, the sudden burst of adrenaline that screams, "Attack, attack, attack!"

I wanted to tell the FBI about JoJo. But one look at the heavy-handed agent who threw me under the bus at SKC, and I saw red. She was tailing me. Or so I thought. The realization pissed me off.

"What are you doing here?"

"Get in." Torres eyed the big lawyer at my side. "What are you looking at, Lumpy?"

"It's Biscuit."

"I should have known."

The two of us hopped into the car, me in the front, Biscuit in the back. We closed the doors. And she hit the gas, speeding down Meeting Street, blowing through every yellow light. A thousand questions raced through my mind. But in my anger, I never asked any of them.

All I could do was lash out. "Why don't you tell us what's going on? Rather than running around half cocked and scaring the crap out of everyone."

"Who's in trouble?"

"JoJo Kincaid. She's been kidnapped."

"Hang on." Torres never blinked. She never slowed down. With a cadaver's pulse, she punched several numbers into her phone and waited to connect. "Walker, get a team to Charleston. Yesterday is too late."

The two spoke for a few moments. When Torres finished—the cavalry on the way—she glanced at me with a no-nonsense look. Eyes steady. Lips pursed. Antennae up. I saw compassion in her features.

Maybe it was the vertical creases between her eyebrows. Or the sense of foreboding. But her expression made me think I had rushed to judgment. Her instructions were simple and to the point. "Start at the beginning."

Over the next forty-five minutes, I poured out the whole story. Everything from my call with Palmer to the mystery package containing JoJo's finger. Didn't hold back. Not once. She gunned down I-26. We crossed the West Ashley Bridge, looped back to Charleston, and the whole way I had one mission, one thought. And that was saving JoJo Kincaid.

Biscuit filled in details. He explained how Highly Intimate Pleasures brought him to the Palmetto Foundation. He described his contact with accountants for the Catholic Fund and its beneficiaries. He complemented my observations with his.

The agent listened and drove. She nodded every so often. Or she requested clarification. She was a good listener, no hint of the angry crab I first met in Palmer's office.

Torres turned onto Gillon Street. She cursed the cobblestones underneath, parked, but left the motor running. In a measured voice, she issued a directive. "From now on, nobody blinks without telling me. We clear?"

"What about Father Ricardo?"

"Not sure."

Her response ticked me off. "First you ordered me to spy on Ricardo. Now you're not sure he's dirty?"

"Your priest keeps hitting our radar," she began. "But we don't know how he fits in."

He's not my priest.

" 'Fits in' what?" pressed Biscuit.

"A Colombian drug cartel."

"Father Ricardo's a pusher?" For a moment, Biscuit forgot JoJo. The word "pusher" crossed his lips like a declaration of victory over Highly Intimate Pleasures.

"Maybe," she replied. "But if I had to guess, he's laundering the cartel's money."

Of course.

Every stockbroker knows money laundering is a risk. Our compliance departments make us watch instructional films about those brand-new eight-figure accounts. The ones too good to be true. There are no happy endings in these videos. Stockbrokers get fined. We lose our licenses. We go to jail.

As a trustee at the Palmetto Foundation, I had not been thinking about new accounts. I was evaluating an orphanage in the Philippines. I was grinding my teeth over photos of kids without limbs—thinking how great it would be to neuter the men who interrupted their childhoods.

"What's money laundering got to do with the Palmetto Foundation?" asked Biscuit.

"Have you ever heard of layering?" the agent replied.

"No," he said.

I had. "Layering is wiring money from one organization to the next, over and over, until it's impossible to identify the source."

"Not bad," Torres said to me. "The Palmetto Foundation is the perfect vehicle to wash money."

"Because we're a charity. Our name legitimizes the cash."

"Right."

"I get it. But the Catholic Fund is a charity too. And they have a great name for washing money. Why use us?"

Biscuit eyed both of us, weighing our words.

"You're just another layer." Torres spoke as though she were in a classroom. "It's that simple."

"I don't buy it. The Catholic Fund paid us six hundred and fifty thousand dollars. That's a big expense for 'just another layer.' How much does it cost to wash money anyway?"

"You got paid one percent, which is peanuts." Torres twisted from the steering wheel in order to face me in the front and Biscuit in the back.

"What do you mean?"

"Money launderers charge anywhere from six to twelve percent to wash money. But I've seen costs as high as twenty-five percent."

"And I thought our problem was tax fraud."

"Who said it isn't?" The agent sounded too casual for my comfort. "I think the Palmetto Foundation gifted money to a criminal operation. That's enough to make the IRS crazy."

"Great."

Torres piled on. "The Patriot Act. The Money Laundering Control Act. A couple of international treaties. I'd say you and your board violated everything in sight."

Biscuit, ever the vigilant attorney, raised his eyebrows and shook his head, signaling me to shut up. I don't think Agent Torres caught the motion.

"You weren't there to see the pictures of the kids." Now, I really didn't like her one bit. She was still holding the $25 million wire over my head like a ball-peen hammer.

"How's HIP fit into all this?" asked Biscuit, deflecting the conversation away from me—or exploring the impact on his clients.

"If I'm right about money laundering," she continued, "your adult superstore is what we call 'placement.' "

"Which is what?"

"When you mix legitimate funds with illegal funds in cash businesses," I explained to Biscuit.

"Which makes it impossible," he said, "to distinguish between the two."

"Right. That's probably why HIP has a bar. It's a cash business."

"Forget the bar," Biscuit observed. "My wife would kill me if she saw any HIP charges on our credit card."

"There's just one thing," I said, growing exasperated, returning my attention to Torres. "I don't buy the money-laundering explanation."

"Why not?" Torres's cell phone rang. She checked the caller ID but ignored the call and focused on me.

"Palmer was too savvy. Not the kind of guy to get duped."

"Don't kid yourself."

Biscuit turned pensive, his face puzzled. Our conversation was troubling him. That much was clear. But I could not tell whether it was my objection about Palmer, or if Biscuit had moved on, mentally that is, and was chewing over a different issue.

"Money launderers are ingenious," Torres continued. "I've seen them infiltrate organizations a million different ways."

"Why don't you spare us the accolades," I said, growing impatient. "And focus on JoJo."

"When the captors make contact, we'll nail them and get her." Torres spoke in cool, confident tones. "My team is on its way now to wire the Palmetto Foundation for sound."

"And what about Claire?" I pressed. "You're following the money, right? They already took JoJo."

"We're watching Claire twenty-four seven."

Good thing, I decided, my mind racing. "What about Ricardo? If you're right, if he's tied into the goons—then you put JoJo's life in jeopardy the minute he sees you."

"Where is he now?"

"Reachable by cell phone. That's all I know." I handed Torres my copy of the contact sheet, the one we had put together in the Palmetto Foundation's conference room.

"Claire's still at the office." Torres's words were half statement, half question.

"She was when we left."

"Get her out," Torres instructed. "So my team can tap the Palmetto Foundation's offices."

"You're kidding. We need to bring her inside the tent."

"The fewer people who know, the better."

"JoJo is her stepmother."

"I don't care."

"It's her father's money at stake."

"I don't care." The agent sounded like a broken record.

"This makes no sense. Why don't you find Ricardo and bring him in?"

"And sweat him out?" For a moment, I thought Torres might add, "Like they do on television?"

I cut her off. "Whatever it takes to get JoJo back."

"We don't have anything on the priest," she explained. "For all we know, he's under duress right now. We nab Ricardo. Moreno kills Mrs. Kincaid and moves on."

"But we still have forty million of the Catholic Fund's money."

"Who's Moreno?" asked Biscuit.

"The Colombian drug lord," Torres said.

"We need to understand the plan," I said, trying to insert order into a three-way dialogue. We were all talking over each other.

"You're meeting at ten o'clock tomorrow morning?" she asked.

"Yes."

"And Ricardo's the only one with access to the kidnappers?"

"Indirect. But yes."

"We won't hear anything until tomorrow. Which is fine, because we're about to spring a trap and take them down." Torres sounded confident.

Too much conviction, I decided. "What do you mean?"

"Because, Grove, you're about to send shock waves all the way back to Moreno."

"What are you talking about?"

"The ransom demand is for two hundred million dollars?"

"Yes."

"You're paying it."

"No fucking way," I snapped.

Torres smiled like the Cheshire cat. "I thought you might say that."

"Look, Agent Torres. I know money. I don't care what you and your team of experts say. There's no way I'm giving up our leverage. Two hundred million dollars. Give me a break."

"Why'd the kidnappers up the ante?" asked Biscuit, the chaos of a three-person conversation returning. "The Palmetto Foundation only has forty million dollars of the Catholic Fund's money."

"It sounds to me," I said, "like we're a target of opportunity. The goons may have a priest working for them. But this isn't church."

"That simple?" asked Biscuit, seeking confirmation from Torres.

"Grove's right," she confirmed. "Opportunity is that simple."

"Simple or not," I interrupted, "we're not wiring them one dime."

"Hey, Grove."

"Yes?"

"I know a little something about the people we're investigating. You pay, you might have a twenty percent chance of getting Mrs. Kincaid back alive. You don't pay, and you have a one hundred percent chance of getting her back in messenger bags."

"Not happening. We're not paying." I was adamant.

So was she. "Yes you will. And here's why."

Fifteen minutes later, I got it.

CHAPTER THIRTY-NINE
BISCUIT'S HOTEL ROOM

"Do me a favor, captain, and send up a vodka martini. Twist of lemon."

Biscuit cradled the receiver. He folded his beefy arms behind his head and swung his size 12 feet onto the bed's golden spread. When he leaned back, the occasional chair begged for mercy and threatened imminent collapse.

Other than room service, there was no reason to stay in Charleston. If Father Ricardo was laundering money, it was only a matter of time before the FBI raided Highly Intimate Pleasures and shut down the operation. Biscuit's clients were on the verge of winning.

The big man considered Mrs. Jason Locklear. He owed her a call but preferred to see her reaction in person. He could swing by her house tomorrow and brief her on his progress. She might even crack a smile, the closest she would ever come to an attaboy.

Nothing like success to shut people up.

He found it impossible, though, to revel in client victory. JoJo Kincaid's life hung in the balance, and until she was free, there was nothing to celebrate. Not only that, but Grove's remark was still gnawing at him: "Palmer was too savvy. Not the kind of guy to get duped." Grove, the FBI, himself—everybody was overlooking something. Biscuit just couldn't figure out what.

His cell phone rang. Biscuit looked at the caller ID and said, "I should have guessed."

"You didn't call on Monday." Mrs. Jason Locklear was on the line, large and in charge, her tone snappish.

"I'm down in Charleston."

"Vacation?" She sounded annoyed.

"Research into HIP."

"What's the store got to do with Charleston?"

"Long story. I'm still sorting through the details."

A knock at Biscuit's door interrupted their conversation. From out in the hall, a man announced, "Room service."

"Hang on." Biscuit slid his legs off the bed, rose from the chair, which sighed in relief, and left his cell phone next to the reading lamp.

"Your martini," the waiter said. "Let me know if it's okay."

"I'm sure it's fine." Biscuit paid and tipped the guy a dollar too much, and the man left.

"You're drinking martinis at five in the afternoon?" Mrs. Jason Locklear was barking now, the disapproval clear in her voice.

Biscuit was well within his rights to say, "Go piss up a rope," or "It's none of your business."

Instead he replied, "We're about to win."

He ran his hand through his thick mop of unruly hair, catching his reflection in the room's mirror. He looked like a meaty Samson, powerful. It was time to take charge of this relationship. Biscuit sipped his martini, let the burn trickle down his throat, and then spoke in a low rumble. "What's on your mind?"

Mrs. Jason Locklear noticed the new tone, the absence of deference. For the moment, she forgot her outrage over Biscuit's cocktail. "Maybe we should back off."

"What are you talking about?"

"Maybe the store isn't such a bad thing."

Her change in attitude was nuts. A few Sundays ago, Mrs. Jason Locklear would have rallied a lynching mob to stampede HIP. Now, Biscuit was tempted to hang up on Client Cocoa Puffs. But as always, he exercised his Southern reserve. "Tell me why."

"Maybe HIP's not so bad."

He detected the quiver in her voice. "You're beating around the bush."

"They hire people from our community."

"We knew that before."

"Maybe I changed my mind."

Mrs. Jason Locklear was married to a chief master sergeant. And Biscuit knew, from childhood, from living in Fayetteville, that military families were always struggling to make ends meet. "Did you take a job?"

"No, nothing like that." Her voice trailed off. She was not used to a full-court press from her attorney. He was always so gentle for such a big man.

"What is it then?"

"Our minister says adult toys are fine."

"Fine for what?" Biscuit couldn't believe his ears.

"Husbands and wives, if you know what I mean."

"I have no clue what you mean." Mrs. Jason Locklear was getting on his last nerve. And he was pleased to have a martini in hand.

"The store keeps marriages interesting."

Give me a break.

"The billboards—what do you tell your kids?"

"Get rid of the ads. But some of us are okay with the store."

Right then and there, Biscuit decided to boot the practice of law. At least for today. He didn't know JoJo Kincaid. But she was in dire straits. And here, his client was flip-flopping over the good and evil of sex products.

What the fuck.

"Okay to be seen but not heard?" he asked.

"Right."

"This one is out of our control. I'll call you back."

"But—"

"But nothing."

Biscuit clicked off the phone, called Faith Ann, and complained that his clients were "too twisted for color TV," which is Southern for "crazy."

"E.T. go home." His wife said that whenever he was away on business and she and the boys missed him. It was their private joke.

They spoke for a while and kissed each other good-bye through the receivers, but only after Biscuit said he'd be spending another night in Charleston. "Something's eating me."

Then, he called room service again. "How about another martini, captain. This time send the shaker." He booted up his computer and Googled Palmer Kincaid.

Grove's right, Biscuit thought. *A guy who makes two hundred million is nobody's stooge.*

CHAPTER FORTY

AROUND TOWN

What the hell can you do?

Your friend's been kidnapped. Through luck, through sheer force of will, you find her. That's the bull case.

More likely she's dead, beat up and abandoned in a Dumpster somewhere. But you can't think about the bear scenario.

"Don't go there," you say. Because uncertainty is all you've got.

That and a Maryknoll priest. Sometimes slick, sometimes twitchy, he gives you the heebie-fucking-jeebies. He's your lead negotiator, the only chance to get your friend back. But the priest, you come to find out, is in league with the devil himself.

Or is he?

You don't know. You're marking time, grinding your way through a personal purgatory, wondering, worrying, waiting for his call with news, any news. Reminding yourself this ball of string would not be unraveling if you had wired $65 million in the first place.

As if anticipation were not bad enough, your most powerful ally is an FBI agent with an agenda all her own. She's as likely to crucify you as she is the kidnappers. Again, you remind yourself, "Don't go there." You try to focus on your friend, getting her back. You put on a brave face. You tell yourself over and over, "I'll deal with the consequences later."

But the uncertainty that offers hope for your friend's release—that's the same uncertainty gnawing your guts. Tearing your insides up like barbed wire. You wonder whether you'll be walking the yard at Club Fed. Doing five to ten with skinheads and the other lowlifes from the wrong side of town.

"You want another drink?" asked Claire. For all the angst of the moment, I was struck by her skin. Beautiful. Ageless. Her complexion looked like it had been poured from a carton of milk.

"Please." I was three shots behind where they would do me any good.

We were sitting on Palmer's second-floor piazza. Every auto on the street looked like an unmarked car, but I didn't breath a word about my conversation with Agent Torres.

She was drinking scotch. I was sipping vodka, because I detest scotch and wine wouldn't do. My watch read five-thirty, and I assumed the FBI was just starting its work inside the Palmetto Foundation's offices.

It was the same spot where JoJo and I had sat the week following Palmer's death. This time, the cool slap from the harbor breezes brought no comfort. My cell phone was on the bistro table, a small slab of white marble between us, gray veins slivering their way through the stone.

Claire's phone was there, too. We were waiting for the call. Waiting for Father Ricardo to tell us he'd made contact. Wondering whether we had done the right thing, which was different for Claire than it was for me.

I hate waiting. I'm no good at it. I see people standing in line, and I start thinking Plan B. There was only one reason I could sit there and pound drinks with Claire. Torres had instructed me to keep her away from the Palmetto Foundation.

She snugged a gray cashmere sweater around her shoulders. "I feel like a jerk."

I knew what she meant. The depth of her anger. The rancor in her garden on Legare Street. At the time, I couldn't believe her acid tongue belonged to the same person I'd known in high school.

But families are funny things. We all have warts of one kind or another, and dysfunctional behavior comes with the territory. We say stupid things that piss each other off. And we stay pissed off. We stop talking and hold grudges long after everybody forgets what the hell was so stupid in the first place.

If anybody deserved a hall pass, it was Claire Kincaid. She was the one who'd agreed to wire $200 million to rescue her father's wife, six years older, a woman she didn't particularly like. She reminded me of that scene from *Chinatown:* "Stepmother, stepsister, stepmother." And so on.

"Don't beat yourself up," I told her.

"You must think I'm a bitch." Tears started running down her cheeks.

"We're all under a lot of pressure."

Claire's hand was on the table. I placed mine on top of hers, trying to punctuate my words with the casual touch that's so foreign to me. Her hand was as icy as the marble underneath, as though the stone's gray veins continued up into hers.

"You're cold." I rubbed her hand to goose the circulation.

"I never gave JoJo a chance."

"You don't—"

"When they got married," Claire continued, remorseful, "I pitched a fit. Demanded my dad get a prenup. Can you believe that?"

"No, actually."

Then she mimicked Palmer's voice. "'Don't need one, sweetheart. I got the poor man's version.'"

"What's that?"

"He never told me."

"Oh."

"Today would break his heart." Claire exhumed her hand, squeezed mine, and poured herself another scotch. "Both JoJo and what's happening to the Palmetto Foundation."

"We're not wiring one dime." Agent Torres had convinced me otherwise, sort of. One way or the other, I wasn't telling Claire about my meeting with the FBI agent.

Kneed-to-know basis.

"Yeah, yeah," Claire replied, remembering my intransigence from earlier that day. "Let's see what we learn from Father Ricardo tomorrow morning."

"I hope we hear something sooner." I considered my words for a moment and then clarified them. "Something good."

Almost on command, the phone rang. Claire reached for hers. But mine was the one ringing. I looked at the caller ID and answered. "Did you hear from Father Ricardo?"

"Who is it?" mouthed Claire.

"Biscuit."

She rolled her eyes.

"No, I doubt he'll call me," the big man replied.

"Are you heading back to Fayetteville?"

"Tomorrow. What are you doing for dinner?"

I looked across the table. "You want to join Claire and me?"

She shook her head no.

"Thanks," he said. "But I'm busy, and Claire may not be ready to hear what I think."

"About what?"

"The thing that's bugging me."

I turned away from Claire toward the harbor, the water gray in the fading light. "What is it?"

"Let me ask you something. What class was Palmer at Harvard?"

"What's that got to do with anything?"

"Just answer the question."

I did.

"Now will you explain why you want to know?"

"What are you doing at ten tonight?" he asked.

"Finishing dinner. Unless of course we hear from the reverend sooner."

"Meet me in the hotel lobby."

"Tell me now," I said.

"It's just a hunch. I'll know for sure by then."

"What if Father Ricardo makes contact?"

"That ain't happening," Biscuit said, no doubt in his voice.

"What makes you so sure?"

"You heard what Torres said. Don't be late."

Dial tone.

"Grove," said Claire. Suddenly, my attention returned to the second-floor porch. "We don't need him interfering. Not now."

"We need all the help we can get."

It was 8:30 P.M. For the last two hours, Torres had been directing the equipment people on her team. She surveyed the spacious conference room inside the Palmetto Foundation one last time.

Windows. They were more than windows. They were architectural trophies from another era: narrow, six feet high, arched near the top, spectacular both inside and out. Check.

Conference room table. The antique was a light wood, definitely not mahogany. The grains were black from age, winding this way and that, a home to untold insects through the centuries. Now the antique housed a different kind of bug. Check.

Finally, Torres eyed the walls: photos of JoJo and Palmer, a few of Claire; old maps of Charleston; and everywhere, pictures of the Palmetto Foundation's projects, like the wing at the South Carolina Aquarium. Von Maur, her go-to guy on the team, worked miracles with surveillance equipment. He had painted his favorite listening device, a single strand of electronic hair, right into the mocha brown walls. Check.

Torres decided the room was perfect. There was no way Ricardo would detect anything askew. Nor would anyone else. Except for the antiques, the conference room looked like any other place to talk business. No hint of all the circuitry inside the room.

There was only one item left to check.

Von Maur had a sixth sense about these things. He appeared just as Torres was about to dial him on her cell phone. "What about the roving bugs?"

"Done."

"Father Ricardo?"

"We got all the numbers from their contact sheet. Everybody's done, Ricardo, O'Rourke, Kincaid, and Hughes."

"Did you try JoJo Kincaid's phone?"

"Won't help." Von Maur rubbed his forehead with his right hand. He was always doing that. "We found the phone in her purse."

"Damn."

The two were discussing a surveillance technique. The FBI had downloaded spyware into all four cell phones—undetected—which enabled the agents to eavesdrop on their conversations. Years earlier, the same technology had been used to convict members of the Genovese crime family.

"Roving bugs" worked not only for telephone calls. The FBI could listen to conversations between Ricardo and the kidnappers, wherever they might be. The sound of a human voice would activate the cell phone's microphone and initiate a call to the FBI. The only way to exterminate the listening devices was to yank out the cell phone batteries.

"Don't worry," Von Maur advised. "I don't care if Father Ricardo's in the confessional. We'll hear everything."

"Frankly, that's the one place I hope we find him."

Bong checked his Rolex. It was 8:45 P.M. He blinked once, twice, and turned onto the Cooper River Bridge heading into Charleston. He had a long night ahead of him. Timing was everything. And right now, he smelled trouble.

O'Rourke was bad news, a real SOB. Bong had known him all of one week. Already, he wanted to grind the guy's face into pulp. Maybe there'd be time for that later, after things played out.

"Anak ng puta," he cursed to himself. Tagalog expletives, "son of a bitch" in this case, were so much more satisfying than their English translations.

There was no telling what O'Rourke had done, whom he had involved. That mountain-sized lawyer was a case in point. Bong knew Highly Intimate Pleasures was gone. All the hard work, all the thought that had gone into the store—it was the perfect Laundromat for money. The bar, the billboards, the capital, they were all fucking gone. The Feds would seize his store and shut it down. All that investment down the drain.

"What kind of name is Biscuit anyway?" he muttered.

In the meeting today, Bong caught the lawyer studying him. The big man said little. But every time Bong looked in his direction, Biscuit was staring at him. Checking him out. It was more than creepy. It was like the attorney sensed something. Maybe he figured things out.

Bong scratched his head. He ran his thumb and forefinger across his clerical collar. He told himself to stop it. He was always touching the damn collar, and it was turning into a nervous tic. Good thing he had purchased two. His one-way sparring session with JoJo that afternoon had left the other one a mess.

Soon, he'd wire $33.5 million to Moreno. That transfer would square things up with the snake. Bong would pay himself the agreed-upon $6.5 million fee and keep the remaining $160 million balance all to himself. He wasn't splitting that money with anybody. He didn't care what promises he'd made.

Details. Details. Everything is about details. And fear is always the greatest before the big score.

Bong eyed the blue canvas bag on his passenger seat. His eyes gleamed, and his lips curled into a cruel smile. Payback would be oh so satisfying, hell for O'Rourke. He retrieved the phone from inside his black jacket, checking the rearview mirror as he pulled it out.

Nobody there.

With his left hand, he powered down the passenger window. And then with his right, he backhanded his mobile out the window. It was a monstrous fling. The phone, $19.95 from Walmart, sailed through the cables and over the edge of the bridge. Down, down, down it tumbled, some two hundred feet to the shrimp and blue crabs waiting in the Cooper River below.

CHAPTER FORTY-ONE
SAVING JOJO

No word from Father Ricardo.

Around 9:15 P.M. I left Claire's home on South Battery, hustled through the shadows of Meeting Street, and phoned Annie. She was aghast by my news about JoJo. "What have you gotten yourself into?"

I could hear the fear in her voice. "Don't worry. The FBI is here."

"They're helping you now?"

"They have their own agenda. I just want JoJo back."

"You're not some kind of bait, are you? You won't do anything stupid?"

I'd do anything for Palmer, even if it meant risking my life to save his wife. Now was not the time to argue, though. "No way."

"Promise?"

"Do me a favor. Get some friends to spend the night."

"What for?"

Then I said to Annie what had been twisting through my mind ever since the first shot of vodka that night. "I'd feel better knowing you're not alone."

"You think I'm in danger?"

"No. But just invite some friends over."

"You're scaring me, Grove."

"I know. Sorry."

"You never answered my question," she persisted. "You won't do any-thing stupid?"

My BlackBerry picked that moment to run out of juice. And I'm not sure Annie heard me say, "I promise."

It was nine-thirty when I returned to the hotel at Charleston Place. Biscuit was nowhere in sight, which was no surprise. We weren't meeting until 10:00, and I assumed he was still doing whatever had prevented him from joining Claire and me for dinner.

A bunch of drunken Shriners boarded the elevator with me. At my floor I raced to the room, stripping off my tie en route. I didn't bother with lights. Afterward, relieved, I washed my hands and brushed away the cardboard taste of delivery pizza from my mouth. And when I emerged from the bath-room, finally flipping on the overhead lights, five words shattered the silence:

"I've been waiting for you."

I almost leaped out of my skin. Father Ricardo was sitting in the room's occasional chair, framed by a blaze of upholstery that was a little too Mar-quis de Sade for my taste. He wore his black shirt and white clerical collar, no jacket this time. His eyes, ringed by anxious dark circles, resembled skull sockets in the gloomy light.

Talk about startled. My heart rate soared from 60 to 150 in three beats. Shivers shot from my legs to my face. And it felt like a million ants were marching up my spine.

"You scared the shit out of me."

"And you interrupted a perfectly good nap, my friend." He spoke in a calm voice.

I went ballistic. "How'd you get into my room?"

"It wasn't hard."

"What do you mean?"

"The lord works in mysterious ways."

"Cut the crap." I was gathering my wits, remembering what Agent Torres had said: Moreno, money laundering, FBI suspicions but nothing concrete.

"That's no way to speak to a priest."

Given what Torres had said earlier, I wasn't sure he was a man of the cloth. So I turned sarcastic. "Fine. Bless me, Father, for I have sinned. How the hell did you get into my room?"

"Saint Benjamin."

It took me a second to process his meaning. "You slipped somebody a hundred?"

"I heard from the kidnappers."

"Your guy spoke to them?"

"I did."

In that second, I forgot my annoyance. I forgot the warnings from Torres. She had been wrong. So had Biscuit for that matter. I forgot Annie's exhortation: "You won't do anything stupid."

I think it was subconscious on my part. But the news, good or otherwise, made me drop my guard. "Is JoJo okay?"

"We're going to get her."

"She's okay?"

"I told you once. I told you before. Nobody pays if these guys develop a reputation for killing hostages."

I ignored Father Ricardo's testiness. "Did you talk to JoJo?"

"She sounds awful."

"But she's okay, right?"

"For now."

"Where is she?"

"I don't know."

"What do you mean? I thought you said, 'We're going to get her.' "

Ricardo was a human boomerang. Every time I asked him something, he returned a bigger question. He tugged at his shirt collar. He rolled his head in a big circle, as though chafing from what he was about to say. "I need you to answer one thing."

"For sure. Just tell me."

"Do you want JoJo back?"

"Stop horsing around. You know I do."

"Are you willing to pay?"

"Once she's safe—whatever they want." I ignored what Torres had outlined. The FBI agent no longer mattered. My instincts were taking over.

"And trade yourself for her?"

"Yes."

"Good. I told them you'd pay. Otherwise she'd be dead."

"We're crazy not to call the police."

"Shut up." His words shook me. "Do you want JoJo back, yes or no?"

"Yes, of course." I nodded my head.

"Then we do things my way. Got it?"

I nodded yes again, even though my instincts were screaming, "No!"

"Where's your phone?"

"Why do you need it?"

"To save you from yourself." He stretched out his hand, palm facing up.

I passed him my BlackBerry. Father Ricardo split it open, yanked out the battery, and disappeared into my bathroom. The gurgle of a flushing toilet filled the room. He returned, minus one battery, and tossed the phone carcass onto my bed.

"Was that necessary?"

"You tell me, O'Rourke. Every time I turn around you're changing the rules of the game. First it was the Catholic Fund's sixty-five million. Now it's the authorities."

"What are you talking about?"

"You spoke with them this afternoon."

"How'd you know?"

Father Ricardo's face clouded over. His features grew dark. For a moment, it seemed like he might answer, "I didn't." He paused, and the silence lasted to the point of discomfort for both of us. He was bubbling up inside, letting his fury build. "You think these guys are stupid?"

"No."

"You think they care about anything other than money?"

"I don't know."

"You're kind of slow," he growled. "What was that refrain in the letter again?"

" 'The woman dies.' "

"But you don't believe them. Is that your problem?"

"I get it."

"Apparently, you don't." He was growing angrier by the moment.

"I just want JoJo back in one piece."

"Then do as I say," he ordered, yet again.

"Okay, okay. But I need to call Biscuit. We're meeting at ten."

"Not anymore."

"Just to cancel?"

"We don't have time."

"I need to tell Claire."

Father Ricardo had been walking to the door. He stopped in his tracks and whirled round. "Who's running the show, you or me?"

"You. But why can't we tell her?"

He never answered the question. Instead, the reverend gestured to the door with a sweeping wave of his arm. "Let's go."

"But I thought you didn't know where JoJo is."

"I don't."

"Then where are we heading, for chrissakes?"

"Watch your mouth."

"Sorry."

"The airport," he explained. "That's all I know."

Five minutes later, Father Ricardo got behind the wheel of his car. I hopped in the passenger side. There was a blue canvas bag on the backseat. After five minutes of driving, not one word between us, I noticed his directions were all wrong. "This isn't the way."

"Relax. I know what I'm doing."

"North Charleston's the other way." I felt naked and defenseless without my cell phone.

"Wrong airport. We're flying private out of Johns Island." He cranked the radio, apparently annoyed by my questions.

Make no mistake. The destination scared me. Johns Island is a hard thirty minutes from downtown Charleston, a remote place where Spanish moss is the only excitement for miles around. It's home to tomato farms and the 1,400-year-old Angel Oak, not to mention the tidal marshlands filled with alligators and crabs, and other bottom scavengers that eat everything but bones. The authorities might not find your remains for days, maybe even years.

"We have a long night ahead of us," he finally said.

"What do you mean?"

"JoJo's captors are running us from one place to the next."

"How do you know?"

"My guy, the mercenary," he started.

"What about him?"

"He said this is how they do it."

"You must have some idea where we'll end up, Father."

"Bermuda. Moscow. Taiwan for all I know."

"Not tonight?" My words were half question, half objection.

"Are you backing out?"

"I don't have my passport."

That's when Father Ricardo began to laugh. It was the strangest thing. He chuckled at first. But his mirth gained momentum and built into a big, roaring belly laugh. The kind that brings tears to your eyes. He almost ran a red light. I was ready to grab the wheel.

"What's so funny?"

"You don't have a clue?" He rubbed the tears from his eyes.

"Guess not." What was I to say?

"We're going off the grid."

"Meaning what?"

"We're about to disappear."

"Hey, it's Grove. This phone is surgically attached to my hip."

Click. Dial tone.

Biscuit finished the greeting. "So leave a message, and I'll call you right back."

The big man was sitting in the hotel lobby. He had left his first message at 10:15 P.M., the second at 10:30. Now it was 10:45, and he knew O'Rourke's voice mail by heart. The stockbroker's absence was troubling. Grove was not the kind of guy to be late or, even worse, to blow somebody off.

Biscuit dialed Claire. "Sorry to call so late."

Half asleep, half surprised, she took a moment to identify his voice. "Did you hear something?"

"No, nothing like that. Is Grove there?"

Claire said nothing for a moment. She was processing the lawyer's words. And Biscuit, suffering through the silence, began to regret what he'd said.

You don't phone a single woman, late into the night, and ask whether some guy's with her. Not in the South.

"I thought you were meeting for drinks." Her tone turned cold, miffed from being woken up.

"He's not here. Sorry to bother you."

Biscuit called Agent Torres next. She answered without Claire's cobwebs. She was awake, all business, her wits sharp. "What's up?"

"Have you spoken with Grove?"

"No. Is there a problem?"

"I'm not sure. We were supposed to meet at ten."

"He's not there?"

"I've tried him three times on his cell phone."

Torres put down her book, dog-earing the page where she left off. The agent didn't know what to think. Fieldwork was always the same—lots of waiting for nothing to happen. Waiting in vans, loaded to the gunwales with surveillance equipment. Waiting for a phone call, not just any call, but one that would betray an adversary's location. Waiting in cheap hotel rooms, like the "Bedbug Express" she was in now. Torres missed her kids and husband.

"Might be nothing," she said.

"Or a real train wreck."

Something about Biscuit's voice, the tone, the tension, made her hesitate. "Did something happen?"

"No. But how much do you know about the Kincaids?"

CHAPTER FORTY-TWO
AIRBORNE

First things first.

Flying is not my thing. I have zero interest in getting a pilot's license, which is odd because my father flew bombers. I do, however, know a little something about planes. You can't help it growing up on an Air Force base. Or when you're a stockbroker and your clients own seven-figure toys.

The Piaggio P180 Avanti is a twin-engine turbo prop. Some call it the "Ferrari of the sky" because the plane is fast, damn fast. It cruises close to 400 mph. And the Ferrari family, in fact, controls the manufacturer. They bought the company back in 1998 with a consortium of other shareholders.

The aircraft is sleek, the styling Italian if somewhat unusual. It has a canard wing, the two horizontal fins mounted just behind the nose. Its engine props face backward, which makes the P180 Avanti a statement. You can't miss it on the runways. It's the last aircraft on earth I would choose for a vanishing act.

But for all intents and purposes, I had disappeared on one.

We boarded a Piaggio P180 Avanti back on Johns Islands and climbed who knows how many feet. Father Ricardo was no ordinary priest in my opinion, if even a priest at all. You don't charter a $5-million-plus plane on a Maryknoll salary. No wonder Torres suspected him of money laundering.

He had sacked out on the plush cream-colored chair facing my direction. His black shirtsleeves were rolled neatly over his wrists, a few inches shy of the elbow. The cabin lights were dimmed, but I could still make out half a tattoo on his forearm. It looked like some kind of spider-sun, disappearing inside his sleeve.

What the hell is that?

His eyes were closed. He was indifferent to the rich smell of leather wafting through the air. The sights out the window, a blue-black night where all the stars had gone into hiding, held no special interest for him. Nor did the bar, stocked with top-shelf scotch, bourbon, and vodka.

Me—I was wired. And it was not the kind of wired where you touch the wooden paneling or ask the pilot about all the gauges in the cockpit. Father Ricardo wasn't telling me everything. I wanted to grill him, find out where we were going.

I reached over to nudge his shoulder. Nothing more than a friendly jostle to wake him up. In that moment, even before I touched him, he exploded into a rolling ball of martial arts. Caught me off guard. Snatched my fingers. Bent them back. Ninety degrees, 110, 125, and still going. Shards of pain stabbed up my right arm. I flipped onto the cabin floor like a rag doll, his choice, not mine. The move saved my wrist from splintering.

But didn't stop the pain.

Ricardo rolled on top of me. His iron knee crushed my chest. His left hand choked my throat. He reared back and readied the right like an open skillet, poising to mash nose and nostrils into the gray of my brain.

I couldn't breathe. But I could smell the violence. Sweat and adrenaline oozed from his pores. Perspiration and fury curdled with his talcum, and I wanted to wretch.

"What are you doing?" His tan face turned crimson with rage, the sides of his mouth damp with spittle.

"Trying to wake you up." I croaked the words in a faint rasp. I could feel my mind shoving off.

"Oh."

Ricardo released his bulldog grip. He backed off my chest. I started to wheeze, gulping oxygen into my lungs, hacking it out at the same time. The act of breathing felt like somebody was rubbing sandpaper inside my throat. Back and forth. Dry and rough. And once my lungs were settled, I watched the stars lift as my consciousness returned.

"Sorry, Grove."

"What the hell was that?"

I rolled onto my side, pushing his knee away, feeling the heat rush to my face in a wave of embarrassment. That's what happens when you get your ass kicked. I hadn't managed any defensive maneuvers. Not one fucking swipe of his hand. Not even a raised elbow for chrissakes. I was down and dying before I knew what was happening. And the words from my kickboxing coach came roaring back:

"You got no street in you."

Ricardo tried to help me back into my seat. I pushed him away. "What kind of priest charters a private plane?"

"Not me."

"You learn those moves in the seminary?" I rubbed my throat.

"No. But they keep me safe in Manila."

Ricardo's eyes twinkled. He had kicked my ass, and now he was savoring the thrill of victory. The momentary smirk was subtle, easy to miss. The smug look washed from his face before most people would notice. But I saw the half smile, the dancing eyes. He had dropped me like a washed-up lightweight, and I wanted another shot at the title.

"Is the Catholic Fund paying for this plane?" I asked.

"No."

"Then who?"

"I told you."

"Told me what?" Damn, he infuriated me. "Would you finish a thought for once in your life?"

"They're running us around."

"On a private plane?"

"Did you go through security?"

"No," I admitted.

"Did anyone ask to see your identification?"

"No."

"Do you think there's any record of us on this flight?"

"No."

"You're finally catching on." Ricardo smiled, the right side turning up more than the left.

"Then where are we going?"

"Fort Lauderdale."

"How do you know?"

"The pilot told me."

"Is he one of them?"

"I keep telling you: I'm a priest, not a cop."

And I'm Mother Teresa.

"What happens once we get there?"

"Planes, trains, automobiles." He rolled down his sleeves, hiding the tattoo. "I have no idea."

I sat back in the gloom of the cabin and didn't say another word. I just watched and waited and paid attention. There was no way Ricardo would get the drop on me again. I visualized a jab to the nose, a roundhouse kick to the chest, an uppercut to the gut that would drive the air from his lungs.

This wasn't over.

CHAPTER FORTY-THREE

Shortly after midnight we landed at Opa-locka, the private airport about ten miles north of downtown Miami. While exiting the plane, Ricardo grabbed a canvas bag. There were no logos on the sack. It was just blue and bland. I wondered, for all of two seconds, if his passport was inside.

Florida feels hot even when it isn't. And outside the balmy night slapped us, a stark sauna against cool cabin air. Ricardo tugged off his white clerical collar and shoved it into the bag. My thoughts turned dark as I remembered that travel documents were the least of my problems.

The worst form of verbal abuse takes place inside our heads. I flogged myself for joining Ricardo. For thinking a posse of two, him leading the charge, could possibly save JoJo Kincaid. Agent Torres had voiced the FBI's suspicions. And Annie had expressed a different concern: "You won't do something stupid?" After Ricardo kicked my ass on the plane, I knew the good reverend was no Maryknoll priest after all. He was in league with the people who'd amputated JoJo's pinkie, with some guy from South America named Moreno.

What the hell was I thinking?

Regret and anger about bad decisions are the wrong mind-set for a rescue mission. But that photo of JoJo, the one we saw in the conference room, kept me going. It was her bandaged hand and duct-taped face. It was the horror that stained her eyes. I wanted JoJo back in one piece and forced myself to forget what might happen to me.

Ricardo hustled to a parking lot outside the terminal, forcing me to keep pace. An unremarkable Lincoln Town Car was waiting for us, one of those black boxes that nobody buys except morticians and limo drivers. The driver said nothing to me. But every so often, he glanced in the rearview mirror and yammered to Ricardo in Spanish.

My sense of direction is the pits. But I have clients in Florida and know my way around. When we turned south on I-95, I spoke out. "Wrong way to Fort Lauderdale."

"Forget it." Ricardo stared out the window. He never bothered to face me. And I stared at the back of his head, hair so black it looked blue.

I thought about confronting him. "Where's JoJo?"

Instead, I pressed around the edges and avoided a direct confrontation. It was better that way. For as much as I distrusted Ricardo, I believed he could take me to Palmer's wife. "Is JoJo in Miami?"

"No."

"Can you tell me where she is?"

"Give it a rest," he snapped. "We have a long night ahead of us."

"I don't see why not."

Ricardo whirled around. For a second, I thought he might throw a punch. Right then and there in the back of the Town Car. His piercing eyes glowed in the ambient light of Miami. His mouth twisted into a bloodless grin, the kind you see on a piranha. But he said nothing and turned away. I said nothing, and we all continued in silence.

We crossed over the Rickenbacker Causeway. Inside Virginia Key, our driver turned left at the Miami Seaquarium and cut right onto a dusty old road circling a monstrous sewage treatment plant. About a quarter of the way around, the Town Car stopped and Ricardo said, "Get out."

If there was ever a time when my fear got the best of me, that was it. No lights. No cars. It was dark, deep into the night, and there was nobody around. Not a soul in sight. There was a sewage plant on one side of the road, trees and scrub on the other. We were in the boonies, a great place to pop somebody. And nobody would be any the wiser.

Ricardo pushed through the bush, a damp tangle of cypress and live oak, cabbage palm and wild coffee. The ground was soft underfoot, the mud a Gucci-eating quicksand. There were black spiders everywhere, waiting and watching from their silky lace. And I'll be the first to admit: the hair, the legs, all eight of them, and the ominous colors—I hate those fucking things.

The air was all mosquitoes and malaria, thick with bullfrog a cappella and the roar of incoming tide. Virginia Key is home to sea turtles and manatees. But every rustle from the underbrush, the flap of wings, the occasional swish of sea grass, and I thought an alligator was charging us. Or a venomous snake was slithering before the inevitable strike.

We pushed through an overhang of mangrove, water coming up to our ankles, and found a rickety old dock that started three feet too late. There was a large boat at the end, forty feet at least, two people on board.

Ricardo hopped up on the rotting planks. "We're here."

"Is JoJo on board?"

"No."

"Where is she?" I stepped out of the water, grateful to see my feet.

"We're going to her now."

"How long before we get there?"

Ricardo ignored my question. "Do yourself a favor, and stay away from the captain."

"Who's the woman?" I asked.

"Girl Louie, the first mate." Ricardo took two steps toward the boat, but stopped and turned around. He waited for my undivided attention. "You really want JoJo back in one piece?"

"I'll do whatever it takes."

"Keep your mouth shut, and everything will work out fine." In that moment, he gave up pretending to be a priest. And I gave up pretending to believe him.

Girl Louie checked her lines on the boat. Hearing a disturbance in the water, a sound unlike any night calls in the Florida Keys, she looked in our direction and gaped at Ricardo.

She stood frozen for a second, two at the most.

Then in a blinding burst of comprehension, she hurdled the boat gunwales and dashed toward him across the weathered planks. Three feet away, she touched off the dock and sailed through the night.

Ricardo caught her midflight, staggered back to the right, and spun around from her momentum. Girl Louie morphed into a human octopus, wrapping her athletic legs around his torso, limbs everywhere, probing his face, his ears, his jet-black hair with her long, practiced fingers.

The two kissed, hard and hungry, none of those cheek-cheek pecks favored by androgynous strains from New York country clubs. The two locked lips and lingered, savoring their carnal past.

"Long time, Bong."

"Too long."

By and by, Girl Louie relaxed her thighs and slid to the creaky old dock. She was fit, trim, chesty, built like a stripper with sea legs. I guessed her to be five foot four, 110 pounds. She wore bikini bottoms and a faded pink T-shirt a few sizes too small. There was a black heart outlining its caption: YOU HAD ME AT BACON.

Yikes.

The scene was weird, discomfiting. Ricardo was dressed in reverend black, halfway to third base with Girl Louie, and answering to the name "Bong." He was definitely no priest. But only a few hours ago, I had been addressing him as "Father." And I found it hard to kick the habit, to stop viewing him as a man of the cloth.

"Who's your friend?" asked Girl Louie.

"My banker." Ricardo aimed 12-gauge eyes in my direction, warning me to stick with his story. His expression made me wonder if there was dissension among the goons.

"Let's go," the captain bellowed.

Girl Louie scrambled across the deck like a spider monkey, gathering up ropes, stowing gear, checking, checking, checking. Ricardo climbed a ladder to the control tower, where he joined the skipper, who had one hand on the wheel and the other on the throttle. The roar of engines drowned the seaside cicadas, which sound like pulsating sprinklers that sweep great jets of water across suburban lawns.

We were under way.

"You want some beers up there?" Girl Louie hollered at the two men up top.

"Yeah," the captain replied.

"How about you?" Girl Louie smiled at me, and I saw her face for the first time. She would have been pretty from thirty feet. Knockout figure, big teeth, and sun-colored hair. But from five feet, she was hard around the edges. The crow's-feet and vertical splits over her lip, all the calling cards from the sun and the booze and the life among men at sea, were gaining momentum.

"No thanks."

We motored out of the cove, pointing in the direction of Fisher Island. Our boat, the *Blue Pearl,* rounded the bend. And that's when the captain gunned the engines, a cone-shaped wake trailing behind, city lights fading into the distance. He remained at the helm, scrutinizing the chop over the bow, occasionally turning to the port or starboard side. He searched, ever vigilant, for floating debris.

Or the authorities.

Fifteen minutes outside the cove, the engines roaring full bore, Girl Louie stood across from me. The night was calm, the sea peaceful. But the boat still thumped across the swells. She was steady on her feet, at ease with the boat's motion. Me—I settled clumsily onto the boat's fighting chair.

"Not what you expected, right?" She suppressed a smile.

"Especially for an old boat."

"Seventy-one Hatteras Convertible refitted with two nine-hundred MAN common rail diesels." The first mate glowed from her words, almost to the point of reverence.

The details meant nothing to me. But I let Girl Louie talk, hoping conversation would prime the pump. That she would disclose where we were going. That I would get the skinny on her connection to Ricardo, Bong, whoever he was.

"What's a nine hundred MAN?"

"A marinized Mercedes engine. We're cruising thirty-four knots, but we can hit forty."

"Sweet." I pretended to be impressed, like I could give a shit about marinized anything.

"The original configuration only did eighteen."

I was about to ask, "Why all the speed?"

"Hold this," she said, cutting me off and handing me her Corona. "Coast Guard, starboard bow."

"Got 'em." The captain's reply came back slow and steady. But an undercurrent of tension gripped the boat.

Girl Louie scurried into the cabin and returned with four stout fishing poles. There was a massive brass reel on each, the Shimano brand etched on every one. She planted the poles in stainless-steel holders and disappeared into the cabin again.

When she reappeared, she was holding a white bucket. It smelled like fish.

"What's that?" I asked.

"Squid."

"What for?"

"Swordfishing."

"Okay." I spoke with "huh" intonation.

She gestured toward the Corona. "Slug some down. I want you stinking like a six-pack if they board."

Ricardo checked me from above. The captain throttled down the MAN engines. Girl Louie pulled off her faded T-shirt to reveal an unsettling bikini, half rubber band and half dare. Nothing hard around the edges about how she looked from five feet now.

"Smile and wave." She threw her hands over her head and cocked her hip, provocative, inviting. But nobody on our boat was thinking sex. This was Hollywood. We were putting on a show. I noticed that Ricardo had rolled up his pant legs and taken off his shoes.

Slowly, the Coast Guard passed off to our left. A beam of light raked across the gentle night swells and onto our boat. Girl Louie waved, beer in one hand, shoulders thrown back, posture chirpy and erect. The Coast Guard's crew, all guys, snapped back two-finger salutes—more lecherous than reverent. And I could feel the tension ease from our deck like air hissing from a balloon.

"Works every time." Girl Louie punctuated her words with a swish of the hips. She disappeared into the cabin again, before returning with a fresh Corona. Though the air was warm, even for an October night off the Florida coast, she pulled her T-shirt back on.

The captain, no longer concerned about the wake, gunned the MAN engines. We were flying at thirty-four knots. Miami's lights vanished behind us, the loom along with them. And after a while, the black sky morphed into the black ocean.

It became impossible to distinguish between air and water, and our world turned into an illusion. Except for the thump of the bow against swells, we were hurtling through space, traveling into infinity. I could almost reach out and touch the stars, our mission to find JoJo the one thing keeping me alert.

"What kind of banker are you?" Girl Louie was now onto her third beer, while the guys up top were still working on number two. The engines droned on and on.

"I'm more of a money manager." My reply seemed innocuous enough.

"That explains it."

"Explains what?"

"Why Bong brought you along."

I glanced at Ricardo in the control tower. He was swigging his Corona, surveying the horizon, and chatting with the captain. "What do you mean?"

"He used to be a banker."

"Oh, right." I pretended to know, but her revelation surprised me.

"Bong never actually managed money. That's probably why he needs you."

"What did he do?"

Girl Louie eyed me warily. "You don't know?"

"He plays it close to the vest."

"Amen to that. He worked in operations for a branch bank in Manila."

Agent Torres, I realized, was right. Ricardo possessed the perfect ré-sumé for laundering money—a procedural background that included open-ing bank accounts and reviewing suspicious activity reports. He had also enjoyed access, as an employee, to sensitive personal information like where wealthy clients were wiring their money. "You know which bank?"

"I don't remember."

"Not important." I backed off.

"But he was pissed."

"About what?"

"Bong discovered that his bank was moving pesos overseas. You know why that's a problem?"

"What makes you think it's a problem?"

"He told me his boss passed him over for a promotion and shipped him off to another department."

"Beats the shit out of me."

Actually, I had a good idea what had happened. Through the years, the Philippines limited foreign-exchange transactions. The government, espe-cially during the Marcos era and the years immediately following, made it difficult for wealthy Filipino families to invest abroad. American dollars and overseas currencies were thought to be safe, at least for those living in that politically fragile land. And techniques, all of them illegal, surfaced for getting money out of the country. Ricardo had probably discovered his bank's participation in the lucrative black market.

"You sure you don't want a beer," she offered.

"No thanks. You make this trip much?"

"All the time."

"What about Ricardo?"

"Who?" she asked.

"I mean Bong."

"Why did you call him 'Ricardo'?"

"Long story."

I kept telling myself, *Less is more.*

"This is Bong's run." Girl Louie wiped her mouth with the back of her hand.

"'Bong's run'?" Repeating phrases is an old trick known to brokers worldwide. I was treating Girl Louie like a prospect, trying to extract information, anything that might help later.

"He needs an escape hatch in his line of work."

"'Escape hatch'?"

"The same reason I drink beer. You want one?"

"No thanks."

Girl Louie grabbed number four, and I decided the coast was clear. "Where are we going anyway?"

"You don't know?"

"I'm along for the ride."

"You ask a lot of questions," she said.

"Trying to pass the time. We've been out here over an hour."

"Great Harbour Cay's worth the wait."

Bingo.

"I've never been."

"The town's a little too Dodge City for my taste." Girl Louie took a big gulp from her longneck. "But the harbor will take your breath away."

"Why's that?"

"The color for one. Gin blue. There's nothing like it."

"Bong come here much?"

"You ask too many questions." She eyed me, grabbed two beers, and ran them up the ladder to Ricardo and the captain. This time, she stayed in the tower.

Uh-oh.

I spent the next hour by myself, propped up in the fighting chair, listening to the drone of the engine, fighting to stay awake. Over and over I played back my conversation with Girl Louie, assessing whether any of my comments would create a problem with Ricardo later. And if I told myself Great Harbour was our final destination—the other side of his escape hatch—I was mistaken.

CHAPTER FORTY-FOUR

INSIDE RICARDO'S ESCAPE HATCH

"There's an FBI agent riding my ass."

In the black of that Wednesday morning, under the stars and surrounded by the sea, I remembered my comment inside the Palmetto Foundation's conference room. I blew it yesterday morning. I tipped off Ricardo. Not on purpose. But it was my fault all the same. And now I was watching the action from my deck chair on the *Titanic*.

No wonder he nabbed me.

The way Ricardo saw it, the authorities were turning up the heat on his operation. He fled the country because arrest and twenty years in prison were his alternatives to a quick getaway. I may have feared the consequences of tax fraud and Patriot Act violations. But his penalties would surely dwarf mine.

As the first hints of dawn cracked through the blackness of night, I bobbed in and out of consciousness, my drowsy thoughts always circling back to JoJo. Call it a hunch or innate stockbroker skepticism. I doubted we would find her in the Caribbean. The abduction—goons spiriting her out of the country while avoiding detection—struck me as too complicated.

But it was possible. JoJo had been gone almost forty hours.

Sometime after four A.M., that's my best guess, I drifted into a fitful sleep. It could have been ten minutes. It could have been forty-five. I have no idea how long I was out.

When the engines throttled down, I snapped awake to Girl Louie and the captain barking information back and forth. The seconds ticked like hours as my eyes focused. The deep space, I slowly realized, was behind us. We were passing through a cut in limestone and coral rock, maybe thirty-five feet wide. The bluffs on either side soared twenty feet high.

Our boat measured sixteen feet wide, meaning there was nine and a half feet of clearance on either side. Not much leeway, despite how it sounds. I could hear our wake slapping craggy walls. I could smell the low tide, the salty whiff of barnacles and decayed shellfish. I had no idea whether the water's depth reduced our margin of error, whether we would scrape the crusty walls or run aground. But the captain and Girl Louie were tense. That much I knew. Here in the dark, they treated our passage like we were threading a needle. The jagged rocks would open nasty gashes in our hull.

Up top, the captain scrutinized his navigation equipment. The scopes glowed red and green, their eerie luminescence piercing the claustrophobic gloom. And just for a moment, I thought he resembled a Wall Street trader checking his screens.

Every so often the captain called below, as though uncomfortable with the sonar, "How we looking?"

"Steady off the bow," came Girl Louie's reply.

Back and forth they pinged. Their consistent rhythm reminded me of Marco Polo, the kids' swimming game. And when we finally passed through the tight quarters, I heard a collective sigh of relief.

"This is why I pay you the big bucks," Bong whispered, his voice raspy from beers and lack of sleep.

He probably assumed I couldn't hear. But I heard all right, and his words were troubling. "They" was the right pronoun. He should have said, "This is why they pay you the big bucks."

He didn't.

He said "I."

"Get ready," barked Girl Louie, interrupting my thoughts about our joyride into hell. "You too, Bong." Whereupon, shoes in hand, Ricardo wedged the ladder between his stocking feet and slid down the rails like an old sea dog.

Girl Louie scrambled to the front of the *Blue Pearl*. She swung the davit, a sea crane holding an eleven-foot Boston Whaler, over the bow rail. The electronic winch whined as she lowered the Whaler into the ocean and kicked a rope ladder overboard. "Let's roll."

The three of us boarded the boat, and she gunned the small outboard. In the distance, I could make out a seaplane rocking with the swells. We approached from the port side, four hundred yards, then three hundred, then two hundred. The plane's small door flipped open, and Ricardo growled at me.

"Get in."

Our plane had been a Grumman Goose once. Now the wings and fuselage looked like a Rorschach test of rust, rivets, and third-rate repairs. Only a whisper of the paint job remained. Every square inch of metal had been dinged or scratched or hammered or shot at or duct-taped or scraped against something. I had serious doubts whether this bird could get airborne.

The cabin was a joke. There were two columns, one consisting of three chairs on the left, the other two chairs on the right. A hole gaped through the floor and out the skin where the third had once been. The ocean water, still black from the night, glinted every so often as swells caught the Goose's landing lights. The sea smacked against our pontoons. And I could feel the updraft of fresh air from outside.

The haphazard ventilation, however, offered no reprieve. An unholy odor wafted through the cabin, the air rank yet sweet, a chemical mix of engine oil and corrosion. I detected vapors from battery acid and vomit crusting somewhere. The remnants of nausea were hardly a surprise. This aircraft would reduce even the most intrepid fliers into jittery white-knucklers.

Our captain—mid-fifties, all muscle, no fat—wore his hair long and left it greasy. His beard was shaggy, his skin as beaten and weathered as our rust-riddled plane. In his tie-dyed T-shirt, he looked like a throwback to the sixties, an LSD flashback around every bend.

I thought Ricardo might join me in the cabin. Instead, he tossed his blue canvas bag onto the copilot's seat and disappeared into the cockpit. For a while, I strained to hear what the two men were whispering. But they kept their voices low, leaving me to wonder.

It was after 5:15 A.M. when the captain sparked the engines, first the starboard, then the port. There was no door separating the cockpit from my hell in the back, and I could hear him yell, "Clear," before we gathered speed.

The plane bounced along the water, thumping against gentle swells. And suddenly, mercifully, we were airborne, barreling through the night and leaving Great Harbour Cay like thieves forgetting a jewel. To this day, I can't believe we ever made it off the water.

Ricardo strode back into the cabin twenty minutes after we hit cruising altitude. He was drinking from a jug of bottled water and handed one to me. "Drink this. It'll clear your head."

"Thanks." I wrestled off the lid, thinking it unreasonably tight. I was eager to slake my thirst and chase the cabin's fumes.

"Get some sleep. We have a three-, maybe four-hour flight."

"Do you know where we're headed?"

"Only the flight time. And tomorrow's a big day."

"More travel?"

"Who knows?" He smiled, his eyes wide and alight with unknown meaning. But the disturbing expression disappeared when our plane thudded into a pocket of air turbulence.

"Shit." I grabbed the rails of my chair while checking the hole in the floor. A body could be wedged through the opening.

"Jumpy?" Ricardo shook his head in a tsk-tsk manner.

The chop stopped, and I said nothing.

"Jake knows what he's doing."

"Who's Jake?" I asked.

"Our pilot."

"It's not Jake I'm worried about. It's this Cooked Goose we're flying." I pointed toward the hole in the floor for emphasis.

"That's nothing. He's flown worse for the Company."

"Who?"

The plane shuddered, more turbulence. Ricardo steadied himself, bracing against the cabin ceiling with the butt of his hand. He had discarded his clerical collar, not to mention the constant references to Maryknoll. "CIA."

"Oh, right. Are they involved?"

"Jake left the Agency years ago."

I was in no mood to fool around. "Is JoJo okay?"

"I hope so." Ricardo turned around and headed back to the cockpit.

Which was fine with me. I was sick of him and all the enigma crap. I was sick of planes, boats, and limos, the running around and chasing after JoJo. I had no idea where Ricardo was taking us, or how I would get Palmer's wife back without my passport.

My eyelids felt like anchors. My head begin to pound. At the time, I blamed the cabin fumes and lack of sleep for the way I felt. Unable to concentrate. Coordination falling slack. It was all I could do to keep from dropping my jug of water. Something was wrong. Way wrong. And that's the thing. Nobody's ever slipped me nitrobenzodiazepine before.

You may know it as a "roofie."

I blinked awake.

The Grumman's salt-pitted windows turned sunlight into confetti throughout the cabin. My vision was blurry, my mind groggy. The world was taking its damn sweet time coming into focus. We had stopped. The propellers whirred much slower now. And the plane was rocking to the gentle surf underneath. Somewhere in the distance a lone seagull squawked, its caustic cry unmistakable over the white noise of engine hum. I tried to turn toward the sound.

But nothing happened.

My head ached. Not inside the brain. The pain came from outside. It came from skin against skull, from stinging and squeezing, from stretching that made my eyes water.

"Brief" does not coexist with agony. Every second is infinite. Every breath is a paroxysm of suffering and regret.

For a moment, I imagined there was a twenty-gallon aquarium around my head. That my tears were home to bloodfin and discus, maybe a pencilfish or two. That my brow would split any second, that my ears were being ripped off in slow motion.

"Comfortable?" I knew that turd of a voice. It was Ricardo's.

I couldn't respond. My lower jaw throbbed. It was cramping, muscle spasms that started at the base of my neck and lurched their way up through my cheeks. Something was on my face and in my mouth, something that didn't belong anywhere near my teeth and gums.

My throat was dry. Parched. I wanted water, lots of water, anything to wash away the taste of sewer. Anything to get the crap out of my mouth. I tried to raise my hands. I just wanted to rip at my forehead, my ears, my neck, at whatever was holding me back. But my arms wouldn't budge. Not one inch.

I rolled my eyes down in their sockets, trying to spot what was holding me back. But the angle of my head made it impossible to see over the swell of my cheek. I strained, my thoughts racing, my horror mounting. Ricardo lorded it over me, grinning, savoring his handiwork.

Who the fuck is this guy?

"Amazing what duct tape does." He picked an incisor with the fingernail of his forefinger. "When I was a kid, we used it to build sets all the time."

I understood everything. I understood nothing.

He had turned me into a mummy with an open mouth. There was duct tape on my forehead, over my ears, and inside my mouth. I could feel the binding under my armpits and around my back. It chafed against my shirt, scratched at my skin. It felt like Ricardo had plastic-wrapped my face and upper torso to the seat. I just wanted to tear the tape off.

But couldn't.

"Now that I have your attention," he said, "let's set some ground rules. Blink twice to show me you understand."

I tried to kick him in the gonads. My legs didn't budge. Nothing.

"There, there," he said. "Blink twice for me."

Despite the circumstance, I glared my best fuck-you into his eyes. Bad decision.

"Maybe you need a little help cooperating." Ricardo reached into his blue canvas bag, the one he had been carrying since the beginning of the trip. "See this stuff?"

He brandished an aerosol can of Great Stuff, infomercial style, so I could view the label and long straw at the end. I refused to blink.

"Foam insulation," he explained. "You should see the way this shit expands. They tell me up to fifty times. Now would be a good time to blink twice."

I scowled.

"Suit yourself."

Ricardo touched the straw to the tip of my nose. I closed my eyes tight, trying to insulate them from the errant splatters of foam. He said nothing. The engines stopped. Silence oozed through the cabin, unctuous and foreboding. Then came the whoosh of aerosol. My nose felt sticky. And when I finally opened my eyes there was a small, misshapen ball of hard foam clinging to me. It was yellowish, disgusting to my skin.

"What we got here . . . is failure to communicate," he said, quoting the warden from *Cool Hand Luke*. "Now would be a good time to blink twice," he repeated.

Nothing from me.

Ricardo raised his eyebrows, surprised by my resistance. "Maybe it's time you understand the product benefits." He pushed the Great Stuff straw against my tonsils. "Take Father Mike. He asked my accountants one question too many. Spooked everybody. There was a draft coming from his mouth. You know what I'm saying?"

I gagged. My stomach was climbing my throat.

"Whoa, Bong. What do we got here?" Captain Jake had joined Ricardo. They were two cats, toying with their cornered prey.

"The thing about this insulation," Ricardo continued, "it keeps everything outside. Heat. Cold. Oxygen. But every space is different. And I can't figure out whether you're a one-can man or a two."

"Uncle," I tried to scream. But the words caught in my throat, the air hissing from my lungs, me sounding like a stroke victim. I blinked twice. I blinked a thousand times. I was caving. I was broken. I could almost feel the backwash from my stomach climbing through my throat.

Please, please, please.

"Does this mean you want to . . ." Ricardo paused. He smirked. And then, his voice singsonging, he asked with exaggerated enunciation, "Cooperate?"

I blinked twice.

"Oh, come on. Spray that crap in there." Jake turned to Bong. "I want to see what happens."

"Think you have it tough?" asked Ricardo, ignoring the pilot.

He reached into the blue canvas bag and pulled out a camcorder this time. With exaggerated slowness, the digital screen in my face, he played a video of him beating JoJo.

The grisly images made my eyes water. I wanted to scream, "Enough." But I couldn't. Instead, JoJo's and Bong's voices pierced the Grumman's noxious cabin air:

"Don't hurt my dog."

"No, Father Ricardo."

"Happy shall he be. Happy shall he be." The final clips showed Ricardo duct-taping her mouth open, just like mine.

"Now do you understand, O'Rourke?"

I blinked twice. I cringed, or at least I tried to cringe. My skin never moved. The tape tore at me, arrested my movement.

"You're a tough one, O'Rourke."

I blinked twice.

"Funny," he said, his smile wan, humorless. "I don't believe in reform. It's so much easier to kill somebody and be done with it."

"You go, boy." Jake's hair was brown and dirty, his face blood-pressure red, his voice whiny.

"I have your attention," continued Ricardo, "right?"

I blinked twice.

"You understand what JoJo feels?"

I blinked twice.

"She's a size two. Think JoJo can swallow a full can of Great Stuff?"

I tried to shake my head no, no, no and started to retch.

"Blink twice, Grover."

I blinked twice.

"All it takes is one call to Sullivan's Island."

She's still there?

"And JoJo gets a can down the gullet. Got it?"

I blinked twice.

"It'd probably traumatize the shit out of the Rafter's maids."

Ricardo smiled, arrogant and smug. I could almost smell his pride, the most serious of the seven deadly sins. And there with my mouth strapped open, me bolted to a tattered airplane seat, I knew hubris would take him down. For Ricardo had made his first mistake.

I know that hotel.

He must have seen recognition flare in my eyes. "That's right. Rafter's. Think you can do anything about it?"

I tried to shake my head no. It wouldn't budge.

"See. This is why I don't believe in reform, Grove."

I blinked twice. I didn't know what else to do.

"You got your knife, Jake?"

The pilot disappeared into the cockpit. When Jake returned, he was carrying what looked like a black handle. But he thumbed the edge and out popped a blade. It was six inches long and serrated, a cruel weapon.

"Here you go, Bong."

Ricardo took the knife and asked the pilot, "You got a coin?"

Jake fished a quarter from his pocket, held it up for both of us to see.

"Here's the problem, Grove. You don't get it. The second I turn my back, you make trouble."

I looked at the knife and tried to shake my head no.

"And you know what I think about reform," he continued, tracing the knife around my throat, his touch light, but firm enough for me to feel the serrated edges. "It doesn't fucking work. But I need you to get my two hundred million."

I blinked twice.

"Sorry, Grove. I don't buy it. Part of me says take your pinkie. Or better yet, a thumb. Give you the full JoJo experience, because that's the only way you'll take orders. And part of me says you walking into the bank with a bandaged hand is a mistake. Bleeding shit all over the cashier. See my dilemma?"

I was too afraid to blink.

"See my dilemma?" he repeated, holding the knife over my small finger, then my thumb.

Don't do it.

I blinked twice.

"We're both businessmen," he continued. "We make decisions without complete information."

I blinked twice.

He dragged the blade perpendicular to my thumb. It was not a cutting motion, just a sensation to assure me the weapon was sharp. "So I want you to call heads or tails. Got it?"

I did nothing.

"Got it?"

I blinked twice.

"Good. You want heads?"

I was frozen. I did nothing.

"Tails it is. Go ahead, Jake."

"I think he craps his pants," the pilot said, flipping a quarter.

End over end, the coin sailed though the air. As it tumbled down, Ricardo snatched the quarter lightning fast from the air. He opened his palm. His eyes widened. He leered at me, his smile sadistic.

CHAPTER FORTY-FIVE

TURKS AND CAICOS

"Tails."

Sweet fucking relief. The word tasted like honey. I blinked once. I blinked a thousand times. The horror lifted from my shoulders.

"Hallelujah," applauded Jake, sniffing the air with exaggerated motion. "Our boy didn't shit himself."

Tears poured from my eyes and streamed down my cheeks like rivers cresting their banks. Only, there were no levees on my face. Just duct tape clawing my skin.

"Not so cocky, are we?" Ricardo was taunting me, asserting his dominance. I now understand that intimidation was all part of the plan. Mission accomplished on his part.

I blinked twice.

Capitulation comes with a certain kind of self-loathing. There is nothing more ignominious than total surrender. Show me a stockbroker willing to take orders, and I'll show you somebody who needs to haul his complaisant ass off the trading floor.

I was bound and gagged. My pride didn't matter. I was relieved, too wounded to care about dignity. "Uncle" was the only word in my two-blink vocabulary, and I was glad to know it.

"Here's how it works." With his forefinger and thumb, Ricardo ripped the hardened chunk of Great Stuff from my nose and tore the skin. "We're in the Turks and Caicos. You will do exactly what I say, otherwise . . ." He paused.

I blinked twice and remembered the warning from my kickboxing coach in Narragansett. "Somebody's gonna pop you outside of class, and you won't know what to do." He was right.

"Otherwise," Ricardo growled, "JoJo dies. Got it?"

I blinked twice.

"This morning you're instructing Claire to wire my two hundred million dollars. Got it?"

I blinked twice. But this time, there were hints of my innate temper. I could feel them stirring inside.

"Good." To make a point, Ricardo tapped my nose with the flat of the knife blade. He cut the duct tape from my ears, mouth, and forehead. When he ripped it from my face, the sting seared my skin and probably turned it pig-belly pink.

The rush of oxygen through your nose into your lungs is a sweet and glorious sensation—especially when your mouth was strapped open the last forty-five minutes. When all you could taste was duct tape and fear. When some asshole was poking a straw down your throat.

The cramps eased from my jaw. My ears relaxed. They were no longer at risk of being torn off my head. The sweep of fresh air cleared my head.

He hesitated at my wrists. "You sure?"

"I swear it."

The words croaked from my mouth like surrender. But my thoughts kept returning to the dingy martial arts studio in Rhode Island. "In a street fight, nobody's gonna wait for you to wake up."

"Funny." Ricardo scraped the knife along the stubble of my morning beard. "I prefer when you call me 'Father.'"

Fuck you.

"Father," I muttered. The word turned my stomach.

"Good." He sliced through the duct tape binding my hands.

Ricardo cut the constraints from my ankles and handed the blade back to Jake. The beatnik captain pointed to the surf. "Watch when you jump. The water's about two feet deep."

Outside the plane, Ricardo nudged me forward every so often. Nothing gentle. The flat of his hand felt like the business end of a cattle prod. We waded toward the sandy beach, private homes hiding behind the palms. The pilot stayed aboard the plane, and I said nothing until there was a quarter mile separating Ricardo and me from him.

"Is JoJo okay?" I asked the question in my most compliant voice.

"Feeling better, are we?"

"You'll get your money. I promise." I couldn't get Palmer's wife out of my head. I had lucked through my ordeal. She was still suffering through hers. And that video, her crazy-wide eyes, infuriated me.

"Your word is shit, O'Rourke."

"What's the point of hurting her?"

"Because I enjoy it." He sneered and pushed me from behind as we walked the beach.

Ricardo's smug self-satisfaction repulsed me. The ocean shimmered like Bombay sapphires, the water so clear I could see our shadows rippling on the sand two feet down. But the pleasures, the visual feasts of an island paradise, were lost on me as we walked. And I think it was that moment when my dignity finally returned.

Palmer's wife occupied every corner of my mind. She was suffering, bleeding, gagging. Ricardo's confederates, for all I knew, were stuffing her full of that damn insulation. I had no idea what was happening back at Rafter's on Sullivan's Island.

"Where are we going?" I asked.

"To clean up. You look like puked-up balut. And that won't cut it at the bank."

"What's balut?"

"Hard-boiled duck embryo."

"What town is this?"

"Providenciales." He pushed me again.

My five senses were kicking into overdrive. I could see, feel, and smell everything. I could still taste the duct tape. And strangely, I heard the slightest note of hesitation in Ricardo's voice. Perhaps it was uncertainty over the $200 million payment.

"Provo?" I asked.

"Yeah."

I had never been to Turks and Caicos. But my clients tell me about "Provo" all the time. Some own houses along the beach. "What bank?"

"You ask too many questions. Pick up the pace."

Ricardo pushed me again, which pissed me off. For a moment, I thought he might be inviting me to throw a punch. Bile was washing up my throat, the muscles in my arms were growing taut, and the spring was returning to my legs.

My head was buzzing. But this time it was Annie's words that came to mind. "Get down there and fight."

Another push. I exercised restraint. You don't suffer total humiliation in one breath and throw a punch the next. Plus, there was JoJo. Ricardo would call his goon at Rafter's the minute I blinked the wrong way.

"Stop shoving, okay?"

"We haven't forgotten our working agreement, have we, dear?"

Dick.

I wanted to kick the ever-living shit out of him. That's the thing about anger. It gets the blood going, clarifies the muddle.

Suddenly, I realized that Ricardo had not used his cell phone since we left Charleston. I looked over, eyed the spider-sun climbing up his arm, and witnessed the most beautiful sight.

No watch.

I slowed down, not abruptly, but one step at a time. "Where'd you get your tattoo?"

"What the fuck difference does it make?"

"Just curious."

"Pasig City."

"Does your tattoo mean something in the Philippines?"

"Just keep walking." Ricardo was all business. He had no interest in the small talk.

Nor did I. "How long before we get to your place?"

"Five minutes, maybe ten."

"You know what time it is?"

"What difference does it make?"

"We've been traveling all night. Maybe we could get some breakfast." I wasn't hungry in the least. I was testing him. Trying to determine whether he would reach into his pocket and pull out a mobile to check the time. Because if he didn't have one, I had a chance of reaching the police before he could reach his goon at the hotel.

"Do me a favor and shut the fuck up."

Inconclusive.

"Just asking." I slowed my pace. Time to do something.

"Jesus, you walk like an old lady." He pushed me again.

Which was one push too many. I wheeled around, instantly feral. Without thinking, I snapped a left jab to his nose. Not an open-palmed karate strike. Just knuckles and wedding band aimed at Ricardo's sad-sack puss.

The move surprised him. But he was fast. He swept my arm off to the left.

That's when I came from below with an old-fashioned uppercut. I caught him on the cheek and tasted the most satisfying crunch of my life. Fist against jawbone, the impact fucking delicious. For a moment, I thought his eyes might roll back in their sockets and flutter skyward until the whites surrendered consciousness.

Wrong.

The shot rocked Ricardo. It was good, solid, enough to raise a red welt on his cheek. But not good enough. I made the mistake of gawking, savoring my handiwork, forgetting the kill. He leered at me, the malice gleaming through two slits. His palms were open, his hands raised in a karate fighting stance.

Ricardo stepped back, way back. He pulled off his black shirt, never dropping his gaze. I had always suspected he was well put together, in a priestly kind of way. But I was still surprised by what emerged. He was thick through the torso, built like a mailbox. His biceps bulged. He had thirty pounds on me.

Girl Louie said "Bong" had worked for a bank. But one thing was certain: Ricardo had developed his physique somewhere else—that and his aura of violence. There was a snake tattooed over each nipple.

For a split second, I worried that my kickboxing lessons had been a joke, that my uppercut to his cheek was a mistake. We were a long way from the controlled environment in Rhode Island.

"You got some training." Ricardo smirked and rolled his head in a circle, stretching the muscles till they were loose. "I'm guessing fifteen, maybe even twenty sessions."

I said nothing, moving backward to my left, angling my body to make the target small—the way they teach in those fifteen to twenty sessions. Ricardo had guessed about right.

"Me," he said, advancing in a straight line, "I should get a goddamn medical degree for all my fights. First time you break somebody's nose, it's pretty fucking exciting. But make somebody spit out a tooth with the roots attached—now, that's a thing of beauty, first time or the fiftieth."

Jab. Jab. Ricardo's second jab caught my right ear. It stung like a bastard. He spun 180 degrees, jumped, and roundhouse kicked through the air. But his right shin only glanced over my head. He was fast. I never counterpunched, not even once.

"You know what happens," he continued, "when you hit guys in the spleen?"

Ricardo dropped his right arm. I jabbed and crossed right with a combo. Missed both. He came back with an uppercut from down low and caught me in the chest, smacking the air from my lungs.

"Sometimes they barf purple shit." Ricardo danced a shuffle and dropped his right hand, inviting me to take a shot. He had yet to break a sweat. "Fucking nasty, if you ask me."

Left jab. Left cross. Nothing. I missed.

One, two steps, and his ferocious sweep kick caught me on the right hip. I almost went down. "There's no 911 out here, Grove. I rupture that little fucker spleen of yours, and you're dead within the hour. We can't have that, can we?"

I felt myself limping. I moved right to work out the pain.

"You enjoyed that last one? I wonder how many teeth you'll have after this." Ricardo feinted right and snapped my head back with a left cross. Then a right jab. Suddenly, my face became his speed bag. Right. Left. Right. Left.

I heard something snap. There was blood everywhere, and maybe a piece of nose. Mine. I brought up my right knee, fast, furious, dirty.

Ricardo deflected it aside and laughed, dropping his right hand, goading me. "You got some street in you."

He stepped on a shell. Or perhaps it was a depression in the sand. I'll never know. But in that second, I saw the opening. His eyes flashed like he was losing his balance. I stutter-stepped and launched into the air, swinging my shin against his head.

Ricardo ducked.

I kicked out, the mother of all lucky shots. You have to understand: I can leg press eight hundred pounds no problem. Most decent cyclists can. The heel of my foot snapped Ricardo's forehead, eight hundred pounds of torque and leg extension crashing into his face. And he went down. Lights out.

"Wake up!" Now I was the one screaming, lording it over him. I forgot JoJo. I wanted to kick him in the face, in the nuts, in the hand with his pinkie exposed. I was raging.

That was a mistake.

I never heard a thing—not the slap of the waves, nor the rustle of running feet, not even the whoosh of a club sailing through the air. There was only pain. There was only my consciousness plunging into a vast, vacant stretch of blackness darker than midnight.

CHAPTER FORTY-SIX
THE PALMETTO FOUNDATION

What would Dad do?

Claire gazed out the window at the pastel office buildings across the street. She could hear the pedestrians below, friends and neighbors greeting each other near the corner of Broad and ennui.

The Southern voices, cured with manners and mellow cadences from the low country, were comforting. She found the consistency reassuring, the way names never changed other than the Roman numerals behind them.

Most days, she felt safe.

Charleston was more than a peninsula. It was an island of manners where family ties ran deep through the generations. Where kids shrimped and crabbed together and later watched each other's back on the high school playing fields. Where neighbors dated and swapped spouses and built their fortunes and borrowed their historic homes until the next generation took over. Where old folks walked through gardens that exploded with the candied scents of magnolias, azaleas, and Confederate jasmine. Where everybody reminisced about the way things used to be. The riffraff were not allowed inside the Holy City.

Today, Claire Kincaid was a wreck.

Her father was gone. JoJo had been kidnapped. And in all likelihood, the Palmetto Foundation would exhaust its resources just to get her back. Claire turned, her brow furrowed behind the bangs, and surveyed the conference room. There were photos of Kincaids everywhere, handing out checks, making other charities more productive. The Palmetto Foundation was the only employer she had ever known. And now, holding the reins less than a month, she was presiding over its demise.

Where's Grove when I need him?

It was 9:58 A.M., and he was nowhere to be seen. Nor had Father Ricardo arrived. Almost on cue, Jill's voice boomed over the speakerphone. "Your guests are on the way up."

For a moment, Claire felt the weight lift from her shoulders. She stopped wringing her hands. But her relief quickly changed to confusion. "You mean Grove and Father Ricardo, right?"

The conference room door was open. Biscuit knocked anyway. Claire rolled her eyes and threw up her arms. "Not now."

"I know what you're thinking," he said, hands flat, palms facing down. "Hear me out."

Claire's clear blue eyes had turned murky and red, casualties of too much booze, not enough sleep, constant worry, or all three. Her sweep of brown hair drifted out of control, the sheen gone, the bangs screaming for help.

Seeing an unfamiliar face, Claire flashed a wan smile. The Hispanic woman standing next to Biscuit was pretty and athletic, even if her outfit did nothing to enhance her appearance. Her intense pupils glowed like shiny ball bearings, her lips a thin pink line. It seemed like there was a question concealed behind every tilt of the head.

"You know we have a meeting, darling." Claire did not think of Biscuit as a "darling." The word just came out, force of Southern habit. "And I need to get ready before Grove and Father Ricardo arrive."

"They're not coming." The Hispanic woman extended her hand.

"And you are?" asked Claire in a dismissive tone.

"Agent Torres. I'm with the FBI."

In that instant Claire Kincaid snapped. It was all too much: how much money to send; when to tell the authorities; whether to trust Grove or a Maryknoll priest. Father Ricardo was not just another chaplain. He was emerging as the family's go-to priest. She'd need his counsel if JoJo died and the Palmetto Foundation vanished down a rat hole of ransom demands.

"What have you done?" Angry as a hornet, she stabbed Biscuit's chest with her forefinger.

"Let me explain." The big man's face turned bright spanking red.

"You have no right to meddle in my family's affairs."

Biscuit backpedaled until Torres intervened. Soft and soothing, the FBI agent caught Claire's hand with her own. "We know how to help."

"Help! Puddin' over here just okayed a hit on my father's wife."

"Stop," demanded Torres.

Biscuit ignored the crack. "Have you seen Grove?"

The question calmed Claire. Her face softened, and her expression grew vulnerable again. "No. I expect him any minute."

"How about Father Ricardo?"

"No. He's not here either. Why do you ask?"

The agent and lawyer traded glances.

The exchange distracted Claire. She turned from Biscuit to Torres, first one, then the other. As the room fell silent, she wondered what they knew. What she didn't. The role of odd one out was foreign to Claire, discomfiting. She had grown up in a community of cliques and took pride in penetrating them. "You want to clue me in?"

"Let's sit down." Over the next few minutes, Torres briefed her about the FBI's ongoing investigation into Ricardo.

Claire listened and said nothing at first. Wary. She glanced over at Biscuit once and caught the big man staring at her hands. She looked down and noticed the slight tremor herself. Claire sat back, folded her arms across her tan cardigan, and waited for the agent to finish. "You've been investigating Father Ricardo how long?"

"Three years."

"And where's Grove?"

"With Ricardo in the Caribbean." There was no emotion in the agent's voice.

"Is he in danger?"

"Probably."

"And I'm supposed to believe you can get JoJo back?"

"Not fair," Biscuit interrupted. He understood how Claire was piecing the events together.

"Easy for you to say. The Bureau's been watching Ricardo for three years. Grove for a few weeks. Now both are gone, and my new best friend tells me she's the cavalry. I don't buy it."

Torres had seen similar frustration in the past. She expected the push-back. And from eleven years on the job, she knew there was only one way to gain Claire's cooperation: change the conversation. "I have questions about your father."

"What's my dad got to do with this?"

"You want to know what happened to him, right?"

"A boom hit him in the head." Claire looked back and forth at the two guests. "It was an accident, right?"

"We're not sure," the agent replied.

The color drained from Claire's face. She was struggling with the revelations. "Are you saying Father Ricardo killed my father?"

"I'm saying he's no priest. His organization was using the Palmetto Foundation to launder money."

"But why hurt my dad?"

"I think your father started to resist. He discovered the scheme. Or he changed his mind." Torres regretted her words at once.

Their implication crushed the air from Claire's lungs. She shook her head no, felt her heart pounding, her eyes moistening. "You think my dad was doing something illegal?"

"We hope not." The agent pulled back and reclined in her chair. She felt no sympathy for Claire. But there were smarter ways than outright accusation to make people talk. "Ricardo is part of a ruthless organization, where people get what they want. Or eliminate the roadblocks. There's no telling what pressure they brought to bear on your father."

The tears flowed steadily now. Claire tried to envision what her father would say under these circumstances. She had watched him take control of meetings so many times before. "Do I need a lawyer?"

"I don't know," said Torres truthfully. "But right now, we need help finding your father's wife and Grove O'Rourke."

Claire dried her eyes with a tissue. "Yes, of course."

"Did your father confide in his attorney?"

"Huitt Young was his best friend."

"You think Mr. Young will answer our questions?"

"He will if I ask him. But I don't see how any of this helps us get JoJo or Grove back."

"We're looking for some lead, some clue, some detail or association, anything to help us find them."

"Anything," consented Claire, wrought with emotion, not sure what to say. She needed the FBI's help. She knew it, no matter how unsettling her decision had been to ignore the kidnapper's threat: "the woman dies."

Agent Torres gunned questions over the next fifty minutes or so. No detail was too small. Her interest in Palmer Kincaid bordered on the obsessive:

"When did your father graduate from Harvard?"

"Who are his business associates?"

"Did he have enemies?"

Claire grew tired of the agent's interrogation, the incessant search for details. Torres began every other sentence with "why" or "how" or "who" or "what" or "where" or "when." Under the benumbing barrage, Claire stopped brushing aside her bangs. Elbows on table, head between hands, she let her hair hang in a long waterfall over her face. She was spent.

There are pains worse than fatigue. Shattered trust is one of them. The mind games are devastating. Especially when the trust was in a parent, whose stature reached epic proportions inside a close-knit community where name and reputation are everything.

Claire had decided that enough was enough. That she needed coffee. That this interrogation was a shit waste of time. It was then that Torres turned to Palmer's second marriage. And the agent's revelations left Claire with one flattening thought:

I don't know my own father.

Around 10:50 A.M., Claire signaled for a break.

Jill placed a tray with coffee, cream, and sugar on a small serving table inside the conference room. She decided Claire looked haggard—drawn face, bags under her eyes, hair on walkabout. "Need anything else?"

"Any word from Grove or Father Ricardo?"

"Not a word. Grove hasn't called his office. And Annie wants to speak with you."

"Why'd you call her?" Claire had never spoken with Annie. But she knew the name all too well. Annie was the difference between Grove being a friend and Grove being a prospect.

"I didn't. She answered his home number." Jill added sheepishly, "And my call upset her."

"What happened?"

"The two of them spoke last night. And she said something about him promising 'not to do anything stupid.' "

Torres, who had been pouring coffee, snapped to attention at Jill's words. "I need O'Rourke's home phone number pronto."

"I'll make that call, captain." Biscuit stood to leave.

"No you won't. It's an FBI matter."

"Don't tell me what to do," the big man argued, surprising himself. "The poor woman is probably sick out of her head. I'll get what you need."

"Do you know Annie?" asked Claire.

"No. But it's time we met." Biscuit exited the conference room with the receptionist.

Torres stirred two sugars into her coffee, no cream. When the agent returned to her seat, she considered the antique chair for a moment and decided to change places. She grabbed her pad and pen, circled the table, and landed in the seat next to Palmer Kincaid's bedraggled daughter.

A rich, almost syrupy aroma wafted through the room. The agent sipped her coffee, savoring the bittersweet taste. She waited for the heat to work through her hands, her torso, for the sugar and caffeine to fill her tanks, for the momentary pause to make Claire Kincaid uncomfortable.

Torres leaned forward, in close, the better to drill down deep. She was ready. Because every second counted.

"How did your father meet Mrs. Kincaid?"

"Through one of his Harvard buddies."

"Does the friend—"

"Gordie," Claire interrupted.

"Does Gordie live in Charleston?"

"No, San Diego."

"How's that make sense?" Torres made a big show of looking confused.

"I don't understand."

"Charleston," the agent said, left palm facing up. "San Diego," she followed, her right hand raised in confusion. "Where did Mrs. Kincaid live before she met your father?" Torres already knew the answer.

"JoJo worked for Gordie in San Diego."

"So that's where your father met her?" The agent was exacting to a fault.

"What difference does it make?"

"We never know," said Torres, "what puts some lowlife behind bars. But it's always there, the fact, the association, the shred of evidence that seems insignificant at first."

"Gordie could have introduced them in Charleston or San Diego. My dad and his college roommates got together all the time."

For a moment Claire's face brightened at the memory of her father and his Harvard cronies, the way they told the same old stories, year in, year out. It was sweet. They were like vinyl records, scratched and dinged through the decades, always skipping at the same refrains or belting out the same punch lines together.

"What do you know about Mrs. Kincaid's previous marriage?"

"What are you talking about?"

Biscuit returned to the conference room. Torres glanced at him, one of those faces that say, "I owe you one, buddy."

"No luck," the big man announced, and sat down. "I'll try Annie in another hour."

Torres resumed the examination. "Your stepmother was married to a sailor once. Biscuit found out surfing the Web."

Claire's eyes widened. Her jaw hung slack. "Which yacht club?"

"U.S. Navy."

"You're kidding," she almost scoffed.

"Chief Petty Officer James Berenson. Divorced from Mrs. Kincaid three years prior to her marriage to your father. Now serving in the Middle East."

"You're wrong."

Biscuit cocked his head. So did Torres. The force of Claire's words dazed them both for a moment.

"Say what?" The agent could not believe her ears.

"You heard me."

"Why am I wrong?"

"JoJo and my father got married in the Catholic Church."

"Not everyone tells their priest," argued Torres.

"My father isn't everyone."

"What priests don't know won't hurt them."

"No way JoJo was married before." Claire shook her head and folded her arms. She was adamant, 100 percent certain.

Torres said nothing. But her head was cocked, her face curious. Her lips curled up to the right and slid down to the left in a thin, colorless line. And her chin was perched between thumb and forefinger. She was the picture of skepticism.

Claire read the signs. "Have you seen the photos of my father at the Vatican?"

"They're everywhere. How could I miss them?"

"Yeah, why do you think my dad was at the Vatican?"

"Every Catholic wants to visit."

"He went to get my marriage annulled."

"Irrelevant," the agent argued. "That has nothing to do with Mrs. Kincaid."

"You don't know my father." Claire kept shaking her head. "He insisted on my annulment. Otherwise, I couldn't get remarried and still take communion."

"Why the fuss over a cracker?" Almost at once, Biscuit realized it was an unfortunate comment. The two women grimaced as though he were the lord of all pagans. "Sorry."

"If my father had married a divorcée," persisted Claire, "he would have told the Church. You can take that to the bank."

"If your father's friend knew about JoJo's first marriage, he'd say something, right?"

"Gordie. Those two finished each other's sentences. What's your point?"

"It's like this—"

Before the agent could explain, Jill buzzed through the intercom. "Father Ricardo's on the line."

CHAPTER FORTY-SEVEN

TURKS AND CAICOS
SEVENTY-FIVE MINUTES EARLIER

My world was black. Crazy, rubbish thoughts eddied through my head. It was cold, so very cold.

There were a thousand shades of blue, disparate hues from azure to turquoise swirling through the lens of a powerful microscope. The slide sucked me down the optical tubes into a vast, hungry void, an ocean of nothing spread across three inches of glass.

What happened?

I had coldcocked a club with the back of my head. Rattled it good. Now I was rolling on a ship's deck, the sea pitching me back and forth. The waves were growing in size and shape, crashing against the hull and gaining strength.

I was swimming, washed over the gunwales by back-to-back breakers. A fierce riptide dragged me down, down, down. Everything was wet and cold, so very cold.

Air. I need air. I can't breathe.

My head broke through the ocean's surface. Consciousness returned but just barely. The light was overwhelming. The back of my head throbbed. I wanted to wretch. I was drenched, sitting bolt upright in a bedroom, my eyes flickering, my head a bucket of mud.

Ricardo came into focus, slowly, unsteadily. It was like viewing him through an ear canal. He had just doused me with a pitcher of water. The bedroom reminded me of the Delano in South Beach, everything white and crisp. We were somewhere in the Turks and Caicos.

Or maybe not.

"Hello, sunshine." Ricardo smiled sadistically, his black pupils surrounded by red. They were piranha eyes, cold and ruthless.

He reared back and crashed a massive right against my cheekbone, opening the skin and bowling me off the bed. I landed on my butt, pain searing through my tailbone and up my spine. Ricardo bounded toward me and stepped on my chest, his foot holding me down.

My cobwebs vanished.

"You got lucky at the beach," he growled, his voice low and menacing. There was a purple lump bulging from his forehead, the spot where my foot had connected.

"You look like a fucking eggplant."

"You double-crossed me." Ricardo leaned with all his weight, the oxygen wheezing from my lungs.

There's one thing I know from Wall Street. The most powerful person in the room is the one who wants something the least, the one who couldn't give a shit about the outcome. Ricardo was obsessed with his $200 million payday. I had stopped caring what happened to me. It was my only hope.

"We can talk a deal when you let JoJo go."

"Hey, Jake," Ricardo called, laughing, amused by my resistance. "The douche bag's still telling us what to do."

That's when I understood what had happened. Standing over Ricardo at the beach, I never heard anyone sneaking up from behind. It was the pilot, who clocked the back of my head. My skull hurt like a bastard. And now, warm blood from a fresh cut was flowing down my cheek.

Jake walked into the room, his tie-dyed shirt annoying as ever. "Just get on with it. You know how anxious Moreno gets."

"But I'm starting to enjoy myself." Ricardo's black clothes were gone. He was wearing jeans and a T-shirt. The heel of his sandal was pressing into my chest, deeper and deeper.

"Did we forget our meds today?" The right opening, and I'd slap his sneer into Sunday.

"Let's get JoJo on the line."

She's still alive.

"Give me your phone," Ricardo instructed the pilot.

"What for?"

"Captain America seems to have forgotten my home movie. I want him to hear JoJo alive and in concert. We'll see who's a hard-ass then." Ricardo bounced on my torso, driving home the point.

"Use your own phone."

"I lost it."

It was now or never. I knew what was coming. I will never forget that video of JoJo. "You assholes really want to swab urinals on the Jersey Pike the rest of your lives?"

Ricardo smirked, his face quizzical.

"I mean, what are washed-out money launderers to do? Moreno won't give you a reference. And the economy's tough these days. After a while, any job will do. You'll be mopping back and forth, doing the math in your head, calculating how many Jersey boys miss the bowl. Won't be long before one of those galvanized squeeze buckets is your best friend."

Ricardo and Jake were both gaping now.

"And every swipe of the mop, you'll be moaning over what could have been. What it's like to have two hundred million dollars. Why you didn't listen to me. Because you'll never see a fucking dime from the Palmetto Foundation if you touch JoJo again."

"Can you believe this guy?" Ricardo shook his head and dialed South Carolina. His heel dug like a spade into my chest.

I had to do something fast. Bong's weight was too much for me to break free. Working on the Street, you learn how to rant. Dishing out insults is both an art and a required form of self-defense. I decided to keep mine short and crisp. "You ever thought about donating your body to science?"

Ricardo took the phone away from his ear. I could hear the other side ringing. He looked at me with an amused expression, curious what I had to say. For a moment, the mailbox relaxed his pressure on my chest. "And why's that?"

"So they can study what happens when a maggot disguised as sperm finds its way into the gene pool."

The call connected.

Ricardo looked at Jake. The pilot's eyes were crazy, like his LSD flashback had finally arrived. "Bong, why don't you take the left. I'll take the right, and we'll kick the shit out of him."

For a split second I thought, *Mission accomplished*. They'd focus on me and forget JoJo. But no such luck.

Ricardo rattled off some Spanish into the receiver, his tone gruff. Every once in a while, he said, "Bueno." But there was nothing "good" back at Rafter's.

He bent over and held the cell phone over my ear. I heard slapping, the sound of leather. Blows rained hard and fast, vicious every one of them. And there was JoJo's voice. Agony with every strike. She wailed and pleaded until I thought my head would explode.

Bong dug his sandal deeper and deeper into my chest. But that's not where I felt the pain. It was in my ears, in my head, me processing the scene at Rafter's. "No," I gasped, arching my back and twisting.

"You like to play?" Ricardo pushed down ever harder.

I managed to dislodge his foot and tried to sit up. But he was too fast, too alert, too strong. He dropped, and his knees pinned my arms. And holding the phone with his left hand, he slapped me open-palmed with his right. Back and forth, one after another, keeping time to JoJo's screams.

"Please stop." She was begging, bawling, the blows raining on and on, both hers and mine.

"That's enough, Bong." Jake pulled him off.

My face was already swelling, the pain searing my cheeks, forehead, ears, everything.

Ricardo jabbered something unintelligible into the cell phone. And almost at once, the screams stopped. The whipping was over. "You ready to call Claire with the wire instructions?"

"And what?" I shot back.

"We let her go."

"You'll kill her."

"We have two hundred million reasons to let her go."

Ricardo eased off my chest. I sat up and stared at him blankly, raging, seething, wanting to feed his face through a shredder.

"What's it going to be, O'Rourke?"

———

A woman takes a beating.

The sounds are hellish over a camcorder, more so over the phone in real time. Smack of leather, moans and labored gasps—it feels like your head is wedged inside a shop vise. Bones are breaking. Flesh is tearing. But you can't do shit, because the attack is going down ten thousand miles away.

It's worse because you're the idiot who drew the line in the sand and refused to pay. You flay yourself from the inside out. You try to remain tough through the whimpering. You keep thinking, *It's the only way*. But upstairs, you know. The bleating and mewling were a decision. Yours. This one's on you.

What could I do?

If I cooperated, Ricardo would kill JoJo. It was that simple. Claire would follow my instructions and wire the money, which made JoJo expendable, which made me expendable.

Game over. As we like to say in my business, "That's all she wrote."

I had never faced anything this dire back at the office. But fourteen bosses in ten years had presented me with some monumentally stupid options. More than I care to remember.

When there are no answers and the outcomes are unacceptable, there's only one thing to do:

Negotiate.

"You watch the details," I told Ricardo. "I'll give you that."

"Glad you approve." He kicked me in the gut, a painful exclamation point to his sarcasm. Something cracked and poked against the walls of my side.

"Ugh," hissed the air from my lungs. It took me a moment to recover. "So why are you dragging your feet?"

"What are you talking about?"

"Nobody knows we're down here in the Turks and Caicos except you, me, and dumb ass."

"Hey," snapped Jake.

"And my guess," I continued, "is that you have the mother of all sweep accounts here. I give the instructions. Claire wires two hundred million. The money arrives for a nanosecond. And then it's automatically whisked off to five different banks."

"Ten countries," he said. "Twenty million dollars to Russia. Twenty to Liechtenstein. Twenty to Nauru and so on until all two hundred million is gone. And the receiving banks all have sweep accounts on their end. You'll never untangle my spaghetti."

"Sweet. Too bad you'll never see the money."

Ricardo was cool. For a moment, I was unsure whether he would bite. "And why's that?"

"I'm the only thing between you and two hundred million. And as long as you have JoJo, I'm never calling Claire. You got that or do I need to walk you through the facts one more time?"

The pilot's eyes widened every time he heard "two hundred million." He said nothing. But I assumed there was something behind the expression, his lips pursed as though he were whistling without making a sound.

Ricardo didn't scare. And at first, he didn't negotiate. "It's time we take JoJo's other pinkie. Make her hands match. Know what I'm saying?"

"You're stressing me out. It's Bong, right?"

He said nothing.

Nor did I wait for the answer. "The thing about pressure, Bong, it's hard to hide. I wear feelings on my sleeve. Can't keep secrets worth a damn. And that's a problem for you."

"You mean JoJo," he interrupted.

"Claire and I have known each other since we were kids. She knows when I'm upset. She knows, Bong. I make your money call and hesitate even for a second, the time it takes to blink, and her antennae pick up the vibes. She calls the police, which is no problem from a safety point of view. Nobody knows where the hell we are. But your two hundred million, well that's another story. It's gone, and you're back on the Jersey Pike choosing between Lysol and Mr. Clean."

I glanced over at Jake. Eyes bulging. Lips like an upside-down U. What was eating him? I assumed Ricardo had promised him a piece of the action. He was worried about his cut.

Ricardo said nothing at first. He was deliberating, evaluating a tough decision. "O'Rourke makes any trouble," he told Jake, "and I want you to make him a soprano."

"Got it."

Ricardo disappeared from the room.

I sat up on the floor and raised myself slowly to the bed. "What's your cut? Is Bong paying you enough to replace that crap plane parked out in the harbor?"

"Shut up."

My fishing expedition ended as quickly as it started. Ricardo returned a second or two later. He checked a paper once, twice, and handed it over to me. I took a quick look and asked, "What are these for?"

"Don't you recognize wiring instructions, bright boy?"

"Claire already has them."

"Change of plans. These are different from the ones you already received."

I looked down and inspected the instructions more closely. The receiving bank was different, the Bahamas Banking Company. No big deal. But my eyes bugged at the receiving account:

Palmetto Foundation.

CHAPTER FORTY-EIGHT
TURKS AND CAICOS

I read and reread the wire instructions three different times. The recipient never changed. Palmetto Foundation. We were wiring money to ourselves. It made no sense.

At first I felt confusion, which shortly gave way to profound anger. Which took me back to bewilderment in a vicious cycle of conflicting emotions. I guess that's what happens when you're struggling to find answers and your demigods start to tumble.

Paragons. Heroes. I mean the guys you trust. The guys you model, because they figured out how to make money and do the right thing. The guys you believe in, until their secrets get exposed and your marrow gets bone-sucked dry of all hope and enthusiasm.

Take it from me, a guy on the Street. I've seen my share of double-dealing, and there are no antidotes. Betrayal breaks your spirit. It steals part of your soul. The wounds leave you with open sores, the unforgettable knowledge that your friend is dirty and all the veneration was a sack of crap. It took me less than two seconds to convict Palmer Kincaid, my mentor, and hang his memory forever.

Ricardo got to him.

The Palmetto Foundation didn't need a bank account in the Turks and Caicos. None of our donors were funding philanthropic projects anywhere in the Caribbean. Nor did we operate a captive insurance subsidiary, a risk-management technique for which the islands are known. Claire, JoJo, and the people in accounting never mentioned a financial relationship with the Bahamas Banking Company.

The bank account served no legitimate purpose, which is why my thoughts returned to Ira Popowski, the trust and estate lawyer from New York City. After my visit to Maryknoll headquarters, he said, "It sounds to me like you stepped on a pile of tax fraud. And the FBI is building its case."

If there's one thing my clients hate, it's taxes. They throw thousands of dollars at lawyers and accountants, a no-expense-spared vendetta against payments to Uncle Sam. Deductions are like free money. And nobody, not even a guy with $200 million, turns down free money.

I'm not proud of my initial reaction.

Ira Popowski, it seemed to me, was right. Palmer had pushed the envelope a little too far. I understood why. In my business, I see the extreme anti-IRS mentality all the time. Some people don't know when to stop. That's why you read crazy stories about Swiss wealth managers checking through airport security with toothpaste tubes packed full of diamonds. It's all about cutting the IRS out of the picture.

But I didn't understand how. For one, my knowledge of the Turks and Caicos as an offshore haven was limited. I suspected their charitable foundations could disburse funds with far less scrutiny than they would attract in the United States. But that was just a guess. For another, I wondered how a fake priest fit into a tax scam.

Ira's words came roaring back. "The money's going around in circles, which sounds like a tax scam if you ask me." How could the Palmetto Foundation have opened a bank account in the Turks and Caicos without Palmer's signature and, therefore, his approval?

Didn't matter. I decided my mentor had slept with a dog and woken up with fleas. His partnership with Ricardo soured. He became expendable. And here I was, racing to defend his family, getting sucked in deeper and deeper.

There was only one problem. I was mostly wrong, which is why my snap conclusion haunts me still.

"Big Mr. Wall Street," Ricardo scoffed with mock disapproval, his eyebrows arched, his mouth a righteous button. "You call yourself a fiduciary? Me. If I'm elected to a board, I'd investigate the banking relationships first thing. Where they're located. Money transfers. Everything. But that's just me. I watch the details."

Ricardo was sounding more like a banker all the time, using the word "fiduciary" rather than "trustee." I asked him, "Did Palmer open this bank account?"

"Amazing what people do before they die."

"Answer the question."

"They go glassy-eyed," Ricardo continued, ignoring my protest. "Some guys sob. Some negotiate. Palmer got down on his knees and begged like a mama's boy."

"Makes me wonder what you'll do."

Ricardo inspected his fingernails, oblivious to my threat. "Now, JoJo— she made me proud. The girl chomped down on a tablecloth and took it like a man. You ask me, that's some stoic shit."

Who is this guy?

In that moment I was struggling with a strange mix of conflicting emotions. Relief—Palmer was clean. Guilt—I was kicking myself for the rush to judgment, however brief. Rage—I wondered what abominations had taken place aboard *Bounder,* how my friend spent the last few minutes of his life.

Temper flaring, I was sitting on the bed. The leverage was all wrong for a quick strike. I wanted to jump up and get in Ricardo's grille, violate his body space. I'd ram my palm against his nose until nostrils were the last things to go through his mind.

But Jake remained vigilant. Any move would have ended the same way as before: more lumps and me counting sheep. That's if I was lucky. The pilot was crazy-sick enough to cut me with that damn black knife of his.

Rather than throw a punch, I did the next best thing and started to trash-talk. "Why don't you send your boy to the next room? We can work things out, man to moron."

Jake made a move.

Ricardo raised a hand for him to halt. "You ask me, the bank account is fucking inspired. Every detail traces back to Charleston, South Carolina. The officers. The philanthropic mission. The Palmetto Foundation, as far as the world knows, has a subsidiary in the Turks and Caicos."

"And you have signing authority?"

"Of course."

"Why use our name?"

"You're the Wall Street wizard. You tell me."

Now it was my turn to ratchet up the sarcasm. "There you go again, Ricardo, always missing the big picture. I keep asking questions, and you keep replying with riddles. Which is unfortunate, because you're starting to piss me off. And I don't know how we'll ever get you two hundred million dollars."

Jake touched the tip of his knife blade. "Maybe I can help you figure it out."

"Not yet." Ricardo cracked his knuckles again. The sound was giving me arthritis.

"You work with me, and I work with you."

Ricardo's coal eyes shimmered. He must have been thinking, *The nerve of this guy.*

Of course, I interpreted the expression as license to continue. "Tell me why it's so important to send money from the Palmetto Foundation to the Palmetto Foundation."

That's it.

By stating the question aloud, I understood. Banks relax their scrutiny when money goes same name to same name. It's when funds go to a third party, John Smith to Jane Doe, that anti-money-laundering units, AMLs for short, kick into gear.

The ruse was brilliant, elegant in its simplicity. Few organizations would prevent a charity from wiring funds to an overseas branch. Somebody's AML division might raise a question or two. But most shops, including mine, were fairly relaxed about organizations they had already vetted. And Charleston bankers, who had wrangled for decades to win the Kincaid business, would never challenge the Palmetto Foundation.

Ricardo saw my flicker of understanding. "You're kind of slow on the uptake. But I knew you'd figure it out. Time to call Claire."

"Not happening."

"Excuse me?" Ricardo did a double take.

"Not until JoJo's safe." My face was throbbing. My heart was pounding. I was doing my best to sound tougher than I felt. "Don't you get it? I'm your hostage. She can't talk to the authorities until I'm safe."

"I don't like it," growled Jake.

"Because your meds won't fix stupid."

Divide and conquer. I had faced group decisions before. There's nothing like riding one guy hard. It creates dissension in the ranks. Brokers do it all the time when they're selling to committees.

Jake clenched his fists, but Ricardo grabbed his shoulder. "Let O'Rourke talk."

"It's not complicated. She'll keep her mouth shut."

"It's too big a chance," argued Jake.

"JoJo needs medical attention."

"Don't listen to him, Bong. One word from her, and we got nothing. And you know what that means to Moreno."

"Hey, good point. How much does he get? I bet you send him forty and keep one sixty."

"Shut up," snapped Ricardo.

"The day's running out," I pressed, pulling out all the stops. "The longer you wait to free JoJo, the longer you wait to see your two hundred. But what do I know about cutoff times for wiring money? I only work in the industry."

"Don't tell me about cutoff times."

"Let me handle this." Jake's eyes were crazy, the glints maniacal.

Ricardo said nothing. There was indecision plastered across his face.

"Cut this guy," Jake persisted.

"Go ahead. And see what happens when I phone Claire." My face was going flush underneath all the welts and bruises.

Ricardo rattled away in Spanish, lightning fast, one word turning into another. And the pilot responded in kind. I couldn't make out what they were saying. Not one word. But the two goons were arguing. That much was clear. I just watched and waited for a resolution.

"Okay," Ricardo finally acquiesced. "You win, O'Rourke."

It took all my self-control to keep from screaming. "Here's how we do it."

"Bong, he's walking all over us."

"When JoJo tells me she's safe," I said, ignoring Jake, "that's when I call Claire. Not a moment before."

"Cut this guy," Jake echoed, his face going pink through the sandpaper skin.

"Nobody asked you." Ricardo turned to me. "I'll let her go."

"I'm not finished with my terms."

"That's it." Jake barreled forward, his body sinew and whipcord, his face bloated with rage, his neck taut. He slashed at my face. I ducked. The knife missed. But his knuckles grazed my ear and stung like a bastard.

Bong grabbed his shoulder, and that split second was all I needed. I drove my knee into his family jewels.

Contact, motherfucker.

It wasn't my best shot. But it was good enough. Jake went down like a sack of bricks. I thought Ricardo would throw the next punch. But instead, he let me off with a warning.

"Next time, JoJo loses her nose."

"I owed him for the beach."

Jake was grabbing his crotch, squealing like a stuck pig.

"We call Claire from a public place," I continued.

Ricardo pulled Jake to his feet. The pilot gasped and grunted. "You're dead, O'Rourke."

I ignored him. Ricardo was in command. "Once Claire wires the money, you have no reason to free me."

"Not till the money arrives," agreed Ricardo. He knew that money transfers are not instantaneous, that back rooms take time to process client instructions.

"Which is why we wait where people can see me."

"And you think it's safer in public?"

I gestured toward the pilot. "Ya think?"

"One shot, Bong. That's all I want." Jake had recovered his senses, but not his pride. He was seething.

"Anything else we can do for you?" asked Ricardo, mocking me.

"Buy me lunch," I said, matching his sarcasm. "I'm starved."

He shook his head in disgust and dialed South Carolina. He spoke his rapid-fire Spanish and then said in English, "Put JoJo on the line."

I thought my heart would beat out of my chest.

Ricardo waited for a second. "Hold on."

Then, he passed the phone to me. "Tell JoJo what happens if she calls the police."

"You okay?"

"Yeah." She sounded weak.

But her voice was the sweetest thing I'd ever heard. "They're letting you go. Just don't call the cops."

JoJo knew I was in a bind. "You're with that monster?"

"Don't worry about me. Call this number from the hospital. Let me know when you're safe. But nobody else. Forget Claire, the police, all your friends. And stay away from downtown Charleston until you hear from me. No other calls, okay?"

Ricardo snatched the cell phone. "You go to the police, and O'Rourke dies."

Fifteen minutes later, we walked through the house into a courtyard bursting with palms and the sun's golden embrace. I was glowing inside. I had just outnegotiated Ricardo, Bong, whatever he called himself. My instincts had served me well, and I felt victorious. Like a guy who prevailed against the odds and kicked an adversary's ass.

Yeah, right.

Ricardo played me.

CHAPTER FORTY-NINE
PROVIDENCIALES, TURKS AND CAICOS

My joy was short-lived.

Every second morphed into a living hell as I waited for JoJo to dial Jake's number from the hospital. Ten, fifteen, twenty minutes, and still there was nothing. No word from her. I knew her drive from Rafter's would take a while. But the anticipation was killing me.

Hot. Humid. Hazy. Outside, we stepped into a small garden brimming with red passionflower and prickly pear cactus. I remember seeing a rough-hewn wall of broad wooden beams fashioned into an island-industrial look. There was a huge Caicos Caribbean pine sitting to the right. But the tree offered no clue to our whereabouts because the species is endemic to the islands.

Even now, I have no idea where we were.

The problem was a pillowcase. Jake bagged my head fifteen seconds into the garden. I couldn't see a thing. But the fabric smelled like a mangy dog, fleas and all. "I can't breathe in this thing."

"Oh, let me help," chided Jake, his tone sarcastic. Then he slapped my nose hard. I could feel my eyes well over.

The two men prodded me like a cow, the difference being cattle don't wear hoods. One of the goons, probably that dumb-ass Jake, sucker punched me in the gut. When I doubled over, the wind wheezing from my lungs, he pushed me into a car and forced me head down on a seat. We drove five, maybe ten minutes, and still no word from JoJo.

The click, click, click of a turn signal. I could feel our car slowing. I could hear the transmission whine. Honking horns. Pedestrians' voices. A bicycle's bell. Jake ripped the bag from my head and snarled, "Sit up, asshole."

I blinked several times, my eyes adjusting to the brilliant light. We were driving through a Caribbean-style business district. There were orange tile roofs and white stucco walls. Postcard palms, their green fronds parched at the tips, lined the streets. The emerald ocean shimmered in the distance, winking at us from every direction. And I would have thought the place a paradise. Except there was a fifty-something beatnik in a tie-dyed shirt holding a knife to my side.

"Try anything, and I'll cut out a kidney," warned Jake.

I stayed silent, trying to get my bearings in the unfamiliar town. Ricardo passed the Bahamas Banking Company, double glass doors in the front, and I thought he would park. But he drove the equivalent of three New York City blocks before pulling over.

The loaner shirt hung like a burlap sack across my frame. The pants bunched under the clinch of my belt. Except for the sandals, which fit fine, my clothes belonged on a fat man.

My teeth had survived intact. But my face was a mess, the beatings ugly. My nose was broken and my left eye swollen shut. My head felt like somebody had inflated it with a bicycle pump. And it hurt to breathe, pain searing through my ribs every time my diaphragm moved.

We walked toward the Bahamas Banking Company, back along the palm-lined avenue. A few tourists passed us, a few executives wearing jackets and collared shirts. They gawked at my face, all dents and bruises, but looked away when I caught them staring. One mother winced. She grabbed her little boy's hand and scooted him away.

Ricardo, ever observant, noticed the commotion. "Give me your sunglasses," he ordered Jake.

"What for?"

"Prince Charming is scaring the local wildlife."

"Give him yours."

Ricardo stopped, turned around, and squared to punch Jake. He could smell $200 million. He could almost taste the cash. But the money's lure was making him a nervous wreck. Earlier he had been so controlled, his words terse, his responses calculated. He answered questions with questions. Now he seemed jittery.

I was glad to see the goons argue. The minute JoJo was safe, I was making a break for it.

Why hasn't she called?

Ricardo's eyes blazed, and Jake melted. The pilot removed his sunglasses, clear frames tinted pink, lenses the color purple. He blinked and made a big show. Like the sun was scalding his vision. Like there was a second hole in the ozone. Like he was taking one for the team. He passed them over to me.

"Put them on," snarled Ricardo.

My nose felt like a puffy snout. It was so swollen, the shades didn't fit. The pain from their touch, the glasses resting on my black-and-bruised flesh, was excruciating. Shivers raced up my spine through the back of my head.

"Shit, that hurts."

"Get over it."

That's when Jake's phone rang.

"Give me that thing," ordered Ricardo. "Yes," he grunted into the receiver. He listened for a moment, rubbing the back of his head, lost in thought. "Oh happy day," he finally said, his tone sarcastic. "Now you can get that manicure you're overdue."

"Is that JoJo?" I grabbed for the mobile. I couldn't help myself.

Nodding to Jake, Ricardo handed me the phone. The pilot pulled in close, too close. I could feel his hot breath, moist and rank. Something sharp poked me in the side. It was Jake's serrated knife.

"I'm begging you to give me a reason." Jake jabbed, not deep, but enough to punctuate his threat.

JoJo was on the line. "Are you okay?" I asked.

"My hand." She was crying.

"Where are you?"

"The hospital in Mount Pleasant."

"Give the phone to the first woman you see." Right or wrong, I assumed her abductor was a guy.

"Why?"

"Hey!" snapped Jake.

"Do it, JoJo. Do it now."

Ricardo snatched my throat and tried to grab the phone from my outstretched hand. "I said no tricks."

"And I need verification. For all I know, your goon has a knife to JoJo's throat."

A thin man in a tan poplin suit passed us, white shirt, no tie. Ricardo eased his grip and nodded for Jake to back off.

"Hello," came a woman's voice over the phone. It wasn't JoJo. In all my life, I had never heard a sweeter Southern accent. No way the woman was one of Ricardo's confederates.

"Ma'am," I said. It was important to start with the South's trademark respect.

"Yes?" Her tone telegraphed discomfort.

"The lady who gave you the phone. Is she okay?"

"I'm not sure."

"What do you mean?"

"She looks shaken up. Are you her husband?"

"No, just a good, good friend. Is she alone?" I tensed for the reply.

"Yeah, except for the dog. They probably don't want pets running around the hospital."

Phew.

"Thank you." I could feel the tension lifting from my shoulders. "Would you put my friend back on the line?"

The stranger handed her the phone.

"Have you seen the doctor?"

"They're calling me now."

"Give me that thing." Ricardo snatched the mobile from my hand.

"Once they finish sewing you up, you go home," he ordered. "You stay out of sight. You're not seen. You're not heard. You're a ghost. The phone rings, you forget it. Your computer is shit. You send any e-mails, even one, and O'Rourke dies. Don't think about the cops. If you do, O'Rourke dies. And guess which body part you get in the mail? I'll give you a hint. It's not his finger."

"Won't take much postage," the pilot sneered.

"So much time. So little brain." I shook my head ruefully at Jake while listening to the phone call.

Ricardo clicked off, though. And he told me, "We're calling Claire."

He punched in the numbers to the Palmetto Foundation and reached Jill, our receptionist. "It's Father Ricardo and Grove. Put Claire on the line."

"Right away."

We held for an agonizing few seconds. The mobile beeped. The battery was going low. And in that instant, I decided the limitations of modern technology were a beautiful thing. A dead phone would delay wire instructions to Ricardo's sweep account.

No such luck.

Jake poked me, deeper this time. Blood was blotting the sack of a shirt they had given me. And he leered like an idiot.

Claire's voice came over the handset's speakerphone. "Father Ricardo?"

He pointed his index finger at me.

"No, it's Grove."

"Where are you?" she asked.

Ricardo shook his finger no. Then he drew it across his neck, the slashing motion of death. Jake's knife blade pierced a little deeper into my skin.

"It's not important."

"What's going on?"

Ricardo cautioned me, the finger, the raised eyes, the furrowed brow.

"JoJo's free," I said.

"Oh, thank God."

"I traded myself for her."

"Oh, dear God." I could almost see her eyes, usually so clear. I bet they were murky, listless and gray with strain from the past few days.

"Listen carefully, Claire. Get a pen."

Ricardo mouthed two words: "No tricks."

"The instructions from the ransom note are no good," I explained. "Write these down."

She stopped me when I read, " 'The Palmetto Foundation.' "

"We don't have an account down there."

"You do now."

"What's the point?"

"Just get going. It's not what you think."

For the briefest of seconds, I wondered whether she would wire the money. What I would do in her shoes. I was not family after all, and it was $200 million. But if I ever doubted Claire Kincaid, I was wrong.

"Yes, yes. We'll do it." She was choking up, but there was no hesitation in her voice. Not even for an instant.

Ricardo pumped his fist.

"Thank you." Claire's generosity humbled me.

"I'll lean on the bank to speed things along." She was trying to be helpful.

No. Not that.

Sure, I was afraid. Ricardo had done his part of the deal. It was time we did ours. But I doubted the two goons would release me. The sooner they got the $200 million, the sooner they'd kill me and hide from the authorities.

"Where's JoJo?" Claire asked. "May we see her?"

Ricardo made the same slicing motion across his neck.

"She's safe."

"But where?"

"Away from Ricardo's people."

"But where?" Claire echoed, this time louder than before. It wasn't like her to press so hard. She was stressed.

"I'm a dead man if I tell you. Just wire the money."

"I'm on it."

Ricardo drew a loop in the air with his index finger, signaling me to wrap up.

"Gotta go."

All we could do was wait and suffer, Ricardo and Jake from greed, and me from my bleak prospects.

CHAPTER FIFTY
CHARLESTON, SOUTH CAROLINA

Claire punched off the speakerphone, and Torres took charge. "What's the name of your father's lawyer?"

"Huitt Young."

"And his firm?"

"Young and Scrantom. They're on Meeting Street."

Torres dialed Von Maur, who had been listening from the FBI surveillance van. "Did you get that?"

"I'm turning onto Meeting Street now." He clicked off.

"I don't know if Huitt's in the office," advised Claire. "He likes to work from home."

Torres dialed the agent back. "Did you get that?"

"Young's behind closed doors with a client."

"I don't feel like waiting," she snapped.

"You won't."

Claire waited for Torres to hang up before protesting. "What if Huitt won't come?"

"Von Maur's a persuasive guy."

"So is Huitt." Wired and Napoleonic, the Charleston lawyer could be a cantankerous old bastard. Claire pushed the bangs from her face. They fell right back.

Torres paused long enough for the silence to turn uncomfortable. "You want to help Grove?"

"You know I do."

"Then do exactly as I say. No pushback. No argument. Okay?"

"Yes, yes."

"Call your bank, and tell them to wire the money."

"It's not that easy." Claire glanced at Biscuit, her uninvited guest, for support.

The big man shrugged with an unspoken expression that said, "Do as she says."

Claire turned back to Torres. "I need to fax the instructions first. Then I need to find somebody way up the food chain. And they may be out to lunch."

"I don't need the details."

"But it's two hundred million dollars." Claire turned icicle white, frozen from stating the number aloud. Her father's fortune was gone. Generations of Kincaid prominence were shot. And at the moment, it seemed like Palmer was Grove's thousandth man. Not the other way around.

"You're not gone yet?" snapped Torres.

Claire shook her head in dismay. "I'll take care of it."

"Good." The FBI agent turned to Biscuit. "You're on deck. When Young gets over here, I want you to ask him what you asked me."

"And what was that?" Claire, standing at the door of the conference room, was still bristling from the dismissal.

"You'll find out soon enough. Now get out of here so I can call the Financial Crimes Unit."

"Washington, D.C.?" Biscuit couldn't keep from asking.

"Turks and Caicos."

"What happened to you?"

"Car accident," said JoJo.

She was standing in the lobby of the East Cooper Medical Center. Her hand was swathed in crisp white bandages. Her face was swollen, puffy eyes the size of tangerines. Her skin, once a stunning blend of gold and mocha, looked like a Goth line drawing. There were blacks, blues, and dark shades of purple spreading everywhere.

Even worse, she was standing face-to-face with Dottie Blanchard, the biggest gossip south of Broad. And before Dottie, JoJo had run into Katie DuBois. Those two could more than hold their own on the SOB grapevine. The hospital lobby had turned into a convention of busybodies. Which was a problem, because Grove and Bong had instructed her to keep out of sight.

"Oh my. Are you okay?" asked Dottie.

"I'll be fine." JoJo squeezed Dottie's arm with her good hand and headed outside, where she found a taxi. Per all the instructions, she needed to hide—and fast.

"Where to?" the cabbie asked. But he spied Holly and reconsidered. "Hey, I don't want your dog in my car."

"She tips well. Just get us out of here."

"You got it."

They pushed into the backseat as JoJo considered her destination. Too soon to go home. That would blow everything. Nor could she drive anywhere. Her car was still at the beach. And lunch downtown was absolutely, unequivocally out of the question. That left one option.

"Charleston Marina."

Twenty minutes later JoJo slipped into the teak lounge below *Bounder*'s deck, her dachshund waddling behind. She pulled off her skirt, blouse, and all the lace underneath. Her clothes had been ridden hard over the past two days. She rifled through her locker and found underwear and a sports bra. She pulled on fresh capris and a thick blue jersey with white horizontal stripes.

For a moment, JoJo was tempted to don shades and a black baseball cap and head upstairs. Too risky. Instead, she headed over to Palmer's bar and rooted around for the Grey Goose and vermouth. There was plenty of ice in the freezer, enough to shake at least ten batches of martinis. For now, one would do.

JoJo carved the perfect lemon twist and placed her martini glass on a folding tray. She loaded some chips into a bowl and double-checked the date on a jar of salsa. Anything post-Jurassic. Finally, she filled a dish with dog food. Holly savaged every bite in less than a minute.

That left one thing. JoJo headed back to the locker and found her stash, the one Palmer had never seen. Nor anyone else in Charleston. She flicked out one cigarette from the pack and lit up.

Sinking deep into a deck chair, JoJo drew in as much smoke as her lungs could hold and savored the glorious hit of nicotine. After a while, she balanced the cigarette on the ashtray and turned to the martini. She sucked on shards of ice, the vodka burning down her throat and into her stomach. The pain, first from her face and then the left hand, steadily dissipated into the cloudy mixture.

Now all JoJo could do was wait. And wait she did—her elbow cocked, wrist bent, a parade of cigarettes hanging between index and third fingers on the right hand. The chips disappeared. So did the salsa. In the background Bob Dylan sang "Forever Young." And the martinis grew sweet, one after another, promising that everything would be okay.

Smoke should have filled the Palmetto Foundation's conference room, single-helix tracers rising from cigarettes and gathering at the ceiling in great clouds of spent tobacco. The four faces were tense, thin lips stretched tighter than piano wire. Angst billowed through the air, and the only thing missing were the Joe Camels.

"What the hell is going on?"

Huitt Young was agitated, annoyed by the FBI agent who had dragooned him over to the Palmetto Foundation in broad daylight. He stood up and circled the conference room. He sat down, unable to make up his mind. His friends often teased that he had been a Jack Russell in a previous life.

"JoJo's safe." Claire labored to sound strong and factual. But the traces of CNN anchor were gone from her voice. And making matters worse, she started in the middle of the story. "Now they have Grove."

Huitt knew nothing about the events since Tuesday. Less than fifteen minutes ago, the guy named Von Maur had flashed Federal Bureau of Idiocy credentials and whisked him out the office, around the corner, and upstairs to the conference room of the Palmetto Foundation.

"What are you talking about?"

Torres smiled. Word had not leaked out about the kidnappings. It was better that way, easier to do her job. "Let me bring you up to speed, Mr. Young."

Huitt sat, his left leg pumping under the conference room table. He listened, his ears cocked. He took in every word, digesting what had befallen his client. When Torres finally finished, Huitt sprang from his chair and started to yap.

"Let me get this straight. Following your recommendation, the Palmetto Foundation wired two hundred million dollars to the Turks and Caicos. To some thug who cut off JoJo's finger, launders money for a South American drug lord, and runs around Charleston disguised as a Maryknoll missionary. Tell me how this transfer is a good thing."

Torres remembered why she'd left the practice of law. "We didn't invite you over for play-by-play."

"No, but Palmer was my friend." Huitt sat down. He drummed his fingers. He stood up, his kinetic impulses taking control. "And the Palmetto Foundation is my client."

Then Biscuit stood up, unrolling his formidable girth in slow motion, filling the room with complete self-assurance. "We don't have time for you to second-guess the FBI, Mr. Young."

Huitt eyed the big man across the table and sat down.

Biscuit sat down.

Claire watched, suffering more than the others. She found the conference room grim and forbidding. The walls were closing in fast, suffocating her. She had no idea how the world had gone so wrong, how her father had become a complete stranger.

"We control the bank account in the Turks and Caicos." Torres clicked through her explanation at a breezy clip, her delivery staccato, the attitude saying, "We've done this before."

"What do you mean?" Huitt eyed Biscuit uneasily.

"Our friends on the island," explained Torres, "are freezing all transactions as we speak. We'll get the money back. But I wish you'd stop playing lawyer and start answering my questions."

She thought about adding, "Your fees are safe." But she decided her previous comments had already been too inflammatory.

"Why am I here?" Huitt pulled a pen from his coat pocket and rolled it around and around with both hands. He desperately wanted to stand.

"We need your help finding Mrs. Kincaid. Any guesses where she is?"

The explanation puzzled Huitt. "I thought you said she's safe."

"According to Grove," Torres replied. "He traded himself to secure Mrs. Kincaid's release."

"But JoJo hasn't contacted any of you?"

"No."

"Why not?"

"We don't know." All eyes were riveted on Torres as she spoke. "Maybe she's afraid that something will happen to Grove. Or maybe it's something else."

"What do you mean?" Huitt riffled his shock of silver hair.

Torres addressed Biscuit. "Why don't you try your theory on Mr. Young."

All eyes turned to the big man.

"I've got five sisters." Biscuit spoke in his trademark speed: molasses slow.

Young tapped his foot and drummed his fingers, when he wasn't fidgeting with his pen. He rolled his eyes.

"They all have kids," the big man continued. "Couldn't wait to get started. It's different for guys, don't you think?"

Huitt looked like he might explode.

"The thing I don't understand," Biscuit continued, "is why JoJo Kincaid never had kids. She was twenty-nine when she met Palmer, right?"

Huitt eyed his friend's daughter before fixing on the other lawyer. "I'm not sure what you want, Mr. Hughes. Or why JoJo Kincaid's maternal in-clinations are relevant. Or any of your business, for that matter."

Claire caught Huitt's look and leaned into the conversation. "It's okay. I want to know."

"It's awkward." Huitt pushed back from the table like a dog straining against its leash.

"I don't care." She pushed the bangs from her face.

"It wasn't possible." The short, feisty lawyer shook his head with clear disappointment.

"What wasn't possible?" pressed Biscuit.

Torres rolled her index finger, this time signaling Huitt to speed up.

"Palmer couldn't have kids."

"Excuse me." Claire's eyes gleamed like sapphires.

"I advised him to get a prenup."

"He was the one," agreed Claire, "sounding air-raid sirens about my love life."

"Palmer refused." Huitt almost whispered his words.

"So he got a poor man's prenup," observed Biscuit, anticipating what Huitt would say next.

"Yes."

"Is that what I think?" Claire suddenly understood.

"Snip, snip," confirmed Torres.

Biscuit rubbed his massive hands. "Did he tell Mrs. Kincaid about his vasectomy before they were married?"

Huitt's face was growing more and more gray. He said nothing.

"Answer the question." Claire Kincaid was not about to be denied. She wanted to know, and she wanted to know now.

"No." Huitt shook his head.

"What happened when she found out?" Biscuit glanced at Claire. He was checking for her support.

"What do you think? You're the one with all the sisters."

"She was pissed?"

"I'm not sure 'pissed' gets the half of it."

Torres shot Biscuit a knowing look.

"Okay," the big man continued. "You know about Mrs. Kincaid's pre-vious marriage?"

Huitt nodded. "Yes."

"What can you tell me about her childhood?"

"I don't see how this helps us find JoJo."

"We can't predict what's helpful," snapped Torres.

"JoJo grew up in San Diego?" interrupted Claire. "Right?"

The cantankerous old lawyer shook his head no this time.

"Where?" demanded Claire. "What are you hiding, Huitt?"

CHAPTER FIFTY-ONE

CHALK SOUND, TURKS AND CAICOS

The chief magistrate was a creature of habit.

At exactly 12:45 P.M. he waddled through the doors of Las Brisas. He held a folded copy of the *Financial Times* and carried himself—shoulders back, chin held high, chest thrust forward—as though moving to the inner beat of "Pomp and Circumstance." The head chef greeted the portly man, as was their custom, and escorted him to a corner overlooking the sound.

The chef seated his patron, their starting bell for the daily ritual. "May I tell you about our specials?"

"No thanks," said the judge.

This is new, thought the chef.

Ordinarily, the magistrate made a big show of listening. And once, just once, he had almost succumbed to conch Bolognese prepared with hints of chorizo, whispers of celery, and sautéed banana peppers.

But the answer was always the same. "Let's go with the usual."

Whereupon the chef would smile and return to the kitchen wondering if he would ever persuade the magistrate to try something else. It was the game called "hope springs eternal," played with creamy sauces, tropical fruits, and fresh catch from the Caribbean. Only today, the magistrate was not participating, which made the chef wonder:

Why the change?

In short order, the waitress delivered a bottle of 2006 Joseph Phelps merlot. She followed with a shrimp plantain appetizer, which the magistrate had long ago decided was the perfect way to start the *Financial Times*. He was halfway through the paper when his beef Wellington arrived, rare, just the way he liked it.

The day was, by most standards, unexceptional.

Except for one thing. The magistrate had received an urgent phone call from the Financial Crimes Unit of the Royal Turks and Caicos Islands Police Force. Try as he might to delay the meeting until three P.M., an officer named Digby insisted the sooner, the better, two P.M. at the latest.

The chief magistrate ordered his customary cheesecake just as an earnest young policeman bustled through the restaurant. He gestured to an empty chair at the magistrate's table and asked, "May I?"

"This is highly unusual," harrumphed the judge with just enough of an Eton accent to annoy the most charitable.

"I'm Digby. We spoke on the phone."

"Oh, right. But our appointment isn't until two o'clock."

"I'm not sure these papers will wait, sir."

The chief magistrate eyed his cheesecake, annoyed by the young officer's interruption. "We're only talking forty minutes, Digby."

"Long enough to wire two hundred million dollars to a drug cartel." Digby smiled wide, all charm and big teeth. Looking at the bottle of merlot, he added, "We wouldn't want to make the British tabloids, sir."

The magistrate considered his *Financial Times* and turned toward Digby. "You have the freezing order?"

"Yes."

"And our communications with Washington, D.C., are in order?"

"Yes."

"You have a pen?"

"Yes."

Digby handed over the paperwork. The magistrate scanned the forms, squinting through half-frame glasses perched on the tip of his nose.

The young officer checked his watch every few seconds. Finally, he said, "The incoming wire was just initiated. We could lose the money any second if we don't hurry."

"Oh, please." The magistrate was exasperated. "It's lunch. Our bankers are half in the bag. You won't get any wires out this afternoon."

Digby checked his watch again. "Something tells me the Bahamas Banking Company will be extremely efficient on behalf of this client."

"This account belongs to a foundation," the chief magistrate began. "You're sure about this?"

"Yes."

"You know what happens if we're wrong?"

"We're right."

"The press will excoriate us." The chief magistrate thought his observation wise, young Digby a little too earnest.

"Sir, it's easy enough to release funds—assuming we freeze an account that ultimately proves to be legitimate. But once two hundred million leaves our control, we can't get the money back."

"No, I suppose you're right." The chief magistrate signed the freezing order.

"Thank you, sir." Digby scooped up his folder and bolted from the room, leaving other guests to whisper and speculate about the commotion.

The magistrate was still holding Digby's pen. He looked at his watch and smiled. It was 1:30 P.M. Now he could enjoy his cheesecake in peace, the pressure of a two o'clock meeting gone.

That's when the chef returned, the other diners buzzing. "Is everything okay?"

"You never told me about your specials," tsk-tsked the chief magistrate.

CHAPTER FIFTY-TWO
PROVIDENCIALES, TURKS AND CAICOS

"Now what?" asked Jake.

"Pay for lunch, dumb-ass."

We were camped out at a local diner, just down the street from the bank. The foundation's $200 million had not arrived. Which, combined with bottomless cups of black coffee, made the two goons antsy.

I barely touched my fries. And I picked at my oil-slick sandwich, which the grease-stained menu billed as red snapper. Even though I had not eaten since the previous night, lunch was the furthest thing from my mind.

Every so often Jake poked me in the ribs with his knife, a pointed reminder to shut up. My blood was trickling. Slowly, steadily, a maroon stain spread through the blue oxford-cloth shirt Ricardo had given me.

The wound stung. I felt like a piece of cut meat and wanted to smash my plate across the pilot's ruddy, 80-grit-sandpaper face. I was wired, alert, looking for the slightest opening.

When our waitress tended the adjacent table, Jake grinned and jabbed me with his knife again. "Don't try anything."

"Next time I break your nose."

Several other diners, locals from the look of them, glanced in our direction. I relaxed my fist, the knife menacing my side. And seeing nothing of consequence, the other patrons continued with their lunches.

Ricardo growled at Jake in a low voice, "Cut it out."

"Liver or kidney?" asked the pilot, his face demonic and red, his tie-dyed shirt a shooting flame. "What body part are you thinking?"

Ricardo glared until the pilot backed off. He never said a word, his intensity warning enough. "I'll be back in a minute."

"Where are you going?" asked Jake.

"To take a leak. Anything else you need to know?"

Ricardo slid out of the booth. *Good.* The goons had gone from zone defense to man-to-man, which felt like an opportunity.

The pilot read my mind, though. He wedged against me in the booth, his hip touching mine, his moist onion-and-batter breath fogging me out. "Just give me an excuse."

Sometimes you're good. And sometimes you're lucky.

I was lucky. The phone rang. Jake relaxed his knife and checked his mobile. The caller ID read UNKNOWN.

"Yeah," Jake grunted into the phone, his tone annoyed at first. But as he listened, his demeanor changed. He turned subservient, and I detected a note of fear. "I'm on it."

Who's calling?

"We're close," insisted Jake. "Really close."

To what—the money?

"He won't leave my sight."

Are they talking about me?

At first I thought Ricardo had phoned from the can. I quickly changed my mind because the conversation was too tense, Jake too compliant. And after clicking off, he muttered, "Fucking Moreno."

Suddenly I understood. They'd been discussing Ricardo. The pilot might be watching me. But he was also keeping tabs on Bong.

Why?

"What are you staring at?" Jake's blade dug deeper, the holes in my shirt and side getting bigger, my blood gushing.

I can take him.

"Just the two of us," the pilot taunted, almost begging me to try.

That's when Ricardo returned. And I must confess, I was relieved to see him.

He looked over the counter booth and down at my shirt, the stain stretching wider and more pronounced. "What the fuck are you doing?"

"You told me to watch him, Bong."

"Why'd you cut him?"

"Couldn't help myself."

"Dammit, Jake. What if we take him inside the bank?"

"Why?" the pilot demanded. "We don't need him anymore."

I watched the knife, checked for the waitress. Anything for an opening.

"We need him until the money arrives." Ricardo hissed his words between clenched teeth.

Some plans take shape through grueling marathons of what-if exercises. Not this time. In those few seconds, I decided to escalate the old divide-and-conquer game. To hit them with everything I had.

"Too bad you'll never see the money, Ricardo."

He gazed at me impassively.

Jake twitched, however, as though he had overdosed on caffeine. "What do you mean?"

"Right about now, the FBI is freezing your sweep account."

The threat seemed plausible. Torres had described her plan in the car yesterday. Plausible—maybe. But I had no idea whether the agent had initiated a freeze. Or whether it would work inside the Turks and Caicos.

"And your point is?" Ricardo's eyes never flickered with concern. He was unfazed, suddenly cool, no longer the anxious goon on the verge of a big score.

"You think he's bluffing, Bong?" Though still wary, the pilot eased the blade from my stomach.

"I doubt it," deadpanned Ricardo, indifferent to the FBI.

He was too cocky, too sure of himself. He knew something I didn't. I wondered why he had grown so confident.

"I wish you'd tell me what's going on," huffed Jake.

"Relax, would you?"

"You can't afford to relax," I chided Ricardo. "Once the money gets frozen, I bet your boy over here calls Moreno first thing. Some guys will say anything to save themselves, and one thing's for sure."

"What's that?"

"Jake's not taking one for you."

"What do you know about Moreno?"

"Only what the FBI tells me." I rolled my eyes toward Jake. "And what I hear on the phone."

"You're fucking dead," the pilot blubbered, exasperated and nervous, his right eye twitching a Morse code of nerves. I could feel the knifepoint vibrating against my flesh.

"And what does the FBI tell you?" Ricardo leaned back, hands clasped behind his head, the picture of cool, daring me to continue.

"That you're a two-bit hood out of your league. That Moreno's coming for the two hundred million." Torres never said any of this. She was sketchy on the facts, uncertain about Ricardo's role. But I was going all in, Texas Hold'em—style. "That about right, Jake?"

The pilot's eyes sparked with anger, but he said nothing.

"Too bad the boss won't get a cent." I was baiting them, trying to make something happen, preferably something other than a knife up my gut.

"You ever seen a freeze order?" Ricardo's voice was calm. He glanced at the half-moons of his fingernails.

"A few," I lied.

"Then you know they come with a date."

"That would be today's date."

"Right you are, grasshopper."

Ricardo's arrogance scared me. He was smug, too pompous and cocksure for my comfort. But I pressed forward anyway. "I bet the FBI already has its freeze in place."

"They push paper with the best."

"Yeah, too bad for you." I was trying to match his breezy attitude, wondering why all the swagger.

"Hey, O'Rourke. It's Wednesday, right?"

"All day long."

"The bank received Claire's wire Monday." Ricardo's face glowed like red-hot coals.

"Impossible. I called today."

"Funny," he replied. "The bank's computers say Monday."

"Where are you going with this?"

"My bank honors all instructions that predate a freeze."

"Bullshit."

"You know what whoosh money is?"

I said nothing.

"Whoosh it were still here."

"Right," I said, unamused.

"The money will sweep," continued Ricardo, "and a week from today, I'll be grading bikinis at my seaside retreat."

My heart sank. Simple lies are effective lies. Palmer Kincaid's fortune, his life's work, would disappear because some clerk took a bribe from this shithead. "Who backdated our money?"

"You ever work in bank operations?" Ricardo was growing stronger and more confident with every word, his plan coming into full view.

"No."

"Too bad. It's amazing what you learn in the trenches." He paused for his words to register. "Take a guy struggling to make ends meet. Wife and three kids at home. One of them big-time sick. Now, there's somebody feeling the pinch. Know what I'm saying?"

I knew exactly what he was saying.

Ricardo's face glowed like hot embers. His teeth glistened pearly white. "After a while, the job screws with your head. Some rich client bitches about not closing on a new yacht. His wire is late. Meanwhile, my guy in operations can't make his mortgage payments on some dump. I'm like fucking Robin Hood to him."

"You keep missing the big picture."

I had no choice but to bluff. Ricardo had outpointed everybody, FBI included, on the money transfer. Once the $200 million arrived, I was a loose end.

"You've got a knife up your ass, and I'm the one missing the big picture?"

I braced for a jab. "Too bad about the suspicious activity reports."

Jake blinked. His smile vanished. His lips turned tightrope thin.

Ricardo stayed cool. "You ever work in a bank's anti-money-laundering group?"

Uh-oh.

"Couldn't keep your job in operations?" I was going down. I knew it. He knew it. My sarcastic response made me feel better but didn't help. Not one bit.

"The bank loved me," he boasted. "Put me through law school in the Philippines. Said I had a big future in compliance. Too bad they never paid me."

"Then you know," I said, leading the Charge of the Light Brigade. "Right about now, there's a guy looking at the SARs."

"Probably so."

"A lot like the guy you know in operations. Wife, kids, mortgage. Except he'd prefer to play soccer on the weekends than chum through the prison showers. He sees two hundred million dollars going out the door today, on an account where there's a freeze order. And he thinks, *Something's rotten in the Turks and Caicos.* And that's when your inside man gets nailed. Do not pass Go. Do not collect two hundred million dollars."

"That guy you mentioned," replied Ricardo.

"What about him?"

"Her name is Olivia. She runs the AML for the Bahamas Banking Company."

"You bought her?"

Ricardo cocked his head to the left and smiled. His elbows bent, he raised his right and left palms to the heavens. But he wasn't praying. He was congratulating himself.

Who isn't on Ricardo's payroll?

CHAPTER FIFTY-THREE

PROVIDENCIALES, TURKS AND CAICOS

I have no history of violence.

Nothing more than a few kickboxing lessons from a coach who says, "Learn to walk away. There's always somebody bigger, stronger, better trained who can kick tomorrow's crap out of you."

I had stayed up all night. Been beaten, bullied, and gagged while two goons probed my tonsils with a can of Great Stuff. My ears were ringing, my head throbbing. But for all the bruises on my face—nose shaped like a pickle and skin tones borrowed from *The Scream*—no permanent damage had been done. Ricardo and I had each been knocked unconscious too soon.

Everything changed in a few seconds.

I erupted, my fury blinding and feral. I was capable of anything. My savagery surprised me then. It haunts me still. And I wonder what vile thing inside pushed me over the line of decency. I had no history of violence.

Now I do.

"Let's go, ladies." Ricardo collected the change and cleared the room with his eyes. No cops. Nobody glancing in our direction. He was drawing closer to his payday and could almost smell the sweet bouquet of dollar bills, pounds sterling, or whatever currency he selected.

"Where?" I made no effort to move.

"One asshole is plenty," he answered. "Get moving before Jake cores you a new one."

Ricardo's face had tensed over the past few minutes. His momentary cool had vanished. The careful planning, all the preparation and bribes, were yesterday's news. Results were all that counted.

His brow creased again. His black eyes filled with an eerie, foreboding glow. Ricardo reminded me of traders with big money on the line, the way they get stiff and jittery and grow old waiting for their bets to pay off.

Or not.

The crowd troubled Ricardo. There had been only a handful of diners before, but now every seat in the house was taken. The patrons were workers, heavyset, with calloused hands, long on perspiration from hours underneath the stinking hot sun. Short on deodorant.

The small concrete-block room was an orgy of eating and drinking. Neon pinks and blues were splashed against the walls, while fourteen-foot ceilings shielded everybody from the midday sun. The room was stained by time and the greasy exhaust from cooking creatures of the sea. It reeked from happy hours that began with Bloody Mary breakfasts and ended when the last sot pitched face-first onto a Formica countertop somewhere.

Waitresses buzzed the tables. Some hoisted huge platters of crab cakes and fish. Others delivered amber glasses of ice-cold beer, their frothy heads jiggling from the motion.

Jake slid out of the booth.

I stayed put.

"Move it," growled the pilot.

"I'm not going."

Ricardo nodded toward me. "Take care of our problem child, Jake."

The pilot slid back in and poked me with his knife. This time he cut a new spot. A fresh stream of blood spurted from the puncture.

I've suffered through my share of pain. That's the thing about distance cycling. You learn to deal with the discomfort and move on, literally, because racing is all about stretching to the physical limit of your legs, your lungs, your head telling you, "This sucks." Cycling is a sport where you make peace with agony, because every turn of the crank brings the finish line that much closer.

But sweet mother of Jesus, Jake's knife hurt.

"You ever had your nose broken?" I asked.

"Shut up." He snarled his words but averted his eyes under my withering stare.

Nobody paid attention to us. The patrons focused on their food and drink. Waitresses scoured for tips. And the hostess took names from the burgeoning crowd.

"Twenty-minute wait," she announced every so often.

A maroon polka dot was saturating my shirt, the radius of blood six inches at least. Four guys, their skin the color of smoke, were standing near the cash register. They should have seen me and sounded the alarm. But they pointed to our empty booth, focused on who would bus the table and how soon.

The diner aisles were narrow, which was good for Jake and Ricardo. The goons could prod me forward, and Jake could keep his knife hidden. The tight quarters, however, were bad for the harried waitresses. Loaded with trays, they shimmied and limboed their way past us. Which, I suddenly realized, was the break I needed.

A slim waitress, her thick black hair a tangle of dreadlocks, hoisted a tray full of beers and shots of Jack. She edged down our lane toward a table of gardeners who looked like commercial fishermen. It was the middle of the day, though, and I decided that anglers would be at sea working their nets.

When the woman squeezed past Jake, he lost his concentration. "You need a management team for your hair, toots."

I grabbed one of the beers.

"Put it back!" she bellowed, wedging into Ricardo. Her loud, angry voice filled every corner, every crevice of the room.

Two quick moves. I rammed the mug into Jake's nose. Beer sprayed everywhere, his flesh and cartilage cracking from my 100 mph thrust, blood spurting across several nearby plates.

Jake's hands shot up. Too little. Too late. I caught him with an elbow to the Adam's apple. The pilot clutched his neck. The waitress's platter blasted from her grasp, amber waves of imported beer splashing the gardeners behind.

Ricardo slapped my right hand. The mug landed three tables over, seated diners bailing from their booth. Everyone in the restaurant craned to see what was happening, too surprised to move, as pain shot up my fingers through my arm.

"Hey!" screamed the waitress.

Ricardo flung the woman onto the table behind him. The gardeners, already doused by the suds, looked up to see a human bowling ball of jeans and elbows and long black dreadlocks blasting into the middle of their booth.

My hand shot forward.

Lucky strike or intentional, I'll never know. My thumb gouged into Ricardo's eye socket. I squeezed with all my might. I gripped and grasped, as though reaching for viscera through his eye socket. Every slide from the Palmetto Foundation, all those kids, exploded through my head in a lightning flash of bloodlust.

Something popped inside Ricardo. Something I was holding. My thumb felt sticky, but I yanked forward, pulling him by the skull.

"Oh my fucking eyeball." Though hurt, he never went down.

Ricardo backhanded the side of my face. I saw stars. He lunged toward me, blood streaming from his gore. The ooze was thick, too thick for me to tell the extent of his injury. I was lost, not thinking, just reacting, breaking away.

The patrons emptied from their tables. They were thick men with thick hands, who worked like mules. Some scrambled out the front door, eager to avoid the ruckus. Others gawked, angry from getting doused with beer.

It was chaos.

The diners were unsure what was happening. Or who had started the brawl. Most watched, their jaws hanging slack. One threw a punch and caught me in the gut, good but not good enough. I stayed on my feet.

Somebody grabbed me, pulled me around. I saw a blur of motion and slipped right.

"What the fuck." A gangly kid with gangly arms threw a long punch. I ducked and pushed past the hostess and out of the restaurant. An angry horde chased me into the street, liquored-up guys furious over a lunch gone bad.

Not one cop on the scene.

Jake lurched through the front door of the diner, Ricardo right behind him. He was holding the sleeve of his shirt against the bad eye.

Somebody pointed at me. "Get him!" another yelled. The crowd lunged forward, united in beer and anger.

No time to explain. No time to turn the crowd against Ricardo and Jake. I spun around, kicked off my loaner sandals, and hit the gas.

Running, running, running. I sprinted past a bank of stucco buildings, bolting between cars on the street. I knocked over a businessman, who landed on his butt. His eyes flared wide from surprise as the wind grunted from my lungs.

I glanced over my shoulder, a classic cycling technique when you're leading the pack. The crowd, mostly men, a few women, stormed after me. Somebody threw a mug that bounced off my shoulder and kicked from my heel.

Damn, it hurt. My head was spinning. Still no police in sight. Pedestrians were parting in the streets, turning their heads to watch all the commotion. They gave me a wide berth. They stepped aside for the people chasing a few lengths back.

Double glass doors, the same ones I had seen before.

I raced forward—focusing, trying to find a cop, no longer daring to look back—and pushed inside the lobby of the Bahamas Banking Company.

CHAPTER FIFTY-FOUR

CHARLESTON MARINA

"Where can we find *Bounder*?"

The cop with salt-and-pepper hair had twenty years on his partner. He wore starched blues and shiny black shoes with rubber soles. He walked with a slight crook in his back, the legacy of a long-ago run-in with a cheap punk on upper King Street.

"Berthed out back." The dockmaster pointed toward the outer docks. "Make a right, walk to the end, then a left and another left."

"Thanks," replied the younger cop, a surprising blend of testosterone and detail orientation. He hated "drive-by directions," the hazy and inexact information that made it easy to miss destinations.

"Can't miss *Bounder*." The dockmaster spoke in the warm, reverent tones that boat people reserve for vessels. "She's got the prettiest lines in the harbor. Just like her owner."

"You know Mrs. Kincaid?" Salt-and-pepper made a mental note to question him later.

"Oh yeah."

"Have you seen her today?"

"Maybe. Maybe not," the dockmaster replied. "I haven't been looking."

"Call me if you see her." Salt-and-pepper handed the dockmaster his card. "We're checking *Bounder* now."

"Not in those shoes?"

"Why not?" asked the younger cop.

"You'll leave marks all over the deck."

"Somehow," said salt-and-pepper, "I don't think Mrs. Kincaid will care."

Five minutes later, the two officers found the boat. The door to the cabin was open, Roy Orbison wailing "You Got It" from the inside. The unmistakable scent of cigarettes wafted into the windless afternoon.

"Charleston police," called the younger cop through the cabin doors.

"Coming aboard," added salt-and-pepper.

Holly barked furiously as the two men poked their heads inside. The rich wood interior was varnished teak. The patterned inlays alternated between chocolate brown and the golden color of country biscuits.

The younger man's eyes hurried from ornate woodwork to brass fittings to galley stove. *It's all so tidy,* he thought.

A woman sprawled on a deck chair, teak with royal blue canvas. She wore large dark sunglasses inside the cabin. Purplish bruises peeked from behind the frames and surrounded her crow's-feet.

Salt-and-pepper had seen it all during his twenty-plus years on the force. Battered women always raised lumps in his throat. His eyes traced JoJo's bruises, her bandaged hand. "You okay?"

"How'd you find me?" JoJo reined back her tears. Holly stopped barking and hopped on her lap. The dachshund licked her face and trembled defiantly at the two men in dark uniforms.

He nodded at her bandages. "You've seen a doctor?"

"I'm fine. Is Grove O'Rourke okay?"

"Ma'am, we don't know, ma'am," replied the younger cop, serving the ma'am sandwich of Southern respect.

"We need you to come with us," said salt-and-pepper.

"And Holly?"

"Bring her too."

JoJo put down her glass and dabbed out a cigarette on her coffee saucer. She took one last look at the teak interior. "Let me get my things."

Outside on the gangplank, the older cop dialed his captain. The chief listened intently and said, "Bring her in."

Then the captain dialed Agent Torres, who answered on the first ring. "Yes?"

"We got her."

Torres said, "Call the hospital and tell them we have Mrs. Kincaid's finger. I'll meet your guys there."

That's when Claire interrupted the phone conversation. "I just heard from my bank."

"And?" The agent's pupils turned into black BBs.

"The money arrived in Turks and Caicos."

"Any word on Grove?" Biscuit stood, walked to the window, and stared across Broad Street, steeling himself for her answer.

CHAPTER FIFTY-FIVE

BAHAMAS BANKING COMPANY

The bank's lobby looked like any other. The ferns were fussy, the stainless-steel fixtures, too. The faux marble floors glistened with a high, slippery sheen. And customers stood in line, waiting to deposit money into an institution that might not lend it back. There were few hints of the Caribbean paradise outside. The room's air was heavy with the torpid inertia of retail banking, nobody moving and nobody giving the day a second thought.

"Everybody freeze!"

My two words changed everything. Customers and staff snapped to attention. Hands over their mouths and faces ridged with fear, they combed the room for a bandit. They waited for the staccato report of automatic weapons—the here and now of a heist going down.

"You're being robbed," I yelled at the top of my lungs as the posse of diners pushed into the lobby behind me.

Somebody gasped. A woman shrieked. I stretched both hands way over my head to discourage trigger-happy cops hiding in the shadows. Several depositors darted out the door. They were petrified even as I was surrendering.

"What's the meaning of this?" One of the bankers marched in my direction. He was bald, save for close-cropped hair on the sides and cactus fuzz on top.

The banker saw no gun. He showed no fear. He was prickly, all attitude and bad mood. He snapped his fingers at a diminutive, bespectacled member of the staff and mouthed the word "Police."

Mission accomplished.

"You're about to lose two hundred million dollars," I hollered, making sure everyone in the building could hear. "Unless you stop all outgoing wires. Now."

Some customers joined the exodus from the building while more diners pushed their way inside. A carousel of angry faces circled me. Ricardo and Jake were nowhere to be seen in the mix.

One man, who had been standing near the restaurant's cash register, pointed in my direction. "That's the guy."

The bald, thorny banker pushed to the front of the ring and winced at my face. He probably thought me daft from a beating. He spoke in slow, elongated tones, soothing and condescending at the same time. "Come sit down on the couch."

"Who's in charge?"

"I'm the manager," he said as the crowd stared at me.

"So you take the hit?"

Now all eyes turned to him.

"What are you talking about?" Elbows bent, he threw both arms into the air. Even his pose reminded me of a cactus.

"First things first," I demanded. "Think you could clear the lobby before somebody throws a punch?"

"A little space here." The banker glared at the crowd.

The shoving stopped. The gawkers backed off, slowly, surely. Some left, but most stayed. Curiosity replaced their fear and anger.

My turn to take control. "What's your name?"

"Smitz. I'm the president."

"Of the Bahamas Banking Company?"

"No. Of the bank's branch in TCI," he clarified, using the abbreviation for Turks and Caicos Islands. "Who are you?"

"Grove O'Rourke. I'm a trustee of the Palmetto Foundation, which is a not-for-profit institution based in Charleston, South Carolina. According to your records, my organization maintains a sweep account with your bank. But we never set one up. It's not ours."

"Whose is it?"

"A money launderer controls the account. And he's bribing your employees. I know him as Frederick Ricardo, though he may be using a different alias." I avoided references to Ricardo's cover, Maryknoll priest, and to his nickname. One mention of "Bong," a common enough name in the Philippines, would have marked me as a nutcase in the Caribbean.

There were at least thirty people in the crowd. They fixed on me, jaws slack, eyes wide. They were no longer disappointed by the lack of punches. Bank robberies were so much better.

Still no sign of Ricardo or Jake.

"You either freeze all outgoing wires from the fake account," I continued, "or tell the authorities why your bank lost two hundred million dollars."

Smitz didn't move. Not until several rubberneckers headed toward the teller stations. I questioned whether my charges would incite a small run on the bank. Apparently, he was wondering the same thing. The banker barked at one of his subordinates, "You heard him."

A diminutive man with rimless glasses began punching instructions into his computer.

"Are the police coming?" Smitz asked him.

"Yes." The man nodded.

"Today, U.S. authorities requested a freeze on that account." I spoke evenly, methodically, hoping Torres had implemented her plan. "In addition, you received two hundred million dollars from my organization. Probably in the last few minutes. But someone in your AML department backdated the arrival time to Monday. So unless you fix this problem now, our money will be swept to ten banks around the world. And we'll hold you liable."

"Our computers don't allow it." Whatever Smitz had thought before, he no longer considered me a raving lunatic. He surveyed the crowd, knowing they could all be depositors.

"I hate to break the news, pal, but you're wrong."

"Our suspicious activity reports pick up anything unusual."

"Yeah, when they're legit. But your head of SAR is dirty."

Smitz turned around. "Get Olivia," he ordered.

"She's at lunch," the other banker replied.

"I don't care."

A tall, thin man pushed through the crowd. He was wearing a police-man's uniform, and at long last, I felt safe. "I'm Digby. Financial Crimes Unit of the Royal Turks and Caicos Islands Police."

"Thank goodness," sighed Smitz. "Would you arrest this man?"

"Are you Grove O'Rourke?" the policeman asked me.

"Yes."

"This man is working with the FBI," he told the banker. Then, address-ing the crowd, he said, "Show's over, folks. Let's break it up."

A few shuffled away. Most stayed.

"Now," he echoed. And the crowd made for the exits.

"Am I glad to see you!" I extended my hand to the officer.

"Who handles the account for the Palmetto Foundation?" Digby asked Smitz, not really responding to me.

"I don't know without checking."

"What are you waiting for?"

"Okay, okay," Smitz acquiesced, no longer combative.

"Has the money been transferred?"

"I just learned about the problem."

"Let's find out." Digby gestured to the back office. And all three of us disappeared into the bowels of bank operations.

CHAPTER FIFTY-SIX
CHARLESTON POLICE HEADQUARTERS

"You okay?" asked Torres.

"What do you think?"

"I'm sorry the doctors couldn't do more."

JoJo gazed at the swathe of bandages. Her hand had been mummified. It was the focus of everyone in the room.

They were sitting inside police headquarters on Lockwood Boulevard. Two detectives had joined Agent Torres to watch the interrogation. A thin manila folder sat on the table in front of her. The label on the tab read "FBI."

"Any news from Grove?" JoJo's face was throbbing, her heart racing. With her good hand, she rubbed her blouse collar between thumb and forefinger.

"Not yet." In fact, Torres knew he was safe.

"I can't believe he traded himself for me."

"Yes you can."

"Excuse me?"

"Cut the crap."

JoJo stopped fiddling. Her eyes were knife blades. Her lips were a garrote. She thought back to her cigarettes aboard *Bounder* and would have killed for one now. "What's this about?"

"Bong Batista."

"That psycho?" JoJo raised her mummy hand.

Torres shook her head, feigning dismay. "Is that any way to talk about family?"

"I don't understand."

"And pigs fly," the agent scoffed.

"You can't talk to me like that."

"Really." Head cocked, brow growing dark, Torres grabbed her chin and feigned concern.

"Chief Mullins is my friend." JoJo shooed the officers, waving her good hand. "You boys get Arthur for me."

"And bring back some tea and crumpets," said Torres, turning sarcastic. Nobody left.

JoJo sulked, the picture of confusion.

"You don't know Bong Batista?" pressed Torres.

"No."

"Never seen him before?"

"Never."

"You're sure?"

JoJo hesitated but only for a second. "I thought you wanted to find Grove."

"Both Grove and Bong," confirmed Torres.

"Then why treat me like a criminal?" JoJo ran her words together without inflection. She wasn't speaking English. She was shooting syllables, rapid-fire, the same way she spoke Spanish.

"Because you're lying."

"That's crazy."

"You know what John Gotti said?"

"What's that got to do with anything?"

" 'You lie when you're afraid.' " Torres reached into the manila folder and pulled out a color photo. Decent quality for an inkjet printer. She pushed it across the table. "And I think you're petrified."

JoJo glanced at the picture. Her face registered nothing.

"That's you, right?" the agent pressed.

"What about it?"

"Yes or no, Mrs. Kincaid."

"Yes."

"Is that Bong Batista standing next to you?"

"How would I know?"

"We have a witness who confirmed his identity."

JoJo said nothing.

Torres smiled and opened the folder again. This time the agent passed over a marriage certificate. It belonged to James and Joanna Berenson.

"Where'd you find Jim?" JoJo shifted in her chair.

"The Navy. Same place you left him." Torres liked this part best. The perp was down, squirming, taking the ten count. Sweet. Sweet. Sweet. It was time to pile on. "But it's Master Chief Berenson now."

"Jim doctored the photo. He hates me."

"Give me a break." Torres looked at the two detectives. "Can you believe she's playing the ex card after fifteen years?"

"How'd you discover my previous marriage?"

"I didn't."

"Who did?"

"I'm asking the questions." Torres sat back in her chair, a kitten toying with her trophy. "But let's just say we had help from a guy named Biscuit."

"I want my lawyer."

Torres ignored her. "It's always the little things, JoJo. You don't mind me calling you JoJo, right?"

"I prefer Mrs. Kincaid."

"Who in the world says, 'Eat all you can'?"

"I asked for a lawyer."

"Here in the States," Torres pressed, "we say, 'All you can eat.' But in the Philippines, they say, 'Eat all you can.'"

JoJo glared, seething through her bruises. "Can someone get me a cigarette?"

No one moved.

"The kids are what sold me." Torres sat back and draped her arm over the chair. "You don't have any."

"None of your business."

"Oh, it's my business all right. And your ex tells us you're fertile."

"I want my lawyer." JoJo looked at the two officers for help. They didn't budge.

"Miscarriages are an awful thing." Torres shook her head. "You ask me, Master Chief Berenson still sounds disappointed."

"I didn't ask."

"Vasectomies, now they're a different story. You found out, and you were furious. You never forgave Palmer, right?"

JoJo stood up. The officers stood up too. One of them motioned for her to sit. She did.

"Your husband robbed you. First you lose your shot at being a mom. Then you lose the house on South Battery. Not to mention one hundred and fifty million dollars. You ask me, Palmer Kincaid's gift to the Palmetto Foundation was 'salt in the womb.'"

The two policemen watched with humorless expressions.

"I'd be pissed, too." Torres cocked her head and pursed her lips.

"I didn't know about the will," mumbled JoJo, her words feeble.

"That's not what your lawyer says," bluffed Torres.

"I need to see Huitt now."

"I doubt he'll take your case."

"Why not?" JoJo twirled locks of hair with her good hand.

"I doubt he'd help anybody who hurt Palmer."

"Huitt will be furious when he hears what you're suggesting."

"He's already furious. And I'm not suggesting a thing. You're a low-life street thug who sold out your husband. We clear?"

"I've heard enough." JoJo was stammering now. "Would somebody get me a cigarette?"

"But what do I know?" continued Torres. "Huitt's a lawyer. Him forgoing fees. It's like saying cobras play nice."

"That psycho hacked off my pinkie, and you're accusing me of murder?"

"That stumped me," Torres admitted, not intending the double entendre this time. "I wonder whether I'd give a finger for two hundred million."

JoJo held up her damaged hand. "You think I like this?"

The FBI agent shrugged her shoulders. "That doesn't change a thing. Bong Batista is your cousin. And you've been lying to us."

"I told you. My ex doctored the photo."

"Not according to records we received from the Philippine government."

"Hah. They get things wrong all the time."

"Which is why my aides double-check everything. You know those two snakes on your cousin's chest?"

JoJo said nothing.

"Your ex told us about those tattoos, too. How'd you piss Jim off anyway?"

"I want a lawyer."

"You stonewall, and I'll get you ten extra years. It'll be so much easier if you tell us what you know about Moreno."

"Huitt will have me out in fifteen minutes."

"Yeah, yeah. You're doing time, lady." The agent flicked her hand dismissively. "Your husband denied you children. He denied you the Kincaid family's prominence."

"I am a Kincaid."

Torres ignored JoJo's protests. "Along comes Bong. That one's a real piece of work. Maybe the two of you don't plan to kill Palmer, not at first anyway."

JoJo shook her head no.

"A little money laundering. Nobody gets hurt. You're living large, and there's plenty of time to fix your husband's will. But bang, the world changes. Palmer discovers the scam, threatens to tell the police, and all of a sudden your cousin has a huge problem with the same guy who let you down. We clear about the motives here?"

"No, we're not clear. Palmer's death was an accident."

"I can't figure out the split between Bong and you. Your face. Your finger. You earned your share, honey."

"You're delusional."

"As good a sailor as Palmer was, there's no way a boom hit him in the head. Hey, I get it. Couples grow apart."

"It was an accident." JoJo's face clouded. Her almond-shaped eyes, the hints of Spanish and Malaysian ancestors, welled over.

"Spare me." Long ago, Torres had decided tears were the last shards of conscience leaving a perp's body. The interview continued for another fifteen minutes before the FBI agent threw in the towel.

JoJo called Huitt. He referred his best friend's wife to another attorney. Under advice of counsel, she stopped talking.

CHAPTER FIFTY-SEVEN
FAYETTEVILLE, NORTH CAROLINA
THURSDAY

At precisely ten A.M., neither a second before, nor one after, twelve FBI agents stormed Highly Intimate Pleasures. They found the manager, asked her to send the employees home, and declared all twenty thousand square feet a crime scene.

The authorities arrived with boxes and left with files and computers. They paid special attention to the store's internal surveillance system, hoping that daily videotapes would provide clues to Ricardo's network. Or better yet, evidence to incriminate Moreno.

No such luck.

Dildos, blue videos, and breast-shaped baking pans became the subject of an ongoing criminal investigation. Lingerie was declared off-limits to everybody, employees and customers alike. A minor scandal erupted when the manager noticed that three *Cathouse 2: Back in the Saddle* DVDs had gone missing.

Word of the FBI's raid spread during the day, steadily, inexorably, into every home in Liberty Point Plantation. By five o'clock that afternoon, Mrs. Jason Locklear had arranged a full-blown victory tailgate. Cars, from compacts to SUVs, flooded into the parking lot at HIP. They arrived with portable grills, Frisbees, and coolers full of steaks and burgers, not to mention beers and martini shakers for when the minister was out of sight. There were two or three bonfires, dogs of every size and shape.

Representatives from the Roman Catholic Church were noticeably absent. Rumors circulated around the lot about a Catholic bishop named Connery. Somebody heard that he would join the party and make a statement, presumably to stymie the growing PR disaster. But nobody from the clergy ever showed.

Biscuit couldn't believe the number of people. The celebration confused him, given Mrs. Jason Locklear's call to his hotel room in Charleston. "I thought you changed your mind about HIP."

"No more truckers. No more billboards. I think our ministers prefer us to get 'marriage help' through the mail."

Around 6:30 P.M.—the crowd at critical mass—Mrs. Jason Locklear decided it was time for official remarks. Her minister stood in front of yellow tape encircling the building that read CRIME SCENE. DO NOT CROSS. He asked everybody to bow their heads and thank the Lord for their blessings. Afterward, he handed his bullhorn over to Biscuit.

The big man, far too gentle for his size and girth, was no stranger to the camera. News teams from ABC, NBC, and CBS affiliates had staked out the adult store parking lot when they learned about the tailgate.

Biscuit kept his remarks brief. He knew the television spots would last a minute at best. "I know where you can get twenty thousand square feet of retail space cheap," he told the boisterous crowd. "And stop digging up the plants." A handful of his clients had arrived with shovels and other garden tools.

The spoils of war.

The camera crews, Biscuit noticed, were ambushing eighteen-wheelers. Every so often, truckers would pull into the parking lot, drawn by the allure of HIP billboards up and down I-95. When drivers stepped from the rigs—backs bent and achy from long hauls—the news honeys shoved mikes in their faces and zinged them with the types of questions that endear journalists to the world:

"Where will you get your sex toys now?"

"What really happens at truck stops?"

"May we show our viewers the sleeping compartment of your cab?"

There were some long faces in the crowd. Twenty-one HIP employees understood their jobs were gone forever. They had nothing to celebrate. But Biscuit passed out cards from his brothers-in-law. "Denny's or Phil's Polynesian. Just tell them I sent you."

For the most part, the evening was all fun and games. But the lawyer grew more and more troubled as the night wore on. In addition to the disenfranchised staff, there was one other potential loser from the HIP fiasco. And over the last few weeks, Biscuit had grown fond of Grove O'Rourke.

FRIDAY

Biscuit dialed Torres at 9:01 A.M. The agent was a hard-ass, no doubt. Their relationship had improved, though, since he reported Grove missing last Tuesday night.

She answered on the first ring. "What can I do for you, Mr. Hughes?"

He cut her short. "For one thing, no more of that."

"Of what?"

"My name. Call me Biscuit." The lawyer felt powerful, confident.

"Okay."

He could almost feel the FBI agent's tough, combat-ready demeanor soften. But he knew her good humor would disappear soon enough. "I'm calling about Grove O'Rourke."

"What about him?"

"Let's cut to the chase. Are you prosecuting him?"

Biscuit's candor surprised Torres. She had grown to think of the lawyer as a teddy bear, however tenacious. "Are you representing him?"

"No." After a moment of silence, neither one saying anything, he pressed the issue. "Well, are you?"

"I don't know."

"Grove put Ricardo out of business. You said so yourself."

"Why do you care? He's not your client."

"He's a friend," replied Biscuit. No hesitation.

"He destroyed our investigation into Moreno. And Ricardo is still missing."

"Not Grove's problem."

"I'm afraid it is. The Palmetto Foundation provided material support to a criminal operation."

"Grove had no idea."

"That charity was the Walmart of money laundering." Torres was adamant. "I'm supposed to turn my back? Give me a break."

"Thanks to Grove, you shut down Ricardo and his machine. I'd say that's a huge win for your department."

"What we do is out of my hands."

"The hell it is." Biscuit had listened to this pit bull long enough. "In five minutes, I'm e-mailing you a document. You have ten minutes to sign it, date it, and return it to me. Otherwise I'm going to the press. And we can try your case in the court of public opinion."

"What makes you think anybody will care?"

"An ordinary Joe getting run over by big government—"

"You want an underdog," she interrupted, "find yourself a plumber. O'Rourke works on Wall Street."

"Fairness and simple math," pressed Biscuit.

"What do you mean?"

"There are three people on the Palmetto Foundation's board. Initially, Grove voted against the wire transfer. Check the minutes."

"And your point is?"

"The two remaining votes were enough to override him. One was fixed. And you're hanging the guy who uncovered the scam?"

"I want Moreno."

"You got forty million dollars of dirty cash and JoJo Kincaid." Biscuit was growing angry, his inflection sharp.

"A bit player who's adorable. There won't be a dry eye in the house when her defense attorneys finish."

"I don't buy it."

"Born to a poor Filipino family. Failed marriage to an enlisted man. Through hard work and market savvy, she becomes a leading real estate broker in San Diego. Marries one of Charleston's elite. It's almost a Horatio Alger story."

"Heroes don't kill their spouses."

"Sorry," the FBI agent said. "Nothing I can do."

Torres was digging in. Biscuit decided it was time to pull out all the stops. There was only one way to save his new friend. "You can Google Cavener Land Development."

"Who are they?"

"A public company I opposed in North Carolina. Check out what the press said about them. And then ask yourself how the FBI will fare once I'm finished."

"You'll be lucky to get the back page in one of those coupon rags."

"What are you doing tonight?"

Biscuit's question caught Torres by surprise. "That's none of your business."

"Don't mean to intrude. But if your plans change and you're in Fayetteville, why don't you drop by Phil's Polynesian?"

"Why?"

"I'm one of the owners. We run a happy hour special every Friday night. Two free Navy Grogs for anyone with a press pass."

Torres stewed for a while. "Fax me what you have in mind."

CHAPTER FIFTY-EIGHT
QUANTICO, VIRGINIA

Torres considered Biscuit's fax. She had already skimmed a dozen stories about Cavener's travails in North Carolina. She no longer regarded the lawyer as a teddy bear. That big lug would get her fired. She couldn't sign his letter:

Dear Mr. O'Rourke:

I work for the Federal Bureau of Investigation. We recently met while I was probing how a money launderer infiltrated the Palmetto Foundation ("Foundation"). You were a trustee of the Foundation at the time and, to my knowledge, remain one today.

During September of this year, your organization transferred $25 million to an account controlled by Bong Batista. He is a money launderer who works with an illegal drug network operated by Hermann Moreno.

We now understand the Foundation was infiltrated by an individual, Mrs. Joanna "JoJo" Kincaid, who came under the control of Moreno's network and its operative, Bong Batista. Mrs. Kincaid systematically misled your organization and, from a position of power, caused the Foundation to wire $25 million to the Moreno drug syndicate.

We have no intention, either now or in the future, of prosecuting you or the Foundation under laws that punish conspiracies, money laundering, or tax fraud. On the contrary, we recognize the extreme personal risk you incurred while uncovering the activities masterminded by Bong Batista.

Furthermore, by copy of this letter, we are commending your performance to the chairman of your firm, Sachs, Kidder, and Carnegie. Through your assistance, our organization has made a significant dent in the war against crime.

It has been my honor to work and serve with you.

Yours sincerely,
Isabelle Torres

CC. Mr. Percy Phillips, CEO of Sachs,
Kidder, and Carnegie
Biscuit Hughes, Attorney at Law

You've got to be kidding.

Torres picked up the phone and dialed Biscuit. "No way in hell I'm signing that letter."

"Can you join us at Phil's Polynesian tonight? This story will make every station in the country, and, frankly, I may take Grove O'Rourke's case pro bono. There's not a jury out there that will convict him. You can take that to the bank."

"I don't have the authority to sign this letter."

"I don't care."

"It won't be valid," she insisted.

"The letter's plenty valid on the *Today* show."

"Is it negotiable?"

"Not one comma. You have ten minutes. Otherwise, I'm warming up the gang."

Biscuit clicked off, leaving Torres to fume.

Her phone rang. She didn't answer it. Several times, incoming messages pinged her e-mail in-box like a submarine's sonar. She never looked. Time running out, she eyed the photos of her son and daughters on her desk, and decided what to do.

FBI protocol required Torres to call Walker, her boss. Instead, she smiled, grabbed her cell phone, and headed outside. Her husband answered on the first ring:

"How are you, sweetie?"

Around four P.M., Torres marched into Walker's office. Her boss was on the phone. But he took one look at her cloudy, uncomfortable expression and decided to hang up. In a hoarse voice, he said, "Gotta go."

Torres was carrying a manila envelope marked "FBI." She sat in his guest chair and slapped the file down on his desk. Not hard. But with authority. She riffled her hair with both hands, mussing the cut that had always seemed so careful and shiny. Now tangled and askew, her locks were definitely not FBI issue.

"You want to head out early and get a drink." Walker wondered why his problems always surfaced on Friday afternoons.

Torres said nothing. She opened her file and pulled out Biscuit's letter.

"What's this about?"

"It's self-explanatory."

"It's a nonstarter," he said, noting her signature. "Totally off the reservation."

"I'm not asking for your approval."

"Then the only decision is which shredder to use."

"I already mailed the letter to O'Rourke with a copy to his firm."

Now it was Walker's face that clouded over. "I wish you hadn't done that."

"I know. That's why you need to see this." She opened her folder again and slid over a second letter, this one more brief than the first.

"You can't resign on me. Don't do this to me."

"I just did."

"It never happened," he said, tearing up her resignation. "Let's go out, throw down a few pops, and talk things out."

Walker turned to the right of his desk. Piece by piece, he fed Torres's resignation letter into the shredder.

She watched and waited until he finished. The shredding done, he stood and said, "Let me get my jacket."

Torres made no effort to rise. Instead, she extended her right hand across his desk, palm flat and facing down. She lowered it steadily. "Sit down."

Walker sat.

Torres reached into her manila folder and pulled out another resignation letter, same as before. She knew Walker, his habits, his charm. She also knew her own vulnerabilities. The folder contained nine more copies.

"It's been a long week," said Torres. "My resignation is nonnegotiable."

"Can't we talk?"

"Yeah, Monday. I'll call you from home. I'm out of the Bureau. It's that simple."

With that, Torres stood and walked into the hall. She was excited about the weekend with her family, the first one in a long time when she was not on call. Movie and a spaghetti dinner at Luigi's. Afterward, Torres and her husband would put the kids to bed, drink too much wine, and watch Jay Leno. Not a bad way to spend the evening. She should have been jubilant.

But for all her enthusiasm about the new life, Torres was racked with guilt. Moreno, Ricardo, all the other scumbags—there was too much unfinished business to feel great about leaving the FBI.

Some end to my career.

"Hey, Torres," Walker called from his office. "I'm getting my coat."

She raised her right hand and waved good-bye, never turning around. "It's Izzy."

CHAPTER FIFTY-NINE

That morning, I meandered my way to the Red Flame Diner and ordered a lumberjack breakfast. The pancakes came with scrambled eggs and enough bacon to worry my arteries into their fifties. I drank two large orange juices and substituted a bagel and cream cheese for the buttery toast.

I was pissed at Katy Anders and Percy Phillips. Neither of them had called me over the weekend, even though my story made all the newspapers. *The New York Times. New York Post. Daily News.* Now everybody knew who I was. A stranger in the diner asked me, "Are you that guy?"

"Yeah."

Even with the pending sale of SKC's brokerage to Morgan Stanley, Wall Street could wait. I read the paper and took my time eating breakfast. I didn't care who said what about the Dow Jones Industrials.

It had been an ordeal getting back. Customs. Immigration. Fortunately, the American embassy took care of logistics in the Turks and Caicos. I had no passport to leave the country, or to enter the USA for that matter. And there was no going off the grid with Girl Louie or Air Ricardo this time.

I arrived in Miami and hopped a flight to Charleston. Claire drove me to the hospital, where the doctors diagnosed two broken ribs. She chanted over and over, "I'm so glad you're back."

"You paid too much for me," I teased her—half jest and half gratitude. The foundation's money was safe. But I kept reminding myself that Claire Kincaid, whatever her weaknesses, risked $200 million to secure my release.

"Let me take care of you," she offered.

"I've got to get back."

Annie took over in LaGuardia. Her face turned gray when she saw mine. I was a wreck, the bruises, the nightmare of purples, greens, and ugly yellows, the stitches over my right eye. She asked, "What am I going to do with you?"

That's how it was all weekend long, nothing quite so glorious as my girlfriend pampering me for two days running. But I still had unfinished business, and no idea how the smiling, dialing cash registers at Sachs, Kidder, and Carnegie would react.

Around 8:45 I arrived at the office. Today was the day. Now was the time. I was about to initiate my plan. To my surprise, the pieces were already falling into place.

The buzz was fairly typical of a Monday morning. Every stockbroker jabbered into his or her phone—each one regaling clients with different advice from the proud brain trust of SKC.

Casper said, "Buy."

One desk over, Scully blasted loud enough to wake the dead. "Sell."

Patty Gershon confessed, "I don't have a fucking clue." Her honesty was noble if you ask me.

But so much for SKC's positioning. Our television ads say we're "one firm with one firm voice."

Yeah, right. The divergent opinions, all the talk, talk, talk with no coherent direction, only increased my resolve. No matter how big the gamble, my decision was the right one. I wondered what Percy would say.

As I walked toward my workstation, the fearsome hum of 149 stockbrokers ended. The world stopped. The eerie silence reminded me of the Bahamas Banking Company, when I yelled, "Everybody freeze."

Colleagues checked out my face, the stitches, the kaleidoscope of bruises. A few clapped me on the back, which bothered the hell out of my broken ribs. Suddenly, the floor returned to normal. Noise erupted everywhere.

There is a certain blackness to our camaraderie. I heard:

"Nice face, Grove."

"Did Goldman do that?"

"Your clients asked me to say hi."

I had seen this rodeo before. Loosely translated, the other stockbrokers were saying: "Glad you're back, man. Really. But would you hurry up and sign the noncompete, so we can close the deal with Morgan Stanley and get our retention bonuses?"

At our workstations, Chloe hugged me hello. Gentle. She knew about the ribs. Same with Zola. "Katy just called," my partner said. "They want us in her office now."

They?

To our surprise, Percy was waiting with my boss. "Sit down," the CEO said. "We owe you an apology." He eyed Anders for a moment and then read a letter from Torres.

I was surprised. And I wasn't.

Over the weekend, the agent had left a short message on my answering machine. "You're off the hook. Let me know if you need anything else." I knew something was up.

But Torres never mentioned the letter. And, clearly, the words were not her voice. During our time together, she never lavished praise on anyone.

When Percy finished reading, he passed me the letter. And seeing Biscuit's name at the bottom, I understood. The big attorney had my back. I owed him one.

The CEO turned right to business. "Can you complete Morgan's paperwork today?"

Translation: "Or you're fired."

Anders handed me the documents, and I looked at Zola. "You signed, right?"

"Waiting for you." She winked, subtle, quick so the others didn't notice.

You're the best.

Percy noticed my hesitation. "We need your signatures."

"Why? The deal gets done regardless." The other three gaped at me. Nobody ever questioned our CEO.

And Percy didn't like the pushback. "Nobody's asking for a favor, Grove. You sign. You get paid. It's that simple."

"Not to me."

Anders shifted uncomfortably.

Percy resembled a blank LCD screen. "We followed the FBI's orders. You'd do the same."

"Maybe. But I had a similar problem with SKC two years ago. You remember that thing with Charlie Kelemen?"

"I wish we had handled things better. Now and back then."

"Me too."

"I'm asking you to move on." Percy rubbed his hands. They looked soft, almost effete. "And sign the deal."

"What you mean is suck it up." I was too much of a veteran to give in, not yet anyway. On Wall Street, the word "yes" is just another security. We trade it for whatever we can get.

"Zola's and your signatures are a matter of optics."

"Optics?"

"We want complete approval from all our brokers."

"Is the deal contingent on everybody signing?" I asked, direct and to the point.

"It sends the right message to investors. Both theirs and ours." Percy shrugged his shoulders. "No deeper than that."

Nobody said anything at first, including me. The person who fills the silence generally makes concessions that sweeten the pot. I didn't expect Percy to be the one.

"Maybe there's something you want." He looked at his watch.

"Actually, there is." I smiled at Zola.

She looked baffled.

"Name it." Percy felt his power returning. He waited, his bearing like the proverbial genie with three wishes to grant.

"Who's running our division after the merger?"

"Not clear yet."

Anders's face clouded over.

"Why not me?" I asked.

"We can run it together." Anders leaned into the conversation, suddenly worried, angling for her slice of a deal.

"I'm not interested in sharing power, Katy."

Anders blanched at my reply.

Zola could not believe what she was hearing.

"You have no management experience." There were question marks written all over Percy's face.

"I've broken in fourteen bosses in ten years."

"Not funny."

"Not meant to be. Every time there's a problem, you throw stockbrokers under the bus. Which is one reason for all the turnover. We don't trust management."

"Keep going."

"Our discards are working for Morgan." I was referring to Frank Kurtz, the guy who left our shop to join theirs.

"You're willing to trade your book for management?"

"Zola and I can work something out."

"I'll see what I can do."

That's how the meeting ended with Percy. We all left with a few bruises to our egos, except for Zola, who came out unscathed. Which was a good thing, because partners watch each other's backs on Wall Street.

Until we don't—but I digress.

"You cool with our meeting?" I asked Zola after we left the boss's office.

"It's kind of a surprise."

"Let's talk. Away from the office, okay?"

Back at my workstation, I called Biscuit first thing. "Torres's letter had your fingerprints all over it."

"What makes you say that?"

"Its tone. The way she CCed you."

"Yeah, I knew you'd put it together."

"You're a good friend," I told the big man. We spoke for another fifteen minutes, and I invited Biscuit to visit New York City. "You can stay with Annie and me. Bring your wife."

He declined at first.

But I persisted. "What about Thanksgiving?"

"What about it?"

"The parade passes our condo."

"All those balloons?"

"Bullwinkle's my favorite."

"We have kids."

"Bring 'em."

"Done," he confirmed. "Under one condition."

"Okay?"

"You visit us and we buy you dinner at Phil's Polynesian."

"Done."

Afterward, I followed up with the victory lap every broker knows. I sent Biscuit a box of Omaha Steaks. It was, I think, the right way to seal our friendship. Something tells me our paths will cross again.

Later that morning, I called Claire. The last few weeks had been interesting. Perhaps the better word is "shattering." After all the drama, I wanted closure.

Not with Claire per se. I'm done with all that Daisy Buchanan nonsense from high school. Annie and I are a team, and Claire will always be a friend. Nothing more than that.

I was closing the books on the illusory perfection of Charleston. For so long, it had been my dream to gain admission into the inner circle. To pattern myself after Palmer. The lure was acceptance, the sense of being an equal in the Camelot of the South.

Now I regard Charleston as a place just like any other, full of warts and foibles and complicated lives where secrets cannot remain hidden over the long term.

Palmer and JoJo Kincaid hid behind stucco-and-brick walls built in the 1700s, inside the colonial colors that had grown softer and more seductive with time.

But Charleston is a front unlike all others. It's the sense that everything is perfect even when it's not. I find it ironic that everybody was looking at the Kincaids. And no one saw what was inside.

Including me.

I often wonder how much Palmer knew about JoJo's past. Whether he named me as the third trustee to sort out his mess or to protect his daughter. Over the past few weeks, she had come undone.

"Hey, you," said Claire, answering my phone call. She was in good spirits, light, full of Southern bubbles. "You feeling better?"

"I'm fine. It's you I'm worried about."

Claire never commented. "Did you hear about JoJo?"

"What happened?"

"She caved."

"Confessed?"

"Over the weekend. JoJo admitted Ricardo was her first cousin. That he killed Palmer on the boat."

"I still can't believe the finger. Or the beatings she took." Every time I pictured her face, all I could think was, *Yeesh.*

"According to my spies at the police station, Ricardo got the idea from the Yakuza."

"The Japanese gangsters?"

"Right. They perform a ceremony known as yubitsume. It means finger shortening. And they start on the left hand just over the knuckle. The gangsters use it as a way to atone or apologize. But JoJo and Ricardo used it to throw us off the scent."

"Good thing Biscuit smoked out the truth," I ventured.

"Puddin' to the rescue."

"That's nasty."

"Yeah, I guess it is." Claire offered no explanation and changed the subject again. Perhaps her reticence was her way to inject some distance into our friendship. "You think Daddy knew about JoJo?"

"Actually, I wanted to ask you the same question. But I know Palmer figured out Ricardo."

"Why?"

"That last Friday. Your dad was upset when he called me. I think he confronted Ricardo, who preferred his chances with somebody else."

"I have my own theories about that," Claire said.

"What do you mean?"

"I think JoJo told Ricardo you're a nice guy. That you'd be a pushover. A family friend who doesn't want to make waves."

Maybe Claire was tougher than I thought.

We both fell silent for a while. Then she asked, "Are you staying on our board at the Palmetto Foundation?"

I considered the question, took too long.

"We need you," she urged.

Staying was the right thing to do. "I get to name JoJo's successor subject to your veto?"

"Done."

That night, Annie and I hopped a cab to Chinatown. I'm a sucker for Asian food, with one notable exception. Something's just not right about glazed ducks hanging by their necks in restaurant windows.

"What will I do with you?" she asked more than once, scrutinizing my face.

I avoided discussions about my career and would have been happier for Annie to talk about hers. But she kept asking questions about the last few days. "What happened to the fake priest?"

"Last I saw, he was bleeding in the diner." I omitted details for the sake of our dinner.

"You think he'll come looking for you?"

Maybe.

"No way." I didn't want Annie to worry. That was my job. "The police will grab him the second he enters the USA."

"But he's out forty million dollars."

"Forty million versus forty years. Ricardo made the choice. He won't come looking."

"What about the pilot?" she asked.

"Same thing. He'd go to prison."

"I don't know, Grove. Claire has all that money. I bet those two guys hold her responsible."

"The FBI took the forty million."

"I know. I mean Palmer's bequest."

"Don't worry. I'm helping her find a bodyguard."

"Which is not your highest and best use." Annie brushed the sutures over my eye, her touch a gentle caress.

We drank too much wine. We relaxed with each other. And our discussion drifted to her career in creative writing. But underneath the light banter, I felt misgivings about my new acquaintances. I was uncertain whether Ricardo would pay a visit. Or whether Moreno, a man I knew only by name, would come in his place.

CHAPTER SIXTY

Providenciales to Port-au-Prince, Haiti, is forty-five minutes by air. Another fifteen minutes, and you're in Kingston, Jamaica. It seems like all destinations within the Caribbean are just a short hop from one another.

Travel times are brief. But the minutes add up when your seaplane is a good twenty, say twenty-five minutes away. And the journeys are punishing when you're hurt, bleeding, and fleeing from the authorities who put the kibosh on a $200 million heist.

Up in the air, your mind plays games. You're either looking over your shoulder or wondering what's waiting on the other side.

The angry diners swept Bong and Jake into the street. The two men were bleeding, the pilot from his broken nose and Bong from his pulpy eye. They had expected to trade punches with the crowd. But to each one's surprise, the fury was aimed at O'Rourke.

"Get him." Jake pointed at the stockbroker, who bolted pell-mell for the bank.

The mob chased O'Rourke down the street. Bong never moved as the swarm jostled past.

"Come on," Jake screamed at Bong.

"Forget it."

"He's got our money."

"O'Rourke was right. Your brain is toast, man."

Jake bristled forward, his stance smug and menacing, the serrated knife in his right hand. "And you're a regular George fucking Clooney. You want the other eye to match?"

Bong, no matter his severe injuries, was still capable. He poked his index finger into the pilot's chest. "Game's over. We gotta get out of here."

Jake backed off, unnerved by entrails and socket. "What about the money?"

"What about twenty years?"

"Moreno's gonna be pissed."

"I'll get the money. Is your plane fueled up?"

"Yeah, of course."

"Let's go."

"Your eye looks like shit." It made Jake wince.

"O'Rourke's a dead man."

The two men stopped at the house first. Bong shredded a clean white bedsheet and bandaged his eye. The blood stopped flowing. And his face stopped throbbing after he downed a few painkillers, which were never in short supply in his line of work. Forty-five minutes elapsed before the two men took off in the battered old seaplane.

"You need to get that thing checked out," said Jake. "I'm telling you, man. It looked like fucking Cyclops."

"I got resources in Port-au-Prince."

"You trust their doctors?"

"Yeah."

"Haiti's a shit hole."

"Just take me there."

The engines droned their lullaby. Bong disappeared into the delicious, satisfying sleep of Vicodin. And Jake manned the controls.

The battered seaplane was rocking, its back-and-forth motion like a cradle atop the Caribbean waters. The stench of fuel wafted through the cabin. And the cockpit's temperature climbed under a relentless blaze of midday sun.

Bong could have been asleep for twenty minutes. Or it could have been two days. Looking out the cockpit window through his good eye, he slowly regained his senses. And he didn't like the view coming into focus. "This isn't Port-au-Prince."

"We're in Jamaica." Jake was sitting next to him.

"You just wrote your obituary, pal."

From behind them, someone said, "I don't think so." The sentence

sounded serpentine, the speaker hissing the word "so" a few seconds longer than necessary.

Bong froze. The slithering *s*'s and bloodless lisp from the bowels of hell
cut through his Vicodin haze. He knew that voice. It was unmistakable. It
petrified him. "I'll get your money."

"Promises, promises." Moreno's hair was pulled tight into a long black
ponytail. His nose was narrow and hooked, the sharp curve of a scythe.
His white shirt was starched, expensive. And he carried himself with a pa-
trician air. But his hands betrayed a rugged past. They were gnarled, too
big for him, and too scarred for an office.

From nowhere, two of Moreno's goons grabbed Bong. They overpow-
ered him and duct-taped his arms. He could almost taste their body odor,
the scent of salt and musk. Their breathing, the gasps of exertion, stank of
fish and rotten fruit, hints of Mount Gay.

"No," pleaded Bong.

The bigger of Moreno's men had arms that looked like howitzers. He
wrapped duct tape around and around his captive's mouth. Subdued and
humiliated, Bong was suddenly suffering the violent déjà vu of Grove
O'Rourke.

"Jake told me about your party tricks," said Moreno. "I'm so happy you
had some Great Stuff lying around."

Bong tried to speak. Didn't work. The duct tape only allowed for nonsense, low guttural gasps that started near the base of his tonsils. His one
good eye begged for mercy.

"We're fishing for shark," Moreno whispered into his ear. "Just you
and me."

When the spraying began, Bong's lungs filled with a strong chemical
odor. The sticky spray latched onto his molars, tonsils, and the roof of his
mouth. He struggled to gag the Great Stuff out. The insulation grew larger
and larger, the foam widening and stiffening.

He heard laughing and cackling from the crew, the slithering sound of
Moreno's satanic *s*'s. The foam grew. It fed on itself, expanding in his
throat like an explosion from inside out. First the foam became a tennis
ball. Then it turned into a cantaloupe. And the sticky substance kept growing and growing, out of control.

Bong's jaw cracked wide open, his pain unbearable. Even the Vicodin, the glorious Vicodin, lacked impact. Darkness descended over him, though not with sweet decisiveness. The seconds lingered into minutes, the blackness hesitant and excruciating. No air. No light. No more. Moreno finally whispered two words:

"Goodnight, Bong."